# LETHAL IN LOVE

THRASHER
PUBLISHING

# LETHAL
# IN
# LOVE

## MICHELLE SOMERS

# ABOUT LETHAL IN LOVE

*A past she can't remember. A time the killer can never forget. And a man who'll do anything to discover the truth . . .*

Homicide detective Jayda Thomasz never lets her emotions get in the way of a case. So when the Night Terror serial killer re-emerges after 25 years, the last thing she expects is to catch herself fantasising over the smooth-talking stranger who crosses the path of her investigation.

Seth Friedin is a reporter chasing the story that'll make his career. When he enters the world of swinging for research, he never imagines he'll be distracted by a hard-talking female detective whose kiss plagues his mind long after she's gone.

Past experience has shown Jayda that reporters are ruthless and unscrupulous. But when the murders get personal and her world begins to crumble, will she make a deal with the devil to catch the killer?

*'It's gritty, it's sexy and it kept me reading long past my bedtime.'*
HELENE YOUNG, bestselling author of *Safe Harbour*

*'A powerful new voice in crime fiction.'*
VALERIE PARV, bestselling author of the Beacon series

*'The romantic tension is almost as dangerous as the killer they hunt . . . An accomplished debut and compelling read. I can't wait for more by Michelle Somers.'*
SANDI WALLACE, award-winning author of *Into The Fog*

*'Sexy and suspenseful. Michelle Somers delivers all that and more!'*
DB TAIT, romantic suspense author of the Dark Mountain series

*'This has all the hallmarks of a great romantic suspense – steamy tension, danger and blade-sharp writing.'*
STEFANIE LONDON, USA Today bestselling author of the
Bad Bachelor series

# A WORD FROM THE AUTHOR

Welcome inside my sometimes frightening, always romantic mind.

I hope you enjoy *Lethal in Love*—my debut, award-winning novel. This story holds a special place in my heart. Not only is it set in one of the best cities in the world, but it's my first foray into a genre I adore—romantic suspense.

*Lethal in Love* is set in Melbourne, Australia, so please note that boots are only footwear when they're not associated with cars. Rubbish bins are for trash, car parks are parking lots, firies are firemen and ambos are paramedics and/or ambulances. Toilets, bathrooms and loos are restrooms, bums are butts and avos are afternoons or avocados, depending on context.

And as for spelling, anything that looks strange reflects how we do it Down Under – S's are Z's and double-L's are single-L's.

And anything else? Well, that's deliberate too.

That said . . .

Thank you for choosing to read Jayda and Seth's story.

I hope you enjoy it!

*Michelle Somers*

*To the four beautiful men in my life.*
*My real life hero, Danny, who believed I could fly.*
*Josh, Nathan and Gabriel. Your love gives me wings.*

# Prologue

*F*ools!

The fifty-inch plasma above the bar flickered.

*Melbourne's beloved police. Futile. Inept. Buffoons, the lot of 'em.*

His lip curled. And her . . . *especially her.* Thinking he'd falter, create hack-work like some wannabe ass-wipe. They didn't know shit. But they'd learn. *Soon.*

He lowered his bottle onto the beer-stained wood, adrenalin charging his veins.

He'd be legend. Transcend death. *In-fucking-vincible.*

Laughter hacked up his oesophagus and his breath caught, phlegm rising, spilling into his mouth. He gulped it back, along with a generous serving of blood. One of the good-for-nothing legacies passed down to him by the old prick.

Then there were others . . .

The pound against his skull slowed. He knocked back a mouthful of ice-cold beer and rode the pain, a wildfire coursing down his throat.

His time had come. They'd pay. Every last fucking one. The bitch included.

He looked up. The camera panned, then zoomed. His gaze latched onto *her,* the woman behind the thick blue-and-white tape. Her eyes avoided the lens, her body drawn tight, erect, watching the shiny black body bag disappear into the back of the State Coroner's van. Then she turned, and he stared into the familiar green of her eyes.

He would carve his name into her heart, the way hers had been carved into his, day after day after day. But no more. Now he had no heart. No soul. None that belonged to him.

He flexed his fingers, cracked his knuckles one by one. Revelled in the pain.

A final glance, then he shifted his sight to the woman nursing her nearly empty glass. The one he'd come for tonight.

His blood quickened, his groin tight. Anticipating.

He inhaled deeply, closed his eyes. The hunter. Testing the air, drawing on her essence, the very taste of it. Blind innocence. Youth. Vivacity. Before he drew each one from her like a vampire draws his blood fix.

He opened his eyes. Lips curving slowly upward, he cut his way around the bar. Her gaze lifted, his smile deepened. She liked what she saw. They always did. Until that pivotal moment, when realisation speared through their bodies and death claimed them.

*Fools.* They were all fools.

He glanced at the wide screen, but the green-eyed witch was gone. No matter.

He'd see her again. And she, him. Soon she'd do nothing but dream of him, in sleep and wakefulness. And then she'd be his.

# Chapter One

'**B**etter make sure you keep your bra on.'

Jayda Thomasz shot Chase Durant a quelling look. As partners go, she could've had worse. She also could've had better. Still, one thing she did know—she could trust Chase with her life. That counted for a helluva lot when it was only your partner and his dependability standing between you and a whole lot of death.

If only she got a little less mouth from him. A little less interest, too.

'Don't worry. This sucker ain't coming off, no matter what.'

'More's the pity.'

Her jaw tightened.

Fellow officer Georgie Tanneras frowned, tweaking the thin wire that now lined Jayda's bra strap. 'How's that?'

'Perfect.' Jayda grabbed the silver lamé top from the bag at her feet and slipped it over her head. She straightened the neckline and tested the mic. Georgie nodded and moved away to twirl knobs and flick switches on equipment straight out of the space age.

Jayda grabbed Chase by the elbow and dragged him away from prying ears—almost impossible while in the back of a van crammed with tech equipment and the two techies that went with it.

Pressing her palm over the microphone on her chest, she forced her next words through gritted teeth. 'What was it about last week's sexual harassment talk that you didn't understand?'

'It's just that when we're talking about such a spectacular pair of—'

'Chase!'

'I was going to say speakers.' He held up the two earpieces. 'What'd you think I was referring to?'

She rolled her jaw, forcing clenched muscles into relaxation. Not much she could do about the knots in her shoulders, or the war of butterflies churning her stomach.

'Your hair may have lost the red, but your temper hasn't. So tell me, is it really true what they say about blondes?'

She stared at the monitor and didn't bother with an answer. It was doubtful he expected one. The time when Chase and his wisecracks had seemed charming was long past.

*He's not Liam.*

She knew that. Knew this situation was nothing like before. But reason wouldn't curb her dread. She'd dodged the aftermath once. Unlikely she'd dodge it a second time round.

Ousting both men from her mind, she tugged an over-folded scrap of paper from her skirt pocket and skimmed the ten points she'd written last night. Each was a definitive check. Warmth frittered through her. She was ready.

Movement on the small screen above the control panel captured her attention and that of her three colleagues in the mobile surveillance unit. As she tucked the list into the bag at her feet, all eyes watched a couple, male and female, perhaps in their early thirties, pause on the veranda of 21 Brayside Avenue, then slip through the barely open front door.

Just a normal Saturday night in the 'burbs. A nice house in a nice neighbourhood, deep in the hub of Melbourne's northwest. Pleasant, quiet, happily dodging the radar. Until now.

She blinked, trying to ignore the unfamiliar scrape of blue-coloured contacts. Just one more facet of her multifaceted cover. A cover that could lead to a badly needed break in the case and stop a killer before he claimed his next victim.

It hadn't taken much to convince Hackett. She was lead investigator and the only woman in the Pacu task force who fit the victim's profile—age, build, apparent innocence. The one thing she'd had to change was her hair colour with a wig. Oh, and the green of her eyes. To a deep, bright tropical blue.

Images flashed through her brain; a young woman slumped against a dumpster, blue eyes gaping and vacant, her mouth a blistered, cavernous maw. She shook her head, wishing away the grasping, biting claws that snatched at her gut and squeezed every time the image appeared. A vision from crime scene photos, and—as of three weeks ago with the Night Terror's return—her ever recurring dreams. Or should she say nightmares?

The victims were all women, like her. The only real difference—

fate. And the unforgiving clutch of fingers around their throat. Impossible to imagine their terror in those last seconds as the oxygen squeezed from their lungs and they fought for existence.

Jayda blinked again. Looking in the mirror, it was difficult not to see the resemblance to her family that she'd longed for as a child. Sleek blonde hair. Blue eyes. When she squinted and tipped her head to the side, she could almost believe she was Bec's real rather than adopted sister.

'Jayda, you're good to go.'

'Thanks, Georgie.'

Her friend's lips tightened, her gaze questioning as it darted between Jayda and Chase.

Fan-bloody-tastic. The force's 'non-fraternising in the ranks' policy may have been loose to the point of non-existence, but she'd learned the hard way how rumours—no matter how false—could turn a career into compost. Georgie was a friend, but others in the squad would be far quicker to comment. And judge.

Jayda's hand dropped to her hip, devoid now of her badge. It didn't matter that life outside the precinct had barely existed for her the past seven years. She'd matched her father's success, made detective before her thirtieth birthday. And she'd done it by keeping her head down and the fly of her pants securely fastened.

*Thank you, Liam.*

There he was again. Elbowing his way into her thoughts.

After seven years, the anger still lingered, a reminder of her promise never to compromise herself again.

Which made her stupidity with Chase all the more regrettable. One drunken night and a blind fumble between the sheets, which almost sealed the end to her reputation. With her partner. With anyone able to read between the tension.

And now she had so much more to lose than back then.

No excuse that she'd been celebrating Ian Trentham's twenty-year sentence for the cold-blooded murder of his family when her mother's news hit—her parents were separating, one week shy of their twenty-fifth anniversary. Both extremes of the spectrum—one high, one low—sending Jayda off on a deleterious tangent.

She'd drowned her disappointment in a string of tequila shots before falling into bed with the wrong man. Thank heavens sense had overthrown insensibility before she'd taken the plunge and slept with him.

Still, dodging the mess of a one-night hook-up hadn't changed that whole 'morning after' scenario, in which she'd stumbled out of his bed awash with mortification and regret, and a mother of a hangover. She'd regretted the slip ever since.

Better she stick to all work, no play. At least her job was the one scrap of her life she could depend on, where she felt safe.

Which was weird, considering what she was about to do.

The screen beside Georgie flickered, the house a fuzzy contrast of black, white and grey in the approaching dark. So sedate. Serene. Innocuous, even. No hint of what was really going on inside.

She could feel Chase's gaze at her back, his crystal blue eyes piercing, hankering for more than she was willing to give. They were partners, and that professional boundary should never have been scaled, would never be again. Regardless of what he thought he felt.

She stepped away from Georgie's over-alert ears, her hand shifting to cover the mic on her chest. The familiar scent of spice assailed her nostrils as she whispered in Chase's ear. 'It won't happen again.'

'I know.'

'It was a mistake.'

He winced. 'I know.'

'We work together, for god's sake.'

'I know, Jayda.'

'Then stop with the wisecracks.'

'I only do it 'cos you're so easy . . .' he paused, eyes sparkling, 'to wind up.'

She fought the rising boil in her blood. The job was her focus right now, not this wannabe stand-up comedian.

'Leave that to some other wise-ass who's not my partner.'

His smile evaporated. 'You know I've got your back, don't you?'

She play-punched his bicep. 'Yeah, I know, you big goofball. I trust you with my life.'

'Just not your heart.'

She searched his expression. Impossible to tell if he was still serious. She knew he was attracted to her, but love? That was a stretch of mega proportions. And top on her 'not in this lifetime' list. *Never date or fall in love on the job.*

'Chase, we've been through this.'

His expression lightened. 'Just kidding, Jayda. Geez, better loosen up before you go in. I've never met an uptight swinger before.'

'I wasn't aware you'd met any type of swinger.' She looked at him then. Really looked. They'd been partners for two years, worked together for the greater portion of that time, saw more of each other than they saw of their own families. Yet how much did she really know about Chase Durant beyond the odd snippets he'd shared?

Lately, something had felt *off*. If only she could put her finger on what that something was.

His gaze darted somewhere in the vicinity of her left shoulder. 'I haven't. Stop reading stuff that isn't there.'

'Now look who's uptight.'

'You guys ready?' The techie who'd been sitting silently beside Georgie turned in his chair. 'The private party's in the house outside, not my van.'

Sam Hathaway may have been joking, but it didn't stop the heat from finding and stamping Jayda's face. Or the alarm from filling her stomach as she imagined what he was drawing from their behaviour.

Paranoia wasn't a valuable commodity when you were about to go deep under cover.

Chase moved away and slapped the other man's arm. 'Stop being such a grouch, Sam.'

'You try sleeping on the couch five nights running and let's see who's a grouch.'

'Christine still not talking?'

Jayda let out a sigh at the shift of spotlight, only half listening to the banter, her mind already on the job.

'Oh, she's *talking* alright. In volumes they can hear way down in Patagonia.'

Georgie's control panel crackled and all eyes zipped to the man who appeared on the second of the three screens lining the wall.

'Enough of the Oprah bloody heartbreak.' Detective Inspector Hackett's voice rumbled out of the speaker. 'We've got an op to run.'

Jayda sipped sparingly at her citrus martini, willing her racing heartbeat to match the sensual murmur of Marvin Gaye. Not a practised spirit drinker, she calculated she could afford one drink, two at a stretch. They were a necessity to blend in, but she also needed to be sharp. Razor senses were the order of the night. One lapse in attention could be fatal.

She closed her eyes, inhaling deep and slow. Reminding herself that if her nerves showed, it only served to cement her role here as a newbie. A first-time swinger looking to skirt the boundaries into a world where inhibitions and limitations didn't exist. Where lines were blurred and sex was free and easy and abundant.

Gaining admittance had been easier than she'd expected, despite the exclusivity of the club. She'd given Gina's name as a reference and while not necessary it had paved the way. They were expecting her.

She'd handed a wad of notes to Clara—the woman who'd answered the door in a black satin corset and stilettos—and won immediate acceptance, after the automatic condolences and niceties, of course. Gina's murder had hit the news two days earlier.

Another sip and she opened her eyes, allowing her gaze to skim the dim-lit interior. Low chandeliers flickered from high, cornice-edged ceilings, their shadows providing obscurity to the guests gathered beneath.

Occasionally she sensed interest, hushed whispers, blatant curiosity and awareness. But as yet, no one had approached, which was fine. It gave her time to scan the layout, get a handle on the group's dynamics. Work out if a ruthless killer could have wangled his way into their ranks.

Lemon zinged across her tastebuds as her gaze roamed, the icy vodka cool and refreshing but not nearly sweet enough. The sensation was, however, sophisticated. A perfect fit with the environment.

Unease shivered up her spine. Stifling the urge to bite her lip, she thrust her shoulders back and turned.

Premonition hadn't prepared her for this. *Him.* Martini clogged in her throat, now drier than the drink itself.

She swallowed, tried to drag her focus back. Failed.

Their gazes locked, and steely eyes the grey of a gun barrel charged the distance between them.

# Chapter Two

The shaking had to stop.

Jayda gulped down a not-so-sparing portion of her drink and tightened her grip on the glass. This might be her first time under cover, but that was no excuse for nerves. Or the quiver sending her body into waves of hyper-awareness.

Intel was the only thing she'd be picking up tonight.

*Get back in the game, Jayda girl. Don't lose it over something as shallow as broad shoulders and tight pecs. Or eyes with the power of a high-speed vortex.*

Sand rasped her throat. She returned his gaze, with confidence and invitation she anything but felt.

His brow arched and he turned, revealing a scar that hugged the corner of his right eye. She shivered. What did Bec always say? *Bad boys make the best lovers.* Great advice from a sister who'd twice married a bad boy and was unashamedly hunting for a third.

The hunk in the corner met her stare for stare. A bad boy if ever she saw one. Although nothing about him could be mistaken for anything less than a man. One who made her body react in ways it never had before.

It was the atmosphere. The low lighting, the sultry music, the burn of gardenia and orange blossom incense, the promise of culmination. The knowledge that just metres away, in nearby rooms, couples and groups were getting it on with an abandon Jayda had never before experienced.

Yeah, it had to be this place.

And yet, every brush of that penetrating gaze stroked flesh already aware and firing. Blood warming, nipples peaking, beckoning to be touched. *By him.*

A face sculpted from the gods. Brick-house shoulders. Firm, lean muscle. His blue shirt hugged a chest broader than should be allowed for common men, tapering down to disappear beneath the waistband of his fitted black pants.

Her gaze roved lower still. After all, it was expected here. In a club of free love and free expression. If she really were one of them, a swinger, wouldn't she check out the merchandise? Unabashed. Confident. *Brazen.*

It was what she'd been sent here to do—fit in and evaluate the male clientele. Not that she needed a reason to appreciate the cling of dark fabric against his thighs. No points for guessing he worked out. And she wasn't talking about weights. Something in his bearing hinted at passion: fervour, wild and unleashed. Hot, sweaty, back-against-the-wall sex.

The air shifted beside her. She dragged her gaze away from Bad Boy and towards the stranger moving in.

'Hi, I'm Brian.'

He was older, a couple of years either side of forty. Blond hair, eyes a cold, glacial blue. Your classic order of calculated good looks. Not something that had ever jerked, let alone yanked, her chain.

'I'm Shana.'

He took her hand and lifted it to his lips. 'A beautiful name. It suits you.'

She tried not to cringe, allowing herself a sidelong glance into the corner again. It was empty. The loss wasn't nearly as sharp as the disgust she directed her way.

*Mind on the job and off your damn libido!*

Bad Boy was attractive. So what? She could handle it, maybe use her reaction to her advantage. It was all part of the act. His presence just made acting all the more easy.

*No matter how hot, he's a suspect, like every male here. Don't forget what happened to those other girls.*

Images of cold, broken bodies assaulted her brain. Innocent prey to the devil.

The grip on her hand tightened. 'Hey. Are you okay?'

She tugged free. *Game face on, Jayda.* 'Yeah.'

Brian's ice-blue scrutiny did nothing but chill her blood. A male version of the Night Terror's victims.

'I'm here to watch. It's my first time.' Words she'd been coached, tailored to allow observation without the pressure of joining activities she neither wanted nor needed.

Her gaze strayed to the still-empty corner. Several open doors led out from this main front room. He could be through any one of them, and what he'd be doing . . .

She shivered, met Brian's stare head-on as she dragged in a deep breath. 'I'm a friend of Gina's.'

'I know.'

'You knew Gina?'

'Everyone here knew Gina.' The smile bypassed his eyes.

She tilted her head, eyes wide. 'Oh. Why's that?'

He shot her a quizzical look. 'She was a party girl. Willing to do pretty much anything.'

Her heart quickened. 'Did you see her the night she . . . you know.' The contacts scraped as she blinked, stemming tears over a woman whose legacy should have amounted to more than Brian's snide assertion. No matter that the assertion provided new direction to the case.

'Died?'

She swallowed. 'Yeah.'

'What night was that?'

'Thursday. Two nights ago.'

His gaze sharpened, piercing her with razor scrutiny.

*Swinger on, internal cop off, Thomasz. Slow down and stop with the interrogation steamroller.*

She gulped. 'I can't believe it's been two days already.' Fingertips trembling against her lips, she blinked some more. 'I wonder if anybody here saw her. If at least she was *happy* those last few hours.' Her hand tentatively touched his arm. 'Did you see her then? Do you know?'

He considered, covering her hand until she tugged it back.

'Don't believe I saw her. Difficult to remember. One night blends in with the next, know what I mean?' His lips twisted into what she assumed he meant to be a grin.

'And Joel?'

'Joel?'

'Her boyfriend. Did you know him?'

That razor scrutiny sharpened. 'First rule of the scene: no questions. Feel free to reveal whatever you wish,' his gaze poured slowly down her body, 'but personal details of other members are off-limits.'

Irritation made her blush genuine. More difficult to mask the evidence in her eyes. She lowered her gaze to her drink. 'I–I didn't realise.'

'I know you're new, so if you need any help . . . adjusting?'

His look, his tone, made her feel dirty—as though a million centipedes crawled the length of her skin. She shivered again.

'You're cold.' He rubbed his palms over her biceps, his beer breath attacking her nostrils. Her first instinct was to pull away. But other eyes watched her reaction, assessing, analysing. This was a test she daren't fail.

'Just nerves.' She forced her lips to curve upward. 'Sorry for the questions. It's just . . . I thought Gina had only been a few times. And if I'd known it was without Joel, I might have come with.'

'How well did you know her?'

'Not as well as I thought.'

One palm remained on her arm, caressing her skin. 'Sure you don't want to do any more than watch?'

She suppressed a shudder. 'I'm sure. I . . .' She dropped her gaze, performing a role not so difficult to feign. The innocent, unsuspecting, in search of a change. Her voice wavered and he leaned in to hear.

'I wanted to see what it was like. To see if I could do it.'

'And what do you think?'

He waited, sharp blue eyes appraising her, weighing every reaction, every word.

'I think I like what I see. So far.' Injecting just the right mix of shyness and innocence to cement her character, she bit her lip. Stared down at her smarting feet, and heels she couldn't remember the last time she'd worn. 'But I'd like to take it slow.'

'That's a shame, Shana.'

She startled at the name that wasn't hers, barely stemming the reaction with a fumbled sip of her drink. The movement gave her an excuse to step out of his grasp. If she was lucky, Brian and her other observers would chalk her reactions up to the nerves of a first-timer.

He indicated to her almost empty glass. 'Let me get you another drink.'

'Thanks.'

Brian slipped through a door to her left and she allowed her gaze to wander.

A delicious fusion of hot and cold rippled through her body as she studied the interaction of singles and couples. To get a feel for the place. Its workings. To understand how a serial killer could infiltrate this closed group simply to stalk and kill an innocent woman.

Now those facts had changed. How much had Joel Vance known?

Brian's words muddled round her mind, looking for a rightful space to settle. Gina was a regular. Not only that, she wasn't an 'innocent' like the vics who came before her. Which meant what? The killer had suddenly changed penchants? Not impossible, but all her instincts screamed it was highly improbable. Which raised questions about Gina's death and its connection to the other Night Terror victims. Something she'd get her head around when her mind could focus.

Brian and her refill never returned. Surveillance caught him stealing out the back and into his new model SUV. Before she could say a word, Chase was on it, ordering a tail on his car and a check on his registration. Leaving her free to return her attention to the room.

With Brian gone, she was seldom alone for long. Others approached, a mix of single men, women and couples, their conversations only serving to cement Brian's assessment of Gina.

Around her the air buzzed, her senses buzzing right along with it. She watched with fascination—the come-ons, the blatant sexual displays, the *lust*.

And all the while, as she overtly studied the comings and goings, she couldn't help but covertly look for *him*. He was just as likely to be of interest as any other male in the room. And while too young to be the Night Terror, he could have knowledge useful to the investigation.

She had to follow every lead.

That's what she told herself as she felt the hot burn of eyes at her back once again. Her goose bumps suddenly sprouted goose bumps of their own, and the hairs on her neck sprung to attention.

Slowly she turned, knowing exactly who she would find.

Beneath the muted glow of a nearby chandelier, Seth Friedin took his fill of the figure painted into her slinky top and short butt-hugging skirt.

He didn't bother to hide his interest, or the obvious appreciation in his eyes, his body. The environment didn't require it. Tonight may have been about work but that didn't preclude him from enjoying the perks. The hottie before him included.

Her cheeks darkened, the flush spreading down her throat to disappear below the neckline of her top. What he couldn't see, he pictured. Generous scoops of flesh thrusting against the silky, fitted top—how they'd pucker and swell at his touch, fill the curve of his palm to perfection. Would her areolae be dusky pink? Or darker, the shade of sweet, plump raspberries?

His taste buds sprang to life with an intensity that surprised him, anticipating the flavour, the rich, ripe texture of her skin beneath his tongue. That wasn't the only portion of his body to spring into gear.

All thanks to the drought of recent months. It had to be. That and the sex-infused atmosphere of the house were toying with his mind. A mind that had focused on work to the exclusion of everything else lately. Perhaps too much.

He raised his gaze to meet the unwavering fix of her stare. A pink tongue flicked over the arc of her lips triggering a keen jolt of muscle below. It was a challenge to his libido to ignore the invitation she offered. So he didn't.

She was too pretty, too soft and innocent to frequent a joint like this. Not a woman he'd pick as typical to 'the scene'. But maybe that was a good thing.

He knocked back the rest of his whiskey and Coke before homing in on his target. After all, she might just be the one he was looking for.

# Chapter Three

**A** panther-like tread brought his magnificent body to a stop before her.

'Enjoying your first time on the scene?' The voice matched the man; deep and rich, full bodied, sexy as all hell.

Jayda's shoulders stiffened. Inexperience was her cover, so she should have been pleased. Only, for some reason she found herself wanting to appear more worldly, more sophisticated for him.

Ridiculous. *Really*. Maybe more than disappointment and drink had led her to fall into Chase's arms. Thank God she hadn't fallen further. But that didn't mean falling was out of the question completely.

She made her body relax.

Once upon a time she'd clung to the misguided delusion of 'saving herself'. *Thanks once again, Liam.* For pounding the final nail on that three-studded coffin, then leaving her without a backward glance. She'd never ventured down that path since. Still saving herself for someone worthy of her all. Just as her mother had.

*Bullshit!*

Knots squeezed at her chest.

That fabled life of love and wedded bliss was a lie. If her parents could walk away after twenty-five years, what was she still waiting for? Perhaps it was time to tend urges other than that to succeed in her career. Time to take the bull by the horns and give him a big, hard yank.

A deep breath and she met that bull head-on. Grinned. Let every sexy, wicked thought swarm that one look.

Feather-light fingers skated up her neck, the tips resting under her chin, raising her eyes to meet and melt in his.

God, she didn't want those fingers to stop. Wanted them to skate downward, touch every part of her that hadn't felt a man in way too long.

'No need to be embarrassed. We were all there once.'

A slow burn rolled out from beneath his touch, the soft murmur of his voice glazing her body, warm and thick like smooth, sinuous caramel.

*Temptation.* Not something that mixed well with the job.

Change might be the answer, but not here. Not now, with her unit listening in and so much on the line.

'You?'

He blinked and withdrew his hand. 'Yes, me.'

'How long since you started?'

'Swinging?'

She nodded.

He contemplated his drink. 'How long is a piece of string?'

She tilted her head. 'That's not really an answer.'

'No.' The admission accompanied a grin that dimpled his chin and made his eyes sparkle. 'But it's better than stringing you along with a lie.'

For some reason her heart stumbled. 'You make a good point.' Her gaze roved the surroundings before returning to him. 'So, help me out here. If no one shares anything personal, how do you work out whether you're compatible?'

'*You feel it.*' He took a step closer. 'Can you feel it, Shana?' Caught between the wall at her back and temptation incarnate, she sidestepped, disregarding his question and the heat it aroused. 'H–how do you know my name?'

He grinned, undeterred by her evasion. 'I'm extremely resourceful.'

Their gazes locked. Impossible to drag her eyes away. *What else are you?*

It was a moment before she realised she'd whispered the words aloud. She refused to be embarrassed—the question was necessary, essential to playing a part. Regardless of the impulse that created it.

'I could demonstrate, but I understand you're only here to observe.'

She stilled fingers that longed to fidget with the stem of her glass. 'Yes. And to satisfy my curiosity.'

'Just your curiosity?'

His entire presence filled the room until there was only him and her and heat. She remembered to breathe. 'So, what else did you manage to discover?'

He looked at her blankly.

She rolled her hand through the air. 'About me.'

His expression said he recognised the conversational ice-pack, but he let it go without comment. 'You're a friend of Gina's and a first-timer.' His gaze softened. 'I'm sorry for your loss.'

'Thank you.' She blinked, the contacts making the show of moisture in her eyes easier. Then she drew in a deep breath. 'Did you know Gina?'

'Not really. But in these circles, word gets around when someone leaves.'

'What word?'

'This and that.'

'More string, I take it?'

His grin completely dissolved her knee ligaments and she reached for the wall to steady herself.

'Something like that.' His gaze narrowed. 'What was Gina like outside of this place?'

She feigned hesitation. 'Fun, but private. In all our years of friendship, I never knew this side of her life existed.'

'That's not uncommon.' The tone of his voice dropped. 'Would you have joined in if you'd known?'

'I . . .'

This time when he stepped in, she stayed.

His thumb skimmed along her bottom lip, rubbing sensation across its circumference until she felt the rush of blood there and other deeper, darker places below. She let out a shaky sigh, eyes widening as he closed the distance and dipped his head, firm male lips ducking to meet hers.

She held her breath, allowing him in. Cementing her cover. This was for Gina, and all those women who'd succumbed to the hand of the Night Terror.

She smelled pine, a woodsy outdoors kind of scent, and man. Pure, virile, aroused man.

Her eyes fluttered closed. She leaned in to meet him, heart gunning in her chest, blood thrashing through her veins, making her body heat and soften. His breath warmed her face, the last swig of his whiskey taunting her tastebuds as the whisper of his lips met hers.

A groan escaped. Hers? Or his?

Hand and glass dropped to her side. Thankfully, she'd swallowed the last of her martini well before he kissed her.

His tongue skirted her lips, sweeping away any last resistance, testing and tasting her as if she were everything. Warmth seared her hip, his palm brushing there, and lower, fingers sinking deep into her flesh, pulling her inward. Her body sighed, sank into him, meeting and melding with heat and hard male muscle. All the while her body buzzed with the promise of more.

Static shrilled in her ear. She flinched. Jerked back.

Room and reality shot into cruel, harsh focus, leaving what could have been and what was in a tug of war with her conscience.

Chase's voice echoed in her earpiece. 'They've found another victim. We have to go.'

Her blood chilled, even while her heart still seemed determined to escape her ribcage. Her gaze darted towards the door.

'What's wrong?'

His hand left her chin as she fought for breath. And sense.

She grabbed his wrist as it drew away, 'Oh my god! The time!' She stared at the Omega watch face, the hot skin beneath her fingers zapping her anew, before she let go to grip her cool empty glass with two hands. 'I was supposed to meet my sister half an hour ago.' The practised words left her lips with superficial confidence.

'Really?' Left eyebrow raised, the word oozed scepticism.

'Bad enough that I'm late, she'll kill me if I don't show.'

Her tone was unequivocal, even as she searched for a place to offload her glass. There was none, of course. She thrust it towards him and those long, sure fingers wrapped it inside. His gaze never once strayed from hers.

'Thank you for—It was—I mean—' Yep, there it was. The unmistakable proof. Her entire unit listening in and she couldn't string more than three words together. Training hadn't prepared her for that kiss.

Not that she expected much when her entire blood supply had rushed south with the promise of—

She shook her head. If only her flustered innocence could be chalked up to acting.

His gaze narrowed, and she pounced before he could call her bluff. 'See you around sometime.'

Her legs carried her to the front door, leaving her brain a few steps behind. She fumbled with the lock. Second try, it gave way. Steeling herself not to turn for one last mind-melting look, she slipped into the cool evening air and tugged the door closed behind her. The clatter of her heels down the front steps did nothing to calm her nerves.

A narrow escape, thanks to Chase.

Her mind whirled, spinning-top style. *Holy hell!*

This stranger with fathomless eyes and the scent of a forest meadow. She didn't know his name, but she knew she'd been willing to kiss him, and more. She was certain she would have done more. And she couldn't blame the drink—she'd hardly had any. Was it the atmosphere in the house? She'd be kidding herself if she said yes.

It was her. And him. Her burning need and some indefinable, uncontrollable attraction. How could she have reached twenty-seven and never have experienced *that* before?

The ground rose before her as she stumbled. A crack in the pavement. Fatal and dangerous, if you didn't take care. Lessons she should well keep in mind.

She rounded the corner and approached the black 'Antenna Solutions' truck hugging the curb.

A cat skittered across her path and she froze, willing her nerves to get a grip. He had her unsettled, frazzled. Men didn't do that to Jayda Thomasz. Not anymore. She was unsusceptible to them, their wiles. Had a lifetime of fortification around her emotions to prevent exactly what had just taken place.

The job had been her single-minded focus for the past seven years. A moment's fancy couldn't be allowed to change that.

One slip. That's all it was. And damn certain it would never happen again.

'What've we got, Teddy?'

Jayda braced her stomach as the stench of decomposing flesh hit her nostrils. The reek of urine from the adjacent lane didn't help. Or the overflowing dumpsters, a consequence of the council rubbish collectors' rolling strikes. The reason this victim wasn't found as quickly as the others. That and the fact she wasn't displayed so publicly and proudly.

Only the occasional car horn and rumble of a city tram disturbed the deceptive calm of the blind alley; reminders they were standing in the hub of Melbourne's city centre.

Medical examiner Rod Bearinger glanced up and nodded. 'Chase. Jayda.'

He pushed up with his cane, leaning heavily against the brass T-handle, his bespectacled gaze giving Jayda a once-over. 'Big night out?'

'I wish.' She tugged at the dipping neckline of her top. 'Undercover op. But because I'm lead on the case . . .'

'. . . you had to bail? Well, good for you. Your dad must be proud.'

'Thanks.' Warmth flooded her cheeks. She ignored the butterflies in her chest, gesturing instead towards the woman who deserved their undivided attention. 'Same MO?'

'Looks that way. Although discovery took longer this time. I'd place time of death around seventy-two hours, possibly more. Which makes her victim number seven, not eight.'

He pushed back a strand of grey hair with his wrist and waved a gloved hand towards the victim. 'Proximate COD appears to be asphyxia by strangulation. Body propped up against the wall. Eyes open. Blistering around the mouth, white chemical burns on the surrounding skin. I'll get the lab to check it out, but from the look of it, I'd say concentrated hydrogen peroxide.'

'And the finger?'

Leaning heavily against his cane, he bent and lifted the woman's left hand. 'Ring finger severed. Surgical incision at the proximal inter-phalangeal joint. Only difference is what appears to be a nick in the proximal phalanx.'

He pointed to a small but clear indentation in the bone. 'Usually a cut of this nature indicates hesitation. Sometimes, even rushing or impatience. Not that I would have linked either of these with our killer before now. I'll know more when I get her onto my table.'

'Do we have an ID?' Chase's breath fanned the hair at the back of Jayda's neck.

She edged sideways, giving him space that didn't invade her own.

The discomfort, she shrugged off. She was being ridiculous.

'Sure do.' Teddy's baritone interrupted thoughts better left till never.

'Angelique Sutton. Twenty-three.' He handed Chase an evidence bag containing a hot pink Cara Vinelli wallet, opened to reveal a Victorian driver's licence.

Jayda braced the hem of her skirt and crouched beside the body, eyes searching. Eventually he'd slip up. He had to. And when he did, that vital clue wouldn't escape unnoticed. She would catch the bastard and see he rotted in a steel six-by-eight until the end of his days.

Chase's hand shook as he handed her a pen. Good to know he shared her anger.

With the nib, she lifted a blonde curl from Angelique's forehead. The hair was coarse, dry, as if bleached without care or conditioner. Recently, too, considering the absence of dark roots to match the chestnut of her eyebrows and lashes.

She inspected lower. 'What's this?'

'Wondered if you'd notice.' Teddy leaned over the top of his cane again. 'Needle mark below the left earlobe, indicating an injection into the glossopharyngeal nerve.'

Jayda's gaze wandered beyond the body. 'I assume no needle was found at the scene?'

'You got it in one. Won't know what was injected until we do a tox screen. But lividity suggests she was killed elsewhere, then posed here.' Straightening, he nudged his specs with the back of his hand. 'I'm all done here. Once you're finished I'll organise to get her back to the lab.'

Teddy limped towards the white coroner's van. Seemed his hip had flared up again. Weird that in a modern, non-wartime society, gout still existed. She'd always associated the ailment with older, ex-military men; Grandfather Joe's generation.

Chase moved to stand beside her. 'He's evolving. What's the bet it's propofol diluted with lidocaine again?' He rubbed his jaw. 'Two vics with needle marks. What do you figure that's about?'

She straightened, her mind racing.

First Gina Hennessey, then Angelique Sutton. Two deaths that didn't add up. Never had she been more certain.

'It's not the Night Terror.'

# Chapter Four

'How can you be sure?' Chase stared at the lifeless human remains, his expression imperceptible. 'Everything else fits, including the bleach around the mouth. Something we've successfully kept from the media. How would a copycat know about that? And let's face it, it's not unusual for these sons of bitches to change MO.'

'I can't explain how he knows what he knows, but something doesn't feel right.'

Chase leaned in, his breath an uncomfortable itch against her ear. 'Could be that's nothing on our vic and more about you locking lips with Mr Macho.'

She stepped back, shooting him a dagger-tipped glare. Just as she'd started to believe her slip in good sense had gone unnoticed, he'd delivered a right hook straight to her false sense of security. If he'd identified that moment of silence in the house for what it was, all bets were on that the rest of the team had too.

She laced those daggers with venom. 'Never heard of playing a part?'

'You were playing alright. I'm just not convinced it was an act.'

'Get a grip on that little green monster, Chase. This is work. If you can't handle it, maybe I need a new partner.'

His smile slipped. 'Damn, Jayda. I was just ribbing.'

'I don't give a rat's. Take your ribbing and shove it.'

'Since when did you lose your sense of humour?'

'Since when did you become an ass?'

He opened his mouth, a whirlwind of thought traipsing across his face before he clamped his lips and cleared his throat. 'Just because there's a shift in MO for the last two vics, doesn't mean there's more than one killer.'

'Not always, but in this case it does. The injections. That hesitation mark. They mean something. The Night Terror's never anything but precise. Hence, the reason he's never been caught.'

She gestured towards Angelique. 'Here's a woman who is immaculate in almost every way. Expensive makeup, hands well cared for, nails long and manicured. Her dress sense is impeccable. That shirt is Gianni Alessandro and wouldn't cost a cent less than three hundred bucks. Yet her hair looks like it's been dumped into a bucket of bleach. That wasn't her doing. It was the killer's, post-mortem. He wanted her to be blonde, to fit the vic profile.'

She squared her gaze on his. 'Someone else killed Angelique and Gina. Someone who wanted their deaths to look like the Night Terror's.'

'I guess that makes sense. Disgruntled boyfriend or partner kills the missus and frames it to look like the serial killer monopolising the media at the moment. But why two girls?'

'I don't know. To perpetuate a pattern? My guess is Angelique was practice. The hesitation indicates inexperience, maybe even remorse. And unfortunately for Gina, once he discovered he could kill, he went after his real target. This bastard is sick, alright. But he's not the Night Terror.'

Chase's brows dipped into an almost perfect vee. 'All great theories, but why don't we wait for Teddy's results before making snap judgements.'

She bit back the words itching to leap from her tongue and slap his confounded complacency. What was up with him? Ever since this case . . .

It had to be the case. Twenty-five years of silence and the Night Terror re-emerges—it had thrown them all. Everyone in the squad wanted to catch the bastard and bring him to the justice he'd dodged last time round.

That had to be it.

Chase hadn't lost his edge, he was just stunned with the killer's return. He'd back her up when push came to shove. They were a team, worked well together. And no two-bit psycho—or momentary lapse in judgement—would change that.

'You're late.' Bec's pink-painted lips dipped into her usual conspiratorial grin.

Jayda retaliated with an eye-roll and lack-of-sleep grumble. 'Good morning to you too.'

Her sister's grin widened. 'If only more than a love affair with your job was keeping you from our crazy addiction to pain, sweat and tears.' Barely a breath, she continued, Bec-style. 'Unless there's a new distraction on the horizon? Or in your bedroom? Last night's hot date transforming into Sunday morning sex?' Perfectly sculpted eyebrows played hide and seek with her side-swept fringe, underlining an expression both ridiculous and hopeful.

Jayda offloaded her gym bag and jacket before joining her sister at the back of the class. With any luck Bec would assume the rush to class put the burn on her face, not truth in her words. Not that there was any. Blue-grey gun-barrel eyes notwithstanding.

'Hilarious, Bec. Let's see if your humour withstands Juz's workout.' She dropped a scrunchie into her sister's waiting hand—why Bec never remembered to bring her own, she hadn't a clue—and watched as she deftly pulled back and secured her long blonde hair.

'Glad you could join us, Jayda.' The man himself, Juz Callum, winked before returning his attention to the group of ten or so other women stretching their quads.

Jayda inhaled, mentally preparing herself for the grind ahead. Juz may be a friend outside class, but he was also the best damn interval trainer in existence. Bec refused to go anywhere else, and she came for Bec.

Oh, and hips, waist and thighs to die for.

The music amped up, pulsing through the thin carpet and her barely broken-in trainers. 'Jog it out, ladies. Soft and slow. This is your warm-up, so don't push it till I tell you.' Flexing his shoulders, Juz dipped his head from side to side.

'Fifteen seconds, then we have power jacks.' He grinned, a look of pure, crazy glee. 'Ready for some insane exercise?'

The group gave a muted mumble.

Jayda shuffled closer to Bec as Georgie slipped into position beside her. Puffing as if she'd already finished a full-fledged workout, she nodded hi to Bec and raised her dark brown brows at Jayda. 'Did I miss much?'

She grimaced. 'Unfortunately, no.'

Georgie mirrored her expression, then rolled her eyes. 'At least I won't feel guilty about that vanilla slice at lunch.'

'An entire chocolate bar for me.'

They grinned.

'I said, ARE. YOU. *READY?*'

Juz wouldn't stop until they gave him what he wanted, and every woman in the room knew it. A unanimous *yes!* erupted as they prepared to jump-jack straight into a low squat. Her muscles were about to hate her, but her thighs would be grateful as all hell.

'I got Dad's pressie. Wanna know what it is?'

She spared Bec a sideways glance, working hard to maintain her balance. And even breathing.

Bec didn't gasp or pant. She didn't sweat or perspire or 'glow' like most normal, earth-dwelling women. Instead, as always, she appeared cool and jumped into the squat with ease. Grace, even. She had the perfect body, a look much like Cameron Diaz and a personality people flocked to. If Bec wasn't her little sister, and an absolute doll, Jayda would have hated her with a passion.

'An "upfront and friendly with a croc" experience.'

Jayda overbalanced, corrected, and only just managed to stop her jaw from dropping to the floor.

Georgie kicked on, oblivious, her sleek brown bob bouncing energetically against her shoulders as she immersed herself in her usual exercise bubble.

Jayda found her voice. 'You're kidding.'

Bec didn't falter, launching into hop squats effortlessly. 'Nope. He always had a thing for Steve Irwin. And he loves animals. Think he'll like it?'

Jayda threw herself into the exercise, taking a deep breath before she answered. 'He loves everything you give him. *Regardless.*'

'Great.' Bec ignored the dig, or maybe she just didn't get it. She hopped, then squatted, making it look a helluva lot easier than it was. 'Know if Mum's coming tonight?'

Jayda's thighs, butt and glutes burned, and something other than the exercise flared in her stomach. 'Why wouldn't she? Dad's still her husband and they love each other, even if they're not living together right now. This is just a glitch. They'll fix it. And tonight is special, his fiftieth.' The words wheezed out from her mouth, but Bec heard.

Georgie didn't. Her concentration was glued with single-minded focus on the workout, to the exclusion of everything around her. Not one to chat through pain, Georgie preferred to breathe through it, never taking her eyes off Juz or his over-enthused movements.

Bec seemed to hesitate, then sighed. 'She's moved in with someone.'

'She's *what?*' Jayda stumbled and clutched at her sister for balance. Georgie jolted into awareness and her expression softened as she mouthed,

'You okay?'

Jayda nodded, her gaze straying to Juz. He shot her a look, both sympathetic and questioning, and she knew she was in for a grilling. The man had a radar for gossip and he relished every shred of it.

Georgie, on the other hand, was more of a there-if-you-need-me flavour of friend. Less inclined to push unless she sensed you were ready to share.

Jayda turned back to Bec, trying to hold it together when every thought made her feel like she was about to fall apart. '*She left Dad for another guy?*'

Her stomach churned, but she still managed the mummy kicks, even if they lacked the energy of seconds before.

'The grapevine says yes, Mum says not, so who knows?'

'Does Dad know?'

Bec shrugged. 'I knew they were having problems, but . . .'

'You *knew*? Why didn't you tell me?'

Her sister's blue lagoon eyes narrowed as she twisted her head towards Jayda. 'I figured they'd work it out. They always do.'

This was getting better by the minute. 'You mean they've had problems before?'

'After Dad returned from that undercover stint on the Highbury Case.' The class dropped to the floor for thirty seconds of moving push-ups. Jayda did the same.

*Three years ago.* Back then she'd been focused on getting her detective's badge, so family life was a blur. They were always there for her. Her rock. But with studies and training, she'd hardly been home.

What she did remember was the tension. She'd shrugged it off as a projection of her own worries over her studies. Never once had she imagined her parents would anything but love each other, or grow old and grey together. Wasn't that why Dad retired last year? They were the perfect couple. A winning team. Bec's words, but she'd always echoed them.

Jayda had spent a lifetime dreaming of exactly what they had. So much so, she'd dreamed herself into love with Liam. Rationalised her disappointment when reality failed to meet fantasy. Made excuses for his failings. Her own.

Because she'd wanted her parents' kind of love with all her heart. Until two weeks ago; the day she'd discovered it was all a sham.

'You bringing that hot partner of yours tonight?'

The shift in topic was as subtle as a g-string. Jayda let it go, her head still spinning from her discovery, not to mention a shortage in oxygen.

'I . . . keep . . . telling . . . you,' she paused for breath, 'he's a work colleague, that's all.'

'So, you wouldn't mind if I . . . *you know?*'

She faltered, noticed Georgie do the same. She always hated the floor part of the workout.

'Really, Bec? You can do so much better.' Her speech was stilted, mere puffs of breath, but nothing her sister wasn't used to deciphering.

'You said he was great.'

'He is.' Jayda pushed harder, wiping the sweat from her forehead with the back of her hand. 'At work.'

'I *am* stepping on your toes.'

'Thirty-second break, ladies.' Juz grabbed his energy drink. 'Then we do it all again! Rehydrate. Re-energise. Check your heart rate. But don't stop moving!'

She collapsed onto the floor, her mind racing in competition with her heart.

*Get a grip, Thomasz!*

Bec lobbed a water her way, then Georgie's. Jayda caught it, the break in her thoughts forcing good old-fashioned reason back into her brain. It was so unlike her, this over-sensitivity, this *angst*, but her parents' breakup had spun her judgement into disarray, causing her to question everything she believed in.

That's all this was.

The cool liquid refreshed as she scrubbed her mouth with the back of her hand. 'You're not stepping on toes, mine or anyone else's. Date Chase, if that's what you want.'

'Sure?' Bec's look was as earnest as the question.

'Loo break!' Georgie shot them a long-suffering grin. The breathless kind that wavers on your lips after you've worked your guts out and are still fighting for oxygen. Jayda's grin in response was pretty much the same.

Georgie jogged off and Jayda returned her attention to her sister. She knew that if she said 'hands off' Bec would do just that. And she loved her for it.

'Yeah, I'm sure. At least if you're out with Chase, I'll know you're safe.'

'With all those muscles.' She whistled, low and suggestive. 'Love a man in uniform. Sex-y.'

'You nut! He's a detective. He doesn't wear a uniform.'

'But he has a gun.'

'Yeah.'

'Double sex-y.'

Jayda laughed. Her first genuine laugh of the day. It felt weird, but a lightness filtered into her chest that hadn't been there for a while. Bec could always drag her out of herself when no one else could.

Georgie rushed back to her side. Flushed. Too obsessively keen over the workout for someone in their right mind.

'Get ready, ladies,' Juz bellowed. 'Ten seconds and we're back into it. Cut the chatter. Save your energy for the insanity to come!'

He shot a wink her way and she retaliated with the mature response. She stuck out her tongue.

He grinned as he counted down, 'Five! Four! Three! Two! One! Jump squats. Go team!'

She threw herself into the workout. Better that than thinking. Her parents. Chase. Bec dating Chase. The Night Terror. The warm, fuzzy feeling every time she remembered that man, *that kiss*. Mixed, tumbling emotions about them all.

Yeah. Better to puff and sweat and ache than think.

The world that had warmed and embraced her for so long was being dragged, kicking and screaming out from under her feet.

Life should be fair. Happy. A comfort.

Difficult to believe in something that no longer existed.

# Chapter Five

'**J**ayda!' Key already in the lock to her apartment, she turned to see Juz striding towards her, a small shopping bag swinging from his hand. 'I missed you after class.'

'Uh, yeah. My car was parked in a one-hour zone.'

'So you weren't avoiding me?'

She returned her attention to unlocking the door. 'Why would I avoid you?'

'For a homicide detective, you're a shithouse liar.'

When Juz grinned it was infectious. The white of his teeth overtook the olive of his face, and the deep brown of his eyes sparkled. 'Time for a coffee?'

'I was going for something stronger.'

He swept past her. 'I'll pour. You relax.'

She sighed and followed the whirlwind that was her friend into her living room. Juz wasn't one to take anything but 'yes' for an answer, particularly if he was on a mission. Like now.

'One drink only, then I need to shower and change for Dad's party.'

'That's tonight?'

'You know it is. You were invited.'

He crouched and opened her freezer, emptying the contents of his shopping bag. 'Remind me to take this when I go.'

He wedged a carton of ice cream between her out-of-date dim sims and a bag of frozen peas.

'Orange choc chip? Not quite your taste.'

'I'm widening my horizons.' Shooting her a grin, he straightened. 'What are you wearing?' He opened the fridge and scanned its contents, then glanced at her above the door. 'The emerald Carrie D'Lor, I hope?'

Dumping her bag on the bench, she perched on the edge of a

barstool and watched Juz turn his nose up at a bottle of her favourite Moscato, grab two glasses and dubiously begin to pour.

'It's dinner with family and friends. I was going for simple and understated, like my LBD.'

'Ah, black. The colour of mourning. We'll get back to that in a second.' Juz stopped pouring and dipped his head to the side, squinting at her over the breakfast bar. 'Family do or not, you never know who else could show. Go with the green. You have those matching sandals, and the necklace and earring set your parents bought for your last birthday.'

He resumed pouring. 'Wear your hair in a loose bun like Carlos styled for you last Christmas. It'll go perfectly with the spaghetti straps and low neckline.'

Grimacing, he set the bottle down and rubbed the back of his hand. 'Now your outfit's set, you can fill me in on what's bugging you.'

Her gaze landed on the red patch of skin as he continued to scratch. 'What happened?'

'I have a suspicion Garry changed washing powders on me.' He slid her glass across the bench.

'Put cortisone on it.'

'Yes, Mum.' He grinned and she grinned back.

'Speaking of Garry, where is he? Shouldn't you be getting ready for your big night out?'

'His boss has him working a double shift.'

'That's rough. Your six-month anniversary is a big deal.'

A zap of passionfruit tangoed across her tongue. She closed her eyes for a second and savoured. 'It's not too late. You can still come to the party.'

'Nah. Think I'll stay in and celebrate when Garry gets home. Better late than never. Right?' He donned his brave face. A mask that showed it hurt that Garry was missing their anniversary. And as much as she hated seeing his pain, she loved that her friend had finally found the happiness he deserved.

'I know he wouldn't miss tonight if he had a choice, Juz. He hates that job. Mind you, it's only since I met Garry that I'm nice to telemarketers. I'd hate to hang up only to find out I'd hung up on my best friend's boyfriend.'

Juz's smile was fleeting. His gaze narrowed. 'Nice deflection, distracting by talking about my favourite topic. Me.' He grinned. 'But don't forget, you're shooting against the best. What's up, Jayda?

'Why do you think anything's up?'

'My radar's on and it's blinking red. You have the body language of a rhino with back pain and everything tells me something Bec said has you spooked. Out with it, hon, or it'll only balloon until you can't hold it in any longer.'

It would take more than a roll of her shoulders to release the kinks in her back, but she did it anyway, knowing Juz was right. 'Do you know what Mum said when she called to tell me about the split? She needed to *find herself*. What the heck is that supposed to mean? *Find herself.* As if she was some lost hippy or something equally ridiculous. And now she's gone, I find out the truth. Mum left Dad for someone else.'

Juz sipped, rolling the liquid expertly over his tongue. He grimaced, almost gagged and spat the mouthful into the sink, dumping the glass with more flourish than required. In the two years they'd been friends, one thing they'd never seen eye-to-eye on was wine. She went for sweet and affordable, he favoured dry and vintage, and never the twain shall meet.

He rinsed his mouth with water, then daubed his lips with a kitchen towel. Slowly. Meticulously.

It was useless to push Juz when he was in contemplation mode, so she bided her time, biting her lip to stop from screaming out loud with frustration.

After what seemed an age, he lifted his gaze to hers. 'Are you sure?'

'Pretty sure.' She tried to read him and got nothing. 'She's moved in with someone.'

He turned to the sink and cleaned his glass. She stared at the broad musculature of his back as his words wafted over his shoulder. 'Your parents split two weeks ago. Don't you think she could have met someone since then?'

Juz never washed, not without gloves.

'You know something!'

He turned to face her, his expression indecipherable. She dumped her glass onto the white granite and leaned forward to force Juz's gaze to meet hers. 'Spill!'

'What could I know about Lydia that you don't?'

'Don't give me that! She goes to your Thursday night attack classes. Did she say something then?'

Juz shook his head. She itched to grab his shoulders and shake every last secret out of him. Instead she made do with slamming her palm on the bench top.

'Dammit, Juz! I've had the day from shit city and I don't need you adding to it. The marriage I idolised is a farce. My parents are separating, there's another dead body in the morgue, and some psycho fucker is running around Melbourne killing women at random. Just once today, I'd like a break.'

He reached across the bench and covered her hand. 'Slow down. You don't get to blow a gasket on my watch. You're doing your best and if you can't catch this guy, nobody can.' He shook his head. 'I'd love to know who comes up with these names, though. The Night Terror. What's that about?'

She yanked her hand back and wrapped it around her glass. 'Some reporter made it up to sell papers.'

A familiar boil scorched her blood. The kind she got thinking about the scum who sensationalised murder. They were almost as bad as the madmen who performed them. Irrational? Perhaps. But not unfounded. Freedom of the press was all well and good, but serial killers sought recognition and it rankled that they got it so readily, and sometimes with an almost-reverence just shy of praise.

'It's all about the signature. Our task force was nicknamed Pacu after a killer fish that bites extremities like fingers from its victims and leaves them to bleed to death. The Night Terror is a sicko who terrorises women at night and he's their worst nightmare.'

'A very clever sicko, mind you.' He sounded impressed, but must have caught her scowl because he waved a hand as if to recant the statement. 'Nowhere near as clever as you, though.'

Her hand sliced the air between them. 'Cut the bullshit, Juz. This isn't about work. It's about my life, and everything I believed turning into nothing but pipe dreams.'

'Happily ever after isn't a pipe dream, Jayda. It's real.'

'Tell that to all the happy, broken couples out there. Even Bec couldn't find it.'

'But at least she's still looking. And as long as she doesn't give up, one day she'll get there.'

'If it exists, which I seriously doubt.' She glared at him over her glass, catching his eye, daring him to look away. 'If we're talking deflections, this ripper of yours won't work. If you know something, it's your duty as a friend to spill.'

'What was that?' He spun around.

Her gaze followed his. 'What?'

'The door clicked.'

'It couldn't have. I closed it behind me.'

'I heard what I heard. Maybe you just thought you closed it.'

Swivelling her chair, she fixed her eyes on the door and slid down from the stool, mentally retracing her steps. She'd closed it, heard the *snap* as it shut behind her. Hadn't she? Or had she just taken it for granted?

The way her mind was flying every which direction right now, maybe she just remembered wrong. Or maybe Juz misheard.

Opening the door, she peered outside at nothing but an empty hallway. This time when the door clicked shut, she double-checked the lock. Whatever the case, the door was closed now.

She slipped back onto her stool and picked up her glass. 'See what you're doing by not telling me. I'm so spun out I don't know what's right and what's *right*.'

'You've a lot on your mind. You're allowed to lose it a little.' He shot her a sympathetic smile, a tilt of his head, and she hated that he felt she needed them. Hated the pity and the weak feeling that followed. *She was not weak.*

'Or perhaps your roving neighbour's back from wherever and it was his door I heard.'

'Darren's in Queensland for business. He's not due back until next weekend.' Her grip tightened round the glass. 'You know I *can* be friends with you both.'

'I never said you couldn't. He just gives me the heebie-jeebies.'

'Sure you're not just a little into him?'

'Pah!' He flicked his hand as if swatting a bug. 'I'm happily taken, thank you very much.'

'Yes, you are. And now you've had your diversion, can we get back on point?'

She glared with intent to intimidate, but his expression didn't falter. He traded stare for stare, completely unperturbed.

'For heaven's sake, Juz. Spit it out!'

'I can't tell you what I don't *know*, and if I'm wrong, guessing will only make things worse. Why not ask your parents?'

'Because they won't tell me. Seems they've had problems for years and I never saw it.'

His palm warmed the back of her hand. 'That doesn't make you a bad daughter.'

'Doesn't it?'

The wobble in her voice surprised her. Thoughts that lurked in the back of her mind pitched forward, dragging at memories and the days leading to her entry into the police academy. Her mother's encouragement. Her father's opposition. It was the one thing over which they'd clashed, until her dad's sudden and unexplained about-turn.

Juz skirted the bench, a cloud of peppermint and clover wrapping her up in warmth and love. 'The fact you never suspected anything just makes them good parents. They were protecting you.'

'From what?'

He shook his head. She'd wring more juice from an MK40.

The day was moving into the surreal; Juz saying so little said so damn much. Her head was spinning, her stomach churning, and it had nothing to do with the wine.

The arms about her tightened. 'Every penny has two sides, hon. Don't go jumping to conclusions before you flip and the coin has a chance to fall.'

'He loved it!'

Bec jostled her way to the bar, elbowing Jayda's ribs with her own brand of 'told you so!'

Jayda raised their empty wine glasses and nodded to the barman before turning to lean her hip against the rustic wood, her lips twitching. 'I never said he wouldn't.'

'But you thought it.'

'Did not.'

'Did too.'

'Damn, I hate how you know what I'm thinking, even when I don't.'

Bec batted her eyelashes and head-nudged Jayda's arm. 'Call it sisterly love.'

Jayda bucked her shoulder. 'Sisterly nosiness, more like.'

'I'm wounded.'

'Doubt it.'

'Yeah, you're right. I'm not in the least bit offended.'

Her sister's grin was infectious, and easy to return. Trading a twenty for their drinks, Jayda slid a glass her way.

'Thanks.' Bec lifted it to her lips and they turned their backs to the bar again, staring across the restaurant floor at the table lined with all of their father's family and friends; bar one. 'It's not the same, is it?'

Jayda shook her head. A sudden thickness coated her throat, making it impossible to speak. She swallowed back the pain, her tense palms smoothing the black fabric of her dress over her hips.

Yes, she'd ignored Juz's advice and gone with comfort rather than fashion. The spectacular, she'd left to Bec, who looked just that in her purple satin off-the-shoulder creation. But then again, her sister always looked spectacular. It wasn't what she wore, it was how she wore it.

'Do you ever wish you were a kid again?' Bec blinked, her over-bright eyes staring at the far wall.

'Not really. You?'

'Sometimes. When shit happens.'

She didn't have to say more. The unspoken words hung in the air between them. *Like now.*

'Dad seems okay.'

Bec frowned. 'He looks tired. And he's lost weight.'

That was just the bad lighting, right? And wasn't it approaching midnight? Jayda shrugged. 'Has he said anything about Mum leaving to you?'

'No. You?'

She shook her head. 'Juz thinks there's more to it than Mum moving out.'

'Like what?'

'He wouldn't say. I tried to call, but her mobile goes straight to voicemail, and she hasn't returned my calls.'

'Mine either.'

Jayda tried to read Bec's normally open-book expression. 'Really?'

'Yes, really.'

Her jaw clenched. 'There are far too many secrets in this family.'

'Not with us. We pinkie-promised.'

Jayda's lips twitched. 'That was over twenty years ago.'

'Pinkie promises don't expire.'

'Amen to that!'

Their shared grin peeled back the years, a rose shedding every perfect petal, and they were kids again, stomping through their primary school playground, conspiring mutiny against Ms Hemmings, their very severe, very ancient headmistress. The poor woman had never stood a chance. Not when Bec had a plan.

'I have a plan.'

Jayda choked on a mouthful of wine. Dabbing at the sudden leak from her eyes, she gasped a reply. 'That's novel.'

'It's simple. We need a disaster.'

'Huh?' Sometimes it was hit and miss when following her sister's weird and winding train of thought.

'You know, a catastrophe. An event that causes serious loss, destruction.'

'Don't tell me. You swallowed a dictionary.'

Her sister swatted her arm. 'There's a tonne of research about how the stress of disaster brings people together. Maybe that's what Mum and Dad need.'

She tried not to roll her eyes. 'What kind of disaster do you suggest?'

'I don't know. But I'm sure we can figure one out.'

'How're my girls?' They turned—surely looking guilty as all sin— as their father wrapped an arm around one, then the other, and squeezed.

The 'girls' shared a look and Jayda bit back a laugh. The toughness in the detective had mellowed over the past few months. Who would have imagined retirement would suit Dean Thomasz? And aside from the wan tinge to his normally ruddy features and his post-split weight loss, he looked pretty damn good for a man who'd just turned fifty.

'How are you, Dad?'

'Never better.'

She searched his face for a hint of concealment and found none. Still, her father was the master of the cover-up.

'Ohh! There's Cynth. I haven't seen her in ages!' Bec disentangled herself and kissed her father on the cheek. Shooting a 'we'll talk later' look at Jayda, she bounded towards a girl of eighteen years with over-teased brown hair and braces. Their second cousin, or was it third? The round of squeals and hugs brought a smile to her lips.

'She's one of a kind, isn't she?' Her father turned and ordered a beer. It was good to see him smile.

'Thank goodness! Imagine two Becs in the world.'

'What a thought!' He passed a crumpled note across the bar in exchange for his pint, raised it in a toast and gulped back a generous mouthful. 'How's the case going?'

No need to ask which one.

She turned, resting her elbows on the dark polished wood. 'We've hit a wall.'

'How so? I thought you had two new vics.'

'They aren't the Night Terror's.'

Her father's brows shot skyward. 'That's not the story I heard.'

'It doesn't add up, Dad.'

'What does, then?'

'The last two were copycat murders. The Night Terror is due to kill again.'

'Evidence?'

'Nothing concrete yet, but Teddy's bound to find something.'

'He's a good man, Teddy.'

'He speaks very highly of you too.'

'We go back a long way.' He contemplated his beer then took another swig. 'So, no regrets about joining homicide?'

'I can't imagine doing anything else.'

'The job does that.'

'Yet you left.'

The instant the words fled her mouth, the air froze and a vacuum rippled between them.

Her father raised his glass, then dropped it again without drinking. His hand seemed barely steady, his nerves barely calm. 'It was time.'

'Was it something to do with you and Mum?'

The line of his shoulders sharpened, his gaze deliberately avoiding hers. 'Why would you think that?'

'Because I don't know what to think and no one's telling me anything.' The print on the blue-and-white bar mat blurred. 'Why did Mum leave, Dad?'

From the corner of her eye she saw him blanch. He coughed, a dry hacking bark deep in his throat, then washed it down with a swig of his beer. 'Sometimes it's as simple as it not working anymore.'

'That's not an answer.'

'No, it's not. But not everything in this life has an iron-clad explanation.'

'You can't tell me you woke up suddenly one morning to find you no longer loved each other.'

'If I did, it'd be a lie. I'll always love your mother. And I know she feels the same about me.'

'Then . . . I don't get it.'

'It's not for you to get, honey.' His hand over hers felt unnaturally cold.

'Accept it. Things are better this way.'

The 'why?' remained stuck to her tongue as Aunt Lorraine dragged him away for more cake.

Her father's apologetic look wasn't fooling anybody. He'd skated around every one of her questions, his practised evasions drowning her stomach in dissatisfaction. Nothing made sense.

The week ahead loomed.

Her parents loved each other but had elected to live apart. And a barbarian still stalked the streets of Melbourne looking for prey.

# Chapter Six

'It's inconclusive.'

Jayda gaped at her father's old friend, her heart so busy nose-diving towards the spotless linoleum floor that for a moment speech was lost to her. She took a desperate swig of double-strength macchiato.

Shame it wasn't vodka.

Teddy brushed his forearm across his brow and shook his head. Clad in his customary blue scrubs, he peered at her over the cadaver on his table.

Nothing in this diabolical case made sense and she'd waited through the entire weekend hoping for more.

'But the injections are a dead giveaway. Not to mention Angelique's hair. It's not the same killer.'

'That's a lot of circumstantial which doesn't necessarily add up to a definitive. I'm not saying you're wrong. I just can't prove at this moment that you're right.'

'There has to be something.' She met Teddy's quizzical gaze. 'I'm not saying you've missed anything. I know you haven't. It's just . . .' She took a deep breath and focused on calming her frustration. 'We need to go back to the vic profiles. The two last girls. There has to be a link that doesn't fit with the other deaths.'

She slipped her notebook from her pocket and flipped through the pages until she reached her latest scrawled list. Her gaze scanned the facts.

Dead end after dead end.

The latest? Brian—née Terence Doogan—may have been a creepy wife-cheating scumbag with two outstanding parking fines and one for speeding, but he wasn't the man they sought. He'd been in LA on business when the two murders prior to Gina were committed, then San Fran after that.

Every lead, another dead end. And the predictability was getting mighty old. Damn! She'd been sure Angelique's autopsy would reveal something new.

Her gut *wasn't* wrong. It was this case. It tied her up and twisted her into tight little knots until she couldn't see straight. Even the nightmares had started up again. Residual memories from a time her subconscious refused to let her forget.

'There is something else.'

Her gaze jumped from the page to Teddy.

'Angelique had intercourse only hours before she died.'

'That's—'

'Another inconsistency?'

She nodded. 'All the other vics were virgins. Except Gina.' Which was the reason she'd gone undercover Saturday night.

Jayda ignored the heat that memory evoked—and the steely grey eyes that accompanied it—to focus on Teddy, who was nodding again.

'There were traces of silicone on the uterine lining indicating a condom was used. But I also found semen. Either the condom split or it leaked, but he must have noticed because the area was washed haphazardly with soap. I've sent what I could to the lab and won't know if there was enough for a conclusive DNA test until I hear back.'

The news jump-started her heart. This was it! The 'something' she'd been waiting for. DNA meant identifying the killer. Which meant they could rule him out of the earlier killings. Then there'd be no doubt, and Hackett would be forced to let them continue the search for the real killer.

The Night Terror hunted innocents, an element too intrinsic to his makeup to change. He'd need a damn good reason to stray that far, and she just couldn't see it in this case.

'It might not be him. The man who had sex with Angelique won't necessarily be her killer.'

Her gut told her otherwise. 'Maybe not. But don't be surprised when it is.'

Teddy shot her a rare smile. 'You've got your father's gut.'

'In most cases that'd be considered anything but flattering.' She managed a grin. 'Thanks for the compliment.'

'I mean it, Jayda. Dean Thomasz was a damn fine detective. One of the best. He could smell a dirt bag a mile away, and you have that same sixth sense. Don't ever doubt it. That gut will serve you well.' Teddy peered at her through half-moon specs, the low timbre of his voice shivering all the way up her spine. 'And it'll keep you alive.'

*. . . so, if you crave the abs of the toned and famous, stick to the un-stickable rule— a teaspoon of peanut butter a day keeps the belly fat away.*

Seth struck the last key on his laptop with flourish, if not satisfaction. His three-part segment on 'Men Shaping Up for Summer' was done, and all he felt was flat. *Fluff and feathers.* His parents' words, not his. But that didn't make it any less true. Or any less agonising.

With a grimace he hit *send*, ten minutes shy of his Friday afternoon deadline. Four and a half years of university, a bachelor's degree in journalism, a master's in media and communication, and all he'd snagged was a couple of two-bit daily columns. Granted, the *Melbourne Telegraph* was this city's equivalent to the *New York Times*, but neither column ever made a showing before page eleven. No *real* reporting was required. Nothing close to what he'd dreamed of when he'd enrolled in his courses, all green-nosed and wide-eyed.

His parents had sworn he'd never amount to much. Turned out they were right.

He shoved back his chair and stood, fighting a restlessness which growled louder day by day. Hands overhead, he arched right, left, back, stretching muscles unused to inactivity.

What he needed was a good dose of grunt and sweat. It was three days since he'd seen the inside of a gym. As for the other kind of activity that loosened tension, well, that had been longer. A dry spell he'd hoped to end last Saturday night, until she'd bolted from him like a mare at the crack of a starting gun.

Seth grunted, dipping his head from side to side. Nearly a week gone and the disappointment still surprised him. But he'd curbed it with a steely admonition—this was work, not play. Distraction was something his geophysicist parents, Brianna and Grant Friedin, had never allowed in their thirty years of staid, stiff-upper-lip marriage. They probably even diarised sex, squeezing it in only when their busy, world-saving schedules allowed.

The chain of thought conjured images that made him want to sear his brain until they receded. It was the age-old paradox. No one liked to consider their parents partaking—let alone enjoying—such acts. And he had the stats to prove it. That was last month's fluff and feathers.

He dipped his head again. The cricks seemed content to remain. Perhaps a run? He turned, and the red-and-black scrawl on his study whiteboard caught his eye. *No.* This story, his hunch, was more important. A one-way pass out of mediocrity and into the limelight.

*The Night Terror.* Something was off. The fact that he'd re-emerged. New additions to his MO. The burning round the mouth—a detail not yet released to the public that Seth had uncovered through a source far superior to the cops on the case.

And then there were the victims, all innocents. Until Gina.

Something about Gina didn't fit. So he'd delved deeper into the swinging portion of her life and gleaned nothing but a raging hard-on. Taut fingers ground into his temple, massaging in vain. He closed his eyes.

She didn't fit the profile of the killer's usual vics. Which meant either one of two things. This death was personal. Or it wasn't the Night Terror.

Instinct inclined him towards the latter. Now all he needed was to outdo the cops at their own game, write the story and collect the accolades. Then he could move his attention to breaking the real Night Terror case—a success impossible for anyone to ignore.

Gina's death provided his first lead. Moving round his desk, Seth dropped into the high-backed chair, pushing the laptop aside to make room for a thick, red folder. The third page yielded what he was looking for. One month before her death, Gina subscribed to a website, *Angels of Harlem*. A place where men hooked up with women interested in the kinkier side of sex. It was while following this lead that Seth had made an enlightening discovery—*Angels of Harlem* was founded by none other than Angelique Sutton, the victim preceding Gina.

His sources in the Department stated that fiancé Joel Vance claimed he knew nothing about Gina's other life. The swinging or the internet.

Sipping at his beyond-cold Nescafé, Seth contemplated. Who was he to question how a man could remain oblivious to such an intrinsic part of his fiancée's life? Still, this fact was like steak cut from the toughest, oldest, meanest bull in the herd—difficult to chew and even harder to swallow.

With help, he'd dug further into the life of Mr Joel Vance. Seemed the man had a past. A couple of quashed misdemeanours and a rape allegation that never stuck. Speaking to 'friends' and neighbours, he'd gleaned that Vance had a history of obsessive jealousy. Why hadn't the police uncovered this? The answer was a flashing neon sign—they believed they'd already identified the killer.

He dragged his laptop back and opened his diary. A page filled with notes leaped onto the screen—thoughts, feelings, hunches. His system for making the world make sense. Without conscious thought his fingers tripped over the keys and the words flowed. His frustrations over his job, the case, the woman who ran before he could get her real name.

Seth's mobile vibrated, followed by the gravelly voice of Mario Puzo's Godfather. *I'm gonna make him an offer he can't refuse.*

Caller ID showed a *Melbourne Telegraph* number—his editor's right-hand man, a friend, and another fluff-and-feathers reporter, but one who loved it.

He answered by clicking on the speaker. Richard Collins didn't bother with formalities, his larger-than-life voice booming out from the phone. 'Turn the TV onto Channel 0.'

'Hi, Richie. Nice speaking to you, too.'

'Yada, yada, just do it, Seth. You're gonna want to see this.' Coffee in hand, Seth moved into the living room and clicked on the widescreen LCD, flicking through channels until he reached 0.

'*. . . one week after her death, detectives have confirmed the latest brutal killing, of Melbourne woman Angelique Sutton, is the work of the man they call the Night Terror.*

*The predator who terrorised Melbourne for more than a decade is back after a twenty-five year lapse.*

*Before the murders ceased, more than forty women fell prey to the serial killer, who hunted and strangled his victims by night. All were unmarried, aged between twenty to twenty-five, with blonde hair and blue eyes. And in every case the ring finger of the victim's left hand was severed. The fingers were never recovered, and it's believed that the killer kept them as trophies.*

*These more recent deaths are identical to those in the past. Detectives leading the case say . . .'*

'Hey, Seth. You still there?'

His lip curled as he hit *mute* on the remote and turned away from the screen. 'Yeah, I'm here.' He positioned a coaster onto the over-polished 1920s buffet and set down his mug.

'Seems your story's no longer a story. Seeing as he did kill those last two women.'

'Just because the police say so doesn't make it true.'

'Amen to that, brother! I'd be first to admit our esteemed police force can fuck up, and fuck up big. But with this case being so high profile and all, it's hard to believe they'd say he did it without being 120 per cent sure.'

'If you're not looking, how can you uncover the truth?'

'Meaning . . .?'

'They're focusing on the similarities instead of the inconsistencies, refusing to believe there can be two sickos out there at one time. Plus, Commissioner Brady is under huge political pressure. State elections run in six months, so his best bet is to pin all the deaths onto one offender.' Seth turned back to the screen. 'Unless they're playing some game, and this is all just a smokescreen.'

'So, what now, man?'

He switched off the set. 'I keep digging. Find out what the police really think.'

Only one place for that.

Ending the call, he grinned, grabbing his jacket and keys. Nothing like going straight to the horse's mouth for the grits and gossip.

# Chapter Seven

*E*xquisite.

His nose twitched. The air hung thick with the scent of her. Frangipani. Coconut. And a whirl of honey. *Sweet.* Just the way he liked them.

They were all sweet, satisfying, but this one was . . . special. Exceptional. The one to make all the difference.

Damp mist swirled around the length of her tiny dress as she walked, the colour of sunflowers glowing incandescent under the blue-grey of the old city lamps. Beads clung to his bare face, sliding from the hair slicking his forehead to run an icy trail down his cheeks. He rubbed the back of his hand across his eyes, flinging the sweat into the gutter, and licked his lips, tasting the night, *her*. Anticipating.

A fox scampered onto the road, pausing, its blood-red gaze latching onto his in silent understanding—one predator to another—before it turned and fled between two towering brick edifices.

The echoing click of her heels stalled, then quickened, matching in perfect synchronicity with his heart. It was always like this. The rush. The heady thrill and anticipation.

*Fear. Hers.* Ambrosia slipping succulently between his lips.

He drew out his gloves, sliding eager fingers into the familiar softness of well-worn leather. *Almost there.* His blood thickened, charging like a wild boar through his body. The hunt, the ultimate.

And this one, the encore.

She reached the corner and turned, disappearing behind the high boundary fence.

*Close now.* He licked his lips, tongue quivering, tasting the air, sucking it in until all he could taste was her. The fear. The untouchable innocence he would suck from her body.

Her footfalls ceased and he smiled. *Close.*

He turned the corner and watched her fear turn to relief.

'You!' She dropped her stiletto and nudged her toes back into its grasp. 'You gave me the fright of my life!'

She stepped forward, only inches from him now. Her hand settled onto his bicep and the muscle flexed automatically beneath her palm. 'I thought you were—'

'Your worst nightmare?' He grinned.

She didn't get it, even then. Not until his fingers wrapped tight round her throat, the tips digging deep into her flesh, her eyeballs bulging clear from their sockets.

Her nails scrabbled at his leather-covered wrists and his groin tightened, his mouth closing in to swallow her final, shuddering breath.

The kiss of death, from the master. There could be only one.

# Chapter Eight

'**W**hat's up with your sister?'

Jayda glanced up from the sprawl of papers on her desk to watch her partner saunter through the door. Not that she'd absorbed a single, blurred sentence for some time. The precinct clock indicated it was past nine on a night that should have been spent celebrating the end of a long week. That explained her heavy eyelids and stiff back.

She closed the file, effectively shutting Angelique's battered remains away from her vision. Removing the slump from her shoulders wasn't as easy. Whatever she sought, it wasn't in the paperwork. If only she knew where the hell it was, where to look next.

Chase shuffled behind her, reminding her of his presence and previous question. She swivelled her chair to face him. 'Nothing, as far as I know.'

He rubbed at a thin bandage on his wrist which hadn't been there two hours earlier.

'What happened?'

'Just an old sprain giving me grief.' He stuffed his hands into his pockets. 'Have you heard from her?'

Jayda stared at him blankly.

'Bec.'

She blinked. 'No. Why?'

'We were meeting at Molino's for dinner but she didn't show.'

'Knowing Bec, she was running late.'

'By two hours?'

The slump left her shoulders. 'That's not like her. Didn't she call?'

'Nope. I even checked with the restaurant in case she left a message.'

'Did you try her mobile?'

'Went straight to voicemail. I thought maybe she'd changed her mind.'

'She'd have told you. And me. And I know for a fact she planned on seeing you.' She grabbed her phone. 'Maybe she's stuck in traffic or has a flat tyre or something. Maybe her mobile died and she couldn't call. She might even be waiting for you at the restaurant now.'

Regardless of all the logical, possible maybes, she couldn't shake the feeling that something was wrong. First her parents, now this. Everything was *off*. As if the entire planet had skewed on its axis.

Her gut squeezed into a macramé of knots, and without thinking she was already speed-dialling Bec's number. After the obligatory five rings, the phone clicked over to voicemail. Jayda's nails tapped the desk, racing her heartbeat. A lifetime later, her sister's greeting ended with a beep.

'Hey, sis. Just checking you're okay. I know you were meeting Chase. What happened? Call me as soon as you get this.'

She tried not to panic. There was a reasonable explanation for Bec's no show and they'd all laugh about it when she called back.

She stared at the phone in her hand and willed it to ring.

It was all about balance.

Seth nursed his first and only whiskey for the evening as his gaze scanned the area surrounding the bar. He picked out a few familiar faces, officers he'd seen in the media in relation to this or other cases—men and women who regularly frequented The Traveller, whether to let off steam or wash away the grit of the job.

He'd seen photos of the victims, waded through anything and everything he could about the Night Terror from twenty-five years ago and now. The images made his usually hardy stomach heave. What did it do to one's soul? To see those dead, debased women in the flesh, revisit almost identical crime scenes day after day after day.

If all it took was a couple of drinks to make the job bearable, who was he to judge?

And it served his purpose well. If you sought information, this was the place. Start up a conversation, buy a round or two. Get a few drinks into a cop and their tongues were looser than Mia Faircliff in twelfth grade.

You just had to find the right one.

His gaze roved, a casual I've-got-all-the-time-in-the-world-and-nowhere-else-to-be type of gaze. Important to give the right impression. A man out for the evening, after nothing more than a drink and a few laughs. He passed over the groups, seeking a loner. Someone not too high in the food chain. Then again, pick someone too low and they'd have no worthwhile information to share.

His head whipped back.

*No*. It couldn't be.

He took in the faded jeans and black tee, wild hair the colour of a rich, full-bodied burgundy. He edged closer so that when she turned he could note her green eyes. *Green*, not blue. The two women looked nothing alike, yet he'd swear it was her. The tilt of her head, that nervous tug on her bottom lip with her teeth.

And she was a cop. He'd bet his life on it. He couldn't prevent the grin attacking his lips, or the tightening in his gut, and below.

Suddenly the night was filled with promise. And extracting the information he needed was looking a lot more enjoyable.

'Is this seat taken?'

Jayda held her breath and turned slowly, as if by delaying she could alter the outcome.

Unsure whether to be happy at the familiarity of the male voice or not, she clutched at her glass and tried to remember how to breathe. In, then out, and repeat. Not difficult, unless your brain had turned to the consistency of pea soup.

Fire blazed up her neck, branching out over her cheeks. Even her ears burned. She refused to acknowledge what was happening in places less exposed. Shaking her head, she lowered her gaze and took a deep sip of her martini.

Hopefully he'd take the hint. If she was lucky, he wouldn't recognise her. Sure, her drink was identical, but any number of women must drink citrus martinis. And, anyway, the similarities ended there. The wig and contacts were gone. Not to mention her sexy outfit. Her hair hadn't seen a comb all evening, her lips were pale and dry, without lippy or gloss. Her old jeans and faded tee were more suited to a rock concert than attracting men in a bar. In short, she was a mess. Not the glamorous woman he'd approached almost a week ago. This wasn't how she'd envisioned their reconnection.

Thoughts of what she *had* envisioned made her blush all over again. Erotic, evocative images best left back in the house where they'd first met.

She sipped, swallowed without spluttering and traded her glass for her mobile, tilting it to stare at the blank screen. No missed calls. Where was Bec?

'Waiting for someone?'

'Just a call from my sister.' Biting her lip, she dropped her mobile back onto the bar. Why'd she say that? This stranger didn't need to know her business. Although, after that kiss, could he still be dubbed a stranger?

'Is she okay?'

She spun round to face him, tangling with familiar blue eyes she'd thought never to see again. 'Of course she's okay.'

The blue darkened to steely grey as he raised a brow. She might be worried—her heart racing like a horse in the Melbourne Cup—but that didn't give her the right to be snarky when he was just being polite.

'I'm sorry.' Now she'd looked up, her focus stuck to the wide curve of his lips.

'I'm a good kisser, you know.'

Her gaze whipped up to meet his. 'W–what?'

'I said, I'm a good listener.'

She'd misheard. Of course, she'd misheard! The poor man had no idea he was talking to a loony-tune who wanted him to kiss her so badly she was even now imagining how he would taste.

'If you want to talk, that is.'

She shook her head, shaking off the images that were making her crazy. 'I'm fine. I expect she'll call any moment now.'

'Let me buy you a drink while you wait.'

'Why?' The word slipped out before she even knew it had been conceived.

'Why not?'

He had a point. Not that she needed another drink. She'd already had two. One with Chase—after he'd dragged her to the bar only to cry tired, deserting her for home. Then 'one for the road'—a 'drowning your bad day in good liquor' kind of drink.

She should be on her way home too. Only she couldn't— wouldn't—rest. Not until she heard from Bec.

'Are you going to make me beg?'

She snorted, the words bringing her back to reality with a colossal thump.

'Would you?'

'I don't know. Do I have to?'

Swivelling in her seat, she faced him, experiencing that familiar bolt of awareness as he stared down at her.

'Much as I'd love to call your bluff, that requires energy I don't have.' She turned to the waiting barman. 'Lemon, lime and bitters, thanks.'

'No more martinis?'

She pushed away her almost empty glass. 'That's my limit.'

He turned to the bar, thoughtfully swirling the lone, dry cube of ice in his tumbler. 'And another whiskey.'

Steel softened to electric blue as he returned every bit of his attention to her. 'I'm Seth, by the way.'

'Jayda.'

His eyes widened, then blanked. Surprise? Had he expected another name? Shana, for instance? Or was her current paranoia getting the better of her?

'Nice to meet you, Jayda.'

Her name melted from his tongue and sinuated its way into her blood. She'd never heard it spoken like that—all soft and smooth, rich and warm and golden, like treacle over a large, hot stack of fluffy pancakes.

'So, tell me, are you a police officer like ninety per cent of people in this room?'

'A detective.'

*What the*—? Since when did she blurt *that* out, least of all to a stranger? It had to be stress, and the drink. And the heady way his eyes seemed to all but consume her.

'Good for you.'

The barman delivered their drinks.

Seth handed the man a twenty, waving away the change. 'Sounds like you love it.'

It wasn't what he said, it was how he said it. As if he really got what being a detective meant to her.

'Most days.'

'But not today?'

Perceptive *and* hot. 'No. Not today.'

'Want to talk about it?'

'Not really.' Her hands tightened around the cool length of her glass. 'What do you do, Seth?'

He knocked back a mouthful of whiskey. 'Communications.'

'Oh?'

'Not nearly as interesting as investigating, I'd bet. Like that serial killer all over the news. Twenty-five years and suddenly he reappears. What's with that?'

'Isn't that the gazillion-dollar question?'

He stared at the golden swirl of liquid in his glass. 'Wouldn't it be great to know?'

He didn't seem after an answer and she gave none.

He drank again, then dropped his glass onto the bar. 'You must have thought about the case at least a little. Any theories?'

Thought about the case? She'd done nothing but eat, sleep and stress over the case since the killer's return. Had theories until they poured out of her skin twenty-four seven and she couldn't sleep at night. But none she was willing to share, least of all with a stranger who made her wary and horny and hot as all hell.

She was tired. Of death and divorce and disappointment, over and over and over again. And more than anything, she was sick of the games.

Staring at the man next to her, she couldn't think of one solid reason not to follow where her dreams had led her after that first, soul-shattering kiss. He was a player. He had to be, considering their first meeting and its location. All that remained was whether he wanted to play with her.

'What is it we're doing here?'

That grabbed his attention. Even toppled him a little off balance.

'What do you mean?'

'The small talk. Idle chatter. Discussing stuff that doesn't come close to what we're really thinking.'

The languid slide of his smile almost saw her slither off her stool. She clenched her thighs, waiting for his response, hoping she could hold it together before she chickened out and fled like she had last Saturday.

Seth leaned in. 'What is it we're really thinking, Jayda?'

She swallowed, then turned in her seat. Each whispered word warmed the air between them. She could taste his drink, him, on her tongue, their lips were so close.

'Whether that first kiss was a fluke, or whether it'd be even better second time round.'

# Chapter Nine

They barely made it through the exit before Seth pulled her into the shadows and backed her up against a wall.

His eyes were more black than blue now, the pupils dilated. All-encompassing. 'I've been dying to do this since you ran away last week.'

She gave no thought to maintaining her cover—that had been blown the moment he approached her at the bar. Now had nothing to do with the case and everything to do with a need unlike any other she'd experienced.

She licked her lips. 'So, you do remember.'

'How could I forget?'

He kissed her then. Only it was much more than a kiss.

His lips rolled across hers, his tongue slashing entrance into her mouth. She moaned, kissing him back with a longing that surprised her. His breath was hot, a familiar fusion of whiskey and hunger, his body hard and unforgiving as it pushed impatiently against hers. The bricks at her back were rough and biting, but she didn't care. She wouldn't hold back any longer. The past seven years had been one lengthy dry spell, and she was ready to banish the drought. With him.

How had she gone for so long without this? If she'd known how incredible—how *liberating*—it would feel, surely she couldn't have held back. Every nerve, every cell, every fibre of her body throbbed with *want*.

His hands roved hungrily and she found herself doing the same. She wanted—no, needed—to feel every inch of him. Know every muscle, every curvature and hollow, with an intimacy she'd never before shared with a man. Liam included.

With a grind of his hips, he wedged his knee between her thighs, opening her up so she could feel . . . She gasped. He was huge. Hard and full and ready.

Her body stiffened, her fingers digging sharply into his back. They couldn't do this *here*. Not in public where any one of her colleagues could stumble upon them and see.

It should be special. Crisp, clean sheets, soft music, dim lighting. Chattels to her old beliefs. But hey, just because she didn't want romance or rings or eternal love, didn't mean they couldn't take things slow and enjoy the experience.

Seth pulled back, his breathing ragged. 'You okay?'

'We can't do this here.'

He looked around, eyes widening as if taking in their surroundings for the first time. 'You're right. Where then?'

Not her place. Or his. But would a hotel be tawdry?

She spared a thought for the wisdom of leaving with a semi-strange man. The Night Terror was out there somewhere, more than likely hunting his next victim. She shivered. Her gut told her she had nothing to fear from this stranger who fell way outside the offender profile on so many levels. She trusted her gut. It was seldom wrong.

It wasn't as if she had blonde hair and blue eyes. Doubtful the Night Terror even knew she existed.

She grabbed his hand. 'I know.'

Skirting the old building, she made for the fire escape, ignoring the erratic beat of her heart. Purse stuffed into the waistband of her jeans, she stretched above her head, gripped the first rung of the emergency ladder, then swung up before glancing down at his upturned face.

'Follow me.'

Where was the siren taking him?

Not that it mattered. She could lead him into the fires of hell right now and he'd willingly follow.

Darkness swallowed her peach-perfect ass as she scaled the ladder and clambered over the edge. Seconds later he did the same, puffing more than he cared to admit. Hunched over, hands braced against his thighs, he worked at catching his breath while his eyes scanned the area.

A rooftop garden.

Muted blue filtered out from four strategically placed security lamps, while a fusion of pungent aromas enveloped him. Basil. Coriander. Mint. Then there was the sweet blend of honeysuckle and jasmine, the white-and-pale-pink blossoms cascading over a large trellised screen, bordering on three sides a low table and a couple of sun loungers.

He turned to her. 'Your place?'

'A friend's.'

There was no time to take in more as she took his hand and led him towards the screened area.

A car horn sounded below.

In the midst of the fragrance and flowers, she released his hand, her fingers toying with the hem of her tee, her teeth toying with her bottom lip. In one swift motion the garment was up and over her head, fluttering down onto the chair beside her. Her hands wavered at her sides, as if she wasn't quite sure where to place them.

His gaze locked on to the rounded flesh spilling from her practical black bra. No frills, no lace. He found it refreshing, the lack of trappings. She didn't need them.

Taut buds thrust at the soft material and his mouth watered, wondering at their taste.

He moved in. She shook her head and pointed to his shirt. 'Your turn.'

Ignoring the buttons, he whipped it over his head by the collar. Then he reached for her jeans, pulling her closer, unhooking the tab at her waist. 'Now yours.'

Her breath hitched as he eased down the zip. His hands slid over her hips and behind to cup her buttocks. God, she felt good. More than good.

He pulled her in, licked her lips, suckled at the bottom one until she moaned and pressed against him. Palms rounding her buttocks, he delved between her thighs. *Hot. Deliciously hot.* He rolled his fingers. She gasped. He bit back a groan, wanted more, *needed* more. He edged the denim over her hips and downward, luxuriating in the satin feel of her skin beneath his touch.

A mingle of scents saturated the air, yet only one made him inhale greedily. Green apples. He'd detected it the moment he joined her at the bar. Had recognised it immediately from their first encounter.

He inhaled again before refocusing on the distraction of her lips. She pulled back, eyes wild and uncertain.

His hands stalled. 'Is this what you want?'

She blinked, her teeth taunting her bottom lip once more. Then she nodded.

'Sure?'

'Would you prefer I change my mind?'

'Hell, no! I just want you to understand, you don't have to do anything that makes you uncomfortable.' She shivered and he rubbed his palms up and down her arms to warm her. 'I can tell you don't do this type of thing often.'

*Oh, God! He knows!*

Jayda clenched her hands at her sides and wavered between denying the truth and grabbing her t-shirt and making a run for the ladder.

Instead, she braced herself and drew in a deep breath. 'Th–this type of thing?'

He nodded. 'The swinging type of sex. Casual.'

'Oh.'

*He didn't know.* He knew she didn't do free and easy. Had guessed it their first meeting. But he had no idea the extent of her inexperience. That she'd had sex a whole, whopping three times in her life. That the last time was seven years ago. That she'd vowed never again unless it *meant* something. With someone she trusted. Implicitly.

Only this was none of that. And she was doing it anyway.

One night. Just once. With a man she'd never see again. 'You're right. But that's about to change.'

Levelling her gaze with his, she trained her lips into an upward curve and began sliding her jeans downward. *Piece of cake.* Until she reached her ankles, that is. Pushing the fabric over her shoes proved trickier. One leg lifted, she rolled the scrunched denim over the arch. It stuck. Her balance faltered. She hopped, tugged, nothing gave.

*Whoever said stripping was sexy was delusional.* There was nothing sexy about this striptease.

Tensing her muscles, she gave one final almighty tug.

Too late to stop the momentum. Fist and trouser leg sucker-punched him in the gut. His eyes widened as the wind all but rammed from his lungs in one loud, immediate *oomph!*

Her body jerked forward, the other leg still trapped in her jeans, and she tumbled. With no time to recover, his hands reached for her and he stumbled backwards, his knees slamming into the sun lounger behind him.

The recliner moaned, legs creaking before giving way, and the whole thing crashed to the ground.

She lay spreadeagled on Seth, her face planted into his stomach, his erection nudging her breasts.

*Oh, God! Magic me away from here. Now!*

It was a mess. *She* was a mess. No way could she lift her head and face him again. He'd known before that she was inexperienced, but now he knew just how much.

The muscle beneath her began to tremble.

*Hell! Not a seizure!*

Visions filled her mind—paramedics, cops, *her squad,* milling the area, questioning her on why they were there and what had triggered the attack.

Her reputation in ruins. *Again.*

A deep rumble erupted from his body.

*Laughter.*

'If you wanted me on my back, all you had to do was ask.'

She tilted her head and looked up. Sighed. He wasn't angry. Didn't seem unimpressed or put off. He just looked . . . amused. And aroused. *That,* she could feel.

Thank Zeus for the darkness and his inability to see that her skin had turned the same shade as her hair.

She shot him a shaky grin. '*Now* you tell me.'

He laughed again, and she joined in, a little uncertainly.

'Much as I find this arrangement enjoyable, I believe you have a pair of trousers requiring attention.' He shuffled up, forcing her to roll over and off until she was sitting beside him. He kneeled before her, easing the jeans over her shoe, dropping the offending garment onto the floor.

'No sense doing half a job.' He grinned as he hooked his fingers over the waistband of her black no-nonsense undies, encouraging her to tilt her hips so he could shimmy them down. Much as he didn't seem put off by the lack of silk and lace, first opportunity she had, she was investing in new underwear. Flimsy, sexy delicates that screamed more than 'warning: inept celibate cowering within'.

Lifting each leg in turn, Seth eased the undies off before dropping them onto her jeans.

She resisted the urge to shuffle, or cover herself with her hands. She'd never been this naked with anyone. Even Liam.

Three times. In a bed, under his crisp cotton sheets. Lights out.

No opportunity to see his body, and small mercies, he'd barely seen hers. A consideration she'd marked as thoughtfulness, a sensitivity towards her shyness. Now she knew the reason had another name—disinterest.

What if she wasn't sexy without clothes? Was she too hairy? It was tidy, her six-weekly waxing took care of that. But she'd never gone the whole hog. A Brazilian seemed over the top, way too painful and—let's face it—grossly unnecessary considering there'd seemed no chance of anyone delving in that direction anytime soon. How wrong she'd been. Perhaps she needed to reassess; pain be damned, maybe the hair should go.

His palms scaled her legs, moving towards . . .

She reached for his biceps and urged him up. The thought of him touching and kissing her *down there* had her hot and throbbing in all the right places. The reality, however, had her freaking out on a grand scale. Some things she wasn't ready for.

'Kiss me, *please*.'

'Well, since you asked so nicely.' His eyes flashed. 'Anywhere in particular?'

'Uh . . .' Maybe he sensed her panic. His finger brushed over her mouth as his expression softened. 'Why don't we start here and see where that leads us?'

He rubbed his finger along her lips and they swelled beneath his touch. Of their own accord they opened and her tongue flicked out, twirling around his fingertip. He sucked in a breath, letting her know she'd done something right. Emboldened, she allowed her hands to run over the planes of his chest. His mouth descended on hers; firm, warm lips massaging her into submission, his tongue teasing her with its lilting play.

Soft, warm skin encased muscles that contracted as her fingers trailed over each plane and trough. Her palms skimmed the hair smattering his pecs, following as it narrowed down his stomach and disappeared beneath the waistband of his jeans.

His mouth left hers, tracing over her jaw and onto her neck. At that point, she discovered one irrefutable fact—the curve where neck and shoulder met was one hell of an erogenous zone. The muscles in her sex gave a massive *whoop*—a hungry, grasping contraction that begged for fulfilment.

Then his tongue dipped between her breasts. Her breath became ragged as he swirled and rasped another killer erogenous zone. Her nipples peaked, begged for more, as his teeth nibbled and tugged at them through her bra. Could a woman die from pure ecstasy?

Her hands shook, her fingers fumbling with his fly. She'd never wanted—or needed—anything so much.

He peeled his lips from her breast, the grey in his eyes darkened to slate. 'Let me.'

She eased his hands away, slowly unfastening the first button. 'I can do it.'

'Am I safe?'

Heat hit her cheeks at his reminder of her earlier befumbled antics, but she ignored it. 'Absolutely not.'

When she released the second button, her fingers slipped inside to brush against his aroused flesh. His breath hitched and she released the final button, her hand gaining full access this time. 'Is that a problem?'

He groaned. 'Not from where I'm sitting.'

She continued her exploration through the fabric of his jocks. He was so hard. So big. The thought of him inside her . . . she shivered.

Her hand stalled, her heart plummeting all the way to the car park below. 'I don't have protection.'

# Chapter Ten

**S**eth's lips twitched. 'I do. Left pocket.'

Her entire body thanked the universe and sighed. She reached in, digging around until her fingers contacted with foil.

'Jayda, you're killing me here!'

She waved it with a flourish. What now? Did she offer to put it on, or would he?

Lucky Seth had no such hesitations. He took the packet and placed it on the seat beside him. Then slipping out of his loafers, he lifted his butt, sliding both jeans and jocks down his hips then his legs and ankles.

Her jaw dropped. She wasn't so naïve as to never have seen a man's penis before. Nothing had prepared her for this.

'Wow.' The word slipped out before she could stop it, and it dragged a flood of heat to her cheeks.

Seth chuckled. 'Thanks.' He reached round to unhook her bra and discarded it, pausing to admire what he'd uncovered. 'I'll return the compliment, and say wow back. You are one beautiful woman, Jayda.' Running his knuckles along the underside of her breast, he bent his head and, *oh, my!* When he sucked it was as if his mouth had a direct connection to every nerve ending below her waist.

She cast her fingers into his hair, soft and warm. And she clutched at the strands as the slide of his tongue had her body clutching for consciousness. Could she climax before he moved past her belly button? Throbbing intensified between her thighs, indicating it was a distinct possibility. She was wet, wetter than wet, and oh, so ready. 'Please, Seth, can we do this?'

Her nipple left his lips with a *plop*, cool air caressing the swollen tip as he lifted his head to meet her gaze. 'I thought we were.'

Need made her bold. Her hand reached between them to wrap round hot, inflexible muscle, leaving him in no doubt. 'I want you now.'

He jolted in her palm, his voice a mere rasp. 'No "please" this time?'

She slid her hand up, then down, delighting in the velvet smoothness of surprisingly soft skin. 'Do you need me to beg?'

'Would you?'

'I don't know. Do I have to?'

His lips twitched as he wrapped his hand around hers. 'Not a chance. Can you tell how much I want you right now?'

She'd guessed. And the realisation was intoxicating.

Dark hunger branded his eyes and she swallowed. 'As much as I want you?'

He tore the square foil packet and rolled the condom on with ease. Just watching him touch himself made her want him more.

'Come here.'

She did. Their gazes locked, and he tugged her round so she stood, straddling his hips, then slowly, gently, he encouraged her down.

His tip nudged her, taunting heat that was wet and hungry and throbbing uncontrollably.

*Buzz!*

'Not That Kind of Girl' pealed from the clothing on the ground. A ringtone she'd stubbornly saved despite Bec's groan that choosing Anastasia over Lady Gaga made her even less 'hip' than choosing clothes from K-Mart over Kate Hill.

She scrambled off, onto her hands and knees, rummaging through the pile of clothes until she found her mobile. 'Bec?'

Silence. She checked caller ID and the bones in her back sagged as she hugged her waist with her free arm. 'Chase.'

'Jayda.'

'Have you heard from Bec?'

Again there was that silence. She shivered, despite the lingering warmth of summer in the air.

'There's been another murder. I think you should come down.'

She dragged in a deep breath. 'Where?'

'Main Street in the city. I'll text you the address.'

'I'll be there as soon as I get a cab.'

'And Jayda?' Another pause. 'I'm sorry.'

'About what?'

The question met an empty ringtone. She stared at her mobile. What the hell had burrowed up his arse? More weirdness. Something was definitely up, something more than their shared non-event.

Which reminded her . . .

Dropping the phone, she stepped into her undies, avoiding the still aroused and naked Seth on the lounger. 'I have to go.'

'I heard.'

His visual disappointment could only have been exceeded by hers.

As she grabbed her clothes, she was vaguely aware of him discarding the unused condom in his trouser pocket before sliding his feet into the trousers and pulling them on. Regret washed through her. The promise of what could have been wrapped once again in fitted blue denim.

Although in her mind, she could still see him—all of him—hard, hungry. The perfect smorgasbord to end her seven-year famine.

Just twenty minutes more and . . . She hesitated, almost dropped her clothes to the ground before making him do the same.

Her phone beeped. Chase's text. She swallowed back a sigh.

The one thing she couldn't—wouldn't—waver on. The job came first.

'Sorry about the timing.' She managed to don her jeans without further embarrassment, sliding the mobile into her back pocket before reaching for her bra. 'Unfortunately the scumbags we chase don't keep regular office hours.'

'The Night Terror?'

'Could be.' She wasn't about to discuss the case.

'Rather than trying to get a cab, let me take you.'

She looked at him then. He was already dressed, the only evidence of their tryst the wayward disarray of his hair. She'd done that. She turned, scouring the area for anything she may have dropped. Her gaze took in the dilapidated state of the lounger. She'd come by tomorrow and pay Carmello for the damage. What explanation she'd give, she hadn't a clue.

'That's not necessary.'

Seth grabbed her arm, more of a caress than a clutch, and she looked at him then. His expression was earnest. 'This doesn't have to be weird, you know.'

Too late. It already was. That dreaded moment after, when you realised the things you said and did were things you would never normally say and do.

She tried for a reassuring smile. 'It's not. But work's work.'

'And I can take you there. No strings. I'll even drop you nearby and leave if that makes you feel better.' His thumb stroked her skin. 'Getting a cab this time of night won't be so easy.'

His offer was genuine and she was being a heel. She'd never been a don't-let-the-door-slam-on-the-way-out kind of girl. Tough, yes. Unfair, no. The least she owed Seth after his gentle understanding was trust.

'Sure. I'd appreciate a lift. I'll need to pop by the precinct for my gun and badge, though.'

'No problem.' He waved in the direction of the ladder. 'After you.'

Seth wasn't one for small talk, and for that Jayda was grateful. The leather of his Mustang was soft and warm at her back, the FM station playing dulcet oldies-but-goodies she'd have hummed to under different circumstances.

She could almost have relaxed, if she hadn't known what waited for her at the end of their short journey.

He lowered the volume. 'Makes you wonder why he's come back, doesn't it?'

It was a question she'd asked herself over and over. 'There are any number of reasons for a killer's sabbatical. He may have moved away from the area or travelled overseas. Perhaps he's been serving a prison term for another crime. Or maybe there's something that triggers his need to kill. Something that hasn't happened for the past twenty-five years until now.'

'What do you think it is, Jayda?' He glanced briefly at her before returning his concentration to the road. 'What does your gut tell you?'

She startled. It could have been her father sitting beside her, posing the same question as she agonised over some niggling facet of a case.

'My gut tells me you're awfully interested in the Night Terror and my thoughts.' She waved her hand. 'My gut also wonders why.'

Seth's eyes were trained on the road ahead. Maybe it was safety, a need to watch for traffic and trams and pedestrians as he negotiated the narrow streets. Or maybe it was more.

He tapped at the steering wheel. 'Morbid curiosity. I imagine the greater public is asking the exact same question.'

'Well, you seem to have given the case a lot of consideration. What do you think his motives are?'

That steely gaze pierced the distance between them. 'His or theirs?'

She turned in her seat to face him, her heart faltering. 'What do you mean by that?'

'What do you think about the last two deaths?'

'What do *you* think?'

'You play a mean game of hardball.' His chin dimpled for one brief moment before his expression sobered. 'I'd say we think the same thing.'

She raised her brows and he answered. 'That there's more than one killer out there at the moment targeting women.'

Falling back into her seat, she felt the beginnings of a smile.

'Am I right?'

'No comment.'

'I'll take that as a yes. So, why did the police release a statement yesterday attributing all the deaths to the Night Terror?'

Her body tensed. 'Good question.'

'You don't agree?'

It was one thing to discover their consensus on the case. It was another to go openly and vocally against the Department. 'I'm not discussing this with you.'

'So, we can do what we almost did, but you can't talk to me?'

'Not about this stuff. I don't even know you.'

'We could rectify that.'

Her heart fluttered. She drew in a deep breath, the clasp of her purse cutting into her palm. 'I need to work, Seth.'

'Now, yes. But not later.'

The promise in his words almost had her forgetting herself, his voice melting her, bone by bone. She shook her head. She couldn't think about that now.

Seth was a one-nighter. No culmination made no difference. They wouldn't be seeing each other again.

The car slowed, then stopped.

Police vehicles littered the area, the criss-cross of their high beams illuminating the otherwise blackened city street. Outside the cordon of crime scene tape, officers diverted passing traffic down one of the wider side-thoroughfares and two uniforms interviewed a young couple.

Beyond the barricade, Chase and Teddy huddled together in deep discussion.

'Just think about it, okay?'

She turned to Seth and nodded. 'Thanks for the lift.'

'No problem. I'm glad we met again, Jayda.'

She managed a brief smile, her mind already beyond the taped area. Opening the door, she stepped out.

'How will I see you again?'

Her hand gripped the door as she wavered. Then Chase looked up and she knew she had to go.

'You won't.'

As she slammed the door and approached the crime scene tape, Chase and Teddy rushed to meet her.

'What—' Tyres screeched and the air singed with burning rubber.

Bustle around the scene froze. Former detective Dean Thomasz charged out of the haphazardly parked blue sedan towards them.

'Jayda!' He clutched her to him, a familiar cloud of leather and sandalwood, and the lean muscle in his body shook. When he pulled back, moisture rimmed his eyes. Her father never cried.

'Dad, what are you doing here?'

'Chase called me.'

'Why?' She looked from one man to the other.

Nausea whirled up from her gut and into her throat, her intuition cemented by her father's next words.

'For Bec.'

Teddy placed a restraining hand on his arm. He shook it free before ducking beneath the tape.

'Where is she? I want to see my daughter. *Now.*'

# Chapter Eleven

Jayda was fine until the first tears slid down her father's cheeks.

Approaching the scene was difficult, but necessary. She was primary on the case and, regardless of the officers who tried to hold her back, she needed to see the victim. Even if the victim was her little sister.

This time there was no needle mark, no hesitation with the cut. No difference bar one—he'd left a note.

*Distinguish the master from the imitation.*

Conceited bastard.

There was no satisfaction in knowing she'd been right.

Her father choked back a moan and their eyes met across the body. She couldn't go to him. She had a job to do and hand-in-hand with that was holding it together.

The air around her was damp, a spring-like freshness that should have skipped through her sinuses with a heady *summer is coming* kind of rush. Instead it curdled with the sour smack of diesel and exhaust, razing the back of her throat with every shallow, tortuous breath.

This time she would find something.

Teddy wrapped an arm about his old friend's shoulders and led him from the scene. She stepped in. A rust-bitten can caught her toe and scuttled across the sidewalk and into the curb, stalling her in a move that would have seen her run into her father's arms.

*No.*

Icy fingertips reached into her pocket, groping for the familiarity of her badge. She turned away, squared her shoulders and continued to scour her sister's broken body.

Her fingerless hand lay slumped in her lap, the yellow flowers of what she'd laughingly dubbed her Van Gogh frock drowning in a crusted pool of blood. The hem had been torn, perhaps when the body was moved?

Jayda swallowed, blinking as her eyes skimmed the area.

There was no obvious sign of the snagged material. She made a mental note to get the uniforms onto it, moving her gaze up towards the neck. Already the thick band of bruising associated with manual strangulation was beginning to show. Teddy would need to dust for prints. No doubt the killer wore gloves again, but who knows—even sick bastards had to slip up at some stage.

Hard metal cut into her clenched palm. She skimmed over Bec's face, blinking rapidly, and inspected the brick wall behind before moving around to inspect the ground. The rutted grey pavement distorted and blurred.

'Jayda, you don't have to do this. Let me take over.'

Her hand jerked from her pocket. She dragged it across her eyes and turned to Chase, avoiding the sympathy she knew she'd see in his expression. 'I have a job to do.'

'Not tonight. Go home and remember Bec in a good way.'

She glared at her partner of two years. 'That won't catch her killer.'

'What the hell is she doing here?' Detective Inspector Terry Hackett stormed through the tape, his round face suffused with its usual red as he glared at Chase. When he reached Jayda, however, his expression changed. She would have said it softened, only her boss didn't do soft. 'Jayda, go home.'

'I can't. I have a case to work.'

'Not now you don't. As of this moment, you're on leave.' The must of stale tobacco hit her nostrils as he extended his arm across her shoulder, forcefully leading her away. 'Take a couple of weeks' vacation, mourn your sister, be there for your family. They need you, and you're going to need them.'

She wrenched free. 'What I need is to find the sick sonofabitch who did this!' Moisture welled beneath her eyelids, threatening to overflow. She blinked.

She would not cry. Not now, not here. Not before she claimed justice.

Hackett scratched at the back of his neck, his gaze centred anywhere but her face. A nicotine patch peeked out from his shirt neckline. His obvious lapse in abstinence wouldn't be helping his mood.

Hackett didn't do emotions, unless they were a variation of mad. Which was why she could tell Bec's death had him thrown, despite his pigheadedness.

'You're off the case.' He looked around until he found his mark. 'Chase, take her home.'

'I'll do it.'

She turned to find Seth standing outside the barrier, the restraining hand of a uniformed officer holding him back.

Her arms crossed against the expanding tightness in her chest as she glared at the man who'd promised to drop her and leave. 'Why are you still here?'

'Instinct.' He turned to Hackett. 'I'll get her home safe.'

And that was it. Like a child, her fate was decided whether she liked it or not. She gritted her teeth. No one fought Hackett and survived. You had to pick your battles.

'Jayda?'

She stared at her boss's upturned palm before dropping her gun into it. Then without a word she ducked beneath the tape and strode towards the road.

A hand grabbed her wrist and she stopped without turning, the strong scent of spice filling her nostrils.

'I'll call you tomorrow, okay?' Chase hesitated, his fingers pinching her skin. 'Just because you're off the case, doesn't mean you can't get updates, right?'

'Sure.'

She twisted her hand and he let go. His narrowed gaze darted from her to Seth, who appeared deep in conversation with Teddy and her father.

She forced a smile. 'Thanks.'

He was still her partner, and he still had her back. In the next couple of weeks she'd be counting on it.

'There's a strip of material missing from her dress. If we find it we may find the primary crime scene. And make sure Teddy dusts her neck for prints.'

'I've got this, Jayda.'

Absently she nodded, her eyes roving the scene and inner circle of cops until she sensed Seth beside her. He moved towards his car and there was nothing left for her to do but follow with her head held high.

Being taken off the case made things difficult, but not impossible. Gun or no gun, regardless of Hackett's dictate, there was no way in hell she intended to lay down and 'vacate'.

The pound inside her skull threatened to explode as she clenched her jaw and yanked the passenger door of Seth's car open.

The Night Terror had made one fatal mistake. In killing Bec he'd killed the best part of Jayda.

And for that he was going to pay.

'Hungry?' Seth pushed open the front door to her apartment and stood aside to let her enter. 'I can make you a sandwich or something.'

Jayda's stomach heaved. She made it to the bathroom, but not the toilet bowl. Staring at what remained of her pad Thai dinner and evening's drinks, she grappled for composure. No time for losing it now. She had work to do.

'Jayda?' Seth joined her in the bathroom and she couldn't dredge up the energy to be embarrassed over chucking her guts in front of a man she'd just been naked with. 'Why don't you change while I clean up?'

When she didn't move, he grasped her shoulders and guided her towards the bedroom.

With robotic obedience she let him push her inside. He walked past and into her en suite bathroom, turning on first the shower's cold water, then the hot.

'Shout if you need anything.' His gaze rested on her for a brief moment, then he slipped out, closing the door behind him.

She stared at the cascade of warm water. It splattered against the acrylic base before spiralling down the drain. And all the while her heart thumped so hard that every beat was a jab against the inside of her temple.

Something banged outside. The sound juddered through her body, dragging her back to the sparkle of ceramic tiles and a wash of thin mist over her skin. She blinked and her fingers trembled as they dragged at the fabric of her top.

Clothes were discarded, layer by layer, and she stepped beneath the spray. Water rolled down her body, but the chill remained.

The hot tap was cool beneath her fingers as she twisted, then waited for the heat to wash away the pain. It didn't.

Bec was dead because of her.

A sob caught at the back of her throat. She gulped and water scalded her tongue. She spluttered, and whatever remained in her stomach heaved out over the shower floor.

Her sister was a message. The sick bastard wanted her attention and that of the Department. And he'd killed Bec to get it.

Her skin began to prick. She watched as a scarlet welt formed on her chest, then deepened and expanded.

And then she began to cry.

Seth dumped the last of the towels used for cleaning into the washing machine and pressed *start*. Then, walking up to the closed bedroom door, he unashamedly put his ear to the wood and listened.

No noise.

He knocked. 'Jayda?'

No answer.

He knocked again. It was only a few minutes since he'd left her, but something inside dictated he check she was alright.

'I'm coming in.' He turned the handle and stepped into a room empty but for the clammy rise of steam from under the en suite door. This time he knocked on the bathroom door. It was hot and dripping with condensation.

'Jayda, are you okay?'

A sob penetrated the wood, followed by a high wail.

He threw open the door. The heavy weight of mist obstructed his vision as he strode to the steam-covered shower stall and yanked open the door. Jayda sat slumped in the corner, her beautiful body a splotchy mishmash of bright pink and red. He reached for the tap, scalding his wrist in the process. Blanking his mind to the burn, he turned the water to cold.

'Jayda, you need to get up.'

Her trance-induced body shook as large sobs wrenched out from her throat. He stepped into the cubicle. Seizing her under both arms, he turned her to face the jets, allowing the cool water to wash over her reddened skin. At first she resisted, almost toppling them both to the floor, but he held her firm and she soon stopped fighting, slumping forward in his arms as if she had just lost the will.

The water seeped into his shoes and through his clothes. His skin chilled as Jayda shivered against him. And still he held her.

They remained beneath the spray for what his watch told him was over ten minutes. By then her teeth were chattering, and his were close to doing the same. He supported her with one arm as he switched off the taps and grabbed a large blue towel from the rail. Patting her skin dry, he noted that the red from the hot water had faded.

He left her wrapped in the towel and shucked his shoes and socks, peeling out of his trousers and shirt before finding another towel to dry himself as best he could.

Jayda stood frozen where he left her, shoulders slumped, eyes staring sightlessly at her feet. Grasping her shoulders, he walked her to the bed; a mere shell of the woman he'd seduced only hours earlier.

Cotton PJs were folded beside her pillow. Much like one would dress a young child, he prompted her movements to slip them on, the unwavering emptiness in her eyes chilling him more than the residual cold from the shower.

Without a word, she curled onto the bed and allowed him to cover her before turning away, wrapping the blankets tightly around her shoulders and back. The message was unequivocal, but he wasn't one for taking hints if they didn't fit.

Her shoulder flinched as he touched it, but he didn't remove his hand. 'I'll be in the living room if you need me.'

Eyes crammed shut, she gave no answer. Not that he'd expected one.

'If you want anything, let me know.' Only then did he go.

Wet towel and clothes in hand, he made for the laundry once more. The first wash was done, so he chucked the towels into the drier and turned it on. Stepping out of his jocks, he tossed them and his clothes inside, setting the machine to wash again.

A blue towelling robe hung on a drying rack and he thankfully pulled it on. It was a fraction tight, and short, but did the job. Just as well Jayda preferred her dressing gowns loose.

Knotting the belt, he headed for the kitchen. He needed coffee.

The only thing resembling caffeine in her pantry was a small bottle of instant that appeared to have survived the dark ages.

On impulse, he checked the fridge. *Jackpot!* If only he could figure out how to work the stainless steel contraption on the bench. Google took care of that.

It wasn't until he was leaning back into a well-worn armchair, a steaming cup of Nigerian blend in his hand, that he questioned what he was doing. He knocked back a strong, hot mouthful and locked his jaw before giving himself an uncategorical answer—he was getting his story.

They both sought the Night Terror. For different reasons, but that made no matter. Pooling their information and insights promised a better chance of success than going the case alone.

It was a match of perfection. A definitive win-win.

He'd watched the face-off between Jayda and her boss. Eyes ablaze, body steeled in determination, she'd surrendered her gun but not her resolve. Grit that made her the perfect partner for his plan.

Jayda wouldn't rest until the Night Terror was behind bars. And he wanted in.

# Chapter Twelve

**A**n odour much like burning hair filled the closet-like room. It wafted through the tiny space, mingling with the residual traces of acetone.

Two final strokes of the round file and he grinned. Even under a magnifying glass no sign of flesh remained. He blew at the dust and inspected his handiwork before discarding the tool on a velvet cloth and selecting another. The abrasive rasp of nail file against keratin was like a lyrebird's song to his ears. Better than, in fact, because it wasn't sickly sweet and filled with promises that were never realised.

Although there was no other sound, it was far from silent. Never was there a moment when the old man's voice didn't burrow into his brain. He should have been accustomed to the bastard's scowl, his never-ending censure and distrust. After all, he'd endured it for twenty-five long years, waiting to procure his legacy, secure in the knowledge that one day he'd snuff it, and everything about the old prick, out.

He squinted, holding the work up, turning it this way and that to get a feel for the grain, its contours. How to best lend justice to its true form.

With practised movements he rotated the fingernail, crafting a perfect droplet in minutes. Replacing the specialty glass file with a buffer, he smoothed the edges before creating the flawless shine across its surface that would provide a base for the next step. His genius.

He didn't even try to suppress the satisfaction which made his lips tighten and split with glee. He may have broken with protocol for this one, but her pain had been just as sweet. More, if he was truthful. The grief in the bitch's green eyes provided ample compensation for the wrath he'd endured from the old man. He wasn't pleased. Well, whoop-de-fuckin'-do. Get used to living with disappointment, *Dad*.

His lips twisted at the word.

A dollop of putty secured the fingernail onto the stand. Adjusting the magnifying lamp, he swung it into place and stared at the blank canvas. His most recent purchase in hand—a soft brush made from the fur of a blue squirrel—he swept the surface of residual powder, then wiped it clean with a wad of damp cotton wool held in place with tweezers.

Turning in his seat, he unlocked the top drawer of the small desk, extracting an old wooden box and positioning it just so, to his right. His palm caressed the smooth oak before he unlatched and opened the lid. On the edge of a new palette he placed the small swatch of material, studying the colour before opening jars of yellow, white and red. The hue had to be precise. On this, he and the old man agreed.

One glance at the wall through the open door, at his legacy, before he dipped his brush into the acrylic and began to mix.

# Chapter Thirteen

The mother of all pinball games was taking place in Jayda's skull and she wanted out.

Scrunching her eyelids against the needles of daylight piercing her blinds, she jabbed at the pressure points on either side of her temple and prayed for peace. Prayed that when she opened her eyes, last night would be just another nightmare and Bec wouldn't be lying on a slab right now in Teddy's refrigeration room.

Something clattered beyond her door. She sniffed, opened her eyes. Freshly brewed coffee. The smell of home. Only this wasn't her childhood bedroom. It was an apartment where she lived alone. And someone was tinkering about in her kitchen making coffee and . . . and bacon.

She buried her face in her pillow, but not before the first tear of the morning fell. Her nightmare had pitched into day and nothing had changed.

The boulder in her chest expanded as she choked back tears she'd believed were spent. Fists pounding the mattress, she beat them off again then rolled onto her back, gulping stinging mouthfuls of air into her lungs. No time for grief now, self-serving or otherwise.

She hauled herself out of bed, erasing all but the promise of retribution from her mind. Fresh underwear on, she rummaged through her wardrobe, pulling on a clean pair of jeans and a tee before heading for the bathroom. Her head pounded, but she had no time for headaches either.

*Suck it up and push on, Thomasz.*

Ignoring the mirror, she brushed her teeth and washed the crust of old tears from her face before tugging a comb through the knots in her hair.

Then she turned to face the day.

She focused on breathing—in, out, in, out—and the cold press of the doorknob against her palm as she opened the door. She fixed on the pale walls, the play of light through the blinds and the spring of cream carpet between her toes.

Her stomach rumbled. Tantalising aromas filled her nostrils, reminding her it had been an age since her last meal. One that hadn't counted for much considering that it wound up splattered all over her bathroom floor. Weird, considering the last time she'd chucked was as a kid with a tummy bug. Since then, her gut had been widely branded as iron-clad. Like her father's.

At the kitchen door, she hesitated. Her hand gripped the doorframe, then she inhaled, bowled in, and . . . stopped. Stared. Dressed in her old towelling robe, Seth looked . . .

She gulped, dragged her eyes away. 'I see you've made yourself at home.'

He looked up and the strength of that gaze dragged her eyes right back to his. 'Ahh, you're awake.'

'And you're still here.'

Staccato heartbeat filling her ears, she moved towards the breakfast bar and grabbed her mobile. One message from her father. She dropped it back down. Not without fortification.

'Glad we've managed to get the obvious out of the way. Although here's one more—I made you breakfast.' He slid a tray with coffee and heaped eggs, bacon and mushrooms across the bench. Her mouth watered at the sight, but her stomach baulked. She couldn't.

She reached for the hot drink and noticed the bottle of instant next to the kettle. 'Please tell me you didn't use *that*.'

He unscrewed the lid and tipped the bottle upside-down. 'Not without a chainsaw.'

'Where'd it even come from?'

'Your pantry.'

'Really?'

'Mmm. I'd say it's been there for years.'

She held out her hand and he passed it over.

No doubt it was from before her time. The previous owners'. Or her dad's. The whirlpool in her stomach churned. She tossed the bottle into her uncharacteristically empty bin. Seth had cleared her rubbish?

He waved his hand at the food. 'Eat.'

Grabbing the steaming mug, she sipped, ignoring the burn on her tongue as she turned away from crispy bacon and perfectly fluffy eggs. 'I'm not hungry.'

Her tummy rumbled and Seth grinned. 'Better tell that to your stomach.'

He slid the tray towards her and the tears she'd fought so hard to tame welled up against her eyelids. Shaking her head, she blinked. 'I–I can't. It's Bec's favourite.'

His smile dissolved and he moved the plate to the sink. He didn't offer any empty reassurances and for that she was grateful. His expression softened along with his voice as he scraped the food into the trash. 'How does toast sound?'

'If it's with peanut butter, great. But I can make it.'

'So can I. Take a seat and drink your coffee.' He dropped two slices of bread into the toaster, looking way too comfortable in her kitchen. And her robe.

Climbing back onto a barstool, she waved her hand in his direction. 'That's a good look on you.'

He cocked an eyebrow, deftly catching the toast that shot out from an element permanently set to eject. Evidence it hadn't taken him long to cotton onto the quirkiness of her appliance.

'My clothes should be dry by now.'

The boulder returned along with memories from the night before. She gripped the mug to her chest, trying to breathe through the tightness. 'I . . . I want to thank you for last night.'

'No need.' He dropped the toast onto a clean plate and applied a generous coating of butter before moving towards her pride and joy walk-in pantry.

'If you hadn't been here . . .'

He stopped and turned. 'It's okay, Jayda. I was and you're fine. I'm sure you'd have done the same.'

The flippant way he discounted his actions made them sound so ordinary, when in fact they were anything but. Few men would clean up puke from a girl they hadn't even slept with, let alone stand under an ice-cold shower with her. Not without ulterior motives.

Her lips trembled. 'I just wish . . .'

'Me, too.'

'Bec deserved better.'

He strode forwards, and she leaned into him, basking in the simple comfort as he wrapped his arms around her. Somehow it felt right.

'They all deserved better. Which is why we won't stop until we find the sonofabitch.'

Her head jerked back. 'We?'

'Let's get to that bit later. First I need an answer to an all-important question.' He brushed the hair back from her eyes and she shivered. 'Smooth or crunchy?'

It took a moment for his train of thought to hit hers. She pulled back and almost managed a smile. 'Nothing but smooth in this house. It's the only kind.'

'No way! Peanut butter should never be smooth. Peanuts are crunchy.'

'Butter is smooth.'

'We might have to agree to disagree.' He grabbed the tub from her pantry, holding it up with mock distaste. 'The old peanut butter conundrum. Up there as one of the big relationship clinchers of the twenty-first century. So, tell me, Jayda, are you a Star Wars girl or a Trekkie?'

'Star Wars, of course.'

'And I'm a Trekkie. If people didn't know better, they'd say we were incompatible.'

Silence.

In an attempt to chase the sadness from her eyes, he'd landed right in the middle of that 'no-go' zone. *Big mistake.* A hint of the R word when they'd barely scaled the one-night-stand scenario. None of which mattered, given the scale of the events that had followed.

Today wasn't last night. He wasn't stupid enough to believe they could go back to that moment before the world had splattered Jayda's heart like a bug on a windscreen. Detours aside, there were other agendas to keep. Sex wasn't one of them.

He passed her the tub. 'Just as well we don't have to worry about that, right?' His brain gave a mental eye-roll. Writing was his life, yet he couldn't string more than two words together with this woman.

*Pathetic excuse for a save, man.*

Her weak smile as she took the jar from his hands said she agreed.

Perched on the edge of her stool, all her energy was absorbed in smearing half of the tub onto her now cold toast. 'I appreciate you waiting to see that I'm okay.' She glanced up at him briefly before returning to her task. 'I am. You don't need to stay.' Then, with a grand sweep of knife, peanut butter and hand, she added, 'I hereby release you from your babysitting duties.'

She dropped the knife into the sink and stared blankly at the toast on her plate. Her hand wavered. Then she picked up a crumb and pushed it past her lips.

'Starving yourself won't help your sister, you know.'

Her head jerked back, eyes glistening. Grabbing the toast, she brought it to her mouth and sunk her teeth into the corner, gnawing at it like it was cardboard.

'Who said I'm starving myself?' The words were muffled, and as if to prove him wrong, she took another bite.

The second hunger overtook guilt, her eyes widened. Not quite enjoyment, but rather some relative of it, filled their depths.

She reached for her mobile, avoiding his gaze, still munching. 'Time's a-ticking and I've a mountain of stuff to do today.' Blinking her over-moist eyes, she polished off the first piece of toast and reached for her second. 'And I'm sure you must have somewhere else you need to be. Like work, for instance.'

This was not where he'd been leading the conversation. Or the situation. Her shoulders were squared, her expression identical to the one she'd worn when she relinquished her gun. He was being dismissed.

He'd hoped for an easier course, but it seemed the opportunity was long gone. That didn't mean this was over. Instead, he'd just have to wing it.

'Let's clear up a couple of things before we continue.' Elbows on the bench, he leaned in to capture her full attention, waiting until he had it. When her head lifted and her gaze met his, only then did he continue. 'I'm here because I want to be, not because I have to. And, just for the record, I don't plan on going anywhere in a hurry.'

Her eyes widened, and he couldn't read whether it was in fear or surprise. No matter. He'd just tethered the rope to her attention, now it was time to tug.

'I have a proposition for you.'

Jayda's heart lolloped in her chest as a thousand different connotations to Seth's words scrambled through her mind.

And this wasn't the time for pretty much any of them.

'What exactly do you think is about to happen here?' She shook her head and realisation clicked. Blow-by-blow, a replay of the past twenty-four hours strobed through her brain, and with every flash the pressure built.

Here he stood in her kitchen, looking like he'd been caught in a pile of cookie crumbs, an empty jar in his hands—a look of guilt, if she'd ever seen one.

'You've got to be frigging kidding me!' Her voice shook, each word a bitter sting against her tongue. 'This is, what? Give me a stroke of TLC and then I return the favour?'

She stormed past him into the laundry. Dragging his jeans and shirt out of her dryer, she turned to find him standing in the doorway.

He opened his mouth, but she didn't need empty excuses or deflections. She thrust her palm into his face. 'What happened last night was nice, but don't kid yourself it'll happen again. I've just lost my sister, for god's sake! Sex is the absolute last thing on my to-do list today, or anytime soon for that matter.'

She tossed his clothes at him and they fell unheeded to the floor. 'I'll leave you to get dressed. No need for you to see me on your way out.'

As she pushed past, his hand shot out and grabbed her wrist. She spun round and glared, her heart gunning like an AK-47.

He loosened his hold. 'You've got it all wrong. What I'm offering here is a business proposition.'

'Business, my ass!' She yanked her hand from his grasp and stepped back, rubbing the brand of his touch from her wrist.

Seth raised his palms in defence. 'Look, Jayda. You're tired, you're mourning and you're pissed. I get that. I really do. Just do me a favour before you kick me out. Let me get dressed and then give me ten minutes of your time to explain myself.' He bent to pick up his clothes.

'And if you still want to kick me out after that, I won't stop you. Just ten minutes, you owe me at least that.'

He had her. Although what he could possibly say to make her change her mind, she had no idea.

'Fine. You get *five* minutes. Just know it's because of what you did after . . .' She swallowed. 'This has nothing to do with what happened before.'

'Sure.'

She watched him saunter towards her guest bathroom and anger had everything to do with the wildfire coursing through her blood. Not the taut thighs and butt moulded to perfection beneath her bathrobe.

Her skin burned. Damn that she should notice that *now*. He turned, caught her staring. *Double damn.*

His chin dimpled. 'And just for the record, what happened before wasn't *nice*.' The slide of a smile stole his lips. 'It was phenomenal.'

# Chapter Fourteen

**A** rustle of denim at the study door told Jayda she was no longer alone. The call to her father would have to wait.

Air huffed out through her lips and only then did she realise she'd been holding her breath. She dropped the phone onto her desk and glanced briefly at the profile on her laptop before closing the lid. She'd catch the bastard. If it was the last bloody thing she did.

'Calling your dad?'

*How the hell did he know?*

She looked up. 'Yeah.'

'How is he?'

'He's just lost a daughter. How do you think he is?' She bit her lip. Since when was she a first-class bitch? Closing her eyes, she massaged her forehead. 'He's stunned. We all are.'

Seth nodded, and she felt his comfort from halfway across the room. What's more, she *wanted* it. When had that happened?

'When's the funeral?'

'Friday.'

'I—'

She stood, palms flat on the polished mahogany of her desk as she leaned forwards, fighting her urge to need someone when the only person she knew she could rely on was herself.

'I appreciate your concern, but I've got a shitload of work to do and half the morning's gone already.'

He entered the room, his presence swallowing vital airspace. She stepped back.

'I understood you were on extended leave.'

With a wave of her hand she brushed his comment aside. 'I promised you five minutes and if you want to waste it discussing my current job status, that's your choice. The timer's on, Seth.'

'I said you drive a hard bargain and I wasn't wrong.' His grin quickly faded. She wasn't a mean person by nature, but this entire situation was bringing out the worst in her. And much as she hated it, she was on autopilot with a brake pedal on the fritz.

'I want to help you, Jayda.'

'Help me do what?'

'Find the man responsible for the deaths of all those women. And your sister.' His voice shook, the words ground out from his lips. As if he were outraged. As if there was no other reason for him wanting to 'help' her.

Her palms left the desk, and she was unable to prevent the constriction of muscles in her chest. 'And why would you want to do that? More altruistic gestures, or do you have some other hidden agenda?'

'In answer to your first question, I'm human and I want a psychopath behind bars. And in answer to your second . . .' He frowned. 'I'm a reporter and I want this story.'

The click in her brain must have resonated on the other side of the globe. She hadn't guessed, but now she knew it made perfect sense. The reason for his interest. His insights.

She forced her gaze to remain locked with his. 'Is that why you approached me in the bar? For information?'

He rocked onto his heels, then his toes. 'That's part of it.'

'And what exactly was the other part?'

He rocked again. 'Our first meeting.'

'The kiss?'

He stilled. 'You can't tell me you weren't thinking about it, too.'

Wild heat skittered through her blood, burning her lips with the memory. The want. How could she lie when he'd experienced her reaction to him firsthand? 'But I never hid what I was after from you.'

'My body.'

She raised her chin. '*A* body. Yours just happened to be there.' That wiped the warmth from his face, and took her the final step towards super-bitch status.

'You lied to me, Seth. How do I know I can trust you now?'

'You don't. And other than to promise there'll be no lies from now on—if you say yes to working together, that is—I don't know what else I can do.'

'Tell me what you can offer that I don't already have with the entire police force at my disposal.'

'The entire police force might be a stretch given your enforced "on leave until further notice" status.' He perched on the corner of her desk.

She edged away until her back was almost at the window.

'I have information you need. And contacts you don't have. And then there's always the old motto, "two heads are better than one".'

'I have a partner.'

'Who's not on your wavelength.'

Her head snapped back. How was a man she barely knew able to detect what had eluded even the closest members of her squad? 'What makes you say that?'

'My gut.'

She flexed her fingers, resisting the urge to cross her arms. 'And you are, I suppose?'

He looked at her blankly.

'On my wavelength.'

'We agreed about the last two murders.'

There was *that*. But to convince her there would have to be more. And if there were... Bec was her priority, and no matter how distasteful the thought, she'd work with the devil if it caught her sister's killer. Tears stung the back of her throat as she swallowed. 'If I consent to working together, there'll be rules.'

He quirked an eyebrow. 'Rules?'

'Yes, *rules*. Provisos. All of which you need to agree to before we proceed.'

'Right.' His gaze never once left hers. Finally he nodded and waved his hand. 'Shoot.'

'I don't sleep with work colleagues. Ever. So if we do this, we'll share nothing but a working relationship.' Heat seeped across her cheeks. With any luck, he wouldn't notice. It wasn't as if anything had *really* happened between her and Chase. And before . . . well, that was *before*.

'I'd be lying if I said that wasn't a shame, but I understand your viewpoint.' He squared his shoulders and performed a three-finger salute. 'I pledge, here and now, that nothing but work will exist between us, unless you change your mind.'

'I won't.'

His smile yelled scepticism. 'Then there's nothing to worry about.'

'Boy Scout, were you?'

'Never.' His expression wasn't even remotely repentant as he dropped his hand.

Tension gripped her jaw and she averted her gaze. 'Number two.' She turned back to face him. 'You tell me everything you know and I decide if it's beneficial to my investigation. If not, I reserve the right to break the agreement.'

'Fair enough.'

Now he just looked cocky.

Instead of slapping the supercilious look from his face, she continued. 'And at any time during our . . . "association", if I decide it's not working, I can do the same.'

He nodded. 'I'm sure that works both ways.'

'I'm *sure*.' Necessity fuelled her restraint, even if her palms were smarting from the dig of her nails. If Seth knew something that helped . . . *Deep breath.* 'And the last rule is this—whatever you write or report in your story, Bec and my family are off limits. You renege on that, and your days of farming info from the force will be toast.'

He hesitated, seemed about to object.

She raised her hand. 'It's not negotiable, Seth. Fail to agree and the deal's off.'

'So we have a deal?'

The thought was like rasping her fingernails across sandpaper. But this was for Bec. And she was going in with her eyes wide open.

Arms crossed and both feet square on the floor, she glared at the man parked dispassionately on the edge of her desk. '*If* we have an agreement.'

She could almost see the scales waver in his mind as he weighed his options. Then he nodded. 'We have an agreement.'

It took a moment for the icy claws of realisation to sink in. She shivered.

*Make a deal with the devil . . .*

He offered his hand and she had to take it. Warmth immediately flooded the cold and she waited the obligatory few seconds before wheedling her grip from his.

*Breathe.*

With fresh oxygen came clarity of mind.

She flipped open the lid of her laptop and ignored the rampant beat of her heart as she pulled up a new screen.

'So, tell me everything you know.'

# Chapter Fifteen

'It'll be a closed casket, but she'll be dressed as she always dressed. With style. Choose something that goes with gloves.' Her father's voice cracked. '*She has to wear gloves.*'

Jayda's grip on the phone tightened. She focused on the far wall of her study, willing back the tears. 'Is there anything else I can do?'

'Catch the sick bastard who did this and give her soul peace!'

She nodded, tried to speak, nothing came out. Her throat rasped. '*Count on it.*' Mentally cursing the open doorway, she swivelled her chair so the man at her dining table couldn't look up and see her face. 'I have to go. I'll try to swing by later today.'

'Sure, honey. Don't worry about me. Your mum's been round, and I'm . . . *okay.*'

She swallowed past the sawdust in her throat. Ironic that Bec's plan might yet work.

That did it. She scrubbed at a tear before it had a chance to fall.

Her father coughed. 'Keep your wits about you, Jayda. I won't lose you, too.'

'You won't.' Her voice wobbled. 'I'm tough like my old man, remember?'

He ended the call, her whispered 'love you' drowned out by the drone of the dial tone.

Loss seized her stomach like gnarly roots at dry earth. Two days and the pain hadn't lessened. Would the emptiness ever go? Unlikely. Not only had she lost a sister, she'd lost her best friend. And nothing that passed hereafter would change that.

She called her mother, left yet another message on voicemail, then let the mobile clatter onto the desk.

The vacuum inside her chest yawned.

Her head dropped into her nested arms. She'd never considered the afterlife before now. Ambivalence and an agnostic upbringing had turned her neither towards nor away from the idea of it, and life had never given her reason enough to care. But somehow it seemed fitting that her sister's soul find peace. And the only way for that to occur was if her killer was removed from the streets, permanently. No matter what the cost.

She waited for her conscience to pull her thoughts back into line and got nothing but a dull murmur.

A chair scraped. She looked up, caught Seth refreshing his email screen for the umpteenth time. A second later he'd switched back to the online media, and the scoop that was her half of their deal—inside news on the case.

In return, she'd gained access to his sourced information. From sources she guessed were so far out of her jurisdiction they made a trip to Mars look like a Sunday stroll.

It irked. Working alongside someone from his profession when she'd vowed she never would. But she'd grit her teeth and bear it. Play as nice as was humanly possible. If their partnership brought the Night Terror to an end, every uncomfortable minute would be worth it.

*He'd made the headlines.*

Only forty-eight hours since his proposal to Jayda and he'd already hooked a ride on the success train.

He edged forwards, fingers almost touching the screen. The static, the heat, Monday morning's *Telegraph*, the front page—all real.

*Night Terror Copycat Kills Two.*

It was all there in cyber black-and-white. How Joel Vance had discovered fiancée Gina Hennessey's secret life. How he'd dug deeper only to find she was having an affair with the *Angels of Harlem* founder, Angelique Sutton. And how after weeks of surveilling the couple, Joel had warned Angelique to stay away, mimicking the Night Terror murders in order to dispose of her when she refused, before doing the same to Gina.

How the police had got it so wrong. And how Seth had uncovered the truth so that, now, a mere two days later, Joel Vance was in custody.

Today's lead story and he'd broken it.

Fluff-and-feathers were a thing of the past. He wouldn't go back.

His lips twitched, but failed to curve further. In her study, Jayda rubbed at her eyes and what he was pretty certain were tears. She pushed herself up and with heavy steps she returned to the dining table and her computer beside him.

The article was a triumph tainted by her loss, and it was a bitch that it had to be that way.

In the newsroom, his editor awaited the next instalment. One which would guarantee his position at the *Telegraph* as a serious news reporter. Catching the killer would be a two-barrelled gun.

One click and the screen flipped to his inbox. He scrolled through the email to his parents, then switched to the automatic response he'd received only minutes earlier.

*Thank you for your message, but we are currently in Libya providing geophysical support for US exploration access opportunities . . . blah, blah, blah!*

He hit delete even as the satisfaction began to fade. He had no phone number for them. No address. No other form of contact.

No doubt at some stage they'd check their emails and then they'd know. Their only son was a success.

And perhaps they'd call.

A *crunch* dragged at his attention.

Across the table corner, Jayda munched on the last piece of her ham-and-cheese toastie and squinted at her computer screen, formulating yet another of her lists. That thought at least brought the smile back to his lips.

She looked up, eyes intent on his. 'Are they pleased?'

He froze. No way could she know his thoughts. 'Who?'

'Your family or girlfriend or whoever you contacted about making the front page.'

'I don't have a girlfriend.'

The fact that she looked relieved did nothing to soften the rocks in his shoulders.

'Ahh, so your family. Parents or siblings?'

Something clenched in his gut and the words shot out too hard, too fast. 'I don't have any siblings.'

'And you talk about me being hard work!' She tapped her fingers on the table. 'Are your parents proud?'

'I have no idea. They haven't responded to my email.'

'So, call them.'

'They're in Libya, saving the world from ruin.'

She stared at him through narrowed lids. He was pissed off. So what? Didn't mean she had to frown and study him like some kind of museum exhibit.

'They don't approve of your job.'

The insight was more statement than question. He grabbed his water glass, for something to do rather than something to drink. 'They have high expectations, that's all.'

Staring at the clear liquid provided no answers. Untenable that at twenty-nine years of age their continued rejection still galled. And even worse, that Jayda should be there to see it.

'And doing what makes you happy doesn't meet those expectations?'

He drank, unsure of how to answer. No need. She seemed happy to continue without him.

'I've read some of your articles. You're good.'

'Glad I can provide light entertainment for you and the minions. Which news-breaking bit of genius did it for you? *Jelly for Geriatrics* or *Rest, Relaxation and Peaches*?'

Her expression said she got that he was irked. But he should have known mere irritation wouldn't deter her.

'You more than entertain. You inform.'

'I suppose you're going to tell me your grandmother took gelatine and fixed her arthritis.'

'My grandfather, actually.' She tapped the table with her forefinger. 'I'm sure there are countless people who include peaches in their diets to combat stress since they read your article on natural sedatives.' Her eyes speared his. 'You change lives.'

'When you say it like that . . .'

'Why so bitter?'

'I'm not bitter.' His fingers stiffened around the glass. 'I just want to make a difference.'

'Well, I say you do.'

He knocked back a mouthful of water. Whiskey would have done better. 'The world won't stop turning if I quit writing those articles.'

'Tell that to the men out there with abs a six-pack of beer would envy.'

'Hilarious, Jayda.'

'I am on occasion.' The way she had of half smiling—her mouth quirked up on one side, the amused sparkle in her eyes—it did something to his gut that he couldn't identify.

He downed another slug of his less than ice-cold liquid. 'How did you know?'

She looked at him, puzzled.

'About the email.'

'Call it a gut-sense. I feel these things.'

His gaze dropped to her mouth the moment her tongue flicked moisture along her bottom lip. When his eyes lifted, they met and tangled with hers. He couldn't look away, and hell knows he tried.

She inhaled, her chest heaving against her tight tee.

Heat thickened his blood and his body hardened. He was on the verge of leaning in.

She dragged her gaze away and shuffled back in her seat. 'Break over. Time to get back to it.'

He suppressed a groan. *Diabolical woman.*

She brushed a red lock from her forehead, tiny furrows deepening between her eyebrows as she stared at her laptop screen. 'Let's recap.'

'And that'd be list number three, five or seven?'

Her chin jerked up, her eyes flashing. 'My lists work.'

He stifled a smile. 'I'm sure they do.'

'Rather than mocking me, how about you suggest a better way of analysing the facts?'

'I wouldn't dare.' He raised his palms, unable to suppress the grin this time. 'Didn't I tell you how much I love lists?'

She rolled her eyes, clearly not susceptible to his wit, and returned her attention to the screen. Her lips pursed and his eyes lingered there. All he had to do was lean across the table and rediscover how she tasted. If not for her hands-off ultimatum . . .

What was with that? It had to be about more than she'd let on. Her expression earlier as she'd talked about work colleagues and relationships had left him pondering a line of question marks. Like the story with Chase and her. How far did their 'partnership' go? The man had called three times in the past two hours. Such dedication screamed of more than just work.

*Messy.*

Something he neither wanted nor needed.

And then there was his own reason for being here. Much as a side trip with Jayda would be pleasurable, it wouldn't get him closer to his story.

He was here for the story.

He stood and moved in to peer at her laptop. His hand gripped the back of her chair and she stiffened, electricity charging the air between them. Her rules were as transparent as her reaction. And he got why she fought it. Guilt and grief were powerful extinguishers.

Still, he wouldn't be human if he didn't feel a modicum of satisfaction that she still wanted him.

Moving closer still, he suppressed the urge to test his theory, his eyes following hers to scan the bullet points filling the screen. She inhaled deeply, then exhaled, the clear light in her eyes hardening. *Cop-mode.* A place with no room for feelings. Her voice was cold and removed, no sign of the vulnerable woman he knew lay beneath as she paraphrased aloud. 'At 0015 hours New Year's Day, the Night Terror re-emerged and, after twenty-five years, killed his first victim.'

He returned to his chair, relaxing back, lacing his fingers behind his head, closing his eyes.

'She was personal assistant Sarah Vaughn, aged twenty-three. He subdued and then murdered her after she stepped out of a friend's birthday party for fresh air. Three days later, he took his second victim, 22 year-old air hostess Tracey Usbourne, after she left her friends in a city restaurant and headed for home. Over the next three weeks there were five more victims, all killed in and around the city centre: shop assistant Clara Gayle, twenty-three; nursing student Sonja Johansson, twenty-one; legal secretary Jeanette Symonds, twenty-four; and psychologist Mikaela Lind, twenty-five.'

Jayda hesitated, her voice a mechanical recitation as if this were some list for her weekly grocery shop. Not for catching a killer. 'The last murder was two nights ago, beautician Rebecca Thomasz, twenty-four.'

Seth opened his eyes in time to see her blink, one hand clamped in her lap, the other clutching the mouse so tightly he wondered if it might crack. Then her body stiffened and rage chased the sorrow from her face, its only residue the sheen of unshed tears warring against her eyelids.

He would have gone to her, but within seconds the mask had returned.

This time when he leaned back and closed his eyes, his threaded fingers rested on his stomach.

'In each case, the MO is identical—petechial haemorrhaging and bruising around the neck, indicating manual strangulation. Left index finger amputated post-mortem. Body propped into a sitting position, publicly displayed. No DNA or fingerprints on the skin, suggesting the killer wore gloves during the attack. Each of these recent murders is identical to those committed twenty-five years previous but for one detail—hydrogen peroxide around the nose and mouth causing white powder-burns to the skin. Which begs the question, why the change?'

He opened his eyes to find Jayda staring. She quickly looked away, but not before he caught the flood of red across her cheeks.

'It's a tough one.' Something darted through the recesses of his mind. The hint of an idea that flickered and fluttered just beyond his grasp. 'What's changed in the last twenty-five years that would require a killer to use industrial strength alkali on a body?'

The refrigerator whirred dully in the kitchen. Someone fired up a lawnmower outside. A clock ticked in a room nearby.

He worked backwards, considered the recent killings, the past ones. Considered the evidence so far. 'Hydrogen peroxide. Why?'

It was there, right in front of him. But he couldn't quite reach it.

'Why?' Jayda tapped her bottom lip, murmuring to herself. 'It oxidises and bleaches, is used for cleaning. It kills germs, can kill skin cells . . .'

Their eyes clashed.

*'DNA!'*

# Chapter Sixteen

'**O**h my god! It's been staring us in the face the entire time.' Jayda jumped up and began to pace.

He nodded, adrenalin slamming through his veins. 'He kisses his victims before he kills them. Not a problem twenty-five years ago. But now, with DNA analysis . . .' His voice trailed at the expression on Jayda's face. Realisation, pain, grief. And then it was gone.

He clamped his lips. *Idiot!* This wasn't just any case to her.

Jayda's hand was steady and deliberate as she grabbed her mobile from the table. 'I have to call Chase.'

Something tightened in his gut. 'Shouldn't we talk this through first?'

'After. I need Chase to pull the cold-case evidence.' Her eyes were shining, only this time there were no unshed tears. 'What if our killer wasn't as careful back then as he is now? What if the means to identify him has been sitting in a box in storage all along?'

He pushed up from his chair and grinned. 'I told you we'd make a good team.'

A tentative smile trembled across her lips. 'I can't believe this is finally happening. We're really going to catch the bastard.'

'Did you ever doubt it?'

'A little at times.' The sparkle in her eyes dimmed. 'If we'd realised sooner . . .'

He grabbed her shoulders. 'We'll get him, Jayda. He won't escape this time.'

She bit her bottom lip. He cupped her cheek, his thumb brushing an escaped tear. Her head tilted, her mouth ready as he made to sweep his lips over hers.

'I have a call to make.' Voice shaking, she pulled back and turned, already scrolling through her contacts as she took up pacing again.

He dropped into his seat and stared at his computer, bugged. That she'd pulled away. That she wouldn't look at him, even now. That at such a ground-breaking moment in the case she felt the need to contact her partner. Something that shouldn't have the power to bug him. Not even a little. But it did.

After all, Jayda and Chase had a history. They worked together, watched each other's backs. He should be glad the other man was there to help. Because when the information came in, he'd be on the inside and get the exclusive he needed.

'Chase, it's me.'

There was a pause. Seth made to type, a string of disconnected letters he'd have to delete later.

'*What* did he say?'

From the corner of his eye he saw her glance his way. She grabbed her empty glass and wandered towards the kitchen. A move made to seem casual, but it smelled of concealment. Was it personal or professional? He shoved back his chair and strode towards the glass doors leading onto her balcony.

He was here for a story. It was that simple.

He released the lock and pushed. The door shuddered for a second before groaning sluggishly along its track.

The air outside was balmy but the breeze had a bite—typical weather for Melbourne, nearing autumn. A few doors down a lawnmower still purred and he caught the whiff of freshly cut grass. Afternoon sun burned his face as he stared at the neighbour's vegie garden below. Even the metal handrail burned. The burn in his gut wasn't weather-induced. He didn't know what the hell it was.

'We should have DNA results in less than two weeks.' He turned in time to see Jayda step onto the balcony.

'That's great. Chase came through for you then?'

'Not Chase.' Her gaze dropped.

'Oh?'

'I didn't tell him.'

'Oh.' He couldn't fathom the relief those four words gave him. 'Any particular reason?'

She shook her head, her eyes still evading his as she joined him at the handrail. 'I called in a couple of favours. Once we get something concrete, I'll fill him in. No point sending the squad off on tangents if we're wrong.'

'Sounds fair.'

'Does it?' Her lips snapped closed, as if the words had escaped without her consent. 'I have to go.'

His hand caught her wrist before she moved out of reach. 'Are you okay?'

'Aside from losing my sister and being benched from the job that would help me find her killer? Sure.'

'We'll find him, with or without the Department.'

Her eyes welled. 'Thanks. It's nice to know at least one person in this mess is on my side, no matter the reason.'

He dropped her hand. It wasn't as if she could delve into his brain and read the images that flashed across his conscience. A computer file containing lists of his own. Lists that included Bec.

He turned back to the railing and stared down at the russet-tiled roof below. It wasn't as if having Bec's details meant he would use them.

She hesitated. Waiting for him to speak, perhaps? Then her expression closed and she moved towards the door.

'I have to go out for a few hours, so let's call it a day.'

'I'll come with. We're a team, remember?'

'It's personal.'

Visions of her and Chase pushed him to ignore the determined tilt of her chin. 'How personal?'

'As personal as it gets.'

At the quiver of her lip, something clicked. 'You're either going to your father's or Bec's.'

She startled, then shook her head. 'Private seems to be a word outside your vocabulary.'

'Let me come with you.'

'This isn't part of your story.'

'I know. Not everything is about the story.' Did he really just say that? He shrugged. 'Can't this be an instance of one friend helping another?'

'Is that what we are? Friends?'

'Why not?'

A blush stained her cheeks and he knew what she was thinking. It was the very same thing his own body felt as he stepped closer.

His heart pounded. 'What are we, Jayda, if we're not friends?'

Heat radiated from her lips, they were so close. He allowed his palm to scale her arm, running up and over her shoulder to her neck, where his thumb rested on her carotid, measuring the racing gallop of her blood.

'Let go, Jayda. Your rules don't take into account this thing between us. I felt it the very first moment I saw you, and I know you felt it, too.'

The moment froze, expanding like the silken filament of a spider's web unfettered in the pull of the breeze. Her eyes never left his as she dragged in a lungful of air.

Then she blinked and turned away, unhinging his hand.

'If you're coming, you'd better get ready.' She was already through the door and halfway across the living room when her final words filtered back. 'We leave in five minutes.'

Jayda's legs couldn't carry her fast enough across the living room floor.

The door shut behind her with an unequivocal *thud*. If only it were as easy to shut out her weakness when it came to *him*.

Her father's old mantra popped up to poke sticks at her folly.

*Mixing work with pleasure is like sticking dynamite under your pillow. At some stage you're gonna wake up with a helluva headache.*

As if to mock, a pound took up residence between her eyes. She jabbed the pressure points at her temple. Involvement with Seth was disaster in the making. Distraction. One which would see her mind focused anywhere but where it had to be.

She hauled on a black hoodie to match her black t-shirt and black mood. Because after her very short and not so sweet phone call to her so-called partner, there was more. Hackett had issued his dictate, and lapdog Chase was following suit—until further notice, Jayda was on a break. Bereavement leave, vacation, the name didn't matter, the outcome was the same. She had orders—stay away from the case. And her squad had theirs—she was out of the loop.

It didn't help that Chase was still pissed about her breaking the copycat murders without him. She squeezed the pressure points again.

If not for her father and his contacts there would have been no one to call. No one to check for DNA and ensure she stayed very much *in* the loop.

The Night Terror was *her* case. Break or not, she wasn't about to let that change.

Collecting her wits along with her keys, she made for the living room.

He was waiting at the front door. Not that she would have gone without him, despite the inner voice that told her she should. It was her apartment, after all—she wouldn't give Seth free rein with all her stuff, her life. No matter how many times he said she could trust him.

'Where are we going?'

'Bec's.'

'Why don't I drive?'

'Because I'm quite capable.' Jayda the bitch was back. 'Look, I can do this myself. I may be mourning, but I'm not weak, so stop treating me like I'm some wounded creature that needs something or someone to lean on.' Blood roared through her brain as she moved past him to open the door. 'I don't lean. I fight. And if you're going to stick around, you'd best remember that.'

She was halfway down the hall before she realised he wasn't behind her. She didn't stop. 'If you're coming, you'd better move. Because another thing I don't do is wait.'

The door clicked and Seth's heavy tread echoed behind her. She sped up, footsteps and heartbeat marking time.

Her body missed its regular weekend visit to the gym. That's what fuelled all this excess energy, not to mention her irrational cravings for sex and Seth. And an intermingling of them both.

Heat doused her blood, the man behind her too damn close for comfort. She strode past the elevator and hit the stairs with out-of-character enthusiasm, reaching the underground car park, only pausing to hold the heavy fire door open for him to follow her through.

The area was unusually dark. Two lights were out, while a third flickered feebly.

A shadow fell in her path, followed by a man with a hood pulled halfway over his face.

She reached for her gun seconds before she remembered it wasn't holstered at her waist. Seth pulled her away just as the stranger pushed back his hood revealing thick, tortoiseshell-rimmed specs and shoulder-length brown hair.

'Eric!' She shook out of Seth's grasp, too aware of him even now, instead narrowing her gaze at her neighbour. 'What are you doing here when your car's near the exit?'

'Hey, Jayda . . .' A shaky forefinger pushed at the bridge of his glasses. 'I heard a noise, like breaking glass.'

His visual tic worsened, and would have indicated nerves, but she knew better. He squinted. Another permanent condition that would take more than glasses to fix. 'Did you hear it, too?'

'We just arrived.' She scanned the area. No sign of glass or offender. 'Where'd the noise come from?'

He pointed towards her car. 'That way.'

'Let me check.' It was the first time Seth had spoken since she'd issued her edict for him to follow.

Eric frowned at him as if he were an interloper. In a mixed-up kind of way, he wasn't far wrong.

'Testosterone versus seven years on the force? Stand down, Rambo. I think experience might just trump your macho instincts.' She left Seth and skirted her vehicle, eyes darting everywhere at once.

'Shit!'

'What?' Both men rushed towards her, Seth effectively blocking Eric's path to arrive first.

She stared at the ground and what remained of her car's headlights. Whoever had smashed them was long gone. But before they left, they'd thought to bash in the windshield and bonnet beyond all recognition.

Seth sidled up beside her and swore under his breath. 'This screams of personal. Someone wanted to leave you a message.'

'This is a secure garage.' Eric's face spasmed again.

'Eric's right. There's no way an outsider got in.'

'So, if it wasn't an outsider . . .?' Seth asked.

She pointed to the security camera above. 'We figure out who it was.'

As far as she could see, all vehicles were untouched bar hers. Much as it galled her to admit it, there was a high probability that Seth was right. This was no random prank.

'We need to contact the police. While you call I'll speak to security and get a copy of the video.' She turned to Eric. 'Sure you didn't see anyone?'

He pressed his glasses back against the bridge of his nose. 'I heard a bang, and footsteps. But by the time I got here, they'd gone . . .'

Seth's gaze narrowed. 'I thought you heard glass breaking.'

'That, too. The bang came first.'

'Just one bang?'

Eric suddenly found interest at his feet, fingers tapping jerkily against his thigh. Signs easily misread if you didn't *know*.

'For god's sake, Seth. This isn't an interrogation, or one of your stories.'

'Stories?' Eric's gaze lifted.

'Of course, you haven't met. Eric, this is Seth Friedin, a reporter for the *Melbourne Telegraph*. Seth, Eric Townsend, my neighbour.'

The men exchanged looks. A metaphorical unzip-your-pants-and-piss-for-dominance match. If only she'd had her gun, she'd have whipped it out so they could all compare sizes. *Men!*

'I'm calling the cops.' Raising his phone, Seth moved away, circling until he had enough bars to make the call.

She was happy to let him go, to relieve the claustrophobia of his constant meddling.

'Jayda . . .' Eric's voice trailed in that way of his. Like he didn't know if he should say what he wanted to say. Like he was measuring how his words would be received.

She nodded, her mind skipping back to her car. It needed fixing, something she didn't have time for right now. Of all days for this to happen—

'Jayda . . .'

She rubbed the back of her neck and glanced at the camera above before returning her gaze to Eric, who was still struggling. Any other day she'd have patience for his nerves. And he was more nervous than usual. It had to be Seth.

Eric and social didn't mix. Unless you had a motherboard, sixteen-gig hard drive and large LCD screen, that is.

'I heard about your sister. If there's anything I can do . . .?'

The ache in her heart spiked. 'Thanks, Eric.'

'I'd like to go to her funeral, say goodbye. Rebecca was always nice to me. Kind, even.'

'Bec would be happy to have you there. Me, too.' Her smile

wobbled but she held it together. 'It's set for Friday morning. I'll drop round with the details when they're finalised.'

'Thanks.' His mouth moved, soundless, as if he wanted to say more. 'She was nice.'

She glanced at her watch—2 pm. She needed her car towed, and she needed to get to her sister's.

Rubbing her brow didn't come close to relieving the pound in her head. 'How the hell am I supposed to get anywhere now?'

Eric's nose twitched. 'I can take you.'

Seth stepped in before she could open her mouth. 'I've got that covered. My car's just outside.'

Eric looked from Seth to her, then back again. 'Oh. Well, if you're okay?'

Her new, ever-present appendage placed a proprietorial hand on her elbow. 'The police will be here in fifteen.'

Shaking her arm until his hand fell away, she hoped her expression was as withering as it felt. She masked it before providing him with the full impact of her turned back. 'Thanks for the offer, Eric. But I'm fine.'

Seth needled his way into her side vision, measuring Eric through narrowed eyes. It would seem he was a dog and Eric was very much the bone. 'You'll need to wait. The cops want to speak to you as you're the only witness.'

'I didn't see anything.'

'They still need a statement.'

Eric looked less than impressed, and she didn't blame him. Much as Seth was right, his attitude set her teeth to grind and she wasn't even the object of his attention. At least, not right now.

Strong fingers wrapped around her elbow as he towed her away, out of earshot. 'After we meet the cops, I'll drive you to Bec's.'

A heavy weight lodged inside her chest. Reality was a bitch. It loved to strike when you were already down. Seth stood beside her acting as if, white horse and all, he'd saved her day, when actually he'd just manhandled her, and the only reason he was there was his damn story. That heavy weight exploded.

She wrenched from his grasp. 'Sure thing. And while you're at it, bend over and tie my shoelaces, won't you?'

He looked at her perfectly tied Skechers. 'You're more than

capable of tying your own laces.'

'Are you sure? After all, until you inserted yourself into my life, I was walking, talking and making decisions all by myself. And now, apparently I need to ask permission to take a piss.'

He stiffened, moved back a step. 'Point taken.' His tight gaze strayed towards her broken car. 'How well do you know Eric?'

'He's my neighbour, has been for the past two years, so as well as anyone ever knows their neighbour. Why?'

'Have you considered that it's possible he wrecked your car?'

'Why would he do that?'

Eric shuffled his feet beside the crumpled metal. Behind their lenses, his eyes were a deep, warm brown, his skin more tanned, his physique more toned than most computer geeks. He wasn't a bad guy, or even particularly bad-looking. If only he'd step away from virtual reality and into the real world.

'He may be a little socially challenged, but Eric wouldn't hurt a fly.'

Seth raised an eyebrow. 'Because no one's ever said that about a psychopath before.'

'You're right. Why let reality get in the way of a good accusation?'

'This is far from a joke, Jayda.'

'I know that more than anyone.' She blinked back the rush of moisture. At least Seth had the decency to look sheepish.

His tone softened. 'If not Eric, who? Who out there hates you enough to do this? Because there's a lot of pent-up anger behind that destruction.'

'The Night Terror?' Not that she believed it, even as she said it. The Night Terror destroyed lives, not inanimate objects.

Seth shook his head. 'He didn't do this. Why would he? Not without a darned good reason for straying so far from his MO.'

It was as if he'd robbed the words straight from her brain. And it was solely because of those instincts that she'd allow him to stick around. For now.

Jayda stared at the closed white door.

No matter how hard she tried, she couldn't make her feet carry her the remaining two steps to open it and go inside.

They'd been in the apartment an hour already, checked phone messages, scoured for any evidence her squad may have missed; a suggestion, perhaps, that Bec had planned to meet someone other than Chase the evening she died.

The search had come up empty, systematically leading them into the bedroom, and to Jayda's other reason for being there.

Searching the apartment was one thing. But there was a vulnerability—a feeling much like snagging a gaping wound on barbed wire and then pulling—that made rifling through Bec's clothes and personal items intolerable.

'If you tell me what you're looking for, I can go in and get it for you.'

Her head whipped round. Seth lounged against the door jamb, arms folded, legs crossed at the ankles, watching her with an intensity that set her nerves on edge. Ridiculous for a detective who dealt with lowlifes and felons on a daily basis without so much as a flutter.

She'd nearly forgotten he was there. How was that possible when he refused to leave her side?

Returning her attention to Bec's walk-in robe, she glared at it as if willing the door to open itself. 'I need to do this.'

'You don't, you know.'

She edged forwards and grabbed the door handle, but something inside prevented her from taking that final step. 'How would you know what I do or don't need to do?'

Like an atom bomb, the silence mushroomed. If not for the flutters in her stomach at his nearness, she'd believe he'd gone.

Then his keys jangled. 'I know because I've been where you are now.'

# Chapter Seventeen

'His name was Callum and he was my older brother.'

The handle slipped through Jayda's fingers as she turned. 'You said you had no siblings.'

'I don't. He died just after his eleventh birthday. I was nine.'

She should have said something then, words of reassurance or even a simple 'I'm sorry'. But her mind was still trying to process why he was telling her this now.

Seth continued, the vacant wander of his voice causing her to question if he remembered her presence through the fog of old wounds. 'Cal wanted to study science, be like my parents. When he died, I always wondered if they wished it was me.'

She blinked. Her parents loved her and Bec equally. Had never distinguished between their biological and adopted daughters. How could any parent worth anything do that? 'That can't be true.'

'You'd think that, wouldn't you? Only he was the genius and I was the screw-up.' He waved her off when she went to protest. 'I'm not telling you this for sympathy or as a distraction. I'm telling you so that when I say you don't have to go into that wardrobe, you know where it's coming from. I can get the outfit for you. You're allowed to mourn without feeling responsible. And you don't need to punish yourself because you survived.'

Vision blurred through the pound in her head and she inhaled sharply. 'It's the blue-lace cocktail dress at the far end of the hanging section.'

She'd meant to say that he was wrong. That none of what he said was true. But when she'd opened her mouth, its connection to conscious thought had severed and *that* came out instead. And there was more. 'There should be matching sandals on the shoe rack underneath. They're the same shade of blue, with a one-inch heel.'

He pushed off the door jamb and she watched the lithe swagger of his black leather jacket and fitted denims disappear into the wardrobe containing memories she wasn't ready to relive.

Averting her eyes, she moved to the dressing table and opened the top drawer. Bec's sunflower address book lay amongst the multicoloured silk and lace. She slipped it into her purse. Perhaps she'd find something useful inside. *Anything.*

She rummaged, locating undies, a matching bra and, recalling her father's tormented request, Bec's black silk gloves, stuffing them into her purse before she could think about the implications of why they were necessary.

Rough plastic scraped her hand and she pulled it out, only to stare at a half-full bag of scrunchies. Her vision blurred.

The scorch on her fingertips was like hot coals and she dropped it back into her bag. *Breathe.* In. Out. In. Out. Blinking drove back the tears but not the burn in her gut at the thought that Bec wouldn't be needing them again.

Snagging a tissue from the blue-and-yellow box on the dresser, she mopped her face and blew her nose, then crammed it into her pocket.

Time to go.

The drawer shuddered closed and the burnished copper frame above it tottered. She caught it before it could fall—partner to a photo on her own bedroom dressing table. The metal felt cold between her fingers, unlike the memory. August twenty-ninth, six years ago, Bec's eighteenth birthday. Her present—a skiing weekend at Mt Buller. Not really Jayda's *thing*, but she'd done it for Bec.

Their two-day spell had kicked off with a private lesson. Marcel, a tall French backpacker, incorrigible flirt and their instructor, was both patient and sympathetic to Jayda's constant grappling with her two left feet, good-naturedly extending his hand whenever she upended onto her butt or flailed about with skis slipping and sliding beneath her.

Her sister, on the other hand, was a natural, at both the sport and capturing dear Marcel's heart. Even in the photo, the man in the middle held Bec tightly against his hip while Jayda clung to his other arm, her expression one of determination—to remain upright until the photo was taken.

'Looks like fun.'

The warm sweep of Seth's breath against her neck jolted her back into the present.

'Who's the guy?'

'One of Bec's many admirers.' An almost-smile wavered over her lips as she replaced the photo.

Seth raised his brows.

Before he could comment, she indicated towards the clear plastic protector and its contents, which were hanging over his arm. 'You found it.'

Bec's sexy-and-single outfit. An indulgence after divorce number two from Mark Graham, a consummate liar who gambled everything they'd jointly owned until there was nothing else to lose. Lucky the apartment was in Bec's name only, so he hadn't been able to access the equity, despite trying his damnedest.

Each outfit in that closet had a name, an event, a memory. Like old and cherished friends.

Gnarly fingers wrapped round her gut and squeezed.

She averted her gaze. Everywhere she looked, something triggered the memories into flooding back. 'We should call it a day.'

Seth nodded. 'What do you fancy? Italian or Thai?'

She followed him from the bedroom. 'I assume you're talking in a hypothetical sense?'

'Nope. Practical. I thought we could grab dinner on the way home.'

Seth watched the play of emotions run across Jayda's face, each one telling him she was less than impressed with his foot-in-mouth slip.

'Home?'

He shot her a placatory grin. '*That* was hypothetical. I meant to say your place.'

Her lips pursed. 'Let's settle this working-together thing before it gets out of hand. You need to go home. *Your home.* Much as I appreciate everything you've done, I'm fine, so no reason for us to be all over each other, twenty-four seven.'

His grin widened.

'Before you get all worked up, that was meant to be figurative.'

'And they say testosterone breeds irrationality. Hold onto your panic, Jayda—I have no raging desire to move in and pick out cushions together.'

'I should hope not.' Fiery amber flecked the green of her irises.

If she was impervious to humour, he'd get her with practicality. Why he had to *get* her with something, to draw out their time together, he refused to mull over too closely. This was a career manoeuvre, nothing more.

'I thought we should discuss strategies for tomorrow. We can't just sit back and wait for the DNA results.'

'I don't intend to. But today has been a shit of a day.' Her lips wobbled and she blinked, gripping the door jamb. 'I could do with some alone time.'

Hell, he was an insensitive bastard. He should have seen she was only just holding herself together. The bravado and determination was her way of dealing with all that had happened.

Grabbing his keys from his pocket, he followed her out the door. 'I'll take you home.'

The ride back was stilted and silent, with Jayda lost deep in reflection. He had his own thoughts to contend with. Ones which reminded him of days he'd tried hard to leave behind.

'Did you hear back from your parents?'

The car swerved. He swore and righted the wheel, the angry horn of an oncoming motorbike trilling harshly through the quiet suburban street.

Her palm rested on his thigh. 'Are you tired? I can drive if you need a break.'

'I'm not tired, I'm just . . .' What? Fed up. Pissed off. *Disappointed, again.* When he should be used to that same old letdown by now. Had been experiencing it since he had the wherewithal to notice.

Grade 3. Was that when it had hit? The school science fair. Callum accepting first prize, his parents sitting front-row centre, clapping, their normally taciturn expressions almost shattered with a smile. Just one month later, Seth was presented with the school's investigative writing award for his article on *Healthier Canteens in Schools.* No one turned up to clap and cheer for him.

And so the trend continued.

'They didn't get back to you, did they?'

'They're working.' He said the words automatically, as he'd always said them.

Her mouth clamped and it seemed as if she'd descended back into her thoughts. He should have known that wasn't the case. She was, after all, a detective. She made a living out of refusing to let things rest.

'An email takes five minutes to write, or less.'

'Not so easy when you're out of phone and internet range.'

She turned in her seat. 'Your parents' lack of acknowledgment doesn't make what you've accomplished any less great. Achievement comes from within. If you don't feel it, it won't make any difference what anyone else thinks.'

His grip on the steering wheel tightened. 'Is that a Jayda Thomasz adage?'

'No, Bec Thomasz.'

Seth spared her a sideways glance.

Her fingers lay clasped in her lap, her knuckles jutting and white beneath her skin. 'Tell me about Callum.'

His throat tightened.

She was looking for distraction. He got that. But after all she'd been through in the past twenty-four hours, he wouldn't lie or try to relate his loss too closely back to hers. They were worlds apart.

He cleared his throat. 'Cal was clever. "My little genius", Mum used to call him. But he wasn't nerdy or a geek or even remotely uncool. He was great at sport, played the violin, always the centre of whatever was going on.'

'Sounds perfect.'

'He was.' The muscles round Seth's jaw tightened as he stared out at the blackened road. 'We weren't close, or even friends. Cal tolerated me, at times, but I learned pretty young not to tag around where I wasn't wanted.'

'Oh.' Her brows knitted, her teeth toying with her lower lip.

And there it was, that whole sympathy and commiseration trap in which those who didn't know better thought he warranted or wanted their pity.

'No reason to feel sorry. If there's one thing I learned growing up, it was self-sufficiency. Cal dying was sad, but since I never really had a brother, I didn't miss him when he was gone.' The hollowness in his chest was nothing more than memories of a time he'd worked hard to forget. A deep inhale went partway to filling the void.

From the corner of his eye he watched Jayda's changing expression. 'I guess you think that makes me callous and unfeeling?'

'No. It makes you a kid dealing with things in the only way you know how.'

He nodded.

It wasn't as if anything much had changed after the accident. He'd buried his brother, his parents had withdrawn further from his life, and he'd continued immersing himself in dreams of a perfect world in which he was adopted, where one day his real mum and dad would appear and declare they wanted him back. Foolish thoughts, perhaps, but they'd kept him focused. Led him to who and where he was today.

'Seth, I'm back there.' Jayda twisted her head as her apartment block flashed past in a blur.

The brakes skidded and he pulled over to the kerb, hands gripping the steering wheel unnecessarily tight. He inhaled, slow. 'Let me drop you outside.'

He forced his fingers to relax, waiting for the road to clear before U-turning the car to park out front.

'Thanks for the lift.' She released her seatbelt and was already reaching for the door handle when he jumped out of the car and sprinted round to open her door.

'I'm coming in.'

The reproach in her eyes as she joined him on the footpath said it all. 'I thought we discussed this.'

'We did. Not sure how else I'll get my laptop, though.' He opened the back door and extracted Bec's dress and shoes from the car.

'I forgot about that. You'd better come in then.'

'So nice of you to ask.'

She ignored his pique and turned up the path to the front entrance. He followed, focusing on the provocative sway of her backside in her jeans. Wondering at his reluctance to leave. He'd barely slept in the past twenty-four hours and should have been anything but invigorated.

It was the case. The knowledge of how close he was to success. His inability to let go when he was onto something good.

She unlocked the main door, then crossed the entrance hall to the lift.

He reached across and pressed 'up'. 'There's one thing about this case that's bugging me.'

'Just one thing?'

His jaw tightened. He glanced across at her before turning back to watch the descending numbers on the LED above the elevator doors.

'I'll ignore the wisecrack and chalk it up to a long day and a short fuse.' He shot her a tight grin. 'I've been going through this in my mind, but whichever way I look, it doesn't make sense. Bec doesn't fit the Night Terror's type, so why her?'

Torment filled her expression. 'To get to me.'

'Why you?' The tarnished aluminium doors slid open and he stepped in after her, waiting until she selected the second floor before continuing. 'He could have targeted anyone in your squad, or the entire police force for that matter, but instead he chose you. Have you thought that maybe this sicko is someone you know?'

'That's ridiculous!' Her eyes shuttered, her lips pressed tight, making him think of a mule refusing to drink.

'Is it?'

'It's like you said—why me? Don't you think I'd know if some psycho-killer inserted themselves into my life?' Her hand shook as she pushed back an auburn lock. 'Look, I'm lead on the case—or at least, I was—so sending me a message is like sending a message to the entire squad.'

She was too close. He'd seen it before, when a detective was too invested, when the case was too personal. He couldn't fathom any other reason for her ignoring the obvious.

The doors opened and he followed her out and along the hallway. 'So, you don't think you should be worried?'

'No more than on any other case.' She shuffled her keys before inserting the right one in the lock.

'Only, this isn't just any other case. It's personal.'

Her hand froze, her head jerking back, eyes widened and moist. He had her attention now.

'He's made it personal, *for you*, which makes me think this is personal for him, too. So, regardless of what you believe, just make sure you cover your back. And be careful.'

The corner of her mouth quirked in that teasing half-smile of hers as she twisted to face him. 'Watch it, Seth. Your maternal instincts are starting to show.'

He stepped in, resting one palm lightly over her bicep, the contact burning his skin. 'Watch it, Jayda. Any witticisms might be mistaken for a sense of humour.'

She swayed. Green apples teased his senses, their promise taunting his tastebuds. He leaned in.

With a jolt, she stepped out of his reach, swinging the door open. 'Your computer's on the dining table.'

His hand fell to his side. She blew hot and cold so fast, he didn't know where the hell he was at. Not that it mattered, considering this was work.

'Sure.' He draped Bec's dress over a chair and packed the laptop into its bag, too aware of her watching his every move. Then he slung the strap over his shoulder. 'Guess I'll see you tomorrow.'

'Not too early.' Air huffed through her lips, as if she were doing him a favour. 'Use my spot in the garage. Number twenty-nine.' She dropped the remote control in his palm, her lip caught between her teeth again. It took all his strength not to move in and kiss it free.

'Nine?'

'Make it ten.'

'Make it nine-thirty and I'll bring coffee.'

'You sure know how to woo a girl.'

'You have no idea,' he muttered. Then he turned and left while he still could.

# Chapter Eighteen

The witch entered the building, but not alone. Scampering close at her heels was her two-bit reporter, like some faithful pound-puppy, tongue lolling, tail wagging.

Fire blazed up from his lungs and into his throat, drowning his tastebuds in a flood of burnt copper and bile. He spat out the phlegm and blood that followed, his hand fisted against the spasming muscle in his chest. Time was running out, and there was still so much to do.

He thought of the reporter. How he'd insinuated himself into her life. So easy, so fast. She flitted from one sap to another. So like a woman. Fickle and faithless. Her only saving grace was that the hound left minutes after arriving, tail firmly tucked between his legs, not hers.

Rendering her alone in that big, empty apartment.

He grinned. What did she make of him now?

He thought about what was to come and his heart began to race. *Let the games begin.*

# Chapter Nineteen

**S**leep was impossible.

Thoughts jumbled through Jayda's mind, elbowing roughly for attention as she lay on her back and stared into the hazy dark above.

First came Juz's allusions regarding her parents' split, her father's evasion. Then her battered car, in evidence being dusted for prints. The parking garage's blank video feed due to unexplained interference with the building's security system. Chase's weird behaviour. His unquestioning compliance in cutting her off from the investigation. Seth declaring the Night Terror was someone she knew.

Bec dead.

She bit her lip and blinked. Yet, despite her squad's stonewalling, she'd made a breakthrough. The end of the week seemed an eternity away, but at least Will Andrews could be trusted to pass his DNA findings on to her given his old-school loyalty to her father.

Flinging onto her side, she punched the pillow and scrunched her eyelids. Bec's scorched face stared vacantly back.

Jayda's eyes catapulted open. She scrambled over the bed and flicked the switch on the bedside lamp. Yellow flooded the room and the image dissipated.

*Not tired enough yet.* Her weary body protested, but her mind refused to follow suit.

Pushing up, she squished her pillow into shape, falling back against it and the bedhead as she checked her mobile. No messages. Her mother hadn't returned any of her calls.

A rapier taunt pierced her heart. *Does she blame me for Bec's death?*

As the thought growled through her mind, she reached for her sister's address book from the bedside table.

*When he died, I always wondered if they wished it was me.*

She shook her head, turned the first page. Her mother was nothing like Seth's . . . and damn the man for unleashing the idea.

Her conscience rumbled.

The hard lines of the book dug into her palms. It didn't matter why he'd said the words, they were out and causing havoc. Irrational thoughts would do nothing but undermine her and her ability to catch the killer. That and nothing else was priority right now. He was becoming too bossy, too know-it-all, and filling her thoughts too much. She'd be better off working the case alone.

*With the new day comes new strength and new thoughts.* Eleanor Roosevelt's words whorled across the top of the first page in Bec's perfect, sinuous hand.

That was Bec. Hopeful. Forever the optimist.

Jayda pushed thoughts of Seth to the backburner and turned to the next page.

*Every path has its puddles.* A line Bec had used on more than one occasion. Much as her heart wrenched, she could feel herself smile.

Each page began in the same way. An inspirational quote followed by a list of contacts, both family and friends.

As she scanned the pages, nothing leaped out. What had she expected? The killer's name and address in Bec's own scrawl?

It was doubtful her sister had known the Night Terror. Just as it was doubtful she herself knew him. Regardless, tomorrow she'd call every number in the book. Someone in it might know something.

The print blurred and she snapped it closed, holding it tight against her chest. What if Seth was right? What if this was personal?

It wasn't as though she hadn't considered the prospect. There was just no foundation for it. And no sense. Or was it that the idea was too terrible to contemplate?

She shivered, pulled the duvet tighter around her arms and shoulders.

Why would a killer from twenty-five years past send *her* a message? She'd been, what? Two or three when he was at his peak, before he stopped killing and dropped clear from the radar. To suggest he was somewhere in her life now . . . Why her? There were other, more prominent members of the force if he wanted to make a statement. Like those who had worked and failed on the case before her, for instance.

Her mobile buzzed. A message—she hadn't heard it ring. More for distraction than interest, she dialled voicemail and switched the phone onto speaker. 'This is Detective Symonds from the OPI. Please call me back as soon as possible on this number.'

She stared blankly at the screen before she remembered to disconnect the call. Why was the Office of Police Integrity calling her? They investigated police corruption and misconduct. Her squad was clean, she'd swear to it.

An image of Chase clasping his bandaged hand sprung to mind. Lately his behaviour seemed off, his explanations evasive. He'd never mentioned an old sprain. Was something going on that she'd missed? Something that had blipped on the OPI's radar?

Her mobile rang again. A familiar number this time. 'Dad.'

'Hey, honey. I missed you today.'

Damn! How could she have forgotten? What with her car, and then Seth hanging around, distracting . . . Still, the last thing he needed to hear right now was that his other daughter was the target of a madman, too.

She picked at a speck of lint on her pyjama top. 'I got caught up with the case.'

'Of course.' There was a quality to her father's voice she'd never heard before. He sounded tired, old, and the knowledge squeezed at her heart. 'What's this I hear about your car?'

She should have guessed he'd find out. 'How do you know about that?'

'I may be retired, but once a cop, always a cop. Any idea who did it?'

She crossed her fingers. 'Probably hooligans. Nothing to worry about.'

'There was a time I would have agreed. Now I'm not so sure. Promise you'll watch your back.'

'I always watch my back.'

'Good.' She sensed his distraction, his attempt to inject an upbeat tone into his voice. 'How're you holding up?'

'I've been better.'

'We all have.'

Papers rustled and she pictured him at his desk, rifling through a mountain of them, his new reading glasses perched low on his nose. Dean Thomasz's idea of method was her personal nightmare. She needed order, everything in its place. And she needed lists. Her father, on the other hand, required everything close at hand, which meant his desk resembled the aftermath of a tornado. Yet ask and he could lay his hands on anything in a matter of seconds.

'Dad?' She clutched the duvet to her chest and forged on before the clamp around her heart made her change her mind. 'Does Mum blame me for Bec's death?'

'Oh, honey, no! *No!* Why on earth would you think that?'

'She hasn't called. I thought maybe . . .'

'This is not your fault, Jayda.'

'Then why hasn't she returned my calls?'

Something clattered, followed by more clattering, this time muffled. Her father swore. Then sound through the phone sharpened again. 'She's coping the only way she knows how. But she'll call you, soon. She just . . . can't right now.'

She wasn't sure if his assurances helped or made things worse. It was like imagining a mug of freshly brewed Jamaican blend and tasting instant instead. Profoundly unsatisfying. But she knew her father well enough to know talk on the subject was over. Impossible to forge through fortified steel.

He coughed, cleared his throat. 'Meantime, we have work to do. I spoke to Will. He's pulled the evidence from storage and says he'll start first thing tomorrow. You've got science on your side, and smarts. I know you'll succeed where we couldn't.'

Cold shuddered through her chest. 'I keep forgetting you worked the case back then.' How had that fundamental detail slipped her mind?

She hauled her attention back to their conversation.

Silence yawned down the phone line. Had he heard? Or had they been disconnected? 'Dad?'

'The Night Terror was my first and last serial killer.' He sighed, heavy. So unlike him. 'He may have been a psycho, but he was meticulous. Organised. Never left a single clue. And without today's forensics, finding him was a hopeless task. The relief when he suddenly stopped . . . Well, we all wondered if he was dead.'

'Seems not.'

'If only he were. If only we'd found something to stop him.' Again, there was that silence. 'But, I know you'll do whatever it takes to put him where he belongs.'

If ever there was a time to read between the lines, it was now. This conversation was about more than just ranting.

'What's wrong, Dad?'

Again there was that throat clearing. 'I called to give you the heads up.' More rustling, this time a delay tactic, but for what?

'Oh?'

'You're going to get a call from the OPI in the next day or so.'

Her heart freefell as she waited for what she hoped he wasn't about to say.

'I'm being investigated.'

By the time Seth knocked on her door one minute shy of nine-thirty, Jayda was halfway through her second cup of coffee. She'd called more than half the numbers in Bec's address book and run a check on her bank and phone records.

Her eyes felt gritty and dry, her body like it'd been dragged backwards through a wringer. Sleep had more than evaded her. She wondered if she'd ever sleep soundly again.

Papers covered her desk, not one of them indicative of who had killed Bec. She tried not to think about the rest. Her father was the reason she'd joined the force. The reason she'd become a detective and set her standards so high. And now he was accused of the unthinkable. Planting evidence with the intent to manipulate an investigation. *Evidence tampering.* By some anonymous caller who didn't have the balls to lay blame face-on. Who'd no doubt manufactured the allegations to combat some warped sense of boredom, discrediting a model cop with an impeccable career in the process.

There was no other explanation.

This time the knock came louder. 'Jayda!'

Finger-combing her hair back from her face, she pushed up from the desk and made for the front door.

A quick check through the security keyhole confirmed her suspicions before she pulled the door open.

Her heart stuttered.

Hands laden with laptop case, coffee and bags from a local

bakery—his hair and jacket dripping wet from what must be rain—Seth looked ready to kick down her door. Patience was obviously not his strong suit. And by the look of him, his night had been as restless as hers.

'You *are* home.'

The way his gaze rolled over her made the heat in her tummy fan up and out through her body. It shouldn't have bothered her that she still wore her old, tatty PJs and robe, the one Seth had worn a few days earlier. She shouldn't have wished for a comb and cosmetics, to look more like the woman he'd first met. She wasn't even happy to see him. Didn't need or want anyone other than herself working the case. 'Where else would I be?'

'Good question.' He shuffled the take-out coffee tray resting precariously on the crook of his left elbow. 'Can I come in?'

She opened the door wider. No sense wasting good coffee and pastries. Her tummy rumbled in agreement as he strode past and dumped everything onto her dining room table.

He shrugged out of his jacket, looking around for somewhere to hang it. 'I've been thinking—'

'A dangerous preoccupation, I'm sure.' She took the leather aviator jacket, ignoring the scent of wet meadows as she draped the collar over the hook on her front door.

'I see a good night's sleep has done jack for your disposition.'

Her jaw clamped. 'My disposition is fine, thank you.'

Turning slowly, he assessed her through hooded lids. Heart pounding, she pulled the robe tighter round her waist. Thankfully he didn't comment on the blotchy red of her complexion or the suitcases under her eyes.

His gaze softened. 'I'm a grouch before my morning caffeine fix, too.' He smiled, passing her one of the two waffle cups, raising the other to his lips.

This time the clamp hit her shoulders, and locked vertebrae by vertebrae down her spine.

If not for the tantalising aroma of freshly ground beans, she would have hurled hers back at him. First he attacked her disposition, then all but called her a grouch. She hugged the cardboard cup in her palms, biting her lip against angry words that jostled impatiently on her tongue. She needed a fight this morning even less than she needed the last word.

'You were saying . . .?'

'Yes I was.' He grinned, and in spite of herself she felt her knees wobble. 'I think we should take a closer look at your dad.'

Her head jerked back. 'What?'

'Last night, I tried to figure out what link you could have to the Night Terror. Then I remembered your father worked the case twenty-five years ago. What if this psycho is targeting you to get back at your father?'

'And why would he do that?'

'They could have crossed paths, either before or during the Night Terror's old reign. Or maybe he didn't like the way your father handled the case and this is his retaliation.'

Lack of sleep and its underlying reasons bombarded her brain. *'My father has never been anything but ethical.'* Each word was bitten out through clenched teeth.

His eyebrow arched skyward. 'I never questioned his ethics. This is about his connection to the Night Terror.'

'Other than his team investigating the murders, there is no connection.' She turned away before he could read her fear. 'This is bullshit!'

'So is a man killing countless women without once leaving a message, then out of the blue feeling the need to do just that. Killing Bec, leaving that note? It was personal. No other explanation makes sense. Who it was personal to is another question.'

Cardboard crinkled beneath her fingers and she battled not to turn them into fists. Disloyalty laced her tongue like the bitter spike of burnt coffee.

She had to fight it. Because not fighting meant she believed there was something in Seth's words. Maybe even something in the accusations made to the OPI.

She dumped her coffee onto the table and threw up her arms. 'Damned reporters! Anything for a story, even if it means accusing an innocent man.'

His head jerked back as if slapped. 'I'm not accusing anyone of anything. I never lied about wanting a story, but I want to catch a killer, too. Something I thought you wanted.' Gun-metal silver glared back at her. 'If you'd just drop the attitude and think logically—'

'Logic? The man's a psychopath. What the hell does logic have to do with that?'

'For god's sake, Jayda. Lose whatever bug is up your ass and think about it. This man is meticulous, a creature of habit. Twenty-five years past, and still his MO is the same. Even to the point where he's started burning his victims to destroy possible DNA evidence resulting from sticking to that MO. Then suddenly he breaks his pattern, kills outside the vic profile, and more, he leaves a message for you. If you can think of another plausible reason for this, I'm all ears.'

His voice softened. 'I'm not saying this because I want it to be true. Hell, the last thing I want is for this madman to be after you. But if you and every other female in Melbourne is to ever feel safe again, we have to get him off the streets. Solve this mystery once and for all.'

It wasn't his words that got her. It was his sincerity, the way his gaze devoured her, as though she meant something to him; something special. The fight in her body dissolved. She slumped to the floor, head so heavy it dropped to rest in her arms, but the tears didn't come. She was too bone-tired to cry anymore. All she could do was shake and clench her lids to block out the world and everything that was closing in.

Liquid splashed as Seth ditched his coffee. 'Dammit!'

Strong arms wrapped around her. She leaned into him, his warmth, his comfort. If only to feel something other than pain.

Woodsy scents filled her nostrils. So familiar now, so calming. And as warm, masculine palms rubbed circles over her back, the tension seeped from her limbs.

Too easy to get used to this. And that wasn't the worst of it. The danger was in wishing she could.

# Chapter Twenty

The body in his arms tensed. Shaky palms found his chest, paused, then pushed.

Jayda edged away, wrapping her arms about her chest as if to hold herself together. As if without that hold she would likely fall apart. 'This is becoming a habit.'

He shot her what he hoped wasn't a goofy grin. 'Not all habits are bad, you know.'

'Falling to pieces in your arms isn't exactly good.'

He couldn't help it. His mind flew back to the rooftop garden and a woman who hadn't been afraid to do just that. The memory instantly had him wanting, and wishing for better circumstances. A simpler life where she wasn't a cop who'd lost her sister to a serial killer and he didn't need her story for his promotion.

He stood and turned, busying himself with setting the pastries on the table. 'They say food is good for the soul. And pastries are one of the best soul foods there is, second only to chocolate, so I'm told. Why don't we sit down and eat, and you can tell me what happened between now and when I left you last night.'

He walked over and extended his hand. She took it, allowing him to pull her to her feet, all the while avoiding his gaze.

'Nothing happened.' The way she dropped his hand the moment she was up, you'd think it was toxic.

'I may not wear a detective's badge but I know when something's not kosher. And your spin just now reeks of pork spare ribs.'

He watched the colour fill her cheeks, a sure indication he was right. Something other than pique at his presence was behind her outbursts. '*Jayda.* I'd like to think we're more than just colleagues in this investigation. That we're friends. If something's happening, you can tell me.'

'And see my words misquoted in the next edition of the *Melbourne*

*Telegraph*?'

The echo of her words buzzed in his ears. 'I promised your family was off limits.'

'Yes, you did.'

'But you don't believe me?'

'Let's just say, once a reporter, always a reporter. You can't turn off who you are any more than I can.'

The accusation stung like a slap to the face. What the hell would it take for her to trust him? Blood spill?

They may not have known each other long, but after the past day and what they'd been through together . . . He'd even told her about Callum, when he didn't disclose his failings to anyone. A lifetime of not measuring up should have taught him to expect as much.

'Fine. I guess there's not much I can do about your lack of trust. Just do me a favour, Jayda. Or make that two. Don't lie to me. I'd rather you tell me to mind my own frigging business than feed me some trumped-up tale.' He speared his fingers through his hair, wishing instead he could shake sense into that obstinate skull of hers. 'And don't blame me for the sins of others.'

'I—'

'If your father's being accused of something and it has no bearing on our case, I don't care if you keep it to yourself. But don't fly off the handle when I throw out a suggestion you know makes perfect sense.'

First shock filled her expression, then anger. He saw clearly how tempted she was to throw his words back in his face. Instead, she clamped her lips and stormed into the kitchen. What followed was a cacophony of banging and crashing until she returned and dumped a tray of plates, cutlery, glasses and apple juice onto the table. The glasses toppled precariously, and his hand shot out to save one before it tumbled over the side and smashed.

She stomped out again, this time towards the bedroom and study.

That hair colour obviously ran more than skin deep. How could he have mistaken her for a blonde? He stifled a grin, tempted to point it out. Or, maybe not. Her temper as it was, his chances for survival bordered slim to nil.

Falling back into a dining chair, he munched on a Danish, determined not to call out and ask why she was taking so long or what she was doing. Let her be first to break the silence, huffing not included.

He heard a low murmur. She wasn't talking to herself, surely? A telephone conversation, then. To who? Chase? His gut clenched. Or perhaps her father? That made more sense. He'd seen the fear in her eyes, the click as her mind gave credence to his suggestion. She was determined to shut him out and too damned stubborn to admit it, to him, or to herself.

No less than ten minutes and two pastries later, Seth heard her return before he saw it, and then the reason for her lengthy absence became apparent. Dressed in jeans and a shirt made from some silky, clingy, burgundy material, the upward tilt of her bottom was the first thing he spied as she dragged a large cardboard box across the tiled floor.

He couldn't look away, and why should he? Her stupid rules said nothing about enjoying the view. This time he didn't suppress the grin. Damn, but she wouldn't dampen his humour. Take that away, and what was left?

'You could offer to help!' She straightened, rubbing her hands up and down the worn denim covering her thighs.

'And be accused of sexism?' He grinned, undeterred by her chip-spitting glare. 'Looked like you had everything well under control. A strong, independent woman like you.'

She harrumphed. 'Enough with the wisecracks!'

'I'm serious. That's exactly how I see you.'

Her eyes glowered, unconvinced. 'Some sexless feminist?'

'Those are your words, not mine. And you should know by now, the last adjective I'd toss your way is sexless.'

The red in her cheeks deepened. She harrumphed again, busying herself with opening the box, pulling out a handful of thick, tatty manila folders. When she next looked up, he could see she'd calmed that red hair of hers.

'I thought we could look back over the cold cases. I've been through them countless times, but perhaps something will jump out that didn't before.'

He left the chair to take a file from her hands. Doris Tombes, twenty-three, shorthand typist. The first murder attributed to the Night Terror.

'What are we looking for?'

'You're the journalist with a bloodhound mentality. I'm sure you'll figure it out.'

Whatever she wasn't telling him had her fired up good. 'You wound me.'

'As if that were possible.'

He dragged his fingers across the tightness in his jaw. 'You know, Jayda, much as you might need a punching bag right now, I'm not sure that person should be me.'

The words mulled aimlessly between them until they hit target. He saw it in her expression.

'You're right.' Her voice cracked. She dropped her files onto the table, the liquid green of her eyes catching his. 'I'm sorry, Seth. Much as I hate this situation, it's not your doing. You just happen to be close enough to be in the firing range.'

'All I can say is, I'm glad you're short one handgun.'

That won a smile, feeble as it was, and the light in her eyes made his heart jump. Pretty much any scraps she threw his way gave that muscle a severe jolt. The realisation caught him off-guard. He wasn't quite sure what to do with the knowledge now it had hit.

She moved closer, placing her hand uncertainly over his, and the blow from the contact struck him square in the chest.

'Let's start today afresh. As friends.'

There was no pattern.

The women were from all walks of life, abducted from a variety of locations. Yes, the killings all occurred in Melbourne's CBD. And yes, the victims were all blonde, blue-eyed innocents. But that was where the similarities ended.

Bec was the only exception.

Staring out at rain that seemed perpetual—and the man on her sheltered balcony enjoying it—she groaned. Much as she hated to admit it, Seth was right. Finding the killer had to lie with Bec. Perhaps even her father. Although, during their brief phone conversation— minutes after Seth watered the seed she'd fought hard to stifle—he denied any possible Night Terror association other than being on the case.

Still, just because he didn't know of one, didn't mean it didn't exist. Her head dropped into her hands.

What was the connection? The tips of her fingers dug into her skull. *Think!* Gut instinct said if she could figure *that* out, she'd find the killer. The same old information whizzed round her brain, none of it leading anywhere. Like a ride on an old-time carousel, she always travelled full circuit and ended up in the same place, like there was nowhere else for her to go.

Even her lists weren't helping.

She cursed, striking her forehead with her open palm.

'Time for a break.'

Was the man psychic or something?

He stamped his feet on the doormat before stepping inside and closing the door. It slid easily. Not only was he throwing out her garbage and making her coffee, he was oiling her doors. Making himself too at home for comfort.

Anastasia belted out from the table beside her, and she checked caller ID.

'Going to get that?'

'No.' Heart pounding, she watched until the song cut off and the call clicked over to voicemail.

He dropped into his seat opposite her. 'That's the sixth time today you've ignored your phone. Who are you avoiding?'

'Telemarketers.'

'You can't evade them forever, you know. Sooner or later, they'll catch up with you.'

And that's what she dreaded. Eventually, the OPI would give up leaving messages and come knocking. And when they did, she had no idea what she'd do. Defend her father, yes. But what did they imagine she knew?

Her gaze lifted to find Seth watching her through narrowed lids.

Ignoring the flutters in her stomach, she closed the file in front of her, stood up and stretched. 'I could use a change of scenery. To refresh the senses and revive the old grey cells.' She tapped her head, eliciting a smile that freshened senses of a different kind.

Why couldn't she get past her adolescent fascination with the man? The first few buttons of his shirt gaped open, revealing tanned muscle she remembered all too well. Even though he'd been under cover outside, his hair was damp and ruffled from being shoved back too many times, while his lips were shadowed by stubble that made her wonder how that rasp would feel . . .

She dragged her eyes away, hoping her top was loose enough for him to miss the reaction beneath it. Her breasts felt weighty, swollen, her nipples hard and sensitive against the restriction of her bra, lost in vivid memories of the attention they'd received. Was it really less than a week ago?

He unfolded himself from the dining chair and reached back to scratch between his shoulder blades. The stretch of fabric over his torso proved deliciously distracting. And the look on his face as his gaze met hers said he knew it.

'Let's go out for dinner. There's a great Italian place not far from here.'

'Like a date?'

His brow shot up as he dropped his hand. 'That'd mean we're romantically interested in each other, which, of course, you're not.' The grin he shot her way stated he thought otherwise. If only he weren't so damned sure of himself, she might have been tempted . . .

*No.* No dating work colleagues. Which for all intents and purposes Seth was. And no distractions. That included the distraction caused by noticing he never denied his interest in her, romantic or otherwise.

'I could go some Italian.'

'But not me?'

It took her all of three seconds to get his meaning. The heat in his gaze helped her translation. 'What is it with men and comedy? Do sexual innuendos get you off or something? Because I can tell you right now, they do zip for me.'

'Just when I'd hoped my irresistible charm and wit would be enough to win you over. How could I have misjudged?'

She rolled her eyes. 'Funny, ha ha.'

'So you do have a sense of humour?'

'When something's amusing, yes.'

His palm slapped his chest. 'Just stab me and smear on the salt, why don't you?'

'Tempting as it may be, sadism's not really my thing.'

'Touché.' He grinned, then gestured at the table's scattering of cups, cutlery, plates and crumbs. 'I'll tidy this while you freshen up.'

'Is that guy-speak for "you look like crap and need to change"?'

His gaze raked her body—the burgundy top she knew made the green in her eyes deeper, and the tight, shape-hugging jeans—leaving spot-fires in its wake.

'What do you want me to say, Jayda? That you could put on one of those old burlap potato sacks and I'd still find you attractive? Because it's true.'

Her face burned, not only at his words, but at the undeniable heat in his eyes, his tone.

'I'll be out in five.'

'Chicken!' The word and its precision followed as she fled the room. It was getting harder. Much as she kept telling herself that he was a reporter, that his profession was ruthless and unprincipled, every one of his actions so far indicated he was anything but.

She rifled through her closet. Even though it wasn't a date—because, as Seth so accurately stated, that would mean something other than work going on between them—she took more time than strictly necessary to choose what to wear.

Three outfit changes later, she scowled at her reflection, then grabbed a fourth. Clothes were Bec's department. When it came to pretty versus practical, no guessing which one she chose. That said, her lack of fashion sense had never worried her before. No reason why it should now.

She pulled the emerald cowl-neck top over her head, refusing to notice the way it hugged her breasts or the display of cleavage designed to tantalise and make a man want to see more. The black skirt wasn't particularly short, but at knee length, with her ankle boots, she knew it showed enough leg to entice. Her black leather jacket completed the outfit, not because it was sexy, but to ensure she wasn't a contender for Melbourne's next wet t-shirt contest if it continued to rain.

Her underwear was still her customary basic black. Not that it mattered. This wasn't a date.

The look on Seth's face, after waiting almost three times longer than she'd promised, said the effort was worth it. Just because nothing was going to happen, didn't mean she couldn't enjoy a little unsolicited admiration.

'Did you want to go home and change?'

He checked his black cargos and shirt. 'Are you saying I need to?'

Her eyes followed his and heat fluttered through her belly. She'd spent the better part of the day struggling—unsuccessfully—to avoid this. Admiring his body, the way it filled her gaze. Remembering how it had felt in those moments when pressed hard against hers.

Their gazes locked, and it was clear Seth guessed the direction of her thoughts.

She swallowed, tried for blasé. 'Rather than incriminate myself, I'll go all American and plead the fifth.'

Humour skimmed across his lips, dimpling his chin. She'd never seen lips like Seth's. They were wide, what some women called 'kissable'. That had to be the reason for her need right now.

'We should go.'

Opening the door, he didn't comment on what was clearly an admission of her attraction—her words and her body's too obvious signs.

The air outside her apartment chilled her skin and she drew the edges of her jacket together.

Hairs on the back of her neck prickled. She quickly forgot Seth's casual swagger down the hall, the way his ass filled his pants. Her fingers twitched, ready to reach for a gun that wasn't there. She turned.

The hall was deserted, yet she could have sworn they weren't alone. Call it gut instinct or a sixth sense, she felt eyes on her back as they waited for the lift. Then she heard it, the softest of clicks. Ten apartments on her floor, which meant nine possibilities. She knew every one of those nine neighbours, had no idea why any one of them would want to covertly watch her.

Unless she was overreacting. Her gut said no.

Either way, visiting her father couldn't wait. She needed her old, pre-force semi-automatic.

# Chapter Twenty-One

'Jayda?' Seth waited inside the lift, finger pressing the open-door button. One last look yielded nothing so she joined him, watching the doors close on an empty hall.

'What's wrong?'

She forced a smile. 'Just wondering if I should've grabbed a raincoat.'

His eyes searched hers, as if he suspected white-washing, but she knew he'd find nothing—it was an art.

'I have an umbrella in the car if you're worried about your hair.'

'I wasn't, but I might take you up on the offer anyway.'

They reached the car without incident, although again she experienced the uncanny feeling of being watched. As if someone or something was lurking in the shadows. Even the security cameras seemed to follow her. Ridiculous, considering the system had been upgraded just under two years ago and not once had she felt uncomfortable with them until now.

She dragged the seatbelt across her waist and clicked it home. Seth sat beside her, keys dangling from his hand.

'What was all that about?'

'All what?'

'The covert surveillance routine back there.'

She sighed. 'I thought someone was watching us.'

He peered out her side window but she knew he'd see nothing but grey concrete and parked cars. What else, when there was nothing to find?

Or was there?

She scanned the area, shook her head. *Get out of the ridiculous and back into reality, Thomasz.* An overactive imagination was something she'd never been accused of. Now wasn't the time to allow one to emerge.

Regardless, first opportunity, she'd run background checks on each of her nine neighbours. Friend or acquaintance, they had to be ruled out.

Seth returned his gaze to her. 'So you agree the killer might be someone you know?'

'It's not a given, but it is a possibility.'

He eased the car out of the garage and shot her a sideways glance. 'You should've been a lawyer.'

'And bore myself silly? No thanks.'

His fingers drummed against the steering wheel as he navigated onto the wet road and into passing traffic. 'If you're right, someone in your building is stalking you, or worse. We should do background checks on them all.'

'Agreed.'

Seth's eyebrows nearly bounced clear off his brow. 'Then you'll agree that we should move the investigation to my apartment.'

She got that he hadn't expected her agreement, and now that he had it, he felt he could push even further. What he didn't get was that she wouldn't be pushed.

'No way. Let him watch.' Her eyes followed the slow back and forth of the wipers as they mopped the smattering of rain from the windscreen. 'At some stage, he'll slip up, and when he does, I'll be waiting. You can't catch a killer without facing him head-on.'

'You can't catch him if you're dead, either. We need to make sure you stay safe.'

'Which is why we're taking a detour before the restaurant. Turn right here.' He indicated, then turned.

She pressed on before he could comment. 'And just for the record, *I* need to make sure, not *we*. I'm the detective here. This is my job.'

The only evidence he didn't agree was the arch of an eyebrow. When it dropped, he shot her another sideways glance. 'Where are we going?'

'Dad's. I need a gun.'

'Oh.'

Silence gnawed through the car like a hungry boar. She issued directions, winning a nod or non-committal grunt in return. It was almost a relief to arrive. *Home.* A word with no warmth since her parents' separation.

Her hands were stiff as she willed them to release her belt and open the door. They seemed intent on refusing.

He cut the engine and turned to her. 'Going in?'

'Of course.' She gave the cobwebs in her head a mental sweep. The pain in her heart wasn't so easy to dislodge.

With a fumble, her seatbelt clicked free. 'I won't be long. So, you may as well—'

The driver's door slammed. Seth skirted the bonnet to meet her on the footpath, disregarding the glare that was supposed to make him turn around and scuttle back inside.

'A tad eager, aren't we?'

'Chalk it up to an empty stomach and the anticipation of enjoying good food in the exclusivity of your charming company.'

She ignored the sarcasm.

He was halfway up the cobblestoned path when she grabbed his arm. 'Before you go in, we need to set a few ground rules.'

Seth's body temp spiked. 'You've got to be kidding.'

'There are some things I never kid about, and protecting my family is one of them.'

'It really is incredible. At times you seem so sane and, well, almost normal. And then there are times like this.' He rubbed at the back of his neck, the muscles protesting angrily. 'What makes you think your father needs protection from me? Unless you think he's hiding something.'

Her hackles rose. 'You're delusional, you know that? He's just lost a daughter to a serial killer he failed to catch twenty-five years ago. It may be a damn good story, but it's off limits if you come inside.'

'From what I know of Detective Thomasz, he's capable of fighting his own battles.'

'I don't care what you think you know. I won't let you loose on my grieving father.'

'I'm not waiting in the car.'

'I'm not letting you in without an agreement.'

Her glare was mutinous, but he was just as determined. 'What the hell will it take for you to trust me?'

'Proof.' The word left her lips devoid of anger, calm almost, and unwavering. 'Do we have a deal?'

'If hearing it again makes you feel better, fine. We have a deal.'

She held out her hand. He took it and they shook, then her fingers unfurled as she wrenched her hand back.

'Good.' She navigated the winding pathway with confidence.

Damn, she was impossible. And her legs looked way too good in that skirt . . .

'Huffing and puffing like an old wolf won't do anything but increase greenhouse gas emissions. I suggest you save your energy for stimulating dinner conversation instead.'

. . . even if the attitude wasn't as hot as the sway of her ass.

His libido needed a vacation, something a meet and greet with good ole dad could well achieve. He allowed his gaze to wander further afield.

Peonies bordered the stony walk, backing onto an immaculately manicured lawn. Retirement had both its price and its advantages, it seemed—boredom and a plethora of free time. Dean Thomasz had left the force just over a year ago. Seth would bet his savings the garden wasn't much older.

They climbed the stairs, the front portico as blazoned with colour as the garden.

Jayda's knuckles didn't quite make it to the door before it was yanked open.

'Jayda! What are you doing here?' Her father's gaze widened, then darted through the fading light to the deserted road. The ravage of the past few days' events were splayed clearly over his face—more than a lack of shaving cream and sleep. Dean Thomasz must have aged ten years in seventy-two hours. And if he noticed, Jayda must see it, too.

She dropped her hand. 'I came to see you.'

'Oh.' His gaze strayed once more to the street before it returned to her. 'You didn't mention a visit earlier.'

So she *had* called her father. About Bec or the case? The way she avoided his gaze, he'd guess the latter. Yet she hadn't shared any insights that conversation yielded. More secrets, a big melting pot that thickened by the minute. So much for their deal being a two-way street.

Jayda pried her father's fingers from the door and squeezed. 'Do I need a reason to see how my old man's going?'

His haunted expression splintered into the semblance of a smile. 'Not so much of the "old" thank you, missy.'

Their hug was genuine and warm, filled with unspoken sentiment. The kind of hug a father should share with his child.

Jayda's head jerked back, her nose scrunching in disgust. 'You've been drinking.'

'Just one.' He stepped away, swiping the back of his hand across bloodshot eyes.

Seth's gaze followed Jayda's, to the backpack and keys dangling from his other hand. 'Are you going out?'

The keyring jangled as he tugged at his collar. 'A couple of errands. I don't suppose you've heard anything from the O—' He stalled when Jayda shook her head, her gaze darting towards Seth. 'Uh, Chase?'

'Not since yesterday. Seth, this is my father, Dean Thomasz. Dad, this is Seth. *A reporter* for the *Melbourne Telegraph*.'

Her tone was as clear as Evian. *No cleaning out of closets or family skeletons right now, Dad.* He would have laughed if he wasn't so damn pissed she still didn't trust him.

Dean measured him from head to foot, a comprehensive dismantling and putting back together, as if by doing so he could uncover Seth's every intention. Only when Dean was done did he nod and offer his hand. 'We spoke Friday night.'

He accepted the gesture for what it was. A token he'd passed muster.

'Good to see you again, Mr Thomasz.'

'Call me Dean. And thank you for looking after my daughter these past couple of days.'

'Dad!'

'Are you telling me it isn't true?'

Seth swallowed a chuckle. Seems he wasn't the only man to rub that beautiful skin of hers the wrong way.

'I came to get my gun.'

If her father was surprised, he hid it well. Instead, he inched the door open and ushered them inside. He fastened the latch and dead-bolted the lock before leading them through a narrow hall and into a spacious living area, well-worn but comfortable.

The blinds were drawn, the globe hanging from the ceiling low-wattage. Light may have been sparse, but it was enough to notice the chaos. If he didn't know any better, he'd say the room had been tossed. But perhaps this was the room's normal state.

Jayda turned full circle. 'What the hell happened here?'

Or perhaps not.

'Spring cleaning.' Dean darted her a look Seth couldn't read. But she sure as hell could. Understanding filled her expression and she clamped her lips, moving towards a sideboard overflowing with flowers and sympathy cards.

Dean shot him a wry grin. 'Sorry about the mess. I guess I got carried away.'

Jayda turned back to face her father, her expression grim. 'I guess you did.'

He could tell she wanted to say more. But damn her obstinacy, she wouldn't do it in front of him.

*Enough already.* 'Jayda—'

She moved to the far door. 'I'm getting my gun.'

Her father ignored the no-argument warning of her tone. 'Why do you need a gun?'

She paused, her hand resting against the frame. 'No reason.' It was a bit like watching two immovable objects battle.

'No reason, like your car being smashed-within-an-inch-of-its-life no reason, or no reason, as in *really no reason?*'

She spun around. 'It's just a precaution, Dad.' This time it was Jayda's turn to come under that intense scrutiny. 'For god's sake! I'm not some hostile witness for you to intimidate.'

His gaze moved to Seth. 'Is it really nothing, son?'

Seth glanced from father to daughter. She looked pretty damn hostile to him. He was going to burn for this.

Turning his attention to Dean, he blocked Jayda's glower from his vision. 'We believe the Night Terror could be someone known to you or your family.'

'Seth!' Jayda shot flame-tipped daggers his way.

Her father, on the other hand, was icy calm. Seth could have been commenting on the oil price in the Middle East for all his reaction. 'Do you have time for a coffee?'

Seth nodded. 'Yes.'

'No!'

Jayda's emphatic denial surprised him and, it seemed, her father. But that wasn't what threw him. It was her disbelief, for once not aimed his way. Bets on, they'd already discussed the possibility. If so, she must agree, even if just in part, with his theory of revenge. Yet she still refused to admit it to him. Was clearly peeved at her father for lending credence to the idea before a witness.

Hell, he wasn't an insensitive ass. The thought that Bec's death was personal, and more, revenge for some past perceived wrongdoing, had to burn like a gallstone on fire. But they were out to catch a killer. How could they work effectively together when she kept shutting him out?

'That's settled, then.' Dean hustled them both towards a puffy white couch, scooping up papers only to shove them into an already open sideboard drawer.

'How do you take your coffee, Seth? I have instant so your options are black or white, straight or sweet.' He shot a look towards a less-than-impressed Jayda. 'Unless you're a coffee snob like my daughter.'

Jayda's lips pressed together so tightly, it was a wonder they hadn't been super-fixed.

He bit back a smile. 'Only so far as I won't touch decaf.'

'None of that stuff here.' He waved his hand. 'Or would you prefer something stronger? I've a magnificent tawny port and I could go a glass about now.'

'Dad! You promised Mum!'

'Well, your mother's not here, and one glass won't hurt.'

Seth looked from Jayda to her father, his gut tightening by the minute. He'd have to be dead not to sense that something else was going on, but if Jayda wouldn't let him in, how the hell was he to guess?

Without waiting for his answer, Dean started pouring from a crystal decanter on the sideboard.

'Port would be great.' It wasn't exactly a lie. Gaining insight into Jayda and her father would be great. The port, on the other hand, would be sweet and sickly, and would probably clog in his throat. But some sacrifices were necessary. And watching Jayda squirm, more than definitely on the back foot with her dad, would be worth it.

'Jayda?'

Throwing her hands up, she forced a sigh that he picked as fifty-fifty exaggeration and genuine. 'We can't stay long.' She evaded the couch, turning towards a doorway off to the right. 'I'm getting my gun.'

He caught her elbow and couldn't help grinning. 'Remember those greenhouse emissions.'

She tugged out of his grasp. 'Remember your promise.'

Palm still burning from the contact, he gave a three-finger salute, grin widening as she left the room. When he turned, it was to find Dean watching.

'She has fire, I'll give you that.' He held out a small glass.

Seth accepted with a wary nod. 'An entire forest of it.'

The other man barked what could have resembled a laugh in other circumstances.

Seth moved to the sideboard. A large frame perched at the end, the typical studio-posed family shot. Bec was easily recognisable, as was a younger, cheerier Dean. An older but no less beautiful ringer for Bec stood in the centre. Then there was Jayda, her cheeky grin framed by a halo of curls. Three blonde heads, one bright, fiery red.

He sensed Dean behind him. 'Nice photo.'

'Sure it's the photo you're referring to?'

He turned to find Dean watching. This time both his words and expression lacked humour. 'All jokes aside, Seth, should I be worried?'

'Worried?'

'That you're using my daughter?'

'I'd be a liar if I said I wasn't after a story.'

'I appreciate your honesty. But in the past seventy-two hours I've already lost a daughter.' He winced. 'I won't see the other hurt.'

'Neither will I. I'm here to ensure that doesn't happen.'

'And to get your story.'

Seth nodded.

'Tell me, what will you do to get it?'

Retired Detective Thomasz wasn't a man to be trifled with. It was obvious where Jayda got her spunk.

'I won't sleep with her, if that's what you're getting at. Not for the story.'

'But you will sleep with her.'

He didn't know whether to laugh or run. Dean's expression

screamed *warning, trifle with my daughter, you trifle with me*. What was the bet an ex-cop's household hid more than one firearm?

'You've nothing to worry about, Dean.' He crossed his fingers behind his back and prayed for lightning not to strike. 'Regardless of what I do or don't want, your daughter has no personal interest in me. So there's no way in hell we'll be doing anything other than solving this case together.'

A door slammed. He spun around to a scowl that could send chills through an Eskimo.

'Male bonding at its finest. Thanks for sharing your intentions so openly, Seth.'

To say she saw red was an understatement. A wild inferno flashed across Jayda's vision as she stared at the two men, who looked like they'd been caught pants-down in a brothel.

'It's not what you—'

Her father's frown cut Seth off mid-sentence. Just as well. Or she might have resorted to other less restrained measures, now she had her semi in her hand.

'Think? It very rarely is.' She slipped the gun into her purse and headed for the door. 'We need to get going.'

Seth seemed out of excuses. Who said miracles didn't happen?

As she passed, her father sprung forwards and grasped her hand. 'Not before we talk.'

Her voice wavered through the constriction in her throat. 'And you haven't already?'

'Not about this.'

She caught the scent of leather and sandalwood, but its familiar comfort eluded her.

His grip tightened. 'Come with me.'

Their gazes clashed, the plea in her father's grappling with the strings of her heart. Then he softened his hold and let go, turning away to leave her standing there. With a sigh, she followed down the hall. Much as she wanted out, something about her father's mood made her need to stay.

She hadn't a clue what was going through Seth's mind as he shadowed behind them. Whatever it was, he'd promised he wouldn't look for a story here and she had little choice but to take him at his word.

They paused at the study door. Her father's hand gripped the doorknob, twisted and pushed. As the door swung inward, he stepped aside. 'In every killer's career, there are moments that define them.'

She froze, the sound of his voice dulled by a harsh ringing in her ears.

'And then, eventually, there's that one moment, an irreversible slip, that marks the beginning of the end. A decision that brings down even those who seem invincible.' He stepped inside.

She couldn't join him. Even if she wanted to move, her legs and the muscles that propelled them refused to cooperate.

The study was no longer simply 'a study'. Each wall displayed a mish-mash of Post-its and photos and string. Thirty-five cold-case deaths and seven recent, all laid out with the hope of uncovering a lead to that one common link—a killer.

Nausea battled against her throat.

'The Night Terror made that mistake when he killed Bec. She was the . . . *slip*.' Her father dragged his hand down his face, over deep, dark lines that hadn't been there a week ago. 'We just need to find out why.'

# Chapter Twenty-Two

'**W**hy a homicide detective?'

Jayda stared unblinking as heat crept across the windscreen, slowly gnawing at the once thick blanket of condensation. She hadn't realised until now how tense she was. The air outside was cold, the air in the car not much better.

She'd never seen her father like that. Single-minded. A man obsessed, without care or consideration for the consequences.

There'd been no opportunity to talk about the OPI. Or the accusations she still hadn't heard him deny. Regardless of Seth's presence, she could tell her father wasn't talking. The implications of which she dared not consider.

'Jayda?'

She blinked. Seth's eyes were directed towards the road ahead, but his hand reached out to rest tentatively on her knee.

Warmth flooded her skin, his touch somehow comforting, without demand or insinuation. Like one friend consoling another. Neither of them had mentioned her father's war cave since they left the house, and she was grateful for Seth's sensitivity in not bringing it up now.

'It has to be more than a love for really bad cop shows with super-hot, kick-ass female detectives.' His chin dimpled.

She focused on the feel of Seth's palm on her knee and the deep familiarity of his voice. The responding warmth that frittered through her body.

'Why choose the "order" part of *Law and Order*?' The corner of his mouth quirked. 'Aside from the boredom factor, that is.'

That pulled a smile to her lips. 'My dad.'

The windscreen was almost clear, the tips of her fingers regaining feeling as she flexed them in her lap. 'It's a Thomasz tradition. Every generation, as far back as you can trace, has produced at least one cop.'

'So you were pretty much destined at birth.'

She hesitated, listening to the slush of tyres rolling over the wet road. At least the rain had stopped, even if the sky was still dull and dark.

She sighed. It wasn't as if Seth wouldn't uncover the truth if he decided to dig. 'I'm adopted. So it's more about upbringing than genetics.'

The car jerked as his gaze left the road to stare at her. His surprise wasn't unexpected. Few people guessed.

Seconds later he turned back to the stretch of headlights over the street ahead, his fingers flexing around the black grip of the steering wheel. 'That explains the hair.'

'And temper?' She gave a wry smile. 'It's an ongoing joke in our household. Everyone else is so . . . balanced and predictable.'

'You say that like it's a good thing.'

'Isn't it?'

'I have a tendency towards the unpredictable.'

His smile tugged at somewhere below her gut. She squeezed her thighs together and stared at the distorted shimmer of streetlamps on wet asphalt as they passed, hunting for words and distraction.

'What about you? Why journalism?'

He manoeuvred the car into a park and killed the ignition. 'Because every question has an answer. And for those answers that aren't obvious, I uncover them.'

'That's almost . . . poetic.'

'It's been rumoured I have a way with words.'

Almost-black eyes gazed at her across the car's interior. Her heart fluttered and she felt his draw, felt herself drowning in that look. Then he leaned in and her lips tingled with memory.

'Don't know about you, but I'm starved.' He released her seatbelt, then his, pulled back and opened the car door. 'Coming?'

It wasn't until she'd stepped out of the car and let go of the door that she knew she could stand on her own. Before that her legs resembled the bellows of an accordion. She felt . . . She didn't know what she felt. Aroused. Angry. Let down.

Rejected.

Back at the apartment, he'd all but told her he found her irresistible. But he had no trouble resisting her now. Had even assured her father, to her mortification, that nothing was going to happen between them.

Then, just now in the car, she'd wanted him. He had to have guessed, yet he'd pulled away as though it was the easiest thing in the world. Did men really lose interest that quick?

She fell into step beside him. What was wrong with her? She was better than this. Didn't go all melty and pathetic every time an attractive guy looked at her.

Until now, apparently.

Well that stopped right here, right now.

No matter how many walls came down tonight, no matter how charming and sensitive Seth might seem, he was still a reporter, and a man. Neither of which she had any use for beyond solving the case.

Jayda was pissed at him. He got it.

Hell, he was pissed at him, too. How'd he managed to pull away? Acting as if he didn't want to kiss her until she no longer remembered her name, let alone those stupid rules of hers. It was a bloody miracle he hadn't thrown her seat back and satisfied the obvious hunger in her expression right there and then.

All he knew was he wouldn't end another evening with a blockade between them.

She didn't trust him. That much was clear, in the way she wouldn't share her thoughts, her feelings, what was happening with her father. And much as it had nothing to do with the Night Terror and catching the bastard, he wanted to *know*.

The aroma of fresh tomato and basil hit his nostrils. Damn, he was hungry. And if he couldn't satisfy one appetite, the least he could do was appease another. He stalked between a pair of large Victorian columns and pushed the door of the bistro, holding it open for Jayda before following her inside.

'*Vecchio amico!*'

Before Seth could answer, he was whipped round and enveloped in one of those old, university, shoulder-grabbing, back-slapping hugs.

'Antonio!'

More back slapping, followed by their old signature handshake. 'I saw your story in the *Telegraph*. Pure genius. You've made it!'

'Almost.' He couldn't help but grin. 'And I see you finally succumbed to the family business.'

'What can I say? When Nonno speaks, we listen.' His friend clutched his shoulder and drew the corners of his mouth downward, stroking an imaginary moustache as he prepared for one of his legendary *Godfather* impressions. '*Nipotini, a man who doesn't spend time with his family can never be a real man.*'

Seth chuckled. 'Nothing like a dose of old-fashioned Italian guilt to pull you into line.'

'We may be the masters, but the guilt-trip's not exclusive to us Italians.' The hold on his shoulder tightened. 'I'm just glad you never gave up.'

'Thanks, man.'

'You made it, Seth. Your mama and papa can't help but be proud now, no?' Antonio grinned, before his eyes wandered and filled with appreciation. Seth followed his gaze.

Jayda stood just inside the door, watching with candid interest. He moved to her side, unable to resist placing his arm firmly round her waist.

'Antonio, this is Jayda Thomasz. Jayda, Antonio Carboni.'

'*Bellissima!*' Antonio ignored her outstretched hand, instead clasping her shoulders, pulling her away from Seth while planting a kiss lavishly on one cheek, then the other.

She flushed in a way he'd imagined was reserved for their kiss alone and his gut tightened.

'*Bellissima come il suono dei violini e il profumo delle rose che trasporta il vento . . .*'

That was a new one. Something about being the wind that brings music and roses? 'You surpass yourself.' He slapped his friend's arm, dislodging his grasp on Jayda in the process. In answer to her raised brow, he added, 'Antonio says it's nice to meet you.'

The corner of her mouth lilted in that gut-tugging way of hers. 'Funny how it always sounds better in Italian.'

'*Everything* is better in Italian.' His friend almost purred the words.

He snorted. 'And only an Italian will tell you that.'

Jayda tilted her head, her gaze darting from Antonio to him, and then back to rest on Antonio. 'So, who normally wins?'

He swallowed his irrationality. New respect lit his friend's expression and he grasped Jayda's hands, chuckling appreciatively.

'*Favoloso!* Beautiful *and* intelligent. *You've* outdone yourself, my friend.' He held her hand to his heart. 'If you ever tire of this *canaglia*, I am yours, Jayda.'

She opened her mouth, but whatever she meant to say was waylaid by the same blast of cold air that hit his face. Welcome distraction, in the form of a large Italian family, bustled in through the front entrance, forcing them to move to the side.

Antonio's smile was laden with Mediterranean charm as he begged the group's patience in his mother tongue before slapping Seth once more on the back.

'Much as it's good to see you, *amico mio*, some of us work for a living.' He indicated to a waitress clearing a nearby table. 'Chanel, *bella*. Show my good friends to table nineteen. And bring them a bottle of *Brachetto d'Acqui*, my compliments.'

'Thanks, man. You don't need to—'

Antonio flourished his hand, in true Italian style. 'Since when have I done anything because I need to?'

He laughed. 'Point well taken.'

'You must try today's special—Taranto stuffed oysters. I guarantee they will capture your heart. *Sono squisiti.*' He kissed his fingers, then bid them *Ciao!* before imparting the full repertoire of his charm to the other group.

Seth turned to follow Chanel, avoiding the question in Jayda's eyes until they were seated.

'Why did you lead Antonio to believe we were a couple?'

At least she'd waited for the girl to leave. 'I didn't *lead* Antonio to anything. He did that all by himself.'

'Yet you didn't deny it.'

'Neither did you.'

Chanel returned.

He watched Jayda bite her lip, and her anger. Damn, but he couldn't lose the memory of her taste, wanted to suck every bit of that lip's sweetness into his mouth, take up where they left off before Bec was killed and any and all chance of something happening between them was killed, too.

After handing them each a menu, Chanel displayed the red label of a dark wine bottle. At his nod, she released the cork and poured a mouthful into his glass. He swilled the berry-rich effervescence over his palate, the wine and its taste the last thing on his mind. What the process did was gain him time, leaving Jayda to stew. When he couldn't delay any longer, he gave the expected nod, allowing his glass to be filled, then hers.

Chanel left with a soft *ciao*.

He opened the menu, ready to leave the thread of their conversation hanging where they'd left it.

'This is *not* a date.'

Her lips drew tight, the green in her eyes flinted with amber fire. She took a deep sip of her wine, and for a moment the moisture on those ripe, red lips had him distracted, until her gaze narrowed and she lifted a brow.

His turn, it seemed. 'I thought we'd already agreed on that.'

'Yes. You, me *and* my father.'

He lowered his menu. 'And now we get to the crux of it all.' The woman was a swarm of contradictions, and driving him bull-crazy. 'You're pissed off because I promised your father nothing would happen between us. Why, Jayda? Because you *want* something to happen? Because you want this to be a date, despite protesting just a little too much that you don't?'

The red in her cheeks brewed to the intensity of her hair. 'I'm surprised your ego didn't prevent you squeezing through the front door. Really, Seth? If I want you so much, why the rules?'

'Those rules are your armour. Without them you have no protection from what you want and feel when we're together.'

'Oh really, Romeo. You're that sure of yourself?'

Palms flat on the table, he matched her glare for glare. 'I'm that sure of you.'

That stopped her. Made her think, her bottom lip growing white under the attention of her teeth. Then she slapped open the menu in front of her. 'Just make sure Antonio knows the truth. This is *not* a date, and we are *not* involved any further than the case requires.'

'If that's what you want.'

Her lips pressed together and she turned the page, eyes scanning the cursive print.

His gut roiled. What was the big deal? Not interest in Antonio. She'd been amused, charmed even, but not attracted to him. He was sure of it.

Damn, but she was impossible. And enticing and intriguing and infuriating as all hell. And he still wanted her, despite her confounded resistance.

And why not? His heart quickened. She wanted him, even if she was too bull-headed to admit it. The signs were all there. The way her eyes devoured him when she thought he wasn't looking, the way her skin coloured when they touched or got too close. The way her nipples thrust hungrily against her top when they clashed. Like now.

He ducked in mock examination of his menu. Instinct told him something more than the case was holding her back. All he had to do was figure out what.

Then they could finish what they started less than a week ago.

Meantime, if she wanted him to back off, then so be it. He turned a page and inspiration hit. *Reverse psychology*. It worked on kids. He should know, he'd written an entire article on it.

Already he'd seen its effect on Jayda, her frustration when he pulled back in the car. A little more unrequited need may help tip her over the edge. In the interim, they had a case to solve and being at odds was getting them nowhere.

He lifted his glass.

'You're right, Jayda. I'm sorry.' He met her gaze and wished he could read the thoughts behind it. 'Our association is about work and I should never have pressured you into something you don't want. Let's start again, no funny business, just the investigation.'

Sipping the wine, he grimaced and stared at the ruby liquid in his glass. What was it with drinks that tasted of fruit and flowers? Antonio should've known better.

He set his glass on the table.

'Let's start by making a list of all the people in your life who could be the Night Terror.'

# Chapter Twenty-Three

'**A***mico*, what is this with the whiskey?'

Antonio indicated to the tumbler in Seth's hand as Jayda polished off her wine and reached for the bottle. If Seth wasn't going to partake, then she would, with gusto. Anything to take the edge off the evening.

As if he read her thoughts, Antonio whipped the bottle from the table, pouring her a generous second glass with flourish and an appreciative grin.

Seth grimaced. 'You know sweet is not my choice of beverage.'

'Ah, but it is your choice of company.'

Jayda returned Antonio's smile with a tight one of her own. He really was charming, loveable even, if only he'd let up on the whole 'Seth and her' routine.

'My apologies for the wine. I thought this time you would enjoy the elegance and *influenzare*. Legend says that Cleopatra believed *Brachetto d'Acqui* had the power to unleash the passions of her lovers. A little help in this area is always welcome, is it not?'

Seth's gaze flicked her way. She nodded.

'And if this were a date, I'd be forever in your debt.'

He shot a wry grin at his friend, and her heart skipped even though the look wasn't for her. Averting her gaze, she gulped back another swig of sweetness.

'Jayda's a homicide detective and we're collaborating on a case together. This is merely a work dinner, so oysters and love potions would be wasted tonight, my friend.'

'What a sin, to squander such chemistry.'

'Not everything is about love, Antonio.'

'And why not? There is too much of the other in the world today. If everyone had more *passione* in their lives, there would be no war.'

Seth chuckled. 'Maybe you're right. Just not in this case.'

Her fingers tightened round the delicate flute stem as she took another sip.

'You Italians see chemistry even where it doesn't exist. We just don't see each other in that way.'

'Then all I can say, *amico mio*, is you are blind.'

Luckily for her and the wayward direction of the conversation, a table of solo, very alluring women called for Antonio's attention, enticing him away.

Seth shot her a triumphant grin and returned all concentration to his medium-rare steak. 'That went well.'

She didn't know what annoyed her more. His apparent lack of concern over the conversation, or her preoccupation with it. After all, he'd only done as she asked.

She stared at the barely touched chicken breast on her plate, stuffed with fetta, spinach and sun-dried tomatoes that had tempted her taste buds earlier, and dropped her fork. Antonio's choice in wine was ambrosia between her lips, and to her nerves. Seth didn't know what he was talking about. The liquid was sweet and fruity, and the bubbles tap danced along her tongue before slipping easily down her throat.

'I still believe Eric trashed your car.' Seth's knife sliced effortlessly through his meat as he spoke. 'But he's too young to be the Night Terror. So, what was his motive? Unrequited love?'

Amusement—and a generous serving of red liquid—spluttered from her mouth.

He raised his brows, using his serviette to first daub his shirt, then his steak. 'I wasn't trying to be funny.'

'Well, that'd be a first.'

'In any other situation I'd say your humour is only exceeded by your beauty. But you might think it was a come-on, which it isn't, of course.'

'Of course.'

He didn't seem at all moved by the snap in her voice. Instead he helped himself to another mouthful of steak with unaffected gusto, then picked up their earlier thread of conversation. 'So, back to Eric.'

'And his unrequited love?' She tried—and failed—not to snort. Just as well it wasn't a date. Spluttering and snorting wouldn't snag a place on any how-to-get-a-man list. 'Only in a world where I sported a mouse and motherboard, and could store twelve or more gig of RAM.'

'A computer geek could easily interfere with the security camera system.'

'But why?'

'To get your attention. To encourage you to turn to him for help. My presence must have put a colossal spanner in the works.'

'If your theory is right, which I doubt. Men don't pine over women like me. That's a role left to the beautiful women of the world. Like Bec.'

The wrench embedded in her heart since last Friday squeezed tighter. Seth dropped his knife and fork onto the plate and reached across for her hand, his voice soft, his gaze softer. 'You are beautiful, Jayda.'

Flutters filled her heart.

She slid her hand from his grasp and dropped it into her lap. 'And that's not a come-on?'

'No. It's a rock-solid fact.'

Her blood heated, and she pushed back the need that accompanied it. 'Either way, this isn't getting us closer to the Night Terror. He has to be around forty-five to fifty-five years old, more Dad's generation than ours.'

'Funny how he came to the same conclusion we did.'

'*You* did, you mean.'

'No, *we* did. Solving this case is a team effort.'

She stared, searching for a hint of insincerity. There was none.

'What? Don't tell me there's a great glob of spinach between my teeth.'

'You just surprise me.'

'I take it that's a good thing.'

'It is. In my experience, reporters don't tend to be so . . .'

'Good looking?' He shot her a cheeky grin.

She rolled her eyes. 'Honest.'

Her gaze threatened to undo him.

He carved another serving of steak, then dropped his fork without bringing it to his mouth. 'What happened?'

She blinked. 'What do you mean?'

'You don't come to have a perspective like that without foundation.'

'I've got plenty.'

'Tell me.'

Teeth frustrated her bottom lip, her stare pensive. Then she sighed. 'I recently worked a case where a man murdered his wife and two daughters.'

He nodded. 'Ian Trentham.'

No surprise that he'd guessed. For weeks the story had been all-encompassing, splashed across every media outlet, Australia-wide. Until the Night Terror stole the limelight.

'We knew he was guilty, but there was no proof. He had an alibi—shaky, but it was still an alibi. And there were no bodies. Trentham told police he and his wife, Noeleen, had fought. In fact, he was open about it, stating he believed she'd followed through on previous threats, that she'd taken the kids and run.'

She double-folded the serviette from her lap and arranged it beside her plate. 'We investigated other suspects, other leads, but the trail always led back to him. So we tapped his phones and watched, waiting for him to slip up. We also put a trace and tap on Noeleen's mobile, in the hope that evidence would surface, if in fact she was still alive. And it did.'

Jayda's fingers toyed with the edge of the serviette, folding, unfolding.

'Twenty-four hours after Noeleen's disappearance, her voicemail was cleared. *Proof she was alive.* New life flooded into the investigation, we pulled out all stops, upped the search. *We had to find her.* No one ate or slept or worked on anything but the case. We couldn't. Not until we'd safely located Noeleen and her two little girls.'

Her hand froze. 'Thirty-five hours later we discovered the truth. The calls were deleted remotely. The person responsible? A reporter. When Noeleen's voicemail filled, he created space in the hope that new messages might come through that he could use in his story.'

Her hand drew into a fist, crumpling the white paper into a tight ball.

'Precious time was wasted hunting red herrings instead of catching a killer. Eventually, we found the bodies and convicted Trentham. But it was despite that reporter's actions, not because of them.' She looked up at him then, her gaze narrowed and intense. 'Can you see why I might be more than a little suspicious of your actions?'

'No.' The word cut across his tongue, low and controlled, through a jaw so tight he thought it might crack. 'From memory, that reporter was some two-bit bottom dweller, digging more for dirt than truth.'

'That may be the case, but he couldn't have sold the story if the media wasn't willing to buy.'

His shoulders met the hard frame of his chair as he leaned back and crossed his arms. 'So, we're all tainted with his brush?'

'Until proven otherwise, yes. You can't tell me you were upfront regarding your motives when we met in the Traveller. You were after an easy mine of information. A cop to ply with alcohol before wheedling out whatever details you could.'

He steeled his chin so it didn't drop to the floor. It wasn't surprising she knew his motives, but his MO was another thing. With a smug expression, she took another swig of her second—or was it third?—glass of red.

He shook his head and her brow arched. 'Surprised? We're not as obtuse as you think. When a cop leaks information from a case, more often than not it's because it suits our purposes, not yours.' She cocked her head. 'Makes you wonder who the real patsy is, doesn't it?'

One minute she was soft, dissolving into a wanton release of sweet, sensual vulnerability, and the next she was as tender and accessible as an echidna. Firmly placing him on the back foot.

His fingers tapped the starched white tablecloth. 'You've made your point.' He heard the grumble in his voice, and hated it. 'What you don't take into consideration is that while we all want the story, some of us have scruples. Unfair to punish an entire profession for the sins of a few.'

'Welcome to the real world, Seth. Where fairness is only an illusion based on pretext.'

'You weren't exactly the woman I thought you were when we first met.'

She blinked, a gratifying surge of red colouring her cheeks. 'That was work.'

'All of it?'

'Of course!'

'Even the kiss?'

She glowered. 'Especially the kiss.'

'Then I congratulate you. Your acting was flawless.'

Her subsequent seat-shuffle, eye-avoidance was a dead giveaway. She knew it. He knew it. That first meeting, she'd been acting as much as he.

'What did Antonio mean, when he congratulated you for not giving in?'

His amusement clotted in his throat. She'd successfully swapped positions and was scrutinising him again, in that way of hers.

'Just old uni talk.'

'Really? Now who's telling pork pies?'

The appetite that had led him to order the 300-gram dry-aged steak fled.

She picked up her fork as he pushed back his plate. 'This is about your parents, isn't it?'

*Never date a detective.* It should be one of those top-ten health warnings, along with cigarettes and too much fried food being bad for you.

Not that this was a date. She'd said it often enough. And yet she wanted into machinations of his mind that even he didn't dare probe.

'Have they got back to you?'

A bass drum took up residence behind his right eye. 'I told you, there's no phone or internet access where they're based.'

'Surely they call once in a while, to keep in touch?'

'Of course.' His fingers weren't crossed, but he doubted the white lie would see him earn God's wrath.

'When did you last speak?'

'Not long ago.'

'When?'

'Damn, you're persistent.' He returned her glare with one designed to make the hardiest of opponents baulk.

Not even a blink. 'And you've just got that figured? Maybe you're not as sharp as I first thought.'

'Ever thought of swapping to comedy?'

'I'd miss the rush too much.' Her gaze narrowed and she tapped the table with her right index finger. 'Are you going to tell me or will I have to drag it out of you?'

His gaze drifted across the restaurant floor, to where Antonio was charming the proverbials off an entire table of women. What was the big deal anyway? It wasn't as if his parents' disinterest still affected him. 'Two years ago.'

'Two . . . You're kidding.'

'Yes.'

She sighed. 'Oh, you—' Something in his expression must have hinted at the truth, because first there was silence, then a soft, almost sorry, 'you're not.'

He positioned his knife in perfect alignment with his fork, then daubed his mouth with his serviette before dropping it on top.

His gaze flicked to the half-eaten meal on her plate. 'If you're done, perhaps we should ask for the bill and get back to work. Unless you want dessert?'

All she did was shake her head. The question was a feeble excuse for a distraction, and unsurprisingly, it failed.

'All over your choice of career?'

'This has nothing to do with—'

'Damn, Seth. Would it kill you to admit it?'

'Much as it'd kill you to let go.' Something inside squeezed at his gut, then twisted. 'Why does my screwed-up life interest you so much?'

'I don't know. Maybe it's just a matter of evening the score. You've seen my dirty laundry, now I want to see yours.'

'If nothing else, at least you're honest.'

'Of course.' The tight set of her mouth said *what else is there?*

'The intrigue lies in the mystery. Once you know, you'll see my story's really not that remarkable.' He reached for fortification, only to discover his glass was empty. Dropping it back onto the table, he drew in a deep breath instead. 'My parents are geophysicists and they expected the same career choice from their son.'

'You mean Callum?'

'And me.'

'But you were never into science.'

'One isn't *into* science, one lives it. Anything else is a phase, something to grow out of. Something a perfect son would never consider.'

'So now you're into the hardnosed reporting, you think their viewpoint will change?'

'They have nothing to do with my wanting success. This for me.'

Raised brows indicated she believed otherwise. Steak and mash churned in his gut as he told himself it didn't matter what she thought.

She opened her mouth then clamped it, her gaze still firmly locked to his. Then her lips bucked in the merest of smiles.

'Funny, your parents wanted you to follow in their footsteps, and my father was dead-set against me following in his.'

His hand froze midair as he reached for the water. 'I never would've guessed.'

'Once he realised it was what I wanted more than anything, he back-pedalled. Although, I now have a funny suspicion my mother might have had a hand in his turnabout.'

He poured himself a glass before offering to do the same for her. She shook her head.

'You were lucky.'

'I am. Was.' She pushed her plate and grabbed her purse. 'You're right. I think we should get back to it.'

He caught Chanel's eye and pulled out his wallet. 'My treat.'

'That may have been Italian, but we're going Dutch.'

He grinned. 'I won't ask for payment in return.'

Her hand flew to her chest. 'Thank heavens you cleared that up! I don't know what I was thinking.'

Chanel arrived, expertly removing the plates and cutlery from the table, balancing them as only an experienced waitress could. 'How did you enjoy your meal?'

'Tell Antonio the chef has outdone himself.'

'He'll be pleased to hear it.'

He handed her his credit card, pushing Jayda's away when she tried to do the same. Chanel shot them both a wide smile before making her way towards the kitchen.

'I told you we'd go halves.'

'And I told you I'd pay. If it's really such an issue, you pay next time.'

'If there is a next time.'

The corner of his lips kicked up as he watched irritation heighten her cheeks.

'Oh, don't worry about that. There will be.'

If not for the dark, everyone they passed en route to the car would have seen steam shooting from her ears in wild, fiery bursts.

Seth was oblivious. He'd paid the bill, man-hugged Antonio, then hustled her out before his friend could do more than kiss her effusively on both cheeks. He was beginning to smell of a control freak, and she wasn't one to roll over or play nice. Not for anyone, least of all for an infuriating, pulse-racing reporter who didn't know when to quit.

'Damn!'

Jayda sidled up next to him and her thoughts stilled in silent agreement. Scrubbing his hand through his hair, Seth scanned the area. She could have told him it was a waste of time. Whoever had slashed all four of his tyres was long gone.

'Still think it's Eric?'

The glower he threw her way said he considered her less than funny. She agreed. The feeling that they were somehow being targeted wouldn't leave. One incident could be disregarded. But two . . .

'Bastard had to wait till I got new tyres!' Grumbling under his breath, he inspected for further damage, the tender stroke of his hand over buffed-within-an-inch-of-its-life silver paint adoring enough to make her jealous.

She left him to his sufferings and reached for her phone, circling the vehicle as the operator answered.

Unlikely she'd find anything after the evidence-lacking state of her own car, but still she had to check. Rounding towards the driver's side, she identified herself to the woman at the emergency call centre.

Her foot planted. Froze. She tried to breathe, tried to speak past the catch of saliva in her throat. *Impossible.*

The mobile slipped through her fingers and slammed the concrete with a sharp *crack!* She wondered vaguely whether the screen had smashed, or if the operator would dispatch the officers now with more urgency than a 34 on a vehicle required.

'What '

Pine wrapped round her mind as familiar hands grabbed her elbows and moved her aside. Seth stepped in and wrapped an arm round her shoulders, shifting his gaze to where hers had frozen. The car door, or rather, what was wedged inside.

A tiny scrap of fabric, the familiar outline of yellow sunflower tinged with blood.

# Chapter Twenty-Four

'**W**e'll get the material to the lab, but it looks a perfect match to the missing portion of Bec's dress.'

Jayda knew it was, without Georgie or Teddy or the three blue-and-whites and her entire squad on the scene to tell her that.

The wind had picked up, moon and stars swallowed by a blanket of puffy grey, while barbed fingers of blue-black leached down from the sky and clutched at her heart.

'Thanks, Georgie.'

'How're you holding up?' Brown eyes assessed her, as if searching for the truth.

She blocked her expression and forced a smile. 'I've had better weeks.'

'Yeah.'

The caring in her friend's voice, the gentle squeeze of her arm, tapped at the thin veneer of her control. Was it only two days ago she'd shared coffee in her living room with Georgie and Chase and assured them she was doing okay?

She swallowed.

Seth reached for her hand and when he squeezed, the rigidity of her shoulders eased. Even the cold night air lost its edge.

Her heart flip-flopped. 'How's everything back at the station?'

'Much the same.' Georgie tapped her fingers, ticking them off one by one. 'Sam's moved off his couch and onto a friend's. Christine's not answering his calls, so if you thought he was grumpy before . . .' Georgie's mock anguish tugged a smile to Jayda's lips.

Sam in grouch mode was anything but pretty. And a regular occurrence for the past six months, since little Robbie had introduced his parents to the concept of three hourly night-feeds. Then, at least, Sam had enjoyed the comfort of his own bed. She could only imagine what he'd be like now.

Georgie lowered her voice. 'Hackett is, well, *Hackett,*' she rolled her eyes, 'and Chase walks round like he's got an entire beehive up his butt. Men and power! Go figure. Everyone misses you.' Her voice trailed off as Chase approached, her gaze cooling, ping-ponging between Jayda and her partner before she made herself scarce.

*What's with all that?*

Ice. Wedged between her two friends, where before their friendship had been warm and fun.

Seth squeezed her hand one last time before following Georgie, as if he sensed she'd want information from Chase, and more, Chase wouldn't cough up with a reporter present.

Her gaze shadowed Georgie. What had changed the past few days? Or had it started earlier, with those glances back in the van? As if she believed something was going on with Jayda and Chase. She should know better. Surely Chase would have set her straight?

She shook her head. She was being overly sensitive again.

Much as Georgie's actions and their implications needled, her leaving was an opportunity she wouldn't let pass. 'Any progress on the case?'

Chase's mouth opened, then clamped, his gaze darting beyond her left shoulder.

'I wouldn't catch you pumping the team for information, would I, Thomasz?' Hackett stormed up and inserted himself between them.

He turned to Chase. 'Liaise with the uniforms. I want statements from everyone—neighbours, shop owners, passers-by, security footage. No stone unturned, understand?'

An apologetic look was all she won before Hackett's dictates saw Chase scuttle away to do his bidding.

'How're you going?' The gruffness of her boss's voice was the only give-away that veiled emotion might lurk below.

'I'd be a darn sight better if I knew where you were at in the case.'

His shoulders stiffened. She'd never questioned him so openly before—no one dared. And if she hadn't just suffered a loss, she didn't doubt she'd be receiving a right royal chewing-out about now.

The idea bothered her a great deal less than it had in the past.

'We're following up on—'

'Not the drivel you tell the public. I want the real stuff.'

The beady brown of his gaze narrowed. 'And if I believed you wouldn't rush off on your own private crusade, perhaps I'd consider it.'

Seth's arm slid round her waist as he returned to her side, and the warmth of that gesture made her throat thicken.

'She was my sister.'

'I know.' Hackett scrubbed the back of his neck, looking anywhere but at her. 'Regulations are regulations, and I won't have you within a flea's butt of anything to do with the Night Terror.'

'What if I promised to stay away?'

'What if I told you someone requested cold-case evidence be tested for DNA?' His squint was probing, accusatory, leaving her with no room for retreat.

'Anyone farts near my case and I know it. Remember that for future reference.' The glare in his gaze lessened. 'What makes you think they'll find something?'

No sense denying what Hackett already knew. And maybe sharing would soften him enough to share back.

'The hydrogen peroxide. Why change MO when you've been so meticulous in the past, unless it's to mask something that never needed masking before?'

His nod was Hackett-speak for 'well done' and his expression was almost paternal before the lines on his face cut away any semblance of humanity.

'Come by the station, give your statement, then go home and rest for the week and a half you have left. I don't expect to see or hear from you until then.'

How could she get it so very wrong? There was no softening stone.

With an awkward pat to her arm, and a nod to Seth, Hackett turned and barked at a uniform leaning casually against the door of his car.

'He's a piece of work, isn't he?'

'He's just doing his job.' There was a snap to her voice she couldn't define. She didn't know why she was defending Hackett to Seth. All it achieved was the drop of his hand from her waist and a distance that made her body shiver.

Seth rubbed his hands together as if he too felt the cold. 'How long until I get my car back?'

'How long is a piece of string?'

'Very funny.'

'Thought you'd appreciate the irony.'

'I'd appreciate a set of wheels more. What do we do now?'

'My car's still in evidence and nowhere near roadworthy.' She swallowed against the constriction in her throat. 'We'll use Bec's.'

The silence was almost as unbearable as the thought of sitting in the psychedelic pink Beetle without her sister beside her. But if using the car meant they were mobile enough to continue investigating . . .

'We'll pick it up on the way to the station.'

That stupid Godfather line barked from his back pocket and he extracted his phone. Eyes narrowed, he returned what must have been a text with one of his own, then replaced the mobile.

'Think we can get a lift from one of your cronies?'

'We'll take a cab.' Not that she didn't trust her team. Rather, it wasn't necessary they know her every move. 'Can you call? My mobile's in dire need of medical attention.' She waved the shattered lump of plastic. Yes, it still worked, but the screen needed an intimate encounter with a roll of tape.

He extracted his mobile again and began to dial.

Spice filled her nostrils. She turned as Chase's palm cupped her elbow to guide her away. 'I thought you hated reporters.'

She edged her arm from his grasp. 'The scum-sucking ones, yes.'

'But not the macho, model-like ones.' Her partner's narrowed scrutiny flicked towards Seth whose keen, directed gaze was eating up the distance, and her.

She wouldn't discuss Seth with Chase, or the fact they were working together. Not when there was no guarantee that what she said wouldn't go further.

'Seth's a friend.'

'A very close friend from the looks of it.'

Her heartbeat stumbled as she glanced again at the man whose gun-metal gaze even now was melting her knee ligaments. 'I'm not sure that's any of your business.'

'Be careful, Jayda. You don't know this guy from Adam. Who knows what he wants?'

She lifted her chin. 'I do. And I'm absolutely fine with it.'

His jaw clenched. 'He's not right for you.'

'You have no idea what's right for me.'

*Damn.* She should have bit her tongue. She bit it now. Or was it more a case of eating humble pie? No good could come from severing her already tenuous link to the case. Unfortunately Chase was it.

'Congrats on snagging lead on the case.'

His smile was distant and not as steadfast as it had been in the past. 'Thanks, but you know I'd rather have you back than the promotion.'

What made her doubt his sincerity? The tone in his voice? The way he avoided her gaze when he said the words? The same way Liam had never looked her in the eye when he said he cared. A mark of untruths.

Rubbing his wrist, Chase glanced over her shoulder, then inclined towards her, his mouth dangerously close to her ear. 'We found nothing of interest in your car, but we're following some leads in relation to your—to the last death.'

He cleared his throat, dropped his hand to his side when he noticed her watching. 'We sent the letter to forensics. Seems the paper is of the home-made variety, constructed from a mix of bleached newspaper and toilet paper. And the glue used to affix the letters is a methyl cellulose derivative. A chemical powder, which, when mixed with water, is most often used in repairing delicate artwork or the spines of antique books.'

'Durant!'

Chase's entire body jolted. He winced, glanced over her shoulder again, before reaching out to shakily squeeze her arm. 'I'll see you at the station. We're going to catch this guy, I promise.'

Her gaze dipped to his bandage. 'How's your hand?'

Snatching it back, he shoved it into his pocket, his eyes darting to her left ear. 'It's mending.'

Shakespeare's words resonated through her mind as she watched a man she no longer knew walk away.

*The man doth protest too much, methinks.*

She needed the hike up the stairs like she needed the headache that accompanied it. But the 'out of order' sign taped securely over the lift doors left her with little choice.

If she'd wanted exercise, she would have hit the gym.

Pain sliced through her chest at the thought of gymming alone.

*Or maybe not.*

Head down, she trudged behind Seth, craving the solitude of her apartment and a long, hot bath to soak away the stench of the past hour. More than that, she wished for a re-enactment of *Groundhog Day*, to wake up to a fresh start—Bec alive, her parents living happily ever after and no OPI investigation. A perfect world.

If only dreams really could come true.

She didn't notice the wall of muscle in front had stopped until it was too late. She jumped backwards before temptation took over and she lost herself in a way she shouldn't. 'What—'

'Who's that?'

She side-stepped in time to see a tall man in a dark grey suit push himself away from the wall outside her apartment and start walking towards them.

'I have no idea.'

Not entirely true. She had some, she just hoped she was wrong.

'Detective Thomasz?'

The voice rang bells. Loud. Clear. Resonating. But she asked the question anyway. 'And you are?'

'Detective Symonds.' He flashed a badge. Her heart did that sinking thing again—something it was doing a lot lately. 'From the OPI.'

'This isn't a good time, Detective.'

'It very rarely is.' His jaw was set, uncompromising, a perfect match to the grit in his brown, almost black eyes as they narrowed on her. 'I've left several messages on your mobile.'

'And as you can tell, it's seen better days.' She held the shattered, less than healthy piece of metal up for him to see.

The man barely glanced at her phone. Instead, he indicated at her door. 'Can we go inside?'

When she hesitated, the grit in his eyes turned to steel. 'Or if you prefer, we can do this at headquarters.'

She traded stare for stare, but his was invincible. And she had no strength left to draw on.

Avoiding the question in Seth's eyes, she brushed past the other man and jabbed her key into the lock. 'You'd better come in then.'

The door swung open. Before she could form the words to tell Seth it was time he left, he'd slipped past, cutting across her living room floor. 'I'll make coffee.'

She closed the front door and dumped her bag and jacket on the dining room table. Symonds didn't wait for an invitation. He walked straight into her living room and sank into her high-backed armchair.

He opened his black briefcase and glanced up. 'Not for me. This won't take long.'

Seth disappeared into her kitchen, a place he'd pretty much made his own. He should be gone. She wanted him gone. And yet she didn't. Because his presence meant she wouldn't have to face this interview alone. Not that she needed Seth. That wasn't the case at all. But living in each other's pockets over the past few days meant that he'd already seen and learned so much. This was just one more gem to add to his growing stash. And news this juicy, well, he'd be bound to find out sooner or later.

Her gut clenched.

He seemed determined to stay, come hell or high water, so why not make the best of it? And trust he'd remain true to his word, that whatever was discussed wouldn't find its way to print.

She perched on the edge of the couch opposite Symonds.

He withdrew a mini recorder and placed it on the coffee table between them. 'Before we start, I must warn you, Detective Thomasz, I intend to interview you in relation to your father, former Detective Dean Thomasz. You are not obliged to say or do anything, but anything you say or do may be recorded and given in evidence. Consider yourself sworn in and think very carefully before you reply with anything other than the truth.'

Her jaw stiffened. 'You haven't done your homework, Detective. If you had, you'd know I never tell anything but the truth.'

The brown of his eyes contained a coldness she'd never before attributed to such a warm colour. 'That seems a good enough place to start.'

The aroma of freshly perked coffee entered the room. Seth passed her one of two inspirational mugs—part of a gift set from Bec. She wrapped her fingers round it, allowing the heat to work at thawing the frost.

The yellow smiley face on the ceramic seemed to mock her, along with the black printed words of Oscar Wilde, *be yourself; everyone else is already taken'.*

She would have laughed if she wasn't so damn nervous and angry and scared. Her father's future and reputation were in her hands, and those of the man before her. And she doubted Symonds cared a tick about destroying a venerated career over a bout of unsubstantiated slander and supposition. A witch hunt. Because that's exactly what this had to be.

Unthinkable that her father would act outside of the law he regarded so highly. The cushions dipped as Seth dropped onto the couch. Her body tilted towards him, his thigh firm against hers, radiating heat along the length of her body.

Symonds flipped the cover of a notebook, pen poised. The man was determined not to miss a thing. Although what he thought she knew, or should know, she hadn't a clue.

Her father had been vague about the accusations. Almost deliberately so. She'd assumed it was to protect her.

Tentative doubts nudged at her thoughts. Was it her father who needed protection?

Symonds checked the recorder, angling the microphone her way. 'Shall we start?' He didn't wait for agreement, and she gave none.

With a nod, he launched straight to the crux of his presence in her tiny, tidy apartment. 'Detective Thomasz, tell me what you know about the Highbury Case.'

# Chapter Twenty-Five

'**W**hy didn't you tell me?'

The lock clicked beneath Seth's fingers as he closed the door behind the sourest man he'd ever had the misfortune of meeting. Jayda was still slumped against the couch cushions, the awry halo of curls framing an expression that said she'd had enough.

'It wasn't something you needed to know.' A weary hand pushed a twist of red back from her face.

Much as he knew he shouldn't push, the irritation which had grown and ballooned throughout the interview spurred him to press on. 'Your father wasn't spring cleaning, was he?' He scrubbed a hand through his hair. 'You must think I'm a damn fool.'

'This has nothing to do with you.'

'Really? Claims of evidence-tampering by a previous key investigator in the Night Terror case isn't something I should know about?'

She reddened. 'Those allegations are phony and have no bearing on this case, now or back then.'

'And you know that, how?'

'My father is innocent.'

'You should have told me. If for no other reason than perhaps I could have helped. We're working together, remember?'

'Not on this.' She stood and grabbed the two empty mugs from the coffee table. 'I think you should go, Seth.'

'This conversation's not finished.'

'It is from my end.'

He fought against the urge to grab her by the shoulders and shake. Instead, he gritted his teeth. 'Tomorrow we re-examine all the testimonies and evidence for anything that could have deluded the investigation.'

'If you want to chase red herrings, that's your deal.'

His phone chimed and he glanced at the reminder on the screen. *Damn.* That was the last thing he needed right now.

He looked up, and encountered Jayda's razer-tipped glare. Then again, perhaps distraction was exactly what he needed. 'I'd stay and argue the point, but I've got a drinks date in half an hour.'

He grabbed his jacket and keys and headed for the door. 'Just for the record, I don't believe your father did it either. But where there's smoke, you're bound to find some guy holding a match. So, if he didn't, who did?'

He twisted the handle and pulled, not waiting to see if any of his bait had caught. 'I'll be back at nine sharp tomorrow. Make sure you're ready.'

Her focus should have been on Symonds' interview or Seth's belief in her father's innocence, but all she could think was *he has a date.*

She wasn't stupid enough to believe Seth had mentioned it for any reason other than to bug her. And she hated that his plan had worked.

Her hands gripped the empty mugs as she made her way to the kitchen.

He'd never mentioned a girlfriend—in fact, had specifically told her he didn't have one—and he wasn't married. At least, he'd never mentioned a wife. He had no ring or ring-line on any of his fingers, but that wasn't a sure-fire indicator. Not all married men wore rings.

Nothing in his background check had flagged a partner or wife. She shook her head and dumped the mugs into the sink.

What did it matter who his date was? Who he was seeing and how he felt about them? Seth seeing another woman only served to make things between them less complex. He wasn't available to her, even if she changed her mind.

The grumble from her stomach had nothing to do with hunger. How dare he pursue her when he was already taken?

Hands operating on autopilot, she readied the percolator and set it on the stove. Next the milk went into the microwave to heat.

Her fist pressed hard against the cold bench tiles. How dare he kiss her! *And* call himself 'a friend', when all the while he was lying and cheating, not only to her, but the other woman. Or was she 'the other woman'?

She would *not* be the other woman.

Thank heavens for her rules. She'd nearly given in. Had wanted him to kiss her again, and more. Lucky for Seth he hadn't, or there'd be even more fuel for her anger right now.

And this time she had her gun.

The thought almost made her smile. She pushed it back, along with any thoughts of *him*, before she let loose, tossed her mug at the wall and screamed.

Fragrant aromas filled her nostrils, closely followed by the gurgle of coffee ready for pouring.

Warring against the shake in her hands, she poured coffee over warm milk, added sugar, then withdrew to the living room, sinking into the couch, legs curled beneath her. Taking a deep, fortifying sip of hot heaven, liquid-form, she tilted her head back and closed her eyes.

She ought to call her father. He should know she'd been cornered and questioned by Symonds. And more importantly, she had questions requiring his explanation.

What was this investigation really about? And why did the OPI believe she had the answers?

She shifted her legs, stretched against the spread of pins and needles, her palms embracing the heat of her mug as she sipped.

Of the many rules governing an undercover cop, one was indisputable—no discussing the case outside the Department, immediate family included. Her father had been a stickler for the rules, especially those ensuring the safety of his girls. Which was why the accusations made no sense, and why she wondered what was really behind Symonds' carefully worded questions.

The Highbury Case. Named after a suburb in Melbourne's northwest, rather than the brothers who'd sparked it. Josef and Johan Syvertsen had gained their citizenship one year before they opened a restaurant and bar in the little pocket suburb of Highbury. Nothing in the move seemed untoward, and not once did they make a showing on the police radar, until known underworld figures in and about the area began mysteriously disappearing.

When police investigated, nothing rang bells. The brothers were clean. So her father was sent in to discover what the uniforms couldn't.

And he hit pay-dirt. But it took him a year out of their lives and—as she'd just discovered—a year in the life of a live-in mistress while working as bar manager at the Copper Cabana.

Undercover was one thing, but unfaithful? Her chest tightened and she fought to swallow the disbelief clogging her throat. The Highbury saga may have begun three years ago, but was this the reason for her parents' split? So many questions, and she doubted her father would have anything but roundabout answers for any of them. Still, she had to ask.

She downed the rest of her drink and dropped the mug onto the table beside her armrest. Her fingers rubbed at her temples, but nothing stopped the heavy pounding inside her skull.

It was a call that could wait until morning. The one to her mother couldn't. More than ever, she needed her hot chocolate brand of comfort. Some soothing words to calm her spiralling disquiet.

Dialling snagged her nothing but the chirpy sound of her mother's voice asking her to leave a message. She hung up before the beep. No point leaving another when there were already a string clogging her voicemail, unanswered.

She closed her eyes, blocked out the world and everything threatening to bury her whole.

Before she faced reality, her father, the boxes of casefiles in her study, she needed something to ease the kinks from her body.

She pushed off the couch, headed towards her en suite bathroom—with a detour to the fridge for a bottle of Moscato—and turned on first the cold then the hot tap in the bath.

On impulse, she nabbed the up-till-now ornamental bottle of jasmine and ylang ylang oil and poured more than half the contents under the hot water stream. Then, dropping her clothes, she took a large swig of wine while waiting for the tub to fill.

Her mobile said it was eleven. Half an hour since Seth had left. And she couldn't stop thinking about what he was doing right now.

Were they still sharing that drink, or had they elected to skip aperitifs in favour of another kind of sustenance?

She stepped into the bath and sank into the heat, the slide of oil and water over her skin making her shiver and sweat all at once. The wine—on top of the numerous glasses of Italian red she'd consumed at dinner—was on a collision course with her head. Rational thought was a thing of the past, and she liked the feeling. Didn't want to think or feel or do anything right now but immerse herself in the moment.

She slid deeper still beneath the water, the roll of liquid over her body like the glide of skin over skin. She closed her eyes, savoured the sensation. Pictured a man with jet-black hair and steely eyes suspended above her. His lips fluttered across hers while one hand pierced the water, gliding slowly along the underside of her breast, over her ribs, across her tummy, down further still to the throbbing flesh, wet and wanting, between her thighs.

Her breath hitched, lips parted, trembling, waiting for Seth to—

Her eyes shot open. They should never have closed. Not when he was all she could imagine.

Damn the man for making her think about him, fantasise over him, want him. While even now he was likely in the throes of what they'd started in Carmello's rooftop garden. With someone else.

She jerked upright and water sloshed over the edge of the tub. She had to know. Didn't know why, didn't want to know why. She just needed to . . . *know*.

She placed her glass on the ledge behind her back. Then, shaking the water from her hand, she reached for her phone.

'I never took you for a teetotaller, Seth.'

Richie's burnt copper brows arched at the tall glass on the table containing Seth's bitter lemon and soda. He raised his tumbler and knocked back a greater portion of his double gin and tonic.

'I've had my fill tonight.'

'And not just of drinks, it seems.'

'I'm not going there, man. Jayda's off limits.'

'To you.' He chuckled. 'Nice to see even the best of us mere mortals get a bit of the no-go, once in a while.'

'Glad to provide some light entertainment.' The muscles in his gut tightened. The fact that Richie had guessed Jayda tied him in knots was almost as vexing as Jayda tying him in knots without even trying.

He discarded the straw and sipped from his glass. 'Now you've lured me here with smoke and mirrors, what's the big news that couldn't wait?'

'Luke Reynolds is retiring in three months.'

His mind skyrocketed in one hundred directions at once. A reporting position up for grabs at the *Melbourne Telegraph*.

'Any idea who's replacing him?'

'You, if you get your ass moving with this story.'

Seth positioned his drink over the water ring on the table, thumb rubbing at the condensation on the glass. 'We still have no idea who the killer is.'

'So you've got nothing else to go with?'

He couldn't help it, his mind automatically jumped to Dean; the battle-room state of his study; the OPI investigation.

Richie's face split into a grin. 'There is something!'

'No.'

'You're holding back, man. Why?'

He looked up then. 'It's nothing.'

Richie tilted his almost empty glass Seth's way. 'Ever since we met, you've wanted out of features and into reporting. Here's your chance.'

'How long have I got?'

'You have an appointment with Carson Monday week. If what you've uncovered doesn't equate to ground-breaking, our esteemed editor will look elsewhere.'

'So there's time.'

'It's her, isn't it?'

'Jayda?'

'The fact you know who I mean has me convinced I'm right. She's a source, Seth. Anything more and she'll hold you back.'

'Says the man who gave up a career in screenwriting for a woman.'

'Who left me for another man.' Stroking the tip of his beard, he narrowed his gaze. 'Trust me, they're not worth it. I'm talking from knowledge, the shitty firsthand kind.'

'This conversation's moot, because there's nothing between us.'

'Not for want of trying.'

The deep gravel of the Godfather's voice vibrated off the table. Seth sucked in a breath at the caller ID. 'I have to take this.'

Avoiding the knowing shake of his friend's head, he dodged nearby tables, accepting the call as he stepped through the exit, leaving the noise and bar behind.

'Jayda.' His greeting met with empty silence. His heart stalled. 'Jayda, are you okay?' He heard a gulp—swallowing a drink?—then a swish of water as if she were—

'Jayda, are you having a bath?' The rasp hit the back of his throat.

Involuntary images of her naked body almost completely submerged in bubbles blasted into his brain. His mind said he was still pissed at her, his body had other ideas.

'How's your date?' Her words jarred.

He couldn't help but grin. 'Jealous, are we?'

She spluttered, and another splash saw his imagination leap into overdrive.

'In your dreams!'

'Then why the call?' Again his question met with silence. 'Perhaps you want me to come over and sponge your back?'

Her sharp intake of breath said that was exactly what she wanted. Every manly bone in his body screamed to desert his friend and go to her before she had the chance to change her mind. Only, wasn't that exactly what he suspected would happen?

'Just checking you're keeping your promise *and* details of the case to yourself.'

Even her rationalisation rang of stonewalling. He could hear it in her voice. Read it between every clipped, cursed word that left her lips.

He gripped the phone to his ear and turned towards the doorway and where Richie waited for him inside. He closed his eyes, cursing himself for every kind of a fool.

Jealousy and alcohol would not be the precursor bringing them together. He'd never taken advantage of a woman, wasn't about to start now. She'd be lucid and willing when they at last tumbled into his bed together. Not *if*. *When*. She wanted him. It was just a matter of time until she fessed up and gave in.

'See you tomorrow morning at nine.' He swallowed, as he tried not to think about what he'd given up. 'Enjoy your bath.'

Then, before he could change his mind and beg her to wait, he disconnected the call and headed back into the bar.

# Chapter Twenty-Six

The noose was tightening around the bitch's pasty, stubborn neck.

His fingers flew over the keyboard, clipping yet another inch from a rope that would see her last breath squeezed from her lungs. It was just the beginning. In time he would steal everything she valued, just as she'd done to him.

He couldn't help but grin as the beep indicated he'd breached the bank's security. Pathetic, really. Their firewalls and encryption were no match for a master.

The account he sought appeared on the screen almost instantaneously. Its security settings were child's play to alter. No need for verification messages or a daily withdrawal limit.

He flexed his fingers. And for his last trick . . . a disappearing act of mega proportions. With the tap of a key, the account balance plummeted, and lost dogs in Melbourne suddenly became all the richer.

Irony at its finest.

It took less than a minute to cover his tracks. Then he logged out and swivelled in his chair to face the window.

Darkness embraced the near deserted street below. Too quiet. Too calm. Perhaps a timely reminder? One to demonstrate the futility of her efforts to conquer him.

Fire burned up his oesophagus and into his throat. He pushed up from the chair and headed for the kitchen. Knocking back a mouthful of water, and the tablets that doctors stated would only give him time, he squinted, staring at his legacy, his one incentive to keep going. That and the knowledge that everyone who'd played a part in his demise would be gone before him.

He dumped his glass in the sink, grabbed his jacket and keys. Time for an evening stroll.

His pulse quickened as he made for the door.

# Chapter Twenty-Seven

Early morning sun glimmered through slatted blinds as Jayda pushed through the heavy laboratory door. She squinted, wishing she'd brought her sunnies. All the while her head spun and her stomach churned, a reminder that she and too much alcohol never mixed well.

At first the room appeared deserted, the hour too early for most in Victoria's Forensic Services Department. But as the door swished shut behind her, she spotted an exception to the rule.

Nodding her thanks to the officer beside her, she approached the overloaded but orderly desk.

Her heart hadn't stopped thundering since she'd received Will Andrews' call at seven-thirty that morning. He wanted her to pop by. His office was an hour's drive from her apartment—not a mere 'pop by' scenario. The request meant he'd found something.

It just had to.

'Will?'

His head jerked up from a large microscope, revealing bushy grey brows and a face that suggested experience, mainly of the good variety. It was a face she remembered well from her childhood—frequent family dinners with friends, and Police Department barbeques.

'Ah, Jayda.' His expression melted into a web of wrinkles that made her think of Santa. A tall, slim, clean-shaven version.

'Sorry to interrupt.'

'No problem. Looking down a microscope is like entering another universe. It's easy to get lost and forget everything, including Margaret and an overcooked pot roast waiting at home.'

She couldn't help but smile. 'Sounds familiar.'

He turned in his chair, his expression measured and circumspect. 'How's your dad?'

The curve in her lips stiffened. Old-school loyalty was the only reason she was here. The only reason she'd been permitted to burden a workload already full to overflowing—a given in the FSD. And while she was willing to take what being her father's daughter afforded her, she wasn't willing to go anywhere near how her father really was—considering the new-to-light facts she still hadn't confronted him with.

'As good as can be expected.'

'I'm sorry about Bec.'

That familiar moisture warred against her lids. 'Me too.' She blinked. 'I don't want to take up too much of your time. Did something come up in the DNA analysis?'

His entire face crinkled into what could only be described as a beam. 'More than something.' His chin lifted, his expression lighting up like an athlete who knows he's won gold. 'We got a match.'

'His name is Roan Madden.'

Jayda wavered between bear-hugging Will and turning cartwheels over the highly polished linoleum floor.

*Gotcha!*

Nut-brown eyes considered her from over tented fingers. 'Heard of him?'

'Should I have?'

Will left his chair and crossed the lab before disappearing into a kitchenette. She followed, heart hammering against her ribs. Not in a good way.

He scrubbed his hands, grabbed two cups from the dishwasher and placed them on the bench next to the sink. 'Coffee?'

She bit her lip and shook her head.

'Tea, then?'

'Uh, no thanks.'

His arms crossed over the starched white of his lab coat as he rested back against the bench. 'After your dad's call, I pulled the cold-case evidence from storage. As you know, Doris Tombes was the Night Terror's first victim. There was a bloodstain on the right sleeve of her sweater. Doris must have fought back, and scratched or cut her attacker.'

'Roan Madden.'

He nodded. 'Seems so.'

'So, who is Roan Madden?'

'A man convicted of murdering his wife just over twenty-five years ago.' At last. Something that made sense.

'He has a history of violence.' She could barely breathe for the excitement. 'I wonder if his wife had blonde hair and blue eyes.'

Will turned back to the bench and poured himself a water. 'She had brown hair dyed red.'

'Oh.'

Where up until now Will had been an open book, suddenly the pages slammed shut. The line of his shoulders appeared awkward and he seemed determined to avoid any and all eye contact.

'Did anything else show up?'

'His wife's dissimilarity to the vic profile is probably why the police never linked Madden with the earlier Night Terror killings. That, and the fact they had no evidence.'

It was as though she hadn't uttered her last question; as though he hadn't heard.

'I'll work through the remaining evidence, but there's no doubt we have a very likely suspect for those cold-case murders.'

Thoughts swirled and ideas formed, an endless stream, one trailing the other. Her mind was running so fast, it was impossible to keep up.

'It fits! He stopped killing when he was caught and convicted, and started murdering again once he was released.'

She grinned. Why wasn't Will grinning back? 'This is great. Better than great. Does Hackett know? Have they located Madden?'

'I sent my full report to Hackett last night.'

The mobile in her jeans pocket began to ring. She ignored it, watching her father's old friend sip then lower his drink before uttering words that made no sense.

'There's no way Roan Madden committed any of the recent murders. Not while he's still serving a life sentence in prison.'

Seth pressed redial, cursing every deity known and a few more untested ones just for good measure.

Five past nine and Jayda wasn't answering her door or her mobile.

He dumped the takeaway coffee holder onto her doorstep as the call clicked over to voicemail once again.

*Damn her!*

He scrubbed the back of his neck, any residual humour long gone.

Sleep had been impossible after last night's phone call. The moment his eyes closed, images of Jayda and bath bubbles had blasted his brain; her auburn tresses slicked back, her body submerged in hot, steamy water, only her head and the taut, raspberry tips of her nipples peeking through the foam.

He groaned. As pissed as he was at her, she still had him hard and wanting. He scanned the hall and tugged impatiently at his fly, the pressure unbearable against a reaction that seemed inexhaustible since the moment they'd crossed paths.

The woman was trouble. In blazing capitals with a trail of exclamation marks a mile long. He should have realised it at their first meeting, and run.

If it wasn't for the story . . .

Richie's words rapped loudly from somewhere inside his subconscious. *Ever since I've known you, you've wanted out of features and into reporting.*

*She's a source, Seth. Anything more and she'll hold you back.*

He had a story. Several, in fact. Every one headline-worthy.

*Detective's sister latest Night Terror victim. Killer's vendetta against cop family. Celebrated cop accused of crooked dealings.*

No need to wait for the Night Terror's capture. He already had what he needed to cement himself as a serious contender for the soon-to-be-announced vacancy at the *Melbourne Telegraph*.

If he had any manner of balls, he'd head for his apartment right now and write the reports. He'd forget about Jayda and the churning unease in his gut, and continue investigating the Night Terror alone.

He stared at the blank screen of his mobile, and swore, even as he swiped and hit redial once more.

'Can you try again?'

Jayda slid her credit card back across the cluttered glass counter and leaned forward. The spiral of unreality that had mushroomed since she left the forensics lab smacked her square in the gut.

The woman, wrapped head-to-toe in red Indian silk with a matching bindi on her forehead, placed her forefinger on the useless piece of plastic and pushed it back. 'The machine is saying I must confiscate the card and contact your bank.' Her gaze darted to the growing queue behind Jayda. 'Do you have another card to use, please?'

'You've already tried my savings account and my credit card. I don't have anything else.' Her hand clenched her wallet. 'You must have pressed the wrong button or something. I know there's money in my account, and my credit card should be clear.'

'I'm sorry. You need to take up that matter with the bank.' The woman indicated to the man beside her. 'If you can step to the side and wait with Nadir, I must serve these people. In the time waiting, is there someone you can call to pay for your petrol?'

'I can pay. If you'd just call the bank.'

'I'm very sorry, Madam, I cannot do that.' Her voice had hardened, her head performing a signature side-to-side bob.

The last thing she needed was a scene in the middle of a crowded petrol station.

The woman waved her hand. 'Please step to the side with Nadir.'

Nadir was tall and wide and would have been enormously intimidating had Jayda not wrestled and subdued men doubly as large, and determined, before. He wasn't a thug so much as massive. And her black belt in taekwondo aside, she could have decked him in five. Or flashed her badge and escaped the stickiness of the situation.

She was loath to do either.

'Do you have a mobile to call someone?' The tone in his voice proclaimed teddy bear rather than villain. She scrambled mentally to regain reason. After all, it wasn't Nadir's fault that her bank had stuffed up.

She just needed to find someone to call.

First she tried the bank, clicking through every red hoop their telephone banking system threw at her until she reached the queue to speak to a customer service officer. She was sixteenth—estimated wait time, forty-five minutes. She hung up.

Juz's mobile clicked straight to voicemail each of the three times she tried. No doubt he was taking a class. Or maybe not. Wasn't the gym closed for renovations? Either way, he wasn't answering.

Neither did Georgie, after two tries.

Garry was working, and telemarketers were banned from taking private calls during their shift. Something she knew firsthand after suffering more than enough of Juz's bitching on the subject.

There was her father, but she wasn't ready to face him yet. Darren was still in Queensland, and not due back until the weekend.

She even considered Eric. The thought made her uncomfortable. Damn Seth for that!

There it was. One person remained. And even as she dialled his number, the misgivings refused to subside.

He picked up first ring. 'Where the hell are you?'

She yanked the phone from her ear and her finger wavered over 'end' on the screen. But what choice did she have? There was no one else to call, and no sense angering Seth further. Her absence at her apartment this morning had obviously fuelled his looming tirade, and rightfully so.

Guilt nibbled at the borders of her conscience. She should have phoned. Regardless of how she felt after her foolish late-night call, leaving him to wait for over an hour was thoughtless and inconsiderate and so not like her. What was with his knack of dragging out the very worst in her?

*Take stock, Thomasz.*

Another serve of humble pie was about to hit her menu, this time with Seth.

*Deep breath.*

'I'm at a service station in Macleod.'

'What the blazes are you doing there when I've been waiting on your doorstep for the past twenty bloody minutes?'

'It's a long story, but I need you to come and meet me.'

'And why should I do that?'

Closing her eyes, her hand clutched the cellotaped screen to her ear when all she wanted to do was fling it at that beautiful, infuriating face of his. 'Because the news I have will be well worth the trip.'

She could hear his exasperated harrumph, then a hefty sigh. A loud bang that sounded suspiciously like a fist slamming against a hard surface.

'What's the address?'

She gave it to him before adding, 'Oh, and Seth, make sure you bring your wallet.'

'Were you planning on telling me the DNA results were in?'

'When I knew there was something worthwhile to tell.'

Seth shoved his wallet inside his jacket. 'And you have doubts regarding *my* honesty.'

Her gaze darted round the petrol station interior, noting the growing interest—evident and otherwise—of nearby customers. So much for avoiding a scene.

She tugged at his sleeve and tried to guide him towards the exit. 'That's unfair, Seth.'

'You've got to be kidding!' He pulled back, carving rigid fingers through hair already spiked from too much attention. 'Want to know what's unfair? A night of tossing and turning because I couldn't get you and bath bubbles out of my mind. Watching the clock slowly tick towards nine, when all I wanted was to see you again. Then turning up to your apartment with coffee and croissants, which are now staring at the inside of a rubbish bin.'

For a moment he appeared as surprised as she did at his outburst. Then determination replaced the daze. He yanked at the door, striding through so fast she had to jump forwards and grab it before it slammed in her face.

Her heart skipped in her chest. He'd thought about her. Still wanted her. Gripping her purse at her side, she shook her head at the irrationality of such thoughts. And their timing.

*Don't forget his less-than-available status.*

Regardless, he'd taken a taxi across town to meet her. She owed him an apology for that at least. 'I'm sorry, Seth. I'll make it up to you.'

'Don't make promises you can't keep, Jayda.' His voice barked back at her, even as he continued his stalk toward Bec's car.

'I meant the coffee part.'

She almost bowled into him as he spun round, his gaze raking hers. 'Of course you did.'

'You have every right to be angry with me for not calling this morning. But not about the rest of it. You had a date last night.'

His lips twitched, his almost thunderous expression softening. 'Which made you jealous.'

She scoffed. 'Don't kid yourself, buddy.'

'I'm not the one here suffering delusions.'

God, she hated that he read her so well. Damn that reporter instinct of his.

'Think whatever you like, we've got work to do.' She jabbed the key into the lock and pulled the door open before sliding behind the wheel. Then she reached across to unlock the passenger door.

He said nothing as he got in beside her.

Her fingers toyed with the key ring and its array of charms, as girlie as they could be and Bec all over. At a time when she and Seth should be celebrating steps forward in the case, they were once again at odds. And it was all her fault.

*Get a grip!* She bit her lip. Time to stop with the verbal and emotional sparring, the constant anger. It was wearing her to the point of madness.

She shook the key ring to find the car key, wishing it were as easy to shake off the strain of the past week.

'Thanks for meeting me and settling the bill. I'll pay you back as soon as I've sorted things out with the bank.'

He sighed, his hand once more spiking his hair. The urge to reach over and smooth it back, to cup his cheek, lean in and kiss his irritation away, was overwhelming.

She slotted the key into the ignition and wiggled until it twisted and the car revved to life.

He turned to her, lines on his face indicating a weariness she'd never seen in him before. 'I don't need your money, Jayda. We agreed to share info and investigate the Night Terror together, and I'm trying my damnedest to make it work. But for that to happen, we need to trust each other.'

She wanted that, too. More than anything. And it wasn't only about the case, although that was all she could extend to Seth. She wouldn't step into another woman's territory, no matter how much she wanted the man. And she did want Seth. She'd lied to herself long enough, and there was no point clinging to the charade any longer.

It was time to face her weakness, and get over it. *Suck it up, Thomasz, and move on!*

They were closer than ever to catching the Night Terror. Now that Roan Madden had come to light, using him as the link could mean solving the case in a matter of weeks rather than months.

When that happened, Seth would take his story and run. All she had to do was bite her lip and steel her senses until then.

She grabbed her seatbelt and dragged it across her body, clicking it into place. He'd said he wanted her to trust him, and in regards to the case he'd given her no reason to do otherwise. Her fingers wrapped round the handbrake and she nodded.

'I'll try.'

The stone in his expression softened.

'That's all I ask.' She felt the warmth of his palm on the back of her hand, and before she could lose herself in the sensation, she released the handbrake and slid her hand out and onto the gear shift.

'We have a DNA match for the earlier Night Terror murders, but the man who killed twenty-five years ago isn't the same man who's killing today.'

'Damn!'

'Yeah.' They shared a grin, and her heart lolloped in her chest.

She dragged her gaze from his. No matter that she'd decided nothing would happen between them, her body was determined to resist.

And it was up to her head to ignore it.

# Chapter Twenty-Eight

She had no money, no credit, and no way of proving she didn't love the Lost Dogs Home so much that she'd donated her entire life savings to its cause.

Jayda tried to breathe past the hulking rock in her throat. Her mind whirled every which way as she stared at the online banking screen and what she now knew to be the truth—a large, mocking zero where the final balance of her old account used to be.

Not only was she on the hunt for some psycho killer, but now she had a hacker to find. Assuming she wanted to see a single cent of her savings again, that was.

She clicked on the 'x' and dragged her eyes from the screen.

As if this little gem wasn't bad enough, she'd finally spoken to her father and come up worse than empty. Something in his reaction rang bells—an entire concerto of shrill, echoing chimes—leading her to broach the topic of his actions undercover. His answers were evasive, stilted. In effect, he'd said jack-shit.

She'd had no energy left to push and had ended the call without trying. He'd tell her when and if he was ready, and she'd just have to accept there was nothing she could do to change that.

One thing he had done was wire money into her new account, an early birthday present to tide her over until next Thursday, payday. He'd also promised to ask a friend to look into what happened; trace the hacker's footprints, discover their IP address. All actions she knew pretty much zip about. Sure, the bank's fraud department would handle it, but it didn't hurt to get a second party to take a look. Either way, she had little choice but to leave that portion of the investigation to the experts.

A hangman's noose squeezed at her throat, every move a scramble for safety, as though the ground beneath her feet was crumbling. And she had no idea how to snatch the stability back.

The chair across from her creaked.

*Snap out of it, Thomasz! You're not this person.*

She didn't wallow. She'd never done it before, and would be damned if she'd start now.

Seth bent over his keyboard, a stray lock of black hugging his left eyebrow and the jagged skin she'd never thought to ask about. His bad boy look. Only, he wasn't the bad boy she'd first thought. He was good. Very, *very* good.

Quivers flared in her tummy, fanning out into each and every portion of her hyper-aware body, parts tingling in reminder of just *how* good he was.

His earlier admission hadn't helped. Since telling her how much he wanted her, the thought had lodged in her mind, never quite forefront, but there, idling in the background, a constant reminder of what could be hers if she threw everything she believed to hell and said yes.

*No.*

There was too much to do, with a clock ticking until the Night Terror's next victim. Her body's urges were the least pressing item on her to-deal-with list. Some things were still in the realm of her control.

She flipped open her pocketbook, clicked her pen and pressed it to the paper.

*The story is the most important thing to him.*

She stared at the page and her first dot-point in a list that would see her take back control and resist every one of Seth's charms.

*No distractions until you solve the Night Terror case.*

If she straightened her mind and what she was supposed to feel, she could return to the job of finding out who the hell had taken over from Roan Madden four weeks ago.

*You're not looking for romance. Love is a lie.*

Not that either had anything to do with Seth.

*Men can't be trusted. No exceptions.*

That one's for you, Liam.

Her mind didn't stop there, much as she hated the thought of placing her father in that same, seedy boat.

*He already has a girlfriend.*

The clincher.

Six points. More than enough to see her through. She tore out the page, folded it into four and slid it into her jeans pocket.

Now to attack stuff that mattered—the flickering computer screen and the case. Not so much at a dead end; rather, she'd hit a snag. But not one that couldn't be budged with a little push.

They had a note constructed by someone skilled in paper-making, someone who had access to the kind of glue used in antique book restoration. And a convicted killer in prison, his crimes recurring.

Who was continuing his legacy? Everything revolved around Roan Madden. He was the answer, or someone close to him. Close enough to learn the tiniest details of the case.

She closed her laptop, her gaze meeting Seth's as it lifted from his computer screen.

'I'm contacting the prison.' She stood, scrolling through the list of contacts in her mobile until she found the number. 'I need to know who's visited Madden over the past twenty-five years. And I want to see him.'

'Will they let you?'

Flinted silver jumpstarted the beat of her heart. She pushed her hand into her pocket, fingertips seeking the comfort of the folded page. 'I won't give them a choice.'

It was bravado of the worst kind. Hopeless. Because without a 464B application and a magistrate's signature she had Buckley's chance of an interview.

Unless she found some way around it.

Appreciation filled Seth's gaze at what was, to her, obvious blustering. The paper scrunched beneath her fingers. 'My battery's almost dead. I need to plug it in to recharge.'

'If you're seeing Madden, I'm coming.'

'The only way you can do that is if he adds you to his approved visitor list.'

*Bingo!* It was like someone had struck a match in a long, dark tunnel. All she needed was Madden's agreement, which meant she needed to lodge a request. The outcome could go either way, unless she managed somehow to pique his curiosity . . .

'Jayda?'

Her gaze refocused on Seth. Too early to let him in on her plan, particularly when its success was far from guaranteed. 'I'll see what I can do.'

She heard the same evasiveness in her voice that she'd heard in her father's earlier. Like father, like daughter.

*No!* The word reverberated through her skull and she flinched, shaking her head as if the action could shake the notion which had once given her pride.

Those all-seeing gun-metal eyes squinted. She moved towards the study and away from Seth's scrutiny. He saw way too much. Plus, she needed to get onto the application now for there to be any chance of seeing Madden this weekend.

'After your call, we need to talk.' He regarded her over his laptop. It didn't matter what sense murmured in her ear, her heart still had the idiocy to jump . . .

'I've been doing some digging into Madden and something doesn't add up.'

And then, crumple.

*Idiot! He's only doing what you wanted. What you should be doing. Focus on the case, not him.*

'Juliana Madden's murder was nothing like the Night Terror killings. He used a knife, three stabs to the chest, then one fatal slash across the throat.'

*What?*

The disparate crimes made no sense. Killers who used their bare— or gloved—hands to kill seldom resorted to knife attack. Strangulation was close-up, personal, leaving the body untouched, virginal, like his victims. She swallowed. His victims, bar one.

He strangled virgins and stabbed those who weren't. Except Bec.

Again the circle returned to Bec. *Why her?*

Anastasia interrupted her thoughts, demonstrating her mobile battery wasn't quite as dead as she'd made out. What had she done to the universe that made it want to bite back?

'And there's more.' Seth continued in a rush. 'I don't think Roan Madden is the man everyone thinks he is.'

She stopped mid-stride and stared. *What was that supposed to mean?*

The persistent ring dragged her mind back to the phone in her hand. 'Hey, Dad.'

'Your mother and I are going away for a while. We want you to come.'

No 'Hi', 'How are you?', 'How's the case going?'—just . . . this. The world had turned on its head. Since when did her father ask her to leave midway through an investigation? Especially this one.

She glanced at Seth before hurrying towards the study. 'I can't. I've just made a break in the case.'

'I know. But, after speaking with Terry, we've agreed you need time out. I should have seen it sooner. We leave tomorrow after the funeral.'

He was conspiring with Hackett to get her off the case? Since when were they so close?

'I thought you wanted me to find the Night Terror.'

The connection crackled, but not enough to mask the weariness in his voice. 'Not at the expense of losing you.'

'You won't lose me, Dad.'

'Then you'll come?'

Hope tugged at her heart. She'd see her mother, get the chance to mend whatever bridges Bec's death had fractured. She closed her eyes and her sister's broken gaze stared back. 'I can't. I'm going to see Roan Madden.'

*'You are not to see that man!'*

The words rumbled through her like an earthquake. She held the phone from her ear and stared at it, her heart so stunned it forgot to beat. Then she pressed her mobile's flat surface back in place. 'Why?'

'He's dangerous.'

'He's in prison. How dangerous can he be?'

Her father didn't answer right away. She almost thought he wouldn't answer at all, and his next words proved she was right.

'Promise me you'll stay away.'

'I can't, Dad. Someone Madden knows is emulating his killing. I'm going to find out who.'

'And nothing I say can stop you?'

'Not unless you have a reason.' The silence was almost as deafening as his earlier outburst. 'Is there a reason I should stay away from Madden?'

'I worry about you. Isn't that enough?'

'Not when it stops me from fulfilling my duty. As officers, we *uphold the good*, remember? If we don't, women like Doris Tombes, Clara Gayle and Bec can never feel safe. And scum-suckers like the Night Terror win.'

He sighed, the way he always sighed when he realised she wouldn't budge. 'When are you going to the prison?'

'I'm hoping this weekend. Why?'

'Just promise you'll keep your wits about you.'

'I always do.'

'Then I guess I'll see you tomorrow.'

The angular edges of the phone dug into her fingers. 'Whoever it is, I'll make him pay for what he did to Bec. He won't get the chance to do it again.'

'I see so much of me in you.' Paper crinkled in the background as her father cleared his throat. 'Just remember, nothing's more important in all this than you. Even when it comes to solving the case. We just want you to be safe.'

She swallowed, tried to pull her voice out from halfway down her throat. 'I know, Dad. You have nothing to worry about. I'll be fine.'

'Love you, Jayda.'

The uncharacteristic words thickened her throat. 'I love you too, Dad.' The dull *beep* of the disconnected call brought her back. She tapped *end*, blinked, bringing the blurred mobile into focus. The home-screen photo stared back. It was old, seven years at least. The day of her graduation from the Police Academy.

She didn't need the photo to remember every detail of that day. It was etched forever into her memory.

Her over-starched navy uniform had pricked at the collar from the moment she put it on, making her want to scratch the entire ceremony. But it hadn't dulled the day. Nothing could. She'd outrun Liam's efforts to undermine her and had come out the other side, top of her class. The pride of that moment still had the power to make her heart glow.

She stared at the photo, her father punch-proud in his dark suit. Bec, well, she looked stunning, as always. Her mother . . . she squinted at the screen. Not once in the past seven years had she noticed the tightness in her mother's smile, the way her body turned slightly outward from the group. Even her eyes seemed focused somewhere else.

The photo was taken just before the Highbury Case trial. Bec had mentioned something was up even back then. Jayda moved her hand to mask the screen.

Was this a sign of her parents' problems? How would she know, with her father's all too professional stonewalling? Not from her mother. She still hadn't called, and Jayda refused to keep asking why when it hurt too much to get the same deflections.

Something inside fractured. Nothing made sense anymore. Growing up, her parents were her idea of perfection. Impossible to imagine a happier, more together family. And she'd wanted the same for herself when she finally met the man of her dreams.

*What a joke.* Perfection was a lie. It existed purely in perception. And dreams, well, they were just that. Dreams weren't meant for the real world.

Her gaze darted of its own accord towards the doorway, her mind picturing the man waiting beyond it.

The most solid of people in her life was changing right before her eyes. Was the entire OPI investigation garnered in lies? The evidence tampering she could explain away. Someone had made a mistake. But the affair? The *photographic* proof? Did she explain that away too and bury her head in the sand?

She'd assumed she knew her father inside and out. He was the archetype for the man she'd always wanted to meet and marry. Now that image was far from reality, and she wondered whether she had ever really known him at all.

*Do you ever really know anyone?*

Where did that thought leave her now? When even her gut couldn't be relied upon to steer her straight?

# Chapter Twenty-Nine

Seth watched Jayda's indecision before she glanced at her mobile and left the room.

*She'll be back.*

The words sliced through his brain and were almost as strange as the growing feeling of emptiness in his chest.

Ever since they'd returned from Macleod, she'd closed off, distanced herself. To use the word 'cold' would be the grossest of understatements.

She was broke. He got that. He could only imagine the violation of having your financials hacked and bled dry. That on top of losing her sister . . .

But he wasn't the bad guy here. Had never been the bad guy. He'd dedicated the past week to helping her find the sick son of a bitch who'd robbed the sun from her life, yet, time and time again, all she'd tossed in his face was a silver platter heaped with an over-generous serving of grief.

He shouldn't care so much.

Only, the more she pulled away, the less she seemed inclined to trust him. And the further he got from the inside of his story.

And that's exactly why he was feeling whatever he was feeling.

'What were you saying?'

He looked up. Jayda hovered just inside the doorway, almost as if she were ready to run.

'How'd you go with the prison?'

'I'm waiting for confirmation, but it looks like two o'clock on Saturday.'

'We couldn't see Madden earlier?'

'Yeah, but I thought it'd be fun to wait.'

There it was again. That bite. Once again, he was the fall guy, and the feeling was getting mighty old.

'I know the saying goes something like "her bark is worse than her bite", but there are times I'm not so sure.'

'Hilarious, Seth.'

'I am, on occasion.'

'So you keep saying.' Her lips twitched as she stepped closer. 'You mentioned something about Madden.'

'I did.'

'And?'

'And, what?'

She rolled her eyes. 'What did you want to tell me?'

'Please.'

'Please?'

He grinned. 'Ah, since you asked so nicely.'

'Are you kidding?' Arms crossed under the curve of her breasts, her eyes flashed with amber flecks. He refused to be so easily distracted, much as her anger sparked other equally animated reactions inside him.

He returned her glare with what he hoped was nonchalance. 'Not remotely. It wouldn't kill you to use a little "please" and "thank you" occasionally.'

'I'll make sure to remember that, *Dad.*'

'Much appreciated.'

'And . . .'

'I've performed every search possible online, and nothing's surfaced about Madden or his wife prior to his arrest.'

'Not so unusual.'

'Really? No bank records? No driver's licence, credit history, birth or marriage certificates? I can't even find a blog or any form of social media entry.'

'Maybe you're looking in the wrong places.'

'This is what I do, Jayda. I dig, and I'm damn good at it. Believe me, I'm looking in all the right places, the info's just not there. Nothing's there. There's even a chunk of missing news reports on the murder. It's like Roan Madden's entire life has been swallowed into some kind of black hole. Like someone has deliberately gone through and wiped out every hint of the man's early existence.'

'Sounds like something the Feds would do to protect witnesses. Only Madden's not in witness protection, he's a convicted murderer still serving his sentence. Why hide his past?'

'Good question. Perhaps we can ask him on Saturday.' He scratched at the stubble on his jaw as if his next words wouldn't completely overhaul the case. 'And there's one more thing.'

Her mobile erupted with that damned song, *again*, and she glanced down at the screen through the mish-mash of tape he could spot even at a distance.

'I have to take this.'

What was with her phone and its godforsaken timing? He bit back a few choice words as she turned away and lowered her voice.

'Chase?'

Seth's gaze followed the gradual drop of her shoulders, the whitening of her knuckles as her grip tightened around the phone that, it seemed, had more than enough battery to spare.

'I'm coming. I don't care what he says, dammit! Tell me where you are.' She grabbed a pen and notebook from her pocket and scribbled in it before ending the call.

'What was that all about?'

'It was Chase.'

He tapped his foot and his rising irritation. 'I got that much.'

Mobile in one hand, Bec's car keys in the other, she headed for the door. 'There's been another Night Terror killing.'

'Where are we going?'

'Not we.'

Was it always going to be uphill with her?

'Yes, *we*.' He grabbed his jacket. 'I have more right to be there than you. You're banned from the case, remember? But I'm media. I'm expected.'

She opened her mouth, then clamped it, leaving the door open behind her as she stalked through it and down the hall.

A mottled black-and-grey cat wrapped its body around her ankles, almost causing her to trip. 'Hey, Tumbles.'

She slowed, crouched, scratched its head and neck as the creature purred and bucked against her fingers.

From nowhere, a growl erupted from the back of Seth's throat. The cat's head jerked up, copper eyes wide as its body tensed. Jayda hugged the animal to her thigh as she shot him a less than amused look. His jaw clenched. Had he completely lost his mind? Jealous of a damned feline, no less.

He slammed the door, and this time the cat didn't hesitate. With what he could only describe as a drunken stagger, it fled down the hall, one of its back legs jutting out at the most ridiculous angle.

Two men appeared through the fire door, saving him from another of her wilting stares. One was Mediterranean, in designer sunglasses and gym gear. The other wore white-collar garb, was slighter and paler, but he guessed most women would find his chiselled features and mismatched eyes, one blue and one green, intriguing.

'*Maldita gata!* Where are you off to now?' The cat disappeared around the corner. Mediterranean Man slipped the glasses off and into his pocket, squinting as he turned towards them. 'Jayda! Where have you been hiding? We've missed you.' He engulfed her in his arms. She buried her face in his over-tanned neck and hugged back.

Something wrenched deep in Seth's gut.

'Hey.' The man cupped her head in his palms and stared down at her with a depth of emotion Jayda unquestioningly returned. 'What's up?'

Their gazes melded. Her lips trembled as she wordlessly shook her head.

Her shaky fingers rubbed at the stain her makeup had left on his shoulder, but he took her hand in his. 'Looks like you're in need of some TLC.' Again she sank into his arms.

Seth and the other man might not have been there, for all the acknowledgement they received.

He pulled at the neck of his jumper. 'We should be going.' He heard the bark in his voice, and couldn't prevent the glare he was sure accompanied it.

She barely reacted, remaining comfortably ensconced within the curve of tanned sinew and muscle as they all turned their attention towards him.

'If we don't leave now, we'll be late.' The bark was still there, and he didn't try to hide it.

'A date?' The man, his arm still circling her shoulders, sounded excited with the idea.

Jayda's head jerked back. 'Hardly!'

The severity of her response made Seth flinch as her fingers dug into her front jeans pocket. 'Seth's a reporter. We're investigating the

Night Terror together.'

Her gaze met and mingled with his for one brief second. Seth's gut clenched, the ground falling away beneath his feet as he tumbled deep into lush shimmering rainforests. Then she snatched her gaze away, and something inside him was lost.

Her hand waved carelessly towards him, 'Seth Friedin,' then moved to muscle-man, 'Juz Callum,' and the other invisible man, 'Garry Wallace.'

They all nodded, his wooden and forced, Juz's unashamedly curious, and Garry's difficult to read.

'Where are you off to, if it's not a hot date?'

For the first time since throwing herself into his arms, Jayda shot daggers towards Juz. 'Crime scene.'

'Another woman?' It was the first time Garry had spoken, his voice soft and low, with an accent Seth couldn't quite pick. Eastern European, perhaps?

Jayda nodded, and was it his imagination or did Garry lean in with more interest than before?

'*Dios!*' Juz's tanned fingers squeezed Jayda's shoulder in an obvious show of comfort. 'But aren't you off the case?'

Garry's eyes seemed to glint. Or was Seth over-reacting? Regardless, he felt his scalp prickle.

Jayda's chin jutted upwards in that 'take no prisoners' look of hers. 'Only officially.'

There was nothing but mild interest from Garry now as the conversation continued, once again completely disregarding him.

Seth shook off his thoughts. He was being ridiculous.

Nevertheless, he made a mental note to check the guy out. He wasn't on a lease in the building, but he knew Jayda. No stone unturned.

Juz smiled, his entire face splitting into a contrast of fluoride white and tanned brown. 'Jayda, you're all guts.'

'Great visuals, Juz.' They shared a chuckle.

*Enough.* Maybe Garry was happy being passed over, but he wasn't. '*Jayda.*'

The bow in her lips flattened. 'We should go.'

She shared a final hug with Juz then moved on to Garry. The man looked plain awkward with the intimate gesture, or was it just with her?

'Will I see you both tomorrow?'

'You need ask? I'm here if you want to talk. And for the next couple of weeks while the gym's closed, I'm even more available. Visit. I'll even buy a bottle of lolly-water for you.'

Her lips quirked, her eyes glowing before she turned to Seth. The glow dimmed, and her hand dug deep into her pocket once more. 'Ready?'

He'd been ready to leave since the moment *they* arrived. 'Yep.'

'Great to meet you' pleasantries were exchanged, Juz's appraisal as he shook Seth's hand too intense for comfort.

Jayda headed towards the stairwell, the lift doors still taped shut by yesterday's 'out of order' sign. Something sharp and acidic hit his nostrils, like paint thinner. His gaze lifted up to the air vent above his head. An artist, perhaps, in a nearby apartment?

Jayda pushed at the heavy fire door, her impatience as she held it open for him so obvious it grated.

'Coming?'

'If only,' he muttered.

'What?' Her gaze was sharp and unimpressed.

'I said, hold your damn horses.'

'That's what I thought you said.'

She let the door go and he caught it, slipping through, leaving it to slam behind him. Taking the steps two at a time, she was already on the second set of stairs when he began negotiating his first. Damned if he'd run to keep up with her.

The blood firing through his veins had nothing to do with exertion. 'Eric!'

Automatically, his steps quickened. He almost flew down the last set of stairs to join Jayda and her neighbour at the bottom.

What was it today? Was the entire damn building on the prowl?

'Seth, you remember Eric?' Her expression warned him before she turned back to the other man. 'I have a computing question for you.'

Eric's myopic gaze seemed to gobble her up. Regardless of what she believed, the guy had it bad. How bad, was the question.

She barrelled on, her only acknowledgement of Seth's hand on her elbow a shake to dislodge it. 'How much do you know about hacking?'

Eric jabbed at the bridge of his glasses, blinking rapidly as his face reddened. 'How much do you need me to know?'

She bit her lip, her mouth tight with that restrained impatience he recognised so well. It didn't preclude her obstinacy, or the fact he had to stop her before she did something stupid.

'Jayda—'

'If someone hacked into my bank account and emptied it, how easy would it be to find them?'

Like that.

Eric blinked at her through his thick lenses, and Seth couldn't figure out if it was his myopia or the fact he was riddled with nerves.

'It would depend on how many routers they used, their method for disabling the action logging capabilities, whether they've installed a RAT into your system.' He paused, whether for a breath or because he'd noticed the lost look on their faces, Seth hadn't a clue.

*Amendment.* Jayda's face. Eric had hardly acknowledged Seth. Perhaps he *was* invisible, after all.

'What's a RAT?'

'A Random Access Trojan. The hacker may have installed it on your computer so he can easily access it in the future.'

'Can you find him?'

Eric blinked. 'Trace him back to his IP address? S–sure.'

'That's great! What do you need from me?'

'Your computer and passwords.'

Jayda didn't even blink. 'I'll drop them round this afternoon.' She glanced at her watch. 'Is three-thirty okay?'

He nodded, jabbed his glasses up the bridge of his nose and continued his amble up the stairs.

'You've got to be kidding!'

She pulled the heavy door open and left him standing in the stairwell. When he caught up, she was opening the fluoro-pink car door.

He grabbed her arm and the door fell shut. 'Dammit, Jayda! Will you listen to me?'

'No.' She wrenched free and stepped away, smacking her back against the side of the car.

Her lips drew tight, the flints in her eyes razor-sharp and uncompromising. He couldn't help wanting to kiss that confounded obstinacy from her. Until she forgot about every other man in her life but him. His fingers jerked through his hair as he drew much-needed oxygen into his brain. 'How do you know Eric didn't steal your money?'

'Because he wouldn't.'

'You can't possibly be that naïve. For god's sake, Jayda, the man knows computers. He's obsessed with you, even to the point of being jealous of me. If he wanted your attention, to ride in on a white stallion and rescue you from some faceless hacker, he's just succeeded. You're giving him exactly what he wants.'

'Eric is not the hacker.'

'How the hell do you know?'

She seemed intent on nibbling the hell out of her bottom lip as she stared at his feet, or hers, he couldn't tell which.

When she finally looked up, the green of her gaze was steeled in decision. Air whooshed from her lungs and her eyes darted to either side before returning to him.

'Because he's former ASIS.'

# Chapter Thirty

**S**eth felt his mouth gaping and slammed it shut. 'Australian Secret Intelligence Service? Eric? No way!'

'Shh.' Jayda's head jerked left then right, scouring the area around them. Ridiculous when she could clearly see they were alone in a deserted parking garage. 'Yes *way*. Satisfied?'

Without waiting for a reply, she pulled the door open again. By the time he reached the passenger side, she'd unlocked his door and the engine was spluttering impatiently.

He waited until she'd negotiated through the car park and out onto the street.

'How could Eric possibly be ASIS?'

'Because of his sight?'

'That, and he doesn't exactly fit what I know to be the ASIS profile.'

She crunched the gears, and the car juddered before increasing speed. 'A year ago he was caught in the periphery of a bomb blast in Afghanistan. Neither his vision or nerves have been the same since.'

'Damn!'

'Mmm. Can we move on now?' She braked at a red light, but her eyes remained fastened on the car in front.

'What's the story with Juz and Garry?'

'There is no story. They're friends.' The light turned green and she switched gears.

'You seem to have a lot of friends who are men.'

'I have a lot of friends.'

'Who are men.'

Lip locked between her teeth, she switched on the radio, catching Freddy Mercury in the midst of breaking free. She turned up the volume. He turned it down.

'He's gay, isn't he?'

'Who?'

'Juz.'

'Does it matter?'

'No.' He sighed. 'What did Chase say about the murder?'

'Just that there was one.'

'Anything to set this one apart?'

'Like a note saying it's my fault?'

Air hissed through his teeth. 'Where the hell did that come from?'

She shook her head, her fingers wrapped with iron-clad tightness around the wheel.

'I'm not a mind-reader, Jayda. If something's up, rather than constantly shoving me in front of a firing squad, just tell me.'

'There's nothing to tell.'

'That's it.' His heart wrenched even as he realised the implications of what he was about to do. His fingers fumbled with the seatbelt clip, before it finally clicked free. The car skidded to a stop at another set of lights. 'This isn't working.'

'What do you mean?' She turned to him, eyes wide, skin robbed of colour. If he didn't know any better, he'd think she was scared.

'I mean, *this*.' He waved a hand between them. 'We agreed to call it quits if things didn't work out.' He checked for traffic before opening the car door and stepping outside. 'That time is now. I can't work like this.'

A car edged past, the driver less than impressed with his invasion of her lane.

'Goodbye, Jayda.'

He slammed the door, heard her call his name but refused to turn. At the pavement, he pivoted back towards the way they'd come, a churn in his stomach he didn't dare identify.

Car horns choroused, and with a crunch of gears he knew the lights had changed and she was gone.

Before he could think about what he'd done, or why, he dug his mobile from his pocket and pressed speed dial.

'Huh! So the celebrity still remembers his old friends.'

'Richie, turn on your police scanner. There's been another murder and I need an address.'

'And you can't ask your girlfriend because . . .?'

'She's not my girlfriend and we're no longer working the case together.' He waved at a passing taxi, dropping his hand when it flew past with a carload of passengers.

'Hell, Seth. Are you sure that's wise?'

'Discussion closed.'

'Just tell me you have a story.'

'We've identified the man who was the Night Terror twenty-five years ago. That copy's with Carson as we speak. But he wants a story on "today", and that's what I intend to give him. I'm going to find the present-day Night Terror before the cops.'

He raised his hand, and this time the yellow-and-black sedan skidded to a stop beside him. 'Do you have a location?'

His friend rattled off the central city address as Seth slid into the back seat and repeated it to the driver.

'Thanks, man. I owe you one.'

'Five, to be precise. But, hey, who's counting?' Seth was still chuckling when his friend coughed and asked, 'So, how are you going to get the inside scoop from the outside?'

'I don't need Jayda for the story.' Rather, he didn't need the constant battling, but Richie didn't need to know that. 'It's called reporting. You should try it sometime.'

The second the words were out he realised what he'd said, and hated himself for it. He was treating Richie the same way she'd treated him. *Unacceptable.*

'Damn! I'm sorry, man.'

'You should be. Lucky for you, I don't bruise easy. Plus, I've known you long enough to get where you're coming from, and I'm with you. Frustration's a killer.'

Seth knew better than to open *that* can of worms.

Up ahead he spotted the lines of blue-and-white tape, the sprawl of police vehicles and uniforms that indicated a crime scene. He ended the call, paid the driver and jumped out of the car.

Chase stood beyond the tape, but Seth continued to scour the area. No sign of a pink Beetle anywhere.

That was no longer his concern.

Striding towards the scene, he shoved at pictures of Jayda amid flat tyres and car crashes and muggings and too much crunching of gears resulting in mechanical breakdowns. She was a big girl, well able to take care of herself. Hadn't she told him so, on every occasion possible?

He checked right, then left, and crossed the road.

There was still a barrel of work to be done. He had a career to forge, a name to make. That was where his priorities lay. Not with fiery locks and lush rainforest eyes and a smile that made everything in the world seem brighter.

He shook his head, almost snorting as the irony hit. Funny that he never got to share with her the coup of all coups. The inconceivable news that explained why Roan Madden hadn't existed until a year before he was married.

Jayda slammed her palm against the steering wheel.

And the moment she did it, she regretted it. The wheel shuddered and wobbled, and the action didn't do a damn thing towards making her feel better.

Anger blazed all the way from her stomach to her throat, until every part of her burned with it.

The instant she'd pulled up at the crime scene and cut the engine, Hackett had rapped against her window, done that stern, no-nonsense thing of his, then directed her back out the way she'd come.

It galled that she had *zip* idea what was happening with her case. If she didn't know better, she'd claim conspiracy; what with her boss's damned unreasonableness and her father's overprotective concern.

Grabbing her purse from the empty passenger seat, she made for the stairs to her apartment. It wasn't until she felt the squelch beneath her feet that she noticed the pool of oil seeping out over the concrete floor. *Great!* Someone had dropped an entire can of the stuff and not bothered to clean up. She'd never been particularly fatalistic, but there was a part of her that couldn't help wondering, *what the hell next?*

She approached the door, scraping at the soles of her shoes until there was no more grease to scrape off.

Something furry brushed against her ankle and she jerked her leg backwards, forcing herself to check before she kicked out and yelled 'rat!' Lucky she did.

Tension whooshed from her lungs. 'Hey, boy. What are you doing here?'

In answer, Tumbles hobbled around her ankle, rubbing the length of his body against her calf, his purr the sound of a well-oiled coffee grinder.

Jayda curled her arm under his stomach and lifted him up. His entire body rumbled and vibrated against her chest as he bucked his head to rub her chin. The strain of the past few hours seeped from her body as she rubbed back, breathing in his warm, fresh scent. A scent of cat and fresh grass.

'How'd you get outside, buddy? Juz'll have a fit if he knows you've been wandering the streets.'

She twisted the handle and pushed at the door with her hip, cradling the cat to her chest as she attacked the stairs. About time someone fixed the elevator. The novelty of traipsing up and down two flights every day was wearing mighty thin.

At the top, she managed to manoeuvre the door open without too much difficulty and headed straight for Juz's door. After two rounds of knocking it was obvious both he and Garry were out.

'What are we going to do with you now, old boy?'

She turned back towards her apartment. Tumbles pawed her cheek and she rubbed her face in his warm, shuddering fur.

'Coffee for me and a treat of milk for you.'

She took his continued purring as agreement and managed to find the lock and twist the key one-handed.

With the door closed behind her, she shucked her shoes onto the mat, somehow smudging grease onto her top. *Great! Again!*

Tossing her purse and keys onto the hall table, she fell back into the couch with Tumbles on her lap. A club thumped against the inside of her skull, sending ripples of tension out over her shoulders and down her spine.

Silence echoed loudly around her. This wasn't how'd she seen the day, or week, ending.

The soft, purring bundle moulded into her lap and she ran her hand over his fur in long, soothing, therapeutic strokes. Her breathing relaxed, the knots in her shoulders and back unfurling. Even the pounding inside her head slowed enough for her mind to move on.

What next?

No thinking about 'before', because if she did, she'd crumble into a thousand pieces, and this time there was no one around to put her back together.

She tugged her notebook from her pocket. The cat mewed, clearly unimpressed with being bumped and shuffled and displaced.

'Sorry, old boy.'

He yawned, stood, arching his back before kneading her lap into an acceptable state of comfort again, the awkwardness of his useless leg causing not even the slightest hindrance.

Jayda opened the pad and started to write.

*To do:*
*Drop computer and passwords to Eric*
*Contact Births, Deaths and Marriages re. Roan Madden*
*Research RM online—murder and trial*
*Contact State Library—check newspaper archives on RM murder and trial*
*Contact Chase re. latest Night Terror murder and visitor log for RM*

Staring at the page, lingering nerves calmed. There was a strange kind of comfort in knowing what she was going to do next.

'But first, old boy, we'd better let Juz know you're safe.'

It took her a matter of seconds to text that Tumbles was with her. As a precaution, she texted Garry, too. Texting Juz didn't guarantee he'd get the message. Much as he loved gossip, modern technology confounded the crap out of him. If Garry hadn't talked him into upgrading, she had no doubt he'd still use the clunky old relic mobile he'd owned since before they'd met.

Dropping her mobile onto the coffee table, she gave Tumbles one last scratch before standing and placing him back on the couch.

'Time for a coffee.' The cat blinked wide amber eyes as it pawed the cushions into submission. 'None for you. How does a bowl of milk sound?' He blinked again, before plopping down into a round, furry heap. Undoubtedly a 'yes'.

She turned. Seth's computer still perched on her dining table where he'd left it. She continued past and into the kitchen, not nearly ready enough to go there. No doubt he'd be back for it. And when he begged her to allow them to continue working together . . .

Her pride told her to throw his pleading back in his face.

But pride be damned, it had been a week since he'd pushed his way into her life, into her apartment. She'd lived alone here for the past three years, and never before this moment had she felt so lonely in it.

That didn't even take into consideration the help he'd given to the case, or her. And her appalling behaviour towards him in return.

The microwave whirred as the milk warmed, and as her hand reached for the percolator, she stalled. An empty weariness filled her chest, calling for something stronger. Like the Moscato sitting open in her fridge right now. Light. Bubbly. Sweet. Uplifting.

Tonic for the soul.

At the ding, she tossed the milk down the sink, then opened a small carton of cat-friendly 'milk' she kept for visits just like this one. She poured the contents into Tumbles' bowl-away-from-home and placed it just outside the kitchen door. Then, wine glass in hand, she grabbed her purse and headed for the bedroom.

A change of top was in order. And a soak for the one she was currently wearing if there was even a chance of saving it. Then she'd take her computer to Eric and he'd find her money. The man was a whizz with anything technology related.

The wine fizzed over her tongue and down her throat, and she took a deep sip before leaving it and her purse on her dressing table and moving into the en suite.

Her white tee went into a sink of hot, sudsy water, then she pulled on another in black.

Splashing her face, she peered at the woman in the mirror. Deep lines rimmed eyes underscored with a smudge of over-weary black.

When had she last slept? Not the fitful, restless sleep of the past week, but a peaceful, satisfying slumber, the kind you woke from feeling refreshed and invigorated and glad to be alive. The kind you woke from on a day when the biggest decision before you was whether to have toast or cereal for breakfast, or whether your coffee should be drink-in or take-out.

With the Night Terror's identity so close now, those days couldn't be far away. They would return, and soon, after the killer was behind bars and she was back working in the job she loved. She had to believe it, if only to retain a semblance of sanity.

She dried her face and looped the towel over the rail, moving back towards the bedroom. The sooner she saw Eric, the sooner she could recover her savings and solve at least one puzzle out of the many vying for her attention. Then she could move onto Roan Madden, and any links or associates who could have stepped into his grubby, bloodstained shoes four weeks ago.

As she reached for the Moscato, her gaze took in the copper frame on her dressing table. Her body jerked. Hand and glass collided, toppling the glass from its perch. It bounced and rolled over the carpet, the fizzy pink liquid spreading and seeping into the spotless cream fibres.

Her gut clenched. Her mind screamed. *No!*

Once the burnished copper had contained a photo much like the one in Bec's bedroom.

Not now.

The picture was one she didn't recognise, but it was familiar. Six hours ago she'd stood in this very spot, dressed in her pre-soiled white tee and jeans, speaking to Will on her mobile, her expression animated.

The realisation came in stages, a gradual *thud, thud, thud* as comprehension unfurled, like a spool of carpet unrolling down a set of stairs, step by step.

Someone had snapped a photo, here, this very morning. Then they'd waltzed into her bedroom and slipped the print into her frame.

But it wasn't the photo which made her reach for the gun in her purse *before* reaching for her mobile. A thousand needles pricked the back of her neck as her eyes flitted in every conceivable direction.

Words covered the glass in scrawled blood-red.

*Peek-a-boo, I'm watching you.*

# Chapter Thirty-One

Ten. Hidden. Cameras. *Ten.* Scattered throughout her apartment. Watching. Filming. Recording her every action.

Breakfast roiled, churning in her stomach.

Jayda jumped from the couch and ran for the bathroom, dodging the forensics officer dusting for prints he'd never find. She surrendered the remainder of her stomach contents to the toilet.

Sinking to her knees, she clung to the cold, ceramic bowl as if it might bring her some semblance of stability.

How long had they been watching?

Her body shook hot then cold. She wrapped her arms round her chest and closed her eyes. Her breathing came in sharp, shuddering gasps as she tightened her grip and rocked back and forth. But the thoughts refused to stop.

Every movement, every day; getting dressed, *undressed*, eating breakfast, taking a bath, kissing Seth . . . every single thing she'd done . . . *for how long?*

'Jayda, are you okay?'

Her arms tensed, then dropped. Georgie's voice was as soft and warm as the towel she pressed into her hands. She opened her eyes, the return of sight and her friend's presence reestablishing a sense of time and place.

Wiping her mouth, she pushed herself up. Only then did she realise how shaky her legs were.

If not for her friend's grip, she'd have tumbled headfirst into the toilet. And fatalistic or not, she wondered almost absently if that would have been a fitting end to the day.

Georgie peered at her with an overflow of worry and compassion. How did she answer?

Was she okay? No.

Would she ever be okay in this apartment? She very much doubted it.

Still, that wasn't what Georgie wanted, or expected, to hear. Who asked the 'are you okay?' question with any real expectation of an honest answer?

Jayda nodded and tried to smile, the bend of her lips unnatural and forced. 'I'm fine, now. It was my lunch that had the problem.' Somehow the nonchalance in her words lent strength to her body, where pandering to her emotional turmoil hadn't.

Straightening her shoulders, she grasped Georgie's hands and gave them a reassuring squeeze before turning to the sink. Her top was still soaking, but she ran the water anyway, washing every bit of grime and emotion from her face, so that when she turned back to face her friend, she didn't feel as if her entire world was tumbling before her eyes.

Work was her only solace.

'Have they found anything to indicate who installed them?'

Georgie shook her head, her shiny brown bob dancing about her shoulders. 'Nothing. But they've removed them all, and lab analysis might reveal something. Do you think it's the Night Terror?'

'It doesn't fit his MO, but neither did Bec or my car.' The thought of not one but two psychos gunning for her wasn't an idea she relished. 'What about the cameras themselves?'

'High-tech. The same calibre used by the Australian army and secret services.'

For the second time that day, Seth's words rapped purposefully against her convictions.

*You can't possibly be that naïve.*

*The man knows computers. He's obsessed with you.*

*How do you know Eric didn't steal your money?*

'There's someone I think we should look at.'

Georgie stepped back, her perfectly-plucked brows drawn in tight. 'Who?'

Vibrations in her pocket had her snatching her mobile out only to discover it wasn't the call she'd been hoping for. She answered anyway. 'This isn't a good time, Dad.'

'Then I'll be quick. Buddy found your hacker.'

The lead in her heart faded. She raised her index finger to Georgie. 'Who?'

'Know an Eric Townsend?'

The lead returned. How could she have got it so wrong? When her gut and her background check had indicated he was clean? Mind you, no flag on a check only meant he'd never been caught. It didn't guarantee he wasn't a crook. Or a killer.

'Are you sure?'

'Very. Supposedly this Eric gave a real chase, rerouting his feed through a series of dummy IPs. And even though he gained root-level access to your account, he got sloppy, removed all but one log entry. That's how Buddy located him.' Air whooshed from her father's lungs. The sound of relief. She wished she could do the same. He gave a throat-clearing cough. 'Make sure you call the Feds.'

She met Georgie's worried gaze. 'I will.' Her fingers dug into her forehead in an effort to ease the tension. A hopeless task. 'Thanks.'

She dropped the phone back into her pocket. 'The man we're after is Eric Townsend. He's a neighbour who lives in apartment twenty-one, two doors down.'

'And we should look at him because . . .'

'He's ex-ASIS. Was head of their IT and technical division until he was injured in Afghanistan. And this morning he hacked into my bank account.'

Georgie knew better than to question Jayda's sources, or intuition. She'd seen both in action before. 'Let's get a search warrant.'

They made for the living room and the bustle of activity that would yield nothing. The Night Terror didn't leave clues unless they were deliberate and premeditated and fundamental to his demented plan. Forensics would find nothing he didn't want them to find.

They'd found Eric—was he a smokescreen or a lead?

Where did he fit in? It was difficult to get her head around. Unless he *was* the killer? And *that* didn't make sense, or seem even remotely possible.

But then, none of what had happened the past week did.

Georgie snapped closed the cover of her mobile. 'It'll be here within the hour.'

The waiting game wasn't something she'd ever done well.

*Sixty minutes.* Every. Second. Dragged.

She sat. Waited. Talked with Georgie about the case. Got nothing she and Seth hadn't already uncovered.

Georgie left to make a call.

She stared at her mobile, finger poised over Seth's number, only to clear the screen and return the phone to her pocket. Much as she wanted to call, what could she say? Talking and bleeding hearts had never been her thing.

She bit her nail until there was no more to bite. Then she moved onto the next.

Knotted claws snatched at her chest and squeezed.

What was Eric's connection to Madden? Were hacker and killer one and the same, or were there two offenders? Two distinct crimes, coincidental, unrelated? Had Eric trashed her car? Did he have access to methyl cellulose? Did he have some vendetta against her? Her family?

The warrant arrived, preventing the spiral of her thoughts from driving her deeper into craziness.

Chase was there, as was Sam, Georgie, the entire Pacu task force. Including Hackett, who instructed her to stay in the apartment. Reading the taciturn in her boss's expression, she didn't bother to argue. Nothing but delays would come from fighting him.

So, she remained on her couch—attacking that second nail to stem nerves she'd never known she had—on tenterhooks to discover whether the man she shared an apartment block with was Bec's killer.

More waiting. It seemed eternal, when in reality only ten minutes passed before Georgie returned.

Her friend's palm felt cold and tense against the back of her hand as she spoke.

They'd knocked, but when there was no reply, they tried the handle only to find the door unlocked. Room by room, they'd cleared Eric's apartment, until they reached the study.

Georgie's voice trailed off. Then her friend blinked and swallowed, her hand tightening as she tore at yet another strand of Jayda's gradually dwindling control.

'Eric's dead.'

Three stabs to the abdomen and one fatal slash to the throat. Juliana Madden's death all over.

This was no coincidence. And she told Teddy so, before he packed up the body and transported it back to his lab.

'You can't stay here, Jayda.'

She stared at Chase. 'Where else am I supposed to go?'

Her gaze swept over the room, empty but for the two of them and the storm of fingerprint powder over the once spotless surfaces of her furniture and window panes. Tumbles had long since fled with the influx of her team. He wasn't one to stick around with strangers.

Chase cleared his throat, the action dragging her gaze back to him. He seemed reluctant to leave her, and much as she dreaded being alone, she craved peace more.

'How about your dad's place?'

He seemed oblivious to what was going on there, and she wasn't about to change that. She moved to stare out the window, wrapping her arms round her body to fight back the sudden wash of cold in the room. 'It's not possible right now.'

'A friend, then?'

Most of her friends lived in the building. What was the point in moving when she'd be right next door?

'Not really.'

'You can stay with me.'

'I appreciate the offer, but I'm fine.'

A shiver took up residence inside that she doubted would ever leave. She felt dirty, violated in a way she'd never imagined could affect her so profoundly.

But leaving the apartment wouldn't change that. If the Night Terror was sending her messages, she needed to stay and watch and wait for him to return. A game of cat and rat. And no way was she the rodent.

'I can't leave you here.' He moved to stand beside her.

'And you can't stay. You're lead on the case and your job doesn't include babysitting me.' She kept her voice soft, but unequivocal. The offer was appreciated, but unnecessary. She. Was. Fine. 'Has anyone spoken to Madden yet?'

He turned to her, eyes gaping, but didn't have the gall to question how she knew. Was that guilt veiled behind his expression, that he hadn't been the one to fill her in?

'An interview's set for tomorrow, late morning. And before you ask, no.'

She almost smiled at Chase's raised hand. Maybe the time would come when he surprised her and acted outside the box. Not letting her sit in on Madden's interview demonstrated that time wasn't today.

'How'd you know that was my next question?'

'Because when you get hold of a rope you won't stop until you've tugged it all the way to the end. Anyway, you have the funeral tomorrow.'

As if the tear in her heart would let her forget. 'What's the length of the 464B application?'

'The maximum.'

'Four hours leaves time for me to come after.'

'And Hackett will have both our asses on a platter.'

She returned his wry grin. It would have been easier with Chase's help, but either way, she'd see Madden. The wheels were already in motion.

Both prisoner and prison had approved her visit application, and in record time. She couldn't fathom Madden's motivation or his speedy response, and didn't care. Whatever perverted reasons he had for agreeing, it landed her face-to-face with the only man who could give her answers regarding Bec's death. And that fact by far outweighed any guilt for going behind the task force's back.

'Make sure you get a list of all Madden's visitors over the past twenty-five years.'

'Already on it.' His lips drew tight. 'I've organised a couple of uniforms to watch outside the building and your apartment for the next day, possibly two if I can stretch resources that far. Their names are Phillip Brandon and Barry Knight. Here are their numbers.'

She stepped back, away from his outstretched hand. 'It's not necessary.'

Chase pressed a scrap of paper into her palm. 'Humour me on this. Hackett insisted. So if you have a problem . . .'

She rolled her eyes and took the paper. 'God forbid!'

Chase's laughter was stilted as it joined hers, but the strain around his eyes eased. 'It's good to see you laugh.'

'There hasn't been much to laugh about lately.'

'I know. I'm sorry I haven't been there for you.'

His eyes held regrets she knew spanned more than the week.

Giving a mental shake of her head, she grasped his hand and squeezed. His palm was warm and soft, and his fingers wrapped round hers to squeeze back. He still wore the bandage, but his grip was firm, even if it did shake a little.

Emotions were getting the better of them both. Jayda swallowed. Something was going on with Chase, but whatever it was, he was a detective first and foremost. 'Just catch this bastard.'

He nodded. And for the first time in too long, she felt they were in sync. It was a feeling she hadn't realised she'd missed.

Chase hesitated. 'I asked tech to leave a spectrum analyser so you can scan the apartment for hidden cameras or bugs.' He indicated towards what looked like a blue TV control on living room table. 'Call me if you need anything.'

She held up her phone. 'You're on speed dial.'

He leaned in, their embrace awkward, when once it had been the most natural thing in the world. God, she hated that one night's idiocy had ruined their friendship.

*Sex.* Even in thought the word sounded tawdry. It tainted, spoiling the most innocent of actions. And it destroyed, ruthlessly. Look at her parents. Her father's affair. *Alleged affair.*

Best to stay clear of it. Not that she had much choice, even in the unlikely event that she'd change her mind.

She double-locked the door behind Chase, clicking the chain into place for the first time since she'd moved in three years ago. Then she grabbed her shoulder holster and slipped it on.

With systematic intent, she walked through the apartment, double-checking all window latches and closing the blinds. An unmarked police car sat on the opposite side of the road, as obvious as a flashing neon sign. Officer number two sat outside her door.

The gesture was solicitous, but if the Night Terror wanted to get to her, a couple of cops, wherever they sat, wouldn't deter him.

Every bone in her body dragged as if iron-clad, but she was far from ready for bed. Even further from sleep. The room resembled the aftermath of a sandstorm and for lack of a better alternative, she felt an overwhelming desire to clean.

Over the next hour and a half she eradicated all signs that her apartment had been the scene of a crime. Surfaces were dusted and sponged and scrubbed, the floors swept and vacuumed and mopped.

Sleep would have been impossible in an apartment that reeked of *him*. Not that cleaning guaranteed sleep. It just upped the odds.

When every visible speck of dust was banished, her face reflected in every furniture surface, she fell back onto the couch in a boneless heap and surveyed the area. Her muscles screamed, but the room looked as it always looked, on any normal, routine day of the week. An easy feeling seeped into her psyche. Not quite peace, but, hell, it felt good.

The one pay-off to come from the evening, apart from the pristine condition of her apartment, was that she'd be getting her money back. Important to focus on that.

'Not That Kind of Girl' crooned from her pocket in gutsy, rich tones. She snatched out her phone, sliding her finger across the screen, her mind mentally finishing the lyrics.

It was time for a new ringtone. This one cut too close, too sharp.

She'd been so sure she knew who she was, where she was at, when she'd downloaded it. Now all she knew was that she hadn't a clue.

'Hello?'

'Jayda.'

Thick emotion coated her throat. '*Seth.*'

'Are you okay?'

The flippant reassurances she'd handed Georgie and the rest of her team wouldn't resurface. Shaking her head, she inhaled deeply, knowing she should say something. 'You left your computer.'

Even if it was lame.

Her voice sounded weird, even to herself. Seth had to pick it.

'I know. That's why I'm here.'

'Here?' Ignoring the very clear message on his reason for returning, she scrambled up from the couch and rushed to the door, peering through the security peephole. No one stared back. 'Where, here?'

'Downstairs. I don't get to come up unless you okay it with security.'

Jayda moved the blinds to see the officer and Seth in a Mexican stand-off. 'Put him on.'

A sudden rush of impatience sent her into a bout of pacing at the front door. What was up with her heart? It was racing, erratic, for what should be no apparent reason.

'Officer Brandon here. I have orders to clear everyone entering the building.'

'I understand. Mr Friedin's a friend. Please let him up.'

'Sure thing. Have a good night, Detective.'

'What did you tell him?' Seth's voice again, puffy and short of breath, as if he was running a race.

'That you were a friend and to let you past.'

'Oh.' A door slammed, followed by heavy footsteps as he scaled the stairs. 'So, today must be Wednesday.'

Her thumb and forefinger kneaded the bridge of her nose as she stared at the closed front door. 'What do you mean? It's Thursday.'

'Not by my calculations.'

Another door slammed. Seconds later there was a rap on her front door. This time flinted grey eyes stared back at her through the security peephole. She unlatched, unlocked and allowed the door to swing inward.

He still looked damn good. His clothes were the same, but rumpled, as though they'd been on his body longer than the twelve or so hours he'd sported them. His chin was shadowed, his hair dishevelled and in dire need of a comb. His hands were empty. No coffee or croissants this time.

But he still had that mind-melting grin.

'Nice to see you, too, Jayda.'

*Hell! Was she really all google-eyed and staring?*

A mental headshake went partway to clearing her mind. Pulling back and noticing a patch of fingerprint powder she'd missed did the rest.

She rubbed at the black specks and refocused on their conversation. 'What calculations?'

'It can't be Thursday. From memory, we've only reached friend status on Wednesdays and Fridays.' He walked past her and into the living room. 'So, why the security?'

Only then did she register the officer standing across the hall. She nodded, then closed the door. Her comprehension was a little slow, but, yeah, Seth was still pissed. While she'd moved on from this afternoon. In leaps and bounds.

She waved her hand, turning to hide the threat of tears. 'Your computer's over there.'

He moved towards the dining table. 'What? No comeback? No gems or words of prophetic wisdom?'

'They take a crap-load of energy and today I'm fresh out.'

His gaze narrowed, piercing her over the lid of his computer, then he glanced down. 'What happened here?'

He swept his finger across the keyboard before holding it up covered in a line of fine black dust. She'd tried to brush and blow the powder from between the keys, and thought she'd succeeded. Obviously she was mistaken.

'Fingerprint powder.'

His hand froze halfway to pushing the lid down. 'Why is there fingerprint powder on my computer? And while we're talking weird and "what's up", what gives with your buddies outside?'

'Didn't Officer Brandon tell you?'

'That man was tighter than a nun's chastity belt in a brothel.'

His words almost dragged the corners of her lips upward. *Almost.*

Of course he didn't know the spiral her life had taken since this afternoon. He'd been somewhere else. With *her* maybe? *His date?* She didn't know why the thought came to her now, or why it felt so damned rough. Her list of worries far surpassed the importance of how Seth had spent his afternoon without her and why he looked like a man fresh out of a woman's bed.

Something she shouldn't give two hoots about.

He'd slammed out of her car five hours ago. When he returned, he'd been occupied with their phone conversation, hadn't continued past her apartment. Hadn't seen the crime scene tape two doors down or Teddy's van as it left with Eric in the back wrapped in a black body bag. Hadn't been there to witness her team pull out ten hidden cameras and their respective mics, or package up the photo and frame as evidence.

The tremors started deep inside, moving slowly to the surface as her shaking hand gripped the back of a chair. 'You don't know?'

Gun-metal softened to almost blue. 'Know what?'

# Chapter Thirty-Two

Seth felt the automatic softening of his resentment, and he fought it like a hound would fight for a T-bone steak.

Something had changed in Jayda. Nothing to do with the dark circles under her eyes or the listless, lack of blush to her cheeks. Although these still tugged at him in a way he tried to ignore, the difference he sensed was intrinsic.

The fight he'd so admired, and endured, was gone. She looked young, vulnerable. Pleased to see him.

Just went to show how fucked up he was over her. And why his decision to quit their work relationship was the wisest goddamn decision he'd made since they'd met.

'Are you okay?'

She eyeballed him as if he was off his rocker. She wasn't far wrong.

The tentative attempt she made at a smile almost shattered his resolve. He'd be a heel not to notice the sheen of unshed tears, or the way her hand shook as it brushed back a lock of flaming red. 'I've had better days.'

'That's saying a lot, considering the crap that's happened lately.'

Her bottom lip quivered and she fought it like a trooper. His glance at the door was fleeting, his censure at his weakness only slightly less so, before he moved away from his computer. 'I'm in dire need of a coffee. How about you?'

Her relief was almost overpowering, and he moved towards the kitchen before she could put her expression into words. He wasn't staying. Not past a drink and checking she was okay. 'Instant or espresso?'

Fire returned to her expression. 'Are you kidding? Putting instant and coffee in the same sentence is sacrilege.'

He bit back a smile. 'Ah, how could I forget? So, espresso?'

'Is there any other kind?'

'A purist. Who'd have thought?'

Her gaze met his, and before he could lose himself in rainforests and dew-swept meadows glinting in the morning sun, he grabbed her percolator from the bench and filled it with water. Adding the grounds, he sat it on the stove and began the process of warming the milk.

Just under one week ago, he'd performed this task for the first time as Jayda slept. Before then, coffee was coffee and he'd have taken it any which way, as long as it had legs. Thanks to Google, he'd become an expert at the perked kind, and it was ruining him for anything else.

Jayda perched at the breakfast bar, same as that following morning. Back then he'd suffered under the delusion that they could work together. That he needed her and she needed him, equally. Now he knew better.

Jayda made it her mission to need no one. And he doubted anything he or anyone else did could change that.

The silence between them was testament to how far they'd fallen towards animosity. Despite his ridiculous need to care for her.

Experts would say it stemmed from his childhood, and his almost child-like yearning to be wanted. And perhaps they'd be right. It didn't matter. The theory wasn't one he intended entertaining, either now or anytime soon.

He removed the percolator before the brew burned, then added the hot, aromatic liquid to the milk.

'Here.' He slid the mug across the bench, and she wrapped her long, fine fingers around it.

'Thanks.'

'Can I ask you a question?'

She sipped, pulling back as the heat hit her lips. 'Sure.'

'Why do you have a hole in your ceiling?'

They both stared up at the gaping puncture in white plaster where her downlight used to be. Haunted grey tinged her skin, her fingers shaking as she plunked her mug onto the bench. Brown liquid sloshed over the sides.

'Careful!' He grabbed her dripping hand and held it under the cold running tap. 'Damn, Jayda. There's no need to make a bad day worse.'

A humourless laugh hacked out from her throat. 'You think it can get worse?'

'What happened?' He fought to soften his voice, when all he wanted was to shake her until she told him what was going on. Instead, he loosened his grip, gently tracing his thumb over her knuckles as he searched her eyes for answers.

She yanked her hand back, hugged it to her chest as she drew in deep, haggard breaths. He turned off the tap.

Old Jayda was back. The one who had to stand on her own and wouldn't accept an ounce of help, no matter what the cost. And yes, there was always a cost.

Damn, would the woman never learn?

'Where to start?' Her voice was high and brittle as she smeared the water from her hand onto her top. 'Let's see . . . someone hid a handful of security cameras in my apartment. Was even thoughtful enough to leave a photo and message for me to find.'

A volcano began building in his brain. 'And still, no doubt, you're defending Eric.'

'Eric's dead.'

He froze. 'He killed himself?'

'That's assuming he stabbed himself three times in the chest before finishing the job with a slash to the neck.'

The thrash of blood through his veins stopped, along with his heart. 'Madden's MO for killing his wife.'

Her lips tightened. 'The apprentice is branching out. What's the bet his mentor isn't impressed.'

'The man has a lot of answering to do on Saturday.'

'If he talks.'

Something twisted inside his chest that he couldn't ignore. It could just as easily have been Jayda and not Eric lying in the morgue right now. The thought wrenched at the ham salad sandwich still sitting undigested in his stomach. 'I should have been here.'

She lifted her chin, fire returning to her expression. 'I'm fine.'

'You might not have been.'

'I don't think he wants me dead. Not yet, at least.'

'And you know this, how?'

A deep breath and she was back. Damn, he admired her spunk, even while he thanked the heavens it had returned.

'He's had more than enough opportunity. Access to my apartment, knowledge of my movements. Not only was he watching, but he was listening. He could have entered anytime and killed me, but he hasn't. So, the question is, why?' She pushed back at hair already secured behind her ear. 'You were right before, you know. This guy is someone I know.'

He nodded and bit his tongue. No need to gloat, it was enough that she'd come round to his way of thinking.

'Tell me exactly what happened since I saw you last.'

'We might need a refill.'

He looked down at his almost-empty mug. 'You might be right.' He grinned across the bench and the natural curve of her lips tugged at his gut.

*Don't be a schmuck! You weren't staying for more than one drink. Drink's over, and so is anything with her.*

*Time to go.*

He dumped the used coffee grounds into the bin.

Just one more drink. That was all he'd share. She'd tell him what happened, he'd make sure she was okay, then he'd pack up his computer and say goodbye without so much as a backwards glance.

Easy.

The heavy patrol outside would see she remained safe.

Coffee made, they moved into the living room. Jayda curled up at one end of the couch. He ignored the obvious invitation to take up the other end, instead lowering himself into the armchair opposite.

She sipped at her drink before peering at him through the rising steam. 'Where shall I start?'

'I usually find the beginning a good place. Starting at the end just gets messy.' The hoot of her laughter filled the room.

'You should laugh more often.' He didn't realise he'd said the words until she stopped, her wide eyes fixed on him with surprise.

Then the corner of her mouth twitched. 'I will when you're funny.'

'Ouch!' He slapped a hand to his chest.

She laughed again, and his resolve melted like an iceberg fallen victim to global warming.

His grip on the mug tightened. All this warmth and fuzziness was too little, too late. Nothing she said or did would make him stay. Even if she fell onto her knees right now and begged.

He cleared the clog in his throat and pushed back his weakness when it came to her. 'Why don't you start from when I left you.'

The laughter lines dissolved, and her armour slipped. The amber flecks in her eyes dimmed, and she looked almost lost. Then, one deep breath and the armour was back.

With the voice of an automaton, she relayed how she was turned away from the crime scene. How she'd returned to her apartment and found the Night Terror's message, and how her squad had located the hidden cameras before entering Eric's apartment only to find him dead.

As every second passed, his mercury edged its way upwards. And when she detailed the picture inserted into her frame, and even worse, the message, he bitterly regretted his decision to stay for that second drink.

His gaze flitted briefly to the door. He should have left when he'd had the choice.

Because now it had been taken from him.

'You can't stay here alone.'

Jayda's head jerked. What the hell was it with men and their almost obsessive compulsion to protect her?

Her fluttering heart, she ignored. This was Seth's Boy Scout altruism at work. Something he'd do for any woman, regardless of who she was and what he felt for her.

'I don't need a babysitter.' She dumped her mug on the coffee table.

Seth's elbows rested on his knees and he leaned forwards, looking at her as if she were something. Everything. 'What about a friend?'

The words tugged at her heart, guilt strings strumming anew over her treatment of him ever since they'd started the whole working-together fiasco. Her fingers trembled in her lap. 'No one ever has enough friends.'

'Then let me stay and be one now.'

She wouldn't let his words melt her. Much as she was tempted—*oh, God, was she tempted*—what then?

If she leaned now, would she ever walk upright again? The fear had been there as long as she could remember. She'd never been able to shake it, no matter how hard she tried. The cost of depending on someone other than herself was too great, when they could so easily walk away, leaving her to fall without any chance of picking herself up. If she thought long enough and hard enough, she'd have no choice but to agree.

Lust had a way of yielding havoc over logic.

Being honest with herself and admitting the truth was half the battle. The sole reason she faltered was her memory and their encounter on the rooftop. And her desire for it to happen again.

Only that was the night Bec died. A clear sign of how wrong the whole episode had been.

What she needed to do was let Seth know she was happy to continue with their original agreement. All rules still effective and securely in place.

But first . . . she inhaled deeply, slowly, before launching into something that was well overdue. 'I'm sorry. For before. For every time I made you feel like you were less than welcome, or that you were the root of all that was wrong in my life.'

She raised her hand when it seemed he meant to interrupt, and barrelled on before she lost momentum. 'There were other, much stronger contenders for that position, but when they weren't available, I took my anger out on you. And that was wrong.' The oxygen shuddered into her lungs as she breathed in again. 'Seth, I'm really, really sorry.'

His expression was one of a man who'd just witnessed a miracle. 'Apology accepted. I guess that means I'm staying.'

'No. It means I'm sorry. And that you can be a friend without staying.'

'Not if I care about your safety, I can't.'

Her hand slid into her front jeans pocket, to the crumpled paper she'd written a lifetime ago. 'I'm happy for us to continue working together. But that's it.'

He unfolded himself from her chair and stood so that she had to tip her head right back to meet his gaze.

'This isn't a come-on, Jayda. But either I stay here with you or you stay at my place. Those are the only two options you get.'

It'd take a helluva lot more than a hot man and height to

intimidate her. She pushed herself up from the couch, and the tilt of her neck reduced to marginal. 'Nothing's changed, Seth. There's still a killer out there and I'm still going to catch him. You can either help me out or not. It's up to you.'

His squinted gaze fastened on her face until she felt it burn. She wanted to squirm, to turn away. Only wouldn't that be a sign he was chipping his way through her resolve?

'I'll leave you to ponder over that, and while you do,' she dragged steel into her shoulders and squared her feet, 'I need to see inside Eric's apartment.'

# Chapter Thirty-Three

**S**eth knew Jayda well enough to recognise a diversionary tactic when he saw it.

But that old saloon door swung both ways and she should have known him well enough by now, too. He wouldn't fall so easily for one of her tricks.

He was staying the night, whether she liked it or not. The conversation wasn't over, just postponed.

'It's a crime scene.'

'And I'm a homicide detective.'

'On leave.'

She waved her hand carelessly as she moved to the window and peered outside. 'Semantics.'

'What are you planning to do with your buddies outside?'

'Lucky for us, they're out the front having a pow-wow. Are you with me or not?'

She detoured to her stereo and switched it on, then turned it up. Frankie Goes to Hollywood blared from the speakers, telling them both to relax.

As she moved towards the door, he noticed for the first time that she was wearing her shoulder holster and gun under her clothes. Something she hadn't done in her apartment before today, or at least, not since they'd met.

'What do you think?' he asked.

'That you still want your story.' She didn't wait for him to answer. Keys in hand, she unlatched and opened the door, first scouring the hall before glancing back. 'Coming?'

He was still floored that she seemed to think his job was the only reason he'd returned. Well, that and his computer.

Did she believe his wanting to sleep with her was all about the story, too? The thought made him sick to his stomach. He may be single-minded, but he wasn't mercenary. And after their time together, she should have known.

He followed her through the door, out of sorts and hating that she had the power to affect him that way.

A cat screeched from somewhere nearby and they froze. Jayda recovered first. 'Georgie!'

She tore down the hallway as the fire door slammed behind a jeans-clad figure, and in the few precious seconds it took him to react she, too, had disappeared from sight. He bolted after her, through the heavy door and down the stairs. It was way too long since he'd hit the pavement and just run, and the past few days' lack of sleep didn't help.

'Georgie, wait!' Jayda yelled again.

Another door slammed and the sound of footsteps ceased. At the bottom, he yanked the door open and nearly bowled straight into her. She stood opposite a woman with bobbed copper hair and unsettled brown eyes who looked vaguely familiar.

It clicked. The detective who'd attended the scene outside Antonio's restaurant.

'Georgie, you remember Seth?'

'Sure.' Her gaze darted between Jayda and Seth before resting on Jayda again. Her cheeks were flushed, no doubt from the hike downstairs, her smile tentative. 'I figured you were out when you didn't answer the door. How are you?'

'Still a little shaken, but fine.'

Again, her brown gaze flicked between them. 'As long as you're okay . . .' She licked her lips. 'I should be going.'

Jayda touched Georgie's arm. 'Come up for a coffee. Or perhaps something stronger?'

'I'm on duty. I just swung by to check on you.' She dipped her head.

'Raincheck?'

'Sure.'

The women hugged, but he could tell from the line of Jayda's shoulders that something was off.

As Georgie left by the front exit, he turned to Jayda. 'What's wrong?'

'I'm not sure. Did you hear Georgie knock?'

'No.'

'Neither did I.'

They watched her approach the officers on the front lawn.

'Just because no one's heard a bear fart in the woods, doesn't mean it hasn't happened.'

The corners of her lips quirked upward. 'You don't say.'

'You find that amusing?'

'What can I say? You're growing on me.'

'If you throw fungi into the mix, I'm going to be wounded.'

'I wouldn't dare.'

She gave a quick wave to Georgie and the two men before shouldering open the door to the stairwell. 'We need to visit Eric's apartment before my security detail returns.'

He followed her through. 'Is that where you think Georgie went?'

'No idea. But if it is, why lie unless her reasons are outside the Department's investigation?'

Up one flight of stairs and they were back where they'd started. He fell in beside Jayda as they continued past her apartment.

Even alone, he would have recognised Eric's place. The door to apartment twenty-one was littered with a haphazard layer of fine black dust, and three bands of blue-and-white tape stretched from one side of the frame to the other.

Jayda leaned in, her eyes flitting across the door's surface.

'What are you looking for?'

She froze. 'This.'

Her finger pointed to a small, almost imperceptible smudge in the black powder beside the lock.

'And that tells us . . .?'

'Either forensics was careless or someone has tried to access this apartment since they left.'

'Georgie?'

'Perhaps. Perhaps not.' She patted her jeans pocket and sighed. 'Wait here.' In seconds she was back. She slipped on a pair of rubber gloves before manoeuvring two lock picks into the keyhole, twisting and turning with the confidence of someone not new to the practice.

'Isn't this breaking and entering?'

The lock clicked and she shot him a look of triumph. 'Only if we get caught.'

'That's reassuring.'

She grinned briefly before passing him a set of gloves identical to hers. They ducked under the tape and slipped inside. Jayda closed the door.

He took in their surroundings and bit back a *we shouldn't be here.* There were times when stretching the letter of the law went with breaking a story. Any reporter worth his salt pushed boundaries now and then. Deny it and they'd be lying. But working this far outside? It made his conscience itch.

Jayda passed him blue disposable shoe coverings, then proceeded to slip hers over her bright red sneakers. 'Touch nothing. If you think something needs a closer look, call me. If you see anything remotely resembling the smudge at the front door, definitely call me. If someone was here after forensics left, I want to know what they were looking at.'

'And we're looking for . . .'

He waited for the smart-alec remark that always came.

She continued to scan the room. 'Anything that's out of place or that ties Eric to the Night Terror.'

Perhaps the change in her was more than cosmetic.

They worked in silence, systematically searching each room, then moving onto the next. Old tensions were gone. In their place came an ease he'd all but given up on finding. It was as he'd always suspected. They worked well as a team.

They finally reached the study—the scene of the crime and only remaining room to be searched. It was Jayda's decision to approach it last, so as not to taint their perspective while searching the rest of the apartment.

He entered first.

If only she'd realised how much the room's contents would taint.

Heat from her body warmed his back before her breath swept his neck and he heard her voice. 'No wonder Georgie was vague when I asked what they found.'

Ignoring her proximity and the strange things it did to his heart, he turned to see if she was disturbed. Seemed not. She had her cop mask firmly in place, appearing more offhand than freaked.

'So, did Eric place the cameras in my apartment, or did he discover their presence and hack into their feed for his own use?'

Seth skirted the chaotic crust of blood and chalked body outline on the cream carpet to reach the far wall. There was no satisfaction in knowing he'd been right about Eric's obsession. He stared at the proof—a mish-mash of photos, most taken inside Jayda's apartment, others in the car park, and others still outside the building using a long lens.

Some showed moments where he and Jayda were together. In others he noted Chase, Juz and Garry, and some other man he didn't recognise. Some model-looking guy, with olive complexion and dark brown hair.

His back prickled, like a trail of millipedes scuttling across his skin. He pointed to the model-man. 'Who's that?'

'Darren.'

A Darren lived on her floor. He knew that much from the checks he'd performed on her neighbours. As of yet, nothing had sparked his interest, other than the exceptionally high male-to-female ratio.

She looked at the photo and smiled. 'Darren's a friend. He lives next door, but he's away for work at the moment.'

Yet another one. She had them circling like moths to nectar. He knew who Jayda chose as friends shouldn't bother him, but it did. Just one more contender for the Night Terror position.

He turned his attention back to the collage. 'Does anything here strike you as strange?'

'Other than someone stalking me both inside and outside my apartment?'

'Well, yeah.'

'What are you thinking?'

'Is his fascination with you or the men you're keeping company with?'

'I don't "keep company" with men.'

He sighed. 'Okay. But do you think his interest might be with the men in the photos?'

'Why place the cameras in my apartment then?'

'You have a point there.'

'And so do you. I'm just not sure what it all means right now.'

His bottom jaw dropped all the way to the floor. Was that praise? And was that flooding warmth in his body a reaction to it? He pushed thought and reaction aside. He'd long since stopped looking for approval outside of himself.

She turned back to the wall, seemingly unaware she'd just broken with her own protocol.

Lips clamped tight, the line of her back was rigid and uncompromising. To any stranger, she was a cop surveying a crime scene. To him, she was a woman battling to hold it together.

Every print earned her attention, some even earned a snap or two with the camera on his phone.

One photo dragged her interest back, over and over. He couldn't see a difference between it and its counterparts, but obviously Jayda did.

She glanced at him before returning her attention to the photo mélange. 'Do you have a video on your phone?'

'You want to film the room?'

'Yes. But first, I want you to film this.' She pointed to the photo. Nothing extraordinary, just Jayda and her father standing beside his blue sedan.

'Why?'

'You'll find out in a second.'

'You're starting to sound like a really badly written daytime drama.'

'Badly written?'

'Yeah. *Tune in next week and discover the unbelievable truth!*'

She rolled her eyes, but her lips twitched at the edges. 'Is it going?' She pointed to his mobile.

His video app was open. All he had to do was point and press record. 'Yep.'

'So, back to that "badly written" soap.' Her fingers bobbed in unison in front of her face before she turned to the wall. 'Drum roll, please, and let's see what's behind photo number one.'

She plucked the photo from the board and turned it over slowly.

The phone slipped. He fumbled, righting it to centre on her once again. One touch and blurred focus sharpened into crystal clarity. He could almost hear the *whirr* as his mind spun and he stared at her hand through the screen. Or rather, what she held in it.

A break in the case, if only they could work out what it meant.

'How the hell did you know?'

# Chapter Thirty-Four

Jayda's expression was as shell-shocked as Seth's as she stared at the photo in her hand.

'It was a hunch.'

'A damn good one.'

'Well, thank you.' Her eyes flashed emerald as her lips kicked upwards, tugging his gut right along with them. 'Now all we need to do is work out what it means.'

'I bow to your vast superiority.' He stopped recording and slipped the phone into his pocket.

'Well, let's not go overboard now.'

Regardless of her words, fire had returned to her expression. The old Jayda was back, and chuffed at her discovery—a small black key taped to the underside of that one photograph.

He scanned the wall, looking for whatever had tipped her off to the key's presence. Impossible, since he didn't have a clue what he was looking for.

'Are there any others?'

Auburn locks bounced over her shoulders as she shook her head. 'I doubt it.'

'How do you know?'

'Ever watch *Sesame Street*?'

'Uh, yeah.' He searched her expression for signs she'd fallen completely off her rocker. Jayda swept her arm across the expanse of the wall and burst into a key that was nowhere near tuneful: *'One of these things is not like the others . . .'*

He snorted. 'Don't give up your day job.'

She wrinkled her nose. 'I never claimed to be anything other than tone deaf.' He couldn't disagree. 'So, are you going to share your secret?'

'Once I do, promise you'll stay impressed?'

'As long as you weren't the one who put the photo there.'

'No. It wasn't me.'

'Eric?'

'No. I'm ninety-nine percent sure it was his killer.'

Seth scuffed his fingers through his hair when what he really wanted to do was shake the entire explanation out of her. 'Stop teasing and spit it out.'

'A tad frustrated, are we?' The bow in her lips deepened.

He forced his gaze upwards and away from temptation. 'Don't make me show you how much.'

That dragged the red to her cheeks. Her tongue slid over her lips and he was tempted to do what he'd threatened, regardless. Kiss her until she couldn't hold back any longer.

Her heel caught a chair leg as she tottered backwards against the bookshelf. After taking a moment to brace herself, she cleared her throat and returned her attention to the wall. 'Every other photo here was taken without my knowledge or my consent.'

'And that one?'

'Was taken by Bec over a year ago. Someone got hold of a copy, or perhaps broke into her apartment and took the original, then placed it here for me to find.' She tugged carefully at the adhesive, extracting the key without tape sticking to her gloves. 'Someone wanted me to find this.'

She turned it over in her hands and he moved in to take a closer look. Her breath hitched, she fumbled and the key slipped through her fingers, bouncing as it hit the carpet. He ducked to rescue it.

Sharp pain sliced through his skull as their heads collided, and an entire solar system danced across his vision.

He staggered back, clutching his temple, watching Jayda do the same. 'You okay?'

Her fingers rubbed just above her right eye. 'Me, yes. My head, not so much. You?'

'Pretty much the same.' He grinned. 'Wanna paper, rock, scissors for who picks it up?'

She grinned back, and he hated that his heart galloped in response.

'I'll get it.' She scooped the key up and tucked it into her wallet.

'Shouldn't we check it for prints?'

'There won't be any. He's too good for that.'

'So, what next?'

'We finish up here before we get caught, then go home and figure out what this key opens. Seen anything in the apartment that could be a contender?'

'Nothing. So unless it's hidden . . .'

'I doubt it. In fact, I doubt this key has anything to do with Eric at all. It's a personal message, and whoever planted it banked on me finding it, not the police.'

Her eyes roved. 'Can you video the rest of the room? Every corner, every surface. Pay special attention to his desk and this,' she swept her arm across her wall of fame, 'and the crime scene, of course.' She pointed to the black chalk and swollen bloodstain. 'Take it slow so you capture everything.'

It was another fifteen minutes before they were done. After the study, he filmed the rest of the apartment, slowly making his way to the front door. Then, under Jayda's direction, he captured close-ups of the doormat and a pair of brown loafers discarded just inside the entrance.

The search had yielded nothing but the key. Eric was neat to the point of compulsive and the photos were the only items in the apartment that seemed out of the ordinary.

Jayda ducked back under the tape, and he followed.

There was no way to avoid detection on the way out. As she locked Eric's door, the officer's glance swung between them and her apartment, confusion quickly transforming into irritation. By the time they'd unlocked Jayda's door, he was already on the phone, no doubt reporting the infringement to her boss.

She had to be aware their actions wouldn't go without consequence. Yet, other than a determined tilt to her chin, he saw no sign Jayda was affected.

She dropped her purse and keys on the little table in the hall, a pointless thing that served no purpose other than taking up space, and turned the stereo down to a murmur before grabbing herself a glass of cold water from the kitchen.

He let it go. If she wasn't worried, then neither was he. And if, as a result, her security tightened, it would only serve to better ensure her safety. He couldn't argue with that outcome.

She sipped at her glass. 'Did you have lunch?'

'A ham-and-salad sandwich.'

'I haven't eaten since breakfast.'

He couldn't help but smile. 'Is that a hint you're hungry?'

'Try famished.'

'Well, perhaps we should feed you then.'

She grabbed a painted, cat-shaped letter holder from above the fridge and scattered its mélange of takeaway menus onto the bench. 'What do you fancy?'

He raised a brow. 'Cook much?'

'Who has time when you're out catching bad guys?' She waved her hand over the array. 'Any preference?'

'Your choice.'

'Pizza?'

'Perfect.' He picked up the crudely painted cat, made of what looked to be chipboard. 'Have a thing for cats, do you?'

'I guess you'd say I'm a cat person. Dogs are too needy for my liking.' As he turned the holder over in his hands, she shuffled through the menus. 'Bec painted that in primary school.'

'She had talent.'

'Not really. Bec was great at most things, but art was her downfall. She couldn't sit still long enough to finish anything.'

'I wondered why only part of it was coloured. So one purple ear and one plain wasn't artistic licence?'

'Nope. More like losing interest.' Her hand paused over a menu for Piergiorgio's Pizzas, and the paper crinkled beneath her taut fingers as she drew in a deep breath before flipping it open. 'Any pizza preferences or no-nos?'

'I'll eat pretty much anything as long as it doesn't include anchovies or olives.'

'How do you feel about vegetarian with beef, no onions?'

'Ambivalent. I've never tried it.'

'Well, tonight's your lucky night.'

His body kicked into gear as she continued, seeming oblivious to the invitation in her words.

'There's beer in the fridge, if you're interested. And while you're there, I'll have a wine.'

Her voice sounded too upbeat. Stretched. As if light and bubbly were a cover for what was really going on in that complex mind of hers.

Peripheral vision allowed him to watch her shaky fingers dial the pizzeria while he made himself at home in her kitchen again. By the time he'd poured her drink, she'd finished ordering and had dropped her mobile onto the bench.

'They said half an hour.'

He handed her a glass of the pink, sickly smelling stuff she called wine and swallowed a mouthful of ice-cold brew. 'You and Bec sound close.'

She collected her purse from the living room and extracted the key. He watched with fascination as she rotated it between her fingers, the wheels of deduction clearly working in her mind.

'We are. *Were.*' Her eyes glistened as she gulped back a generous serving of lolly liquid. 'She was my best friend.'

What to say to that? Rather than get it wrong, he nodded and said nothing.

She dropped the key onto the bench and swirled the liquid in her glass, staring at the rising bubbles as if one might hold relief from her pain. Then her body jolted and she pulled herself out of wherever she was, back into the present. 'I've been thinking about Eric.'

Another swerve in conversation to avoid getting close. Just when he thought she'd open up and let him in, when he thought her guard was dropping, the damn thing went back into automatic snap-shut mode.

He took a jerky swig of his beer, stemming the temptation to knock the entire bottle back in one gulp. After the ease between them in Eric's apartment, he'd hoped for more. Guess he should have been used to expecting the unexpected when it came to Jayda.

'There are two scenarios.' She ticked them off with her fingers. 'Eric either hid the cameras in my apartment, or knew who did. Either way, he stumbled onto something or someone, and was killed before he could reveal what he'd found.'

She stared at some indefinable spot across the room. 'What we do know is that he was in the parking garage just before he was killed.'

'Of course. We passed him on the stairs.'

'I mean later. After we left the building.'

'And you know that how?'

'The oil on his shoes. A whole can was spilled down there sometime between 12.30 and 2 pm. I'll get Chase to check the surveillance cameras, but after what happened last time, I doubt we'll find anything.'

'And the significance of the oil?'

'No idea. It's all linked somehow, like a jigsaw. Unless the spill is mere coincidence, something I'm inclined to doubt. It's more likely that Eric was killed or captured down there and the oil was spilled to cover up the crime scene. Teddy's report will help determine either way. Whatever the case, the more pieces we uncover, the more we can connect. And by the time we complete the puzzle, we should have found our killer.'

'That's almost poetic.'

'You're not the only one who knows their way around a dictionary.' The way her lips curved into a slow, wide arc made his heart kick more than it should.

He cleared his throat, and his mind, of that mouth. 'Eric hacked into your account; he was stalking you. He had the expertise to set up the surveillance system, and the pictures on his wall prove he was using it.'

'*If* he was the one who put them there.'

His chest tightened. Even now she was defending the guy, when they had rock-solid proof of his guilt, for the hacking if nothing else.

He was sorry the man was dead—he *really* was—but Eric was far from the innocent she seemed hell-bent on defending.

'Who else would pin photos of you on Eric's wall?'

'Didn't it strike you as odd that everything in his apartment was orderly and precise, but the pictures were haphazard, showing no logic or sequence?'

'I didn't—'

'And that there was no sign of a camera or zoom lens for those long shots?'

'It could be in his car.'

Her gaze narrowed, but her voice remained steady and low. 'Or someone else's.'

'So, you think the Night Terror's muddying the waters?'

'I think he's trying to throw us off track. Only reason he'd do that is if we're getting too close.' She sipped at her drink. 'Roan Madden must be the key.'

Getting her to see sense over Eric was a waste of time. And passé now the man was dead. It was time to move on. 'Speaking of keys . . .'

'Yes. How does that fit in?' She glanced towards the black metal object on the bench. 'Either the killer left it as a message, or someone else banked on me searching Eric's apartment and understanding the significance of the photo. When we discover what the key opens, we might get a better handle on who planted it.'

She moved towards her computer. 'I have an idea.'

That ridiculous song belted out from her phone. She backtracked and looked at the caller ID.

'But first we need to deal with this.' Sliding her finger across the screen, she held the mobile to her ear. 'Officer Brandon . . . yes. What's the topping? . . . That's it. Please let him up . . . No problem . . . Thanks.'

Within minutes there was a knock at the door.

'Pizza!' Her face was a city of lights as she scooped up her purse and raced across the room.

He noticed that no matter her hurry—or hunger—she still peered through the security peephole before unlatching and unlocking the door. And as she opened it, one hand rested on the gun at her hip.

It wasn't necessary. Her security detail was back outside her door, and the pizza guy really was a pizza guy, bearing a couple of appetite-inspiring pizzas. But it was reassuring to know that she was on the alert.

'You're gonna love this!' She handed one box to the cop outside, brandished a winning—and perhaps conciliatory?—smile at him, before double-locking the door and turning to drop the other box onto the coffee table. Perching on the edge of the couch, she flipped open the lid, scooped up a slice and held it out to him.

He took it and sank into the armchair opposite. Sliding her wine across the table towards her, he watched her capture another slice before drawing it into her mouth. She munched, licking a glob of sauce from her lips. He swallowed a groan along with a large bite of his slice.

'Good pizza, right?'

Her contented, pizza-sauce grin tugged one in return from him, even while he fought the impulse to lean across the table and taste a different, more tantalising alternative.

'Want to talk about what we found in Eric's apartment?'

She wiped her mouth with the back of her hand and assessed the remaining pieces before selecting the biggest and nabbing a bite. 'We just did.'

'I mean, about how it made you feel.'

The pizza froze midair. 'Touchy-feely doesn't solve cases. Hard facts do. We need to dig deeper into Madden's past.'

'I tried that and hit a cyber-wall. His past doesn't exist on the web pre-trial.' Now was as good a time as any to share what he'd found. 'At least I thought it didn't, until I realised the truth.'

'What truth?' She popped the last bit of crust in her mouth and polished it off with a mouthful of wine. It was obvious she didn't consider his news significant. He couldn't wait to see her expression when she realised it was.

'Roan Madden was born Rose Madden.'

Jayda's jaw dropped. 'You mean . . .'

He nodded. 'Roan Madden was a woman.'

'No way! Will would have told me.' She frowned. 'I asked him if the DNA analysis revealed anything else. I *asked* him.' Her gaze slipped. *'He would have told me.'*

She blinked. The glass in her hand dipped. He jumped up and saved it seconds before she snorted and collapsed into laughter.

He set her drink on the table.

Chortles bubbled up her throat as she clutched at her stomach and flopped back against the couch. Tears rolled down her cheeks. Her mouth opened. She gasped, lips moving, only she lacked the breath and ability to form the words.

He'd missed the joke.

With any luck, she'd pull it together before her heart seized up and he had to call emergency triple 0.

Her breath burst out in pants as she tried again. 'Y . . . you . . . don't . . . get . . . it!'

*Nope. Not a clue.* 'Get what?'

'Th–the irony.'

She dissolved into another bout, scattering the couch cushions. The tone changed. Her laughter lost its humour. He leaned in. *Her tears were real.*

He skirted the table and pulled her into his arms. 'Hey, it's okay.'

She shuddered beneath his palm, collapsed into him, her sobs deep, shattering.

'It'sssnot!' She sniffed, pulling away to drag the back of her hand across her eyes.

He reached for the tissue box with the tips of his fingers and dropped it into her lap, watching as she yanked a handful out and mopped her face.

'Th–thanks.' She hiccupped, then slowly shook her head. 'A woman killing all those women.'

'For all intents and purposes, when he became the Night Terror he was a man.'

'Still . . . I don't get it.'

'He's a psycho-killer. What's to get?'

She snatched another wad of tissues and blew her nose. A couple of deep, shuddering breaths later and she was right but for large splotches under her eyes and nose.

For an age she sat, fingers clenched around the hem of her top, staring into some distant place Seth could neither fathom nor see. Then she jolted and the haze in her eyes cleared.

She grabbed his hand. 'Show me.'

He let her pull him towards her computer. A couple of mouse clicks and he found it. 'Here.'

They stared at the screen. He clicked through the series of photos he'd uncovered until he reached the last. He'd seen it before, but it didn't lessen the shock of staring at the image again.

Madden as a woman turning man, dressed in maternity clothes and about to pop.

# Chapter Thirty-Five

'**H**e was *pregnant?*' Jayda's eyes widened, her lips full and open and waiting for him to . . .

Seth dragged his gaze back up to those eyes. 'She.'

'When was the photo taken?'

'A year before his marriage to Juliana. By then he was on his way to becoming male as a result of the hormones and injections. He must have stopped the hormones to have the child, then continued on with them and had the gender reassignment operation soon after.'

'*He has a kid.*'

'Not a kid. He or she would be in their late twenties by now.'

'We need to find them.' She moved to the kitchen counter and grabbed her phone.

'Who are you calling?'

'Will Andrews. I need him to run a familial match on the NCIDD.'

'What makes you think he'll check the criminal DNA database for you?'

'Not for me, for the investigation. And this time I'll make sure I get straight answers from him.'

'You might want to reconsider calling him this late, in that case.'

She glanced at the screen before dropping the phone back onto the bench. 'I'll call first thing tomorrow.' She grinned, remnants of the laughing, crying woman from seconds before gone. 'This kid is the link. I know it!'

'Which would explain why we're coming up against that cyber black hole. He's covering his tracks.'

'You're assuming Madden had a son.'

'What's the likelihood he had a daughter and she also had a sex-change?'

'Now you're assuming today's Night Terror is male. Much as the profile suggests a man, what if the killer is a woman? Madden could be running the show from prison with his apprentice as his proxy. A woman could easily lure other woman into a trap without suspicion. It would explain why none of the victims felt threatened when approached.'

'Yet a woman still doesn't fit the profile. Most female serial killers target male victims they share a relationship with. And more often than not, their motivation is financial.'

'You have a point, but there are exceptions.'

'There are always exceptions. Why don't we wait and see what Will comes up with?'

'You're right. We have other angles to work in the meantime. Like this black hole you keep referring to.'

She wandered back to the couch. 'Do you think someone with ASIS-level computer skills could wipe all mention of Madden off the internet for that period?'

'Maybe, if they had the means and the access. I assume we're talking Eric again?'

She finished her glass of wine and refilled. 'Either Eric was working for our killer, or our killer has skills that equal, or even surpass, Eric's.'

'Skills that could empty a person's bank account and donate the funds to charity.' Eric may have died, but Seth wasn't convinced that made him any less guilty. At the very least, he was a hacker. At the most . . .

She snagged another wedge of pizza. 'If Eric didn't do the hacking, it makes perfect sense that the person who trashed both our cars and stole my money is the same one who killed Bec and who's stalking me. Eric was just the fall guy, a red herring. What I don't get is, why target me? I'm not even officially on the case anymore. Why not target the investigation?'

'Because this was never about the investigation.'

She gaped, wine glass in one hand, pizza in the other. 'What was it about then?'

'Some deep-seated hatred for you or your family. *History*.'

'I don't have history with someone who'd want to kill me.'

'How do you know? You said you were adopted. What about your birth family?'

Her brows knitted as she contemplated the jumbled topping on her pizza. 'My parents were killed in a house fire. I was two at the time, and the only keepsake I have from that day is this.' She set her glass onto the table and scrunched up the left leg of her jeans to reveal a jagged scar from ankle to knee.

How the hell could he have missed that before? *'Ouch.* What happened?'

'A metal bookshelf collapsed while the fireman was rescuing me. He managed to shield my body, but my leg caught a slashing.'

'Damn!'

'Yeah. That pretty much sums it up. Still, it could have been worse.'

His stomach churned just thinking about it. 'Any other siblings, then?'

'I was an only child until Bec was born.'

'Was Dean connected to you in some way before you were adopted?'

'All I know is that he was good friends with my biological dad, and he also happened to be my godfather.' She eyed the last slice of pizza. 'You going to eat that?'

'Take it. I had lunch.' He knocked back a mouthful of beer.

She snatched it up as if she believed he'd change his mind, all attention centred on devouring the food.

'Jayda, we need to go there.'

Her hand stalled.

When she'd already been pushed to her limits, here he was, pushing her more. For the case, for her own peace of mind. Was it too much?

Air hissed from her lungs. *'I know.'*

Weight lifted from his chest. It was a concession he never thought he'd hear.

'My life pre-adoption is a mystery.' She stared at the half-eaten slice in her hand. 'Pretty much everything from that time was destroyed in the fire. There were no photos, no mementos. Even my original birth certificate and other records were lost.'

'Couldn't you ask your father?' Silence stretched. He tried again. 'Surely Dean would know more.'

'I'll ask him when I see him next.'

'That'll be the funeral. Wouldn't it be better to call him now?'

She closed her eyes and bit through the thick, cheese-covered crust. Her expression declared 'do not disturb', her focus solely on the food in her mouth. She chewed, swallowed, blinked, sipped at her wine.

By the time her gaze reconnected with his, any and all emotion was gone. 'Heard from your parents yet?'

His head jerked back as he waited for that familiar emptiness to swallow his insides. It did, although with less vigour than in the past. 'This isn't about me.'

'Maybe not. But I'd like to enjoy my food without being reminded there's someone out there who wants me dead, or worse. Just five minutes' respite. Is that too much to ask?'

Her whole diversion tactic and conversation round-about made his head spin. Not that he didn't get how hard this all was for her. But how the hell was he supposed to keep up?

'No, I haven't heard from them. But they probably haven't received the message yet.' Automatic pilot had kicked in, making him tell the same old story, all the while hating himself for defending them.

She reached for her wine, gripping it to her chest, her knuckles glistening starkly against the clear glass.

Barely a movement, then her next breath shuddered out through her lips. 'I haven't spoken to Mum yet.' Her voice was soft, her head bent so the words were almost lost in her drink.

'You mean lately?'

'No. I mean yet. As in, since Bec.'

His beer stilled en route to his mouth. 'Why?'

'I don't know. She won't return my calls.'

'What does your dad say?'

'That she's not coping. That she'll call me when she can.'

'Maybe it's just as he says.'

She shook her head, her bleak expression a reflection of his own in pasts not yet distant enough. Her eyelids fluttered as she chased back a fresh flow of tears. 'Growing up, I was always Daddy's little girl and Bec was Mum's. They were close, really close. Now that Bec's gone . . .'

'You'll be daughter to them both.'

'I don't know if I'm enough.'

Her words wrenched at memories, dragging them up from his heart to his throat so that he struggled for breath.

'Seth, *what if I'm not enough?*'

Jayda gulped down her wine, the alcohol scalding the back of her throat in the process.

*Just desserts.*

As soon as she'd said those five needy words, she regretted them. Words like that defined a person, and they weren't her. *This* wasn't her. She was a homicide detective hunting a killer. Now was the worst possible time for her defences to crumble. She'd already had one lapse of control for the evening. The last thing she needed was another. She pushed up from the couch. 'So, let's see if my theory on the key holds up.'

Grabbing it and her laptop, she sank back into the couch, balancing the key on the computer just below the screen. Her fingers raced over the keyboard without waiting for Seth to comment or offer input.

He did, regardless. 'It's from a security deposit box.'

Pine filled her nostrils and the cushion beside her dipped. He made himself comfortable, too close for sensible thought. Heat scampered across the side of her body adjacent to his, their thighs so close nothing more than a cat's whisker separated them.

She riveted her eyes to the screen. 'You got part A of a two part question right, Einstein. Now for part B. A security deposit box from where?'

He took the key and turned it in his hands. 'It could be from anywhere.' His breath fanned her hair and she fought the urge to turn, to bring her lips in line with his.

'Not just anywhere. Here.' She turned the screen, so he could see better, so he didn't have to lean further in and send her body's already screaming senses into hyperventilation.

'Black Keys Security? You know this, how?'

'The colour of the key, along with its size and shape. When Dad was undercover we used a deposit box there as a means to get messages to him safely. And once he returned home, he decided to keep it for a bit of fun, every once in a while leaving little notes and surprises for Bec and me to find.'

The memory thickened her throat. She swallowed. Focused on the blinking cursor in the middle of the screen.

'There must be other places that use black keys.'

'Perhaps. But I've a hunch this is the place.'

She turned. So close she could see silver lights shimmer in his irises. Her lips parted, tingled. *Closer.* She wavered, he moved in.

Her head jerked back and she averted her gaze to stare once again at the computer screen. 'I guess we'll find out tomorrow.'

'You have Bec's funeral.'

His mouth was still so close. So reachable.

'In the morning. Our afternoon is free.' She moved off the couch, out of his heat, and set her computer aside. 'Now we only have two things left to figure out.'

His brow arched, dragging her mind back to their initial meeting and the bad-boy look that had her hooked from that very first moment.

She swallowed. 'What's for dessert and where is Madden's child now.'

Jayda watched Seth all but lick his bowl clean of Ben & Jerry's Chocolate Therapy and sprinkles. He was like a little boy in an ice-cream parlour for the first time. At a guess, the treat wasn't something he'd enjoyed much as a child. If ever.

He eyed her bowl. She wrapped her arm around it and moved it closer. Countering any designs he may have on stealing hers, she scooped up the last few melted, multi-coloured spoonfuls.

They worked well together. She'd even moved past the fact that he was a reporter and not to be trusted. So far, every one of his actions indicated otherwise. They'd long since finished their coffee, so Seth made another. The caffeine helped her think. Sleep was overrated, and unlikely with or without the buzz she was all but throwing at her system. Munching on a packet of salt and vinegar chips—a weakness they discovered they shared—they outlined what needed doing over the next couple of days. An extension of the list she'd started earlier.

As she chased the last crumbs in the almost empty foil wrapper, Seth glanced at his watch. Then his mobile. Then her.

'It's past midnight.' He pushed himself up from the armchair. 'We should get some sleep.'

Her heart jolted and she grabbed at her computer, thwarting its slide down her legs and onto the floor. 'There's still a heap to do.'

'Nothing that can't be done tomorrow.'

'I'm not ready for bed yet.'

'Well, I am.' He stretched and looked around. 'Where's your spare room?'

Everything in her body froze. 'You—you're not *staying*.'

She inhaled. Deep. To steady the shake in her voice, along with the nerves jumping like crazy, everywhere. It didn't help that the scent of pine and spring was making her dizzy. Dumping her computer onto the cushions, she stood. He wouldn't intimidate her with height. And he wouldn't stay when there was a tiny, unsubstantiated part of her that wanted it. *Needed it.* To feel alive.

Bad idea. At this point, she didn't need protection from outside forces. She needed protection from herself.

'I'm not asking, Jayda. I said I wouldn't leave you alone, and I meant it.' Less than two steps away, his skin radiated heat; wild flames that licked and snatched and caressed the length of her body. Made her want to burn. Unashamedly.

Every instinct said *retreat*, but with the couch at her back, it was impossible. She wouldn't run, not again. The action was cowardice, and a coward she was not. It was time to face Seth head-on and strip him back, layer by layer, until the power he had over her receded.

Then they could move forward and all this ridiculous sexual nonsense would be behind them.

She squared her shoulders. 'Bully tactics won't work. I've seen and tried them all.'

He moved in. Everything stopped. Including her breath, which jammed inside her throat along with any chance at speech. She wanted to breach that final distance. So much. To feel live, pulsing flesh pressed hard against hers.

She wanted all that ridiculous sexual nonsense.

# Chapter Thirty-Six

**S**eth cupped her cheek, brushing his thumb along her trembling lips, his voice shivering up her spine. 'I don't bully. I play nice. Very. Very. Nice.' Humour slid a path across his lips and his chin dimpled in that way which stole every bit of staunch from her knees. 'Would it kill you to let me in?'

She swallowed, her voice coming out all husky. 'I told you, I don't mix—'

'Business with pleasure?' He leaned closer, the whisper of his breath tantalising her to open up and do as he asked. Let him in. 'It would be pleasure, Jayda. We both know you know it. And that's why you're running scared.'

Seth slid his hand back, combing his fingers through Jayda's hair to cup the back of her head.

'You've got a girlfriend.'

'I do?' His lips twitched, fighting a smile that would surely aggravate her.

'Yes! You had a date.'

'With a work colleague. And believe me, there is no stretch of the imagination large enough to place Richard in the role of my girlfriend.'

Her eyes widened, then narrowed. 'You misled me.'

'No. You did that all by yourself.' He moved closer. 'With maybe a little help. But you were so . . .'

'Irresistible?'

'Immovable.'

The scent of windswept meadows and green apples intoxicated

him. He inhaled, drowning in the sensation. 'You hooked me so bad I tried that juvenile stunt just to get your attention. And I'd say it worked. Jayda, we want each other, we're both available, consenting adults. No reason now to hold back.'

'I have rules.' The words toppled out in an agonised whisper, from lips which trembled and taunted him.

He dragged his thumb back across her mouth and watched the bottom lip plump and darken. 'I don't care.' He dipped his head, slow, giving her time to back away.

Her pupils glazed, almost swallowing the lush green of her irises. She didn't move, so he didn't stop. When their lips merged, the past days' anticipation exploded between them.

She moaned. Memories of unfinished business drew his hand to her hip, urging it to slide behind and pull her closer. Her tongue skimmed along his teeth and entered his mouth with unequivocal need, the sensation slamming his groin with the force of a supersonic cruise missile.

No way could she deny it now. She wanted this. No trumped-up rule system would let him believe otherwise. They'd been inching towards this moment since the second they met. It was inevitable, the most natural progression in the world. And regardless of guilt—misplaced or not—stopping wasn't an option.

He needed to feel her skin, beneath his fingertips, against his body. He found her waist and slid his hand beneath her tee. Soft, warm silk waited for him as he smoothed his palm along her back and up towards her shoulder blades. She shivered and he pulled her closer, the throb of his erection finding solace between her thighs.

Peeling his lips from hers, he made to drag her top up and over her head. She pulled back, her chest heaving with every gasping breath as she tugged the hem down over her jeans. 'We can't do this.'

His heart continued to thump, even as it plummeted towards the plush carpet at his feet. 'You're kidding.'

She turned away. 'That never happened.'

'Felt pretty real to me.'

'It was wrong.'

Tense fingers slewed through his hair. 'How can something this good be wrong? It doesn't make sense, Jayda. You wanted that kiss as much as I did.'

'I have rules, Seth.'

'Which you want to break.'

'Maybe so, but that doesn't mean it's right.' Her voice wobbled.

Sliding his hand around her waist, he pulled her in. 'Giving in to your desires isn't weakness, Jayda. It's strength. It's following your convictions and saying to hell with everything but what you feel.'

His hands slid under her tee and up over her back, and she shuddered into him. Whatever her rules, whatever she wished to believe, this reaction was real. She wanted him. And God, he wanted her! He rolled the fingers of one hand down her back to clutch her bottom and pull her closer still.

They fit, the perfect complement, like pizza and cheese.

Jayda's heart galloped through her chest like a stallion on steroids. Every part of her body bar her brain agreed with Seth. A majority vote.

*To hell with everything but what you feel.*

If she could . . . Just. Stop. Thinking. About everything. Escape the blunt reality of her life and trade it for a few moments of peace.

This could be the way.

Not leaning so much as giving in to temptation for one brief, beautiful moment. She'd wanted Seth the second she'd seen him in that house. It'd be stupid—and untrue—to admit any different. The more time passed, the more her reasons for holding back became forfeit. Or so lame that she couldn't dredge up the means to fight anymore.

Even with that damned paper in her pocket.

His fingers tightened about her waist and she trembled. The anticipation and *need* to feel them on her breasts, taunting, stroking, squeezing . . . She groaned, and his expression told her he knew she was his. *Tonight only.*

Need ribboned through her quivering body like flames stroking the logs in a fire. She couldn't keep saying no. Had lost all strength to deny herself any longer. She wanted Seth. He just didn't need to know how much.

'This is a bad idea.'

He inched her tee up and she lifted her arms, letting him slide it over her head before her trembling fingers moved without conscious thought towards his buttons.

'Yeah, bad,' he agreed, never once detaching his gaze from hers as he tossed her top behind him.

'Very bad.' She did the same with his, leaving his chest bared, beautiful. Just as she remembered.

Running her palms along the planes of his stomach, her fingers explored along the waistband of his trousers.

His breath hitched, his mouth swooping to capture hers. 'Mmm.'

'Terrible.' Her words were muffled as he worked at the clasp of her jeans.

'Uh huh.' His hand slid between the denim and black cotton briefs, and the flesh between her thighs gave an almighty shudder.

She still hadn't bought those lacy, silky panties. Too late now. And what did it matter when she'd be out of them soon anyway?

The thought sent another shudder coursing through her.

His fingers slipped down further still, and her sex contracted as if he were inside. As if it had been waiting her whole life for this moment and couldn't bear a second longer.

'You're way overdressed for what I have in mind.' The breath against her ear blew hot and wet, his voice low and deep as his words sent thrill after thrill though her body.

She closed her eyes and sank into the sensation. 'This doesn't mean I like you.'

'I know.'

'Or that I want you to stay.'

'I know.'

'This is the one and only, the absolutely last time this is going to happen.'

He raised his head, his face melting into that to-die-for grin. 'We'd better make the most of it then, hadn't we?'

# Chapter Thirty-Seven

'**K**iss me.' Seth grabbed the open tab of her jeans and tugged.

She stumbled into him and clutched his shoulders for balance. Taut muscle flexed beneath her palms, heat and hunger zapping every living, breathing cell in her body. Not the pizza-craving hunger she'd felt earlier. This was deeper, earthier. Animal.

*To hell with everything but what you feel.*

Her heartbeat drummed in her ears. She wanted to feel Seth. Lose herself in him, in *this*. Until every heart-wrenching, soul-slamming bit of her life receded into obscurity.

She wrapped her hands behind his neck, pulled his head down and lifted her lips to meet his. Her breath caught, firelights erupting inside her brain. Lips so soft, so gentle. Seemingly impossible when their touch was charged with such fire and tempest.

At first he let her own the kiss, a slow, erotic trail into mindlessness. But when she dared flick her tongue between his lips, they hardened as he at once reclaimed it, and her. He reached back to unhook her bra, and she tugged the straps down her arms, curving her body away from his to allow the fabric to fall somewhere at their feet. Then blissfully, mercifully, her skin coupled again with his.

His hands found her breasts, the powerful length of his thighs marching her backwards, slamming her into the wall, rattling the keys on the hall table beside them. He threaded his fingers with hers and locked them above her head, making the air whoosh from her lungs as he took her lips and swallowed every last breath. He tasted of coffee and pizza and promises to come.

Rough denim bit into her flesh. The pain mixed with pleasure and she moaned into him as she felt the thrust of his erection between her thighs.

His lips found her neck, and that wondrous curve where it joined her shoulder. She shivered, every nerve in her body firing on full-throttle. Then he sucked, and her sex pulsed. Needy. Hungry. Impatient.

He nibbled her earlobe, drawing it into his mouth, robbing oxygen clear from her lungs. But when his hand skimmed her tummy and slid between her thighs, her heart faltered, then stopped beating altogether. Her hands dropped to his shoulders before the jelly in her legs could make her slither to the ground. The tortuous, barely there stroke of his fingers had her eyes slamming open and her hips bucking uncontrollably.

*'Oh!'*

He rubbed again and her body shuddered, her sex contracting in hungry, grasping need. For him. Then his breath fanned her ear and he yanked at her waistband. 'These need to go.'

*Yes.*

Their fingers scrabbled at her jeans, dragging the material down her thighs as his mouth slipped lower still and found her breast.

*Holy hell!* Her legs buckled, everything below her waist a boneless, liquid, quivering stupor. Fists of denim filled her palms as she clung to him, his hands on her thighs, her jeans scrunched at her ankles the only things keeping her from dissolving onto the floor.

She tried to widen her legs, feel more of him where she wanted him most. Impossible with her jeans stuck. She kicked off her shoes, then wriggled and stomped until her feet were free. Knees locked, she fumbled at his zip, moaning as his teeth rasped over her nipple before he moved to the other.

Every nip, every graze, sent her soaring body higher than she'd imagined possible. She shoved at his waistband until it inched past his hips, allowing her to forage beneath his jocks to hard, throbbing muscle, hot and, oh, so big. Ready for her.

She ignored the inner quiver of her stomach muscles.

Wrapping him in her fingers, she squeezed, his groan and the thrust of his hips making her feel powerful. Decadent. Ready.

Seth wanted her, with no other agenda but satisfaction. One night of passion, no strings. That was enough.

He lifted his head, his eyes gun-metal grey and all-encompassing. Sweat slicked his chest, a smorgasbord of bronzed skin and muscle, hers for the taking.

She ducked. His nipple, hard and flat beneath her tongue, tasted of salt and Seth; a virile, sexy, all-male tang that exploded against her taste buds and made her crave him all the more.

Strong hands cupped her bottom and squeezed, pulling her towards him. She moved to the other nipple, this time grasping it between her teeth and tugging as she recalled him doing to hers. His nails clutched deep into her flesh as he groaned and bucked his hips.

She seemed to be doing all the right things, could tell he was clinging desperately to control, even if only by a thread.

Eternal love may not exist, but this hunger, this aching, empty need, was real.

*No. More. Waiting.*

'Seth, I want you.'

'You have me.'

He growled into her skin as she squeezed her hand again, running her palm up and then down his length, feeling the pulse of his need as surely as hers was making itself known between her thighs.

'Not all of you, yet.' She opened her legs, guided him closer, rubbing his tip *there*.

*So good.*

'I want you inside me. *Now*. I can't wait any longer.'

Seth's cock pulsed, the only thinking, cognisant organ in his body.

Whatever control he'd clung to fled in a blast of sensation as tentative fingers slid lower still to cup and squeeze his balls. He shuddered, so tight that bursting like some feverish adolescent was a real possibility. He'd never wanted anything more than he wanted Jayda right now.

Two sidesteps right and he lifted her onto the little table beside them; not such a useless hunk of wood, after all.

Her keys clattered onto the floor. He didn't care. He eased her knees apart and moved in. Her eyes widened. Skimming his hands over her buttocks, he urged her forwards until she was right where he needed her.

Gaze locked in an ocean of liquid green, he shifted his hips and perched just shy of heaven, her trembling wet heat taunting his tip with the promise of more.

He leaned in, inhaled apples and arousal, shuddered as her hands grazed his chest, scraping his nipples, lower, stopping short where he nestled between her thighs. Her lips hovered inches from his and he took them again, hard and hungry, and thrust inside. Slick, tight.

She stiffened, gasped, her surrounding flesh constricting until he felt he might explode.

Her shock became his. He froze.

*Shit!*

He'd swear this wasn't her first time, but he'd bet it came pretty damn close. Her reaction spoke volumes. She'd tensed, that very last second. As if expecting something other than enjoyment. Like she'd been hurt in the past. Like he was hurting her now, making her relive that moment.

The thought slumped like wet cement in his chest.

He tried to withdraw, tried not to hurt her further. Her lips clamped, her hands scrambling to his butt, pulling, her hips bucking to maintain the contact. 'Don't stop.'

'I'm hurting you.'

'You're not.'

The lines cutting her brow told another story.

Pain. Surprise. Shock. She'd displayed it all. And he wanted to know why. Palms pressed against the wall either side of her, he pushed back, painfully aware he was still inside her—and that this wasn't how he'd envisaged this moment.

'What happened?'

She locked her gaze to somewhere beyond his left ear. 'We were having sex.'

'Not that. You know what I mean.'

'You want to have a D and M *now*, while we're like *this*?'

He raised a brow. Waited.

She scrunched her eyelids and inhaled. When she opened her eyes again, a mask drove the uncertainty from her expression. The cop was back. 'Don't make me hurt you, Seth Friedin.' The words rasped, the fingers on his buttocks digging into his flesh. 'You're not stopping now.'

Discomfort. Forced bravado. Humour. It was all there. She tried so hard to be tough, to be strong and stand alone. If only she'd let go, for just a moment, let him in . . .

Even now, so close, her mask forged a distance between them. Always a distance.

He was going to breach that void if it killed him.

His right hand cupped her cheek, then slipped beneath her hair to caress her neck. 'I don't want to stop any more than you do. But I won't hurt you either.' His thumb brushed her cheek. 'Do you trust me?'

Her eyes widened, their gaze piercing his soul. Her breath caught mid-inhalation. *'Yes.'*

One whispered word, a hundred-pound weight on his chest.

He should have said something then. Anything. But his throat was so thick, he couldn't for the life of him find his voice.

The hold on his buttocks wavered then loosened. He eased out.

*Shit! No condom.* What was he thinking?

Precisely the problem. He wasn't. Didn't seem capable of that one process where Jayda was concerned. He tugged his jeans back up over his hips, and stared into her wide, unfathomable eyes for seconds that felt longer.

She blinked. Averted her gaze.

A lock of red covered one eye and he swept it back. 'It'll be amazing between us. You'll see.' Dropping a kiss to her forehead, his lips lingered, his senses drenched in windswept orchards and her, then he whispered. 'Come with me.'

She nodded, allowing him to slide her down from the table, wrap her fingers in his and lead her to the bedroom. Then, with a quick squeeze of her hand and a whispered 'back in a sec', he headed for her en suite.

The bathroom door clicked to. Even before it closed, he slumped against it, mentally kicking his butt from here to the deepest, darkest jungles of Africa.

*What the hell is wrong with you? Ramming into her like a frigging bull on heat. Forgetting to use protection.*

Losing every modicum of sense he might have owned. For what? All he'd managed to do was scare the shit out of her, and remind her of some past hurt she'd rather forget.

He slammed his head back, achieving a well-deserved pound against his skull. He'd known Jayda didn't do casual. Didn't sleep with just anyone. Until that night at The Traveller.

His heart thudded.

He still didn't have a clue what had driven her to act so out of character. He hoped it was him. That he was the difference. The thought froze, like stalactites jutting from the walls of his chest, and the next thought only added to the frost. Because she was the difference for him.

Realisation hit. *Hard.* Jayda was more than just a one-night fling, or—shoot him for even thinking it—more than a story.

He couldn't put a name to what he felt right now, it was just *more*.

He sluiced water over his hands and face, didn't stop to think what he was about to do. About the responsibility.

Jayda didn't trust anyone. Yet tonight she was willing to trust him. Despite all she'd been through, all *they'd* been through. No time now to consider the implications or how that made him feel. Or the importance he could place on this moment if he allowed his thoughts freedom to take root and grow.

It was just enough to know that she was giving him a second chance.

# Chapter Thirty-Eight

Jayda checked the blinds. The wooden slats rattled beneath her fingers as she tried to still them.

*Impossible.*

Her robe chafed her bare, still buzzing skin and she shivered despite its warmth. Her heart wouldn't stop ramming against her ribcage.

Was it possible to bungle sex? Heat scampered through her body and she scrunched her eyelids closed. The answer had to be *yes*. Otherwise she'd just managed the impossible.

*Idiot!*

She was acting like a twenty-year-old virgin. Like she didn't know a thing about sex. She *did*. She'd had sex before. Mediocre, missionary and three times.

And not one of those experiences had prepared her for Seth.

Her body still hummed, yearned. Wanted him. All the more for his tenderness, after she'd acted like some wide-eyed teenage innocent.

Her scorched skin burned anew. How could she face him now? What did he think of her? Would it bother him, now he knew just how inexperienced she was?

Should she care if it did?

A somersault of craziness crammed her brain.

*Sex with Seth.*

Every list she'd devised against this moment evaporated. Their connection, their attraction. It was electrifying. Heart-racing. Terrifying as all hell.

Did he still want her?

Her grip on the blinds tightened. Memories of Liam would *not* taint this moment. If Seth was willing to see this through, she would *not* freeze a second time round.

Hard, masculine heat welded itself to her back and she couldn't stem the impulse to sink into it.

Warm breath fanned her ear. 'Miss me?'

Her laugh erupted without warning, relaxing her shoulders. 'I'd hate to pander to your ego.'

'God forbid you ever do that.' His palm rode up along her arm before encouraging it away from the blinds. 'The blinds are fine.'

She glanced at the spectrum analyser and, much as he couldn't see her face, he guessed her thoughts. 'We've already checked twice this evening. The room is clear.'

Her hand dropped to her side as his skimmed up to cup her breasts. His palms weighed against their underside, the thumb and forefinger of each hand reaching up to taunt the nipples beneath the fabric into submission.

Her gaze fell to the gap between photos on her dressing table before darting to her bookcase, and the now empty shelf where her books had screened the camera from view. How could she have forgotten?

In the heat of the moment. A storm of sensation.

*Seth didn't use a condom.*

The thought slammed her chest, robbing the air from her lungs.

*Hell!* If she hadn't frozen . . .

But she had, and now in the light of the aftermath, the real world had nudged back inside her thoughts to haunt her. 'It needs to be dark.'

'I want to see you.' His fingers tugged ecstasy into the taut, sensitive buds, and she fought the well of sensation which would have her forget everything.

*Not yet.*

'You'll have to see me with the lights off.' She wriggled out of his arms, and the loss of his warmth sent chills up and down her torso, regardless of the thick towelling that covered it.

A flick of the switch transformed the room into a jumble of shadows, stretching and dancing within the gentle glow of the hallway light.

He caught her hand and tugged her to him. 'Why the robe?' His fingers made to untie the belt.

She stalled his hands, and for the first time since he returned, met his gaze. 'I'm sorry, Seth.'

'That was my line.' His grin faltered. 'Want to talk about it?'

'No.'

He nodded. Let it go. But there was a light in his eyes that said he wouldn't let it go forever.

He refocused his attention on her belt, tugging gently until it loosened and fell free. Her breath stalled. With feather-like touches he inched the lapels apart, his gaze rolling across her bare skin like a desert sandstorm. Only the muted darkness stopped her from crossing her arms over her breasts.

His hands slid over her shoulders, edging the material down her arms until it slithered to the ground. 'I'm glad we're starting over. This way I get to enjoy every inch of you.'

Hands on her hips, his jeans-clad body melded to hers, and he walked her backwards until her knees hit the mattress, tumbling her onto the bed.

She shimmied back against the pillows. His heavy heat gone, she shivered.

*Missing him.*

She wouldn't give weight to that notion.

And she wouldn't freeze now, when she wanted this. Needed this. Seth filling her body, her mind, her everywhere, until the outside world receded and there was no room for anything but him.

Pushing up onto her elbows, her eyes strained through dusky shadows to glimpse the body she'd waited forever to see again. A contrast of light and shade; hard, sculpted muscle encased in taut, supple skin. Her memory hadn't lied.

The rasp of his fly charged the silence, followed by the swish of fabric as he eased the denim down his thighs. There was a slap as they fell to the carpet, then a softer whisper as his jocks followed suit.

His palms seared her thighs as he kneeled between her legs, hands skimming upwards, head dipped, mouth inches from where she throbbed uncontrollably. And much as she craved his touch, the darkness wasn't enough to make her feel comfortable about him being there.

She grabbed his wrist. 'Something up here needs your attention.'

She could sense his smile as his body slid up hers until their mouths were only inches apart.

'And that is?'

'This.' She brushed her lips to his, her stomach quivering beneath the tormenting trail of his fingertips.

Almost enough to make her forget.

Seth revelled in Jayda's unchecked reaction to the play of his hand across her skin. She still wanted him, regardless of his blunder earlier, and this time he'd make damn certain he didn't mess up again.

Light from the hall allowed him access to her awkwardness. Something she needed to move past before they could move on and lose themselves in each other.

But first, he needed to check one last time. He turned her to face him, framing her face between his palms. 'Do you trust me?'

Her body tensed, her gaze riveted to his. She held her breath, blinked once, twice, and nodded. The slightest of movements, slow, imperceptible, but it blasted his brain.

He swallowed, somehow locating his voice. 'I want you to enjoy every second of this, so you need to relax. Can you do that?'

She nodded again, her hands curled in front of her chest as if she were suddenly shy of using them.

'For you to relax, you need to understand what's about to happen.' He rubbed his thumb across her bottom lip, felt it soften and swell beneath his touch.

'First, I'm going to kiss you thoroughly, starting here.' His fingers trailed over her lips, over her chin, downward.

She held her breath, her wide-eyed gaze never once leaving his.

'Then I'll kiss my way to your neck, your shoulder, your breasts, sucking each of your nipples in turn.'

With every word, his hand mimicked where eventually his mouth would follow and her body shuddered in reaction. His fingertip circled a nipple and it puckered, tightened, raspberry-ready and, oh, so deliciously ripe.

He crossed to the other. 'Next I'll kiss every inch of your ribs, your belly, and keep going until I reach here.' He cupped her sex and her muscles tightened.

*Anticipation.* He felt it too. Wanted her so damn much his voice had lodged halfway down his throat. 'When I'm between your legs, my tongue will taste you and taunt you and make you crazy until you come against it.'

His finger pressed against her clit. Her eyes closed and her mouth plumped open, emitting a soft, silent sigh.

The invitation was unequivocal, so he gave in on a growl and dropped his lips to hers.

# Chapter Thirty-Nine

Jayda trembled.

Seth's mouth sashayed down her body, every suck and sweep driving her further into mindlessness. The thought of where he was headed . . .

But he'd asked her to trust him. Strangely, it wasn't a stretch. In all the crazy, mixed-up lunacy that was her life, he was the one constancy she could depend on. Even in those moments when she'd treated him like crap.

So, she focused on the whisper of his lips and tried not to think about how she'd feel when he reached his destination.

His palms revered and caressed, as if she were special, treasured, as if he couldn't imagine anything more exquisite. Warm lips followed his hands and her stomach quivered, starting a slow, resonant throb deep between her thighs. Anticipation. Impatience. *Need.* Every bone in her body as liquid as the blood that raced through it.

He edged downwards, his lips skimming lower—through the triangle of hair she'd considered trading for a Brazilian—and he didn't stop. The abrasive sweep of his palms slid upwards to ease her legs apart. Her heart thundered, breath caught in her throat.

First instincts screamed for her to freeze, to clamp her legs and pull away. She tensed.

Feather-like touches rolled over her breasts, his thumb and forefinger plucking her nipples, tweaking, twirling . . . and she forgot. Lost sense of everything but Seth.

Fire swirled low in her tummy as sensation exploded between her legs. Then he licked.

*Oh. My. Lord.*

Every muscle inside clenched. Nothing had ever felt so *good.* So decadent. Like double-whipped triple-chocolate ice cream, steeped in steamy-hot chocolate fudge sauce.

His tongue swirled and a deep, guttural moan filled the air. Hers. He laved and swirled and laved and tugged, and she lost the part of her mind centred on coherent thought. Sheets fisted in her palms, her head twisting and turning, each new sensation hitting with the force of a tidal wave. Tension rose and whirled, a feeling of tottering on the edge of an abyss, wanting to plunge in, yet wanting to draw out every second.

And she would have done just that, if his fingers hadn't left her breast to delve between her legs and deep into her flesh. She gasped, drowning, reeling in wave after rapturous wave.

In a haze, she felt his withdrawal, heard his fumbled search on her bedside table. The tissue box thumped onto the floor. Foil rustled distantly. Only vaguely did she thank him for remembering this time.

Her body cried out. Empty. Impatient. She reached for his shoulders, enjoying the slide of his skin and the gentle nudge of him just where she needed him.

His lips found hers, tasting of musk, soft, sensual caring, and Seth. As his tongue swirled inside her mouth, she felt the pull of flesh between her thighs. He edged inside, then stopped. There was that brief sensation he was too big, she too small. She gripped his shoulders, her flesh pulsing, stretching, moulding.

*God, it felt* . . . words didn't describe how frigging amazing it felt. Better than anything she'd experienced. Ever.

His mouth left hers in a rush of breathlessness to find that spot between neck and shoulder only he knew how to find. The brush of his lips was slow, luxurious. Exquisite.

The muscles hovering above her tummy tightened as his hand crept down to touch her—

*There.*

White light burst across her vision and the easing spasms intensified. Her sex tightened, clutching, pulling him inward, greedy for more.

She wanted more.

Lifting her hips, she pushed, a delicious slide of flesh against flesh. Solid muscle rippled beneath her palms as her hands skimmed from his shoulders out over his back. Their heated breaths mingled, her heart pumping so hard it should have leaped clear from her chest.

No thoughts now but one. *Don't stop!*

She closed her eyes. Losing herself, in the moment, in Seth. The feeling new and unusual, but strangely comfortable. And right. Sure fingers strummed between her legs, growing the sensation, zinging nerve endings throughout her body until every part of her hummed with mindless pleasure.

Her eyes fluttered open.

He lifted his head, his hazed outline suspended above her, the deep lines on his face tight with restraint.

'Okay?'

Her heart faltered and she choked her reply. 'More than.'

*'Good.'* The whisper was lost as he kissed her mouth, moving his hips, gently drawing out and in, building the pressure with slow, soft attention.

Her hands circled his back and dropped downwards, clutching his buttocks, matching the clench and release of muscles as he filled her and then pulled back. Sensation swirled, her body light, detached, until she toppled over the edge, erupting in surge after surge of mind-melting rapture.

He stilled, as if sensing her need. As if her pleasure was steadfastly linked to his.

The rampant drum of her heart slowed.

Their gazes locked, gun-metal grey banishing the world outside. Everything but the man joined so wondrously to her. He ducked, brushed her lips and thrust, once, again, his magnificent body shuddering into her with abandon that stole her breath.

He collapsed, his weight on hers so natural, *so right.*

She sank back into the mattress as languor eddied into conscious thought. The race of her body slowed. The room returned. Dusky shadows on the ceiling above, the soft brush of the sheets below.

*Wow.*

*Spectacular* joined wow. Along with *mind-blowing.*

Imagination hadn't come close to what had just happened. Nothing had. And each time, it would only get better.

*Whoa!*

She blinked, double-time. What was she thinking? That this was permanent? Real?

Last time she boarded that hope-train, she'd barely avoided disaster. Not that Seth was anything like Liam. Then again, she wasn't anything like the girl she'd been back then.

Now she knew the value of restraint. Which made her thoughts all the more wayward. A female detective in a man's world. Scandal, even a hint, would only undermine how far she'd come.

She wouldn't undo years of control for one moment's pleasure.

*Perspective. Now. Deep breath.* The scent of pine and sex filled her nostrils. His lips brushed hers. Perspective dwindled.

He rolled off.

She shivered, missing his blanketed warmth, the removal of his weight and contact leaving her with an odd feeling of loss. Inexplicably contrary to her thoughts.

'You're cold.' He reached across and pulled the duvet up to cocoon her from behind.

Care. Concern. The realisation he'd ensured her pleasure— multiple times—before taking his own. They stole the words from her tongue.

Impossible to stall the rush of those thoughts through her heart's door. He caressed her cheek for seconds longer than a simple action required, before sliding out of bed.

'Back in a sec.' He shot her a grin that warmed her like no blanket before disappearing into the en suite.

Thoughts which had abandoned her only moments ago now surged back with a vengeance.

If she allowed her mind's ramblings free rein, she'd wonder at Seth's caring when he didn't love her, and Liam's lack after professing he did.

*If* she allowed it.

Before she'd wandered too far down that muddied track, Seth was back, edging onto the bed beside her, giving her reason to toss any thought that threatened her bliss. She tugged the duvet over his shoulder, feeling the warmth of the cover, the radiant warmth from his skin.

Hair flopped over her forehead and he softly tucked it behind her ear. The action tingled her skin, there, lower, before burrowing inside and tugging her heart.

If she closed her eyes and lost herself in the moment, she could almost believe it meant more . . .

*No.*

Maybe if they'd met under different circumstances, in a different life, where she still believed in love and marriage and fidelity and happy ever after.

Her hand jerked and she clenched it firmly beneath her chin. She had no idea where those thoughts came from, but they could go straight back where they belonged. There was no place for them here, in her bedroom, beneath her duvet which had never experienced a man until now.

She exhaled, let go of everything but the languorous aftermath of Seth's lovemaking.

His hand reached over to tug hers into its warmth. 'Okay?'

She nodded, fighting buffeting emotions triggered by his concern, her thoughts, the mess that was her life.

'Thank you. For . . . making just now special.' Benign sentiments after he'd turned the world on its axis for her. But what else could she say, with her senses still humming and her thoughts in a state of flux?

She watched the race of Seth's mind through his eyes, a wealth of unspoken questions just waiting to be voiced. His mouth opened, stalled, then slammed shut, delaying curiosity she knew would need satisfying.

Just not now.

His thumb rubbed across her knuckles, luxuriant, lulling, drawing her deeper towards drowsiness. Weight dragged at her eyelids and she gave in to the pull, allowing them to close, locking out the world and all that had gone wrong today so she could focus on what had gone right.

And maybe—just maybe—the fact that something had meant her sleep would be sound.

# Chapter Forty

Jayda whimpered.

*No!*

She shucked her bedcovers. Moaned. Tossed her head. One side. The other.

Arms flung outwards. Images. Scorching her brain. Flickering frame by frame across the insides of her eyelids.

*A woman weeping.*

Breath caught. She flipped onto her side. The other. Lips moving, soundless. Pleading.

Nothing changed. The motion picture sliced through her subconscious, rolling, never-ending, as if the reels that fed it had a life of their own.

*A scream.*

*A name that slipped her mind before it had time to stick.*

*A banana moon. Legs running. The smell of wet dirt. The sense of loss. Death.*

Her eyes shot open.

She bolted upright, shaking, cold, slathered in sweat. Her hands flew to her face, her cheeks a dry crust of makeup and tears.

'Jayda?'

She turned to the voice, only then registering she wasn't alone.

Seth pushed himself up, his bare torso reminding her of the night before. The fact that she was naked, too. She grabbed at the sheets and pulled them up to her chin.

Her bedside clock said it was 4 am.

The hour varied, the dream never did—a runaway rollercoaster of colour and sound that made no sense. It charged full-throttle through her brain, leaving her alone and grasping for some missing link always just there, barely beyond her fingertips.

'Are you okay?'

She nodded, sure if she tried to speak he'd guess just how un-okay she was.

He looped an arm around her shoulders. 'What happened?'

'A dream.' Her hands clenched tighter into the sheets.

'Nightmare, more like.' He pulled her into his arms and she buried her face, breathing in everything about him that gave her comfort. The race of her heart slowed.

'Want to tell me about it?'

She dragged in another mouthful of Seth-rich air and let it shudder out from her lungs. 'There's not much to tell.'

The words mumbled against his skin, and as they left her lips the rub of his hand over her back ceased.

*Please don't stop.*

She steeled herself and pulled back, just a little. Not ready to leave the cocoon of his warmth. 'Sometimes I have bad dreams.'

Cold still managed to shiver up her spine until he pulled her closer into his side.

'Dad told me they started after the fire, the day my birth mum and dad died. Then when I was five, some guy showed up to the precinct with a gun. I hid under the desk while he shot two officers.'

*Chair legs scraping. Blood dripping. Screams buffeting her eardrums.*

She clenched her eyes against the memory. Inhaled. 'He was finally subdued, but the nightmares started up again, this time much worse.'

Disparities between that day and the dream's images she wouldn't delve into.

'How recurring are they?'

'You mean, how often?' She swallowed. 'Lately, most nights.'

The arm around her tensed. 'That's a mighty big reaction for something that happened so long ago.'

'It's not as if we can choose what affects us and what doesn't. One image mixed with a child's imagination is all it takes to throw things out of proportion.'

'Have you ever talked to anyone about it?'

'You mean a shrink?'

He nodded.

'After my parents died, of course. But I was two, and didn't remember much of what happened. Then a few months after the shooting I saw a police psychologist, and the nightmare disappeared for a while. Most times I don't dream at all. But since the Trentham Case they've resurfaced. They tend to do that when I'm stressed or working a particularly bad case.'

'Do you remember what you dream?'

Like countless times before, she searched her memory and got nothing but a dry mouth and rabid pound against her skull. And a chaotic jumble of picture fragments that made no sense.

She floundered, lost, grasping. As if something were missing. *What?* She shook her head.

Seth considered her through hooded lids. 'Ever wondered if the nightmare could be about more than something you saw twenty or so years ago?'

She pulled back. 'Why would I?'

'I don't know. Perhaps seeing someone as an adult would expose the real source behind it.'

'Perhaps.' She edged out of his arms, still grasping the sheet to her breasts, and shuffled downwards to rest her head on her pillow.

'Promise me you'll think about it.'

'Sure.'

Seth's expression left her in no doubt that he wasn't fooled by her answer. It wasn't as if she'd made a habit of taking his advice before.

Her yawn was genuine, but timely. And hopefully enough to waylay conversation she'd rather have *never*. Although she knew enough about Seth to know *that* was wishful thinking.

He dropped down beside her, head on his pillow so they rested nose almost to nose, chin almost to chin. She edged back to gain breathing space but his gaze still bored through the distance, its heat scorching her head to toe.

'Why, Jayda?'

Her breath caught and stuck. 'Why what, Seth?'

Not that she needed to ask. *Never* had come all too soon. And much as she dreaded the conversation, neither did she want it hanging above them, mushrooming into something bigger than it was.

Light from beyond the doorway illuminated his face, and she was glad hers was masked by shadows. She didn't need him reading her, a talent in which he seemed to excel. His gaze burrowed into hers and she matched it until she wondered whether he could see more after all.

She quickly closed her eyes. 'What are you asking? Why the

inexperience or why now?'

He seemed to consider. 'Both.'

She opened her eyes to find his still on her. It was unnerving, the intensity of that gaze. She dropped hers to the three o'clock shadow dusting his chin and wondered how a smattering of unshaven hair could be so sexy.

'I guess it's almost unheard of these days. A twenty-seven-year-old homicide detective with less sexual experience than most teenagers.'

She paused and his lips kicked upwards. 'Unusual, yes. But not necessarily in a bad way.'

She didn't know how to take that, so she didn't try.

Sorting through the jumble that was her thoughts, she let out a sigh. She'd never been a hasher and rehasher of life's crap. But something in Seth's gaze, some little flutter in her heart, made her want him to *get* why she was who she was.

She blocked her mind as to why him, why now, and forged on before she lost her nerve. 'My parents' marriage was always my idea of happiness. I grew up watching them love and support each other, always loving both Bec and me equally.'

A little corner of her heart twisted as she considered her mother's lack of contact lately, and whether that, too, was something she'd gotten wrong.

'You weren't wrong about that.'

Her gaze flew to his. Why was she surprised at Seth's insights into her mind? You'd think she'd be used to it by now. That uncanny knack he had of reading her.

'And you know this, how?'

'Gut instinct.'

Difficult to argue, considering her intuitions ran on the same oily rag. But it didn't mean she had to believe it.

'Since forever I'd wanted what my parents shared. I thought if I did what Mum did, I'd find what she found in Dad. It sounds ridiculous when I say it aloud, but back then it just seemed to make sense.'

She didn't wait for him to comment. Didn't need his thoughts on how naïve and stupid she'd been.

'I was twenty, the same age that Mum met Dad, when I met Liam. I was top of our class in the academy, he was second. We wanted so many of the same things. To excel, to reach detective before our thirtieth birthday. To meet and marry our soulmate.'

She couldn't help it. Her lips twisted. 'The one thing we didn't have in common was the one thing that counted most. He didn't feel the same way about me that I felt about him.'

Bitterness laced her tongue, the old pain an echo of its former self, but still there, still wreaking its havoc.

'It took a while, but when the rumours came full circle, I realised our relationship was about nothing more than undermining my reputation. He'd been spreading all kinds of lies behind my back. That I got into the academy because of my father. That I was succeeding because of my father. That everything I achieved was because of my father.' She swallowed. 'And then there were the other digs—I was a spoilt bitch using any means possible to get to the top.'

The cringe was instinctual. Even this many years past, the cut of Liam's words still stung. And even though those who knew her should have known better, the stain back then had still stuck. 'He used me to get what he wanted.'

Seth's expression hardened. 'I hope you got the bastard kicked out.'

'I'd have liked nothing more than to cut off his balls and play ping-pong with the damn things.' She inhaled, slow, tempering the burn in her chest as she dragged calm back into her body. 'I could have lodged a complaint, made him suffer for every nasty, bitter-stained word he uttered. But what would that accomplish? The stigma of ending a man's career before it started would have followed me. I'd be the bitch who got Liam expelled because I couldn't handle a bit of flack.'

'Sexual harassment's more than a bit of flack.'

'I know how these things play out, Seth. My complaint would have read like nepotism and Liam's lies would have taken on more than just a whiff of legitimacy.' She sighed. 'I didn't want my career tainted any further than it already was. I distanced myself, picked myself up, worked my butt off and graduated top of my class regardless of his aspersions. Even then, it didn't stop some from questioning whether I'd earned it or not.'

'The bastard.'

'And then some.'

'And you haven't been with anyone since? How long?'

'Seven years. And no.'

Seth looked thrown enough to hit something. No doubt Liam. Hell, she'd felt the same back then. Then she'd vowed to leave it all behind, had focused all that burning energy on her career instead.

Her fingers tightened around the duvet. 'I didn't give up on love, I just looked for it outside of the job.'

'Hence your business and pleasure, oil and water parallel.'

'Yeah.' She couldn't help the tug his words gave to her lips. 'And until recently, I still believed that love was out there, that I just hadn't found it yet.'

'Enter, your parents.'

She swallowed. Nodded. 'When Mum announced she and Dad were splitting—just before their twenty-fifth wedding anniversary, mind you—it threw me. Mum called Dad her first real love, said he was the first, last and only man, ever, for her.'

Tears pressed against her eyelids. She swallowed them back. 'It's not that I'm belittling everything they shared until now. Twenty-five years of marriage is a milestone and it shouldn't be underrated. But to end this way . . . If two of the most perfect people for each other can't make it, what chance do the rest of us have?'

'Happy ever after is a long time. If people are happy in the moment, what's wrong with that?'

Liquid green blinked, measuring him so thoroughly he had to temper his need to squirm. Then she licked her lips. 'Because when the moment's gone, they're all alone again.'

Seth watched the roll of emotions spill across Jayda's features. Pain, disbelief, yearning.

He got it. They were worlds apart on so many levels, yet their visions of love weren't so different. But where his came from longing, hers were born from a more tangible source—experience.

He shook the thought and the feeling it tugged along with it. What they both wanted or didn't, and why, weren't part of this. Helping Jayda, helping the investigation, was. Better he focus on her momentary slip, rather than his. 'We're still talking about your parents, right?'

Her fists clenched beneath her chin. 'Don't try to psychoanalyse me with the whole adopted kid, feeling abandoned, seeking security scenario. My biological parents didn't abandon me, they died. And my adoptive parents are still there for me, even if they're no longer there for me together.'

Her lips twisted and he knew she was thinking about her mother. Damn but the woman better have a ripper of an excuse for leaving her daughter when she most needed her.

Jayda's chin tilted. 'I'm simply making an educated decision based on precedent. Once upon a time I wanted what my parents had, but now I know what I wanted doesn't exist.'

'Just because it didn't happen for them, doesn't mean it won't happen for you.'

'Or Bec? Twice divorced. Even Grandpa Joe and Grandma Emily couldn't stick it out back in the days when you pledged to stay together for better or worse and meant it. Us Thomaszes aren't cut out for marriage.'

'Love and happiness aren't genetic, you know. And if they were, you wouldn't suffer the same end. You don't share the same genes.'

Her lips pressed tight. 'I'm as much a Thomasz as any member of my family.'

'I never said you weren't.'

She shook her head with that 'closed for business' sign he knew so well. 'It doesn't matter. You asked, I answered, discussion over.'

'I know why you closed off for so long. I still don't know why now, or why me.'

He saw the moment fight came to blows with flight. Her eyes widened. Narrowed. She double-blinked. 'That's enough open heart surgery for one day.' She flopped onto her back, glanced at her bedside clock before sheltering her face in her elbow. 'Three hours before I have to get up, listen to a stream of robotic condolences and mourn my sister. I need sleep.'

The words may have been harsh, but the tremble in her voice told another story.

He wheedled his arm beneath her shoulders and edged in until her head rested against the crook of his neck. While she didn't move closer, she didn't pull away either. Her moment of what she no doubt viewed as weakness was gone. The Jayda who sought nothing and no one was back. A woman he knew was just fooling herself.

They may not be destined for the same happily ever after, but that didn't mean she couldn't use his help. She *did* need someone other than herself to rely on. And, if nothing else, he'd convince her of that before the case closed and they were both left to go their separate ways.

# Chapter Forty-One

The lamp light above stuttered, then died.

His blood quickened.

He drew in a mouthful of car fumes and death. Most people found the dark terrifying. But then, most people were weak.

The lamp ahead flickered, and he waited a few seconds before it too went out. Amazing what one learned on the internet these days—bombs, makeshift firearms, how to short-circuit the city's street lighting. All there for any Tom, Dick or killer to find.

He dropped into a squat and slid his hand down limp flesh and bone, counting fingers until he'd located the one. The soft *crack* of cartilage slicing between the metal blades barely disrupted the silence.

He grinned into the nothingness. Revelled in it.

*Find something you enjoy and you'll never work a day in your life.* He didn't know where he'd heard the idiom, but it was first-rate advice. Life should be a thrill, and it was, every single day.

Both finger and cutter were dropped into plastic, along with his gloves, and he slid his forefinger and thumb across the top to seal the bag before slipping it into the hole in his jacket lining.

He straightened his legs and gasped as phlegm pitched up into his throat. His days may be numbered, but his legacy would far outlive the man who sustained it. Him. Not that useless waste of space who'd grown soft all those years in his prison cell. His demise was long overdue. Soon he'd join the woman who was good enough to fuck, but never good enough to marry.

A growl chased the bile burning up his oesophagus.

The old prick's decision had made him into the bastard he was today. That and his advice.

*Man up, boy. Who wants a pussy for a son?*

How about it, *Dad?* Am I man enough for you now?

# Chapter Forty-Two

Funny how the weather failed to reflect the mood at ground level.

Jayda tilted her face to the heavens. Clumps of puffy white clouds chased the sun across the broad, mostly blue sky. If the day were in a novel, no doubt the author would have written an expanse of looming grey and a sense of doom. There was none of that. She could revel in the warmth of the sun's rays on her skin and lose herself in the wonder of being alive.

If only her limbs didn't feel as though they were newly carved from a tree stump.

She stood at her father's side and, for the first time in twenty-plus years, felt as if she didn't belong.

People filled the grassy stretch of back garden for the post-funeral gathering, spilling up the stairs, past the life-sized placard of Bec's smiling face and into what was once her parents' home. Now her father lived there alone and her mother hadn't even bothered to show up to her own daughter's funeral.

If she'd had a hint of where to find her, Jayda would have confronted her and demanded answers. Only, she hadn't a clue. The situation stunk of dodge and she was left with nowhere to turn. And no one to turn to. Her father was no help.

An emotional storm brewed in her stomach as she nodded and smiled and returned inane comments with ones of her own. When all she wanted to do was kick and scream and throw things, and be anywhere else but here. 'I have to go.'

Her father's touch was like ice. 'You just got here.'

'I arrived an hour ago and I have an appointment.'

'What could be more important than being with your family?'

'Don't know, Dad. Perhaps you should ask Mum.' He withered before her eyes.

*Hell!* She was frustrated and disappointed and angry, but with her mother, not him. He'd been through the wringer, they all had. Last thing he needed was a dishing of more angst from his only surviving daughter.

'I'm sorry, Dad, I just . . .' Her vision blurred and she swallowed, fighting back the tide that would surely wash her away.

'Thought you might need this.' Seth sidled up between them, pressing a cool drink into her palm.

Memory skidded through her body as his fingertips brushed lightly over her hand and up her arm.

'Thanks.'

Their gazes tangled and a wild heat braised her cheeks. Surely every one of her emotions was bared for him to see.

She blinked. Shifted focus from his eyes to his lips and tried not to reflect how for a few amazing moments last night he'd made her forget the emotional soup that was her life. How she needed that distraction now.

He handed an identical glass to her father and proceeded to exchange niceties, effectively dissolving the tension between them.

She lifted the glass to her lips. Lemonade chilled a path down her throat, the cold inside warring with the radiant warmth from his body's proximity.

She edged away. This was all wrong, on more levels than she could put a list to. How could she think about sex, about wanting him again? *Here. Now.*

The moisture returned to her eyes, like a damned yo-yo forever bouncing back, and she blinked with more determination than before. There was still a killer to be caught.

Then, and only then, would she be free to mourn the loss of her sister. She felt a tap on her shoulder and turned.

'Darren!'

Without a word he wrapped her into his warmth, his arms around her like hot chicken soup for her soul. 'I'm so sorry, Jayda.'

The shudder of those relentless tears scuffled at her eyelids and she pressed her face into the wool of his sweater. Her hand dropped and she barely acknowledged someone saving her glass before it slid from her fingers.

'I thought you were back tomorrow.' Her voice was muffled against his chest, but she couldn't seem to pull herself back.

'I changed my flight when I heard the funeral was today. I'm so sorry I missed the service. Why didn't you tell me?'

She shook her head. She had no explanation for a lot of the things she'd done this past week. Avoiding calling a friend so he couldn't be here for her today was just one. 'How did you find out?'

'Juz.'

'He called you?'

'Yeah. He said regardless of how we felt about each other, we both felt the same way about you, and that was what counted now.'

Warmth seeped into her skin where the sun's rays had failed. Darren's breath fanned her hair and she didn't care that this moment would fuel weeks of scandal with her family and friends. Thankfully her squad had already been and gone, were no doubt this very moment on their way to question Madden. Her arms tightened.

He flinched.

She pulled back. 'Are you okay?'

Darren's hand flew to his chest as colour leached from the olive of his complexion. 'I overworked on the bench press yesterday.' He squeezed her hand. 'So, tell me, how's the case going?'

She shrugged. 'It's going. We're getting closer.'

'That's great.' His *you can't fool me* gaze scanned her face. 'How're you holding up?'

'She needs a break.' Her father stepped closer and she cast him a look she hoped was withering and effective.

He still looked pale, unwell even. Grief did that to a person. For some, it could even steal the thunder from their storm. But looking at him now, at the vigour in his eyes, she realised she should have known better than to place her father in that category. Nothing could stop him when he set his mind to something.

'Thanks for coming, Darren.'

'I'm sorry for your loss, Dean. Bec's death was a terrible shock. She'll be missed.'

They nodded, shook hands, exchanged the type of look two men exchanged at the funeral of a loved one.

'Now you're here, perhaps you can convince Jayda to see sense. To take time away from Melbourne and work.'

The workaholic calling the kettle black. The anomaly didn't sit well, as though a man other than her father had spoken.

Darren hid his discomfort well. More a save-the-world, Kumbaya kind of guy, he was the last person her father should have enlisted for his cause.

She planted her heels. 'Plenty of time for that when we find Bec's killer, *Dad*.'

The air thickened, words spoken and unspoken hovering between them. Her father's expression was grim, as if he were steeling himself to push further.

'We should get moving.' Seth cupped her elbow. She'd almost forgotten he was still there, white horse and all.

Darren turned, treating Seth to a slow trek from head to toe before he nodded and offered his hand. 'You must be Seth.'

Heat slinked across her cheeks. At a guess, Darren was stirring, and the question in Seth's glance said his mischief was noted, and working.

'You must be Jayda's until-now absent neighbour.'

'And close friend.' Darren gave another nod, this time the knowing kind. Seth's expression tightened.

He looked . . . *jealous*!

Warmth frittered up from her tummy, fanning out through every cell until she wondered if it were possible to combust on attraction alone.

She didn't know why Seth's possessiveness had her heart racing so fast, a feeling all new and too delicious to question. Having a man want her so bad—she couldn't mistake the heat in that look, regardless of his motives and the headline he chased—was enough to make her want a re-enactment of the past night's activities.

*Why not?*

Reasons for and against waved their arms, screaming *pick me!* She'd be a liar if she said she gave both sides equal weight. Against was hazy, while for . . . she wanted *for* to win. It was simple. They were adults, free agents, neither one looking for anything past the crazy attraction they shared.

Seth's 'happy for now' scenario.

First, they had a list to work through. The job was priority. But once they were done . . .

The heat in her body spiked. When they were done, she'd be able to forget everything again, but the wondrous slide of Seth's skin over hers.

Seth's chest clamped under a surge of green mist. Yet another man to add to the 'who loves Jayda?' fan club. Did the woman have no female friends?

Her eyes glazed over at Darren's cheesy expression and he wanted to deck the guy. This from someone who abhorred physical violence in any form.

Yet, something about Jayda continually dragged the caveman out in him. She glanced at her watch. 'We should go.'

'Right.' He hated the bite in his voice, but couldn't do a damn thing about it. She lit a fire in his gut and he should resent her to hell and back for doing it so easily and inadvertently. Instead he resented the men she had falling out of the woodwork and into her life.

Darren returned his attention to Jayda. 'Where are you going?'

'A lead.'

Dean perked up. 'A lead?'

Her gaze slipped from Darren as she eyed her father warily. 'I'll let you know if it comes to anything.'

'You're not going to the prison now?'

'I told you, I couldn't get anything until tomorrow.'

'Good.'

'But I *am* going.' Her eyes sparked, and he knew firsthand how intimidating it was to be on the receiving end of that fire. 'When are you and Mum leaving?'

Dean's expression shuttered. 'After we've tied up a few loose ends.' His gaze sharpened. 'Sure you won't reconsider?'

'Not while a killer's loose.'

He nodded, as if he'd suspected nothing less.

She turned to Darren. 'I've lots to tell you.'

'Then I'll put a Moscato on ice. Tonight?'

'I'll call. It depends how I go—'

'—working through your list?'

The corners of her lips kicked upward. 'How'd you know?'

Darren raised his brows. 'How long have we been friends?'

'Long enough for you to know me too well.'

'I'll be waiting for your call.' Darren winked, and it was impossible for Seth's gut to wind any tighter.

Even blind he could have sensed their camaraderie. They were close. Closer perhaps than her and Juz. And this man, with his model physique and looks, was not remotely gay, despite his almost embarrassing scrutiny seconds ago. So where did he fit in?

'Bye, Dad.'

Seth watched Jayda steel herself before their hug, this one rather less easy than the last.

'I wish you'd change your mind.' Dean's voice was gruff.

She pulled back. 'I can't. You know I can't.'

Her father appeared to hesitate, then he nodded, and understanding flowed between them—the kind Seth had never known. It sparked a longing inside that he'd long since suppressed.

*Idiot!*

'Ready?' She turned to him, rainforest eyes wide and waiting.

He nodded, shaking the trouble from his thoughts to exchange pleasantries with Dean and Darren before pressing his palm to her back in an action that he knew was petty and pathetic.

Half an hour later they'd worked through the crowd, Jayda's expression closing a little further with each offer of sympathy.

They clicked their seatbelts in silence. Jayda worked the ignition of the pink beast, her shaky hand grinding the gears painfully upwards until they cruised almost smoothly into fourth.

'There's no rush to get to Black Keys Security, you know. We could have stayed longer.'

She shot him a sideward glance. 'I was thinking we should have left earlier.'

A car darted into their path. She slammed the brakes and horn in unison, only just preventing the beast from stalling.

He clutched at his seat, thankful for the tight grip of his seatbelt. 'Never a cop around when you need one.'

'Funny, ha ha.'

'It was, wasn't it?' He relaxed as the car's speed steadied. 'So, do you think the key could be the answer to finding the killer?'

'Only time will tell.'

Strange how changing the topic from the funeral to a murderer saw the rigid line of her shoulders relax.

'And if it does belong to Black Keys, what then? Have you considered that you'll need a locker number, maybe even an access code to get into the place?'

'The locker numbers are made up of four-digits and I doubt they've changed the six-digit passcode or the protocol to get into the building since I was here last.'

'That's a lot of assuming.'

'Maybe, but it's calculated.'

'Only time will tell.' He couldn't help the words, or the grin that hijacked his lips. It was gratifying to see Jayda smile, even more so since that smile was directed at him.

She reached across and fiddled with a knob on the stereo until music bounded out from the speakers.

Mile after mile of Princes Highway whizzed past his window until they reached the turnoff for Koo Wee Rup Road. The same turn-off they'd take tomorrow for their visit with Madden. Odd that the storage facility was located less than five minutes from the prison.

Black Keys Security was a large, grey box of a building guarded by an iron gate worthy of a medieval fortress. As the car idled beside the security keypad, Jayda reached through the window, her fingers hovering over the numbers. He watched her indecision before the keys beeped with each punch of a number.

There was a moment's silence when he wondered if she'd guessed wrong, then the gates creaked and juddered and slid slowly open, and he knew he shouldn't have been surprised. Jayda had instincts sharper than the razor edge of a knife. When she wasn't conceding to obstinacy, that is.

She cut the engine and jiggled the key until it slipped from the ignition. 'Time to find out whether we're trailing a flock of squawking birds.'

He followed her lead and got out of the car. 'What makes you think we're on some kind of wild-goose chase?'

She skirted the bonnet and made for the wide, double glass

entrance. 'Nothing yet. But with this case, it's always a distinct possibility.'

She pushed the doors open and entered a narrow stairway to the left of a wide goods elevator. When they reached the first floor, she hesitated in front of two arrows marking the direction of locker numbers. Taking a deep breath, she turned right.

He didn't question her choice. She had to be working a theory, and who was he to question her methods when he hadn't Hades' chance in offering an alternative?

From the dimensions of the roller doors either side, these were not security deposit boxes, they were rooms, possibly more than a square metre in size, each one secured by a large, black padlock.

Jayda stopped almost a third of the way down the corridor and Seth checked the number above the door.

'2101?'

'January twenty-first. The date the photo was taken.'

'How can you be so sure?'

'It was my father's birthday.'

The theory was as good as any other, but he didn't hold out much hope of her being right, first guess.

'Here goes.' The key fit when her trembling fingers pressed it into the lock, but when she made to turn, it resisted. 'Damn!'

'Let me try.'

Her look scowled *give it your best shot, sunshine!* but she stepped aside to allow him space. He took the key and jiggled it lightly before feeling the snap as it connected. Slowly he turned.

The lock clicked and the arm sprang loose from its shackle.

'Way to go, Seth!'

He pushed back a ridiculous glow from her praise and stood aside. 'You should open it.'

She nodded, slipping the padlock free before yanking the handle until the heavy metal door gave way. It creaked and wailed and lurched in protest, the din echoing off the walls, floor and ceiling before lumbering down the hall.

The beat of his heart stuttered, then stopped.

He could feel Jayda beside him, mouth gaping, her body as rigid and stunned as his.

He didn't know what he'd been expecting. Before they'd arrived and seen the size of the door, something a lot smaller. The size of a safe rather than a very small room.

Perhaps files or notes or some type of evidence to help them move forwards in the case. There were a variety of things he'd anticipated. But not once had he considered the possibility of what they'd just found.

# Chapter Forty-Three

***N****o way!*

The words battered round Jayda's brain as she stared at what was supposed to have been a break in the case.

She stepped inside, turning full circle as she surveyed the area, looking for something that was clearly not there. All she got was a dull thump against her skull and a faint whiff that made her think of nail polish.

Pressure rumbled inside her chest. 'You've got to be frigging kidding!' No matter the angle, the outcome was the same. The room was empty.

Back against the whitewashed wall, she slid to the ground, sinking her head into her hands.

*Think.*

'This can't be it.'

She shook her head, the beat of her heart a listless thud against her ribs. There had to be more. The key's concealment, the cloak-and-dagger mystery of it all. Why send her halfway across Melbourne unless there was a reason? There *had* to be a reason.

Pressing the tips of her fingers into her skull, she tried to massage action into her brainpower.

A light sparked, faint and brief. But a light, nevertheless. Her heart hammered. She pushed herself up, renewed energy waking her limbs as she relocked the roller door and headed back in the direction they'd come. 'This way.'

'What are you doing?'

'Following a hunch.'

It cost nothing to follow, and more often than not her hunches reaped dividends. With luck, this was one of those times.

Up another flight of stairs, then turn right. The path was embedded in her memory. As she walked, she fumbled with her key ring, hoping it was still there. It was. The little black key she'd been meaning to take off and return to her father.

The security boxes here were smaller, the size of an average desk drawer, and they spanned floor to ceiling. A lot like the inside of a bank vault.

One hundred metres or so and then she was there.

Number 2018. Her age along with Bec's, back when her father was undercover.

'Surely the key won't open two security boxes.'

'No, but another key will open this one.'

Seth's expression cleared. 'Your father's?'

'Uh huh.'

'What makes you think something's inside this one?'

'Because I'm out of ideas. We were led here for a reason, and perhaps to find that reason we need to improvise.' She waved her key. 'This is me improvising. Maybe whoever planted the other key meant to lead us to this building so I could access Dad's old security box.'

'And find something of your father's, or something else?'

'Won't know until we open it.' She inserted the key and twisted. This time the lock turned easily.

'This is getting creepier by the minute.'

She shot him a grin. 'Ahh, but it'll make a good story.'

He returned her grin without comment. Breath clogged in her lungs as she tugged the door open and peered inside.

Seth leaned in, and lush meadows and pine filled her nostrils as they both stared at yet another empty interior.

Seth tried to imagine the force of Jayda's disappointment when weighed against his own. It was like being thrown one end of a rope and hanging on only to discover the person at the other end had just let go.

'It was a good deduction.'

'But wrong.'

'For the lack of an alternative, it was better than nothing.'

'And still wrong.' She slammed the door.

It bounced back, hitting her knuckles with a loud *crack*. He winced. She clutched her hand and stared at the slow ooze of blood, her temper a rumbling volcano one quake short of an eruption.

He closed the door and turned the key, giving her the time and space she needed to calm down. Last thing he wanted was to be a stand-in for that locker door.

'We should go.' Her voice low, her jaw tight and clamped, she grabbed a tissue from her pocket and wrapped it over the cut.

He fell into step beside her. 'We should dig deeper into Madden and his mystery progeny.'

'I couldn't agree more. We also need to check who rented the space and whether that,' she waved towards a security camera, 'is functional or just for show.'

This time they took the goods elevator down and there was none of their light banter and anticipation as they pushed through the double glass doors and headed for the car.

She stopped just shy of the Beetle, fists clenched.

'Damn the sick bastard to hell!' Eyes blazing, she turned to him. 'He's playing some twisted power game and I refuse to be his bitch!'

'We're closing in and this is his way of claiming back control. But we'll get him.'

'Oh, I know we'll get him. I'm going to mop the floor with his ass until he rues the day he was ever born.'

He dropped the keys into her outstretched palm. She stalked the short distance to the car, jammed the key into the lock and yanked the car door open before dropping into her seat.

The ugly grey expanse loomed beside him. Something didn't sit right. Why lead them here if there was nothing to find? There were far less complex—and risky—ways of wasting their time than this uncover-a-key-in-a-dead-man's-apartment scenario. So, if time-wasting wasn't his motive, what was?

He dug his cold fingers into his jacket pocket. Nothing in this damned case made sense.

Neither did standing there, waiting for Jayda to unlock the door. He ducked and peered through the glass.

Jayda sat slumped, deathly still. Wide eyes stared at the contents of a large manila folder, her knuckles jutting stark and white, clutching fast at the cream-coloured cardboard.

He knocked.

Slowly she dragged her eyes towards him and what he saw there froze his blood. Her hand shook as she released the lock on his door so he could join her in the car.

'What's wrong?'

She didn't react, her eyes still on the folder, both wild and trapped at once.

'Jayda?'

'How do I get Will to stop his DNA search now?'

He shook his head, sifting for sense in her words. 'Why would you want to do that?'

'We don't need to keep looking.' She waved the papers in her hand. 'We've found Madden's child.'

His heart leaped. 'But, that's great! We find the kid, we find the killer.'

'Not quite.' It was only then she turned and the lacklustre of her eyes hit him square in the gut. 'You've already found her. It's me.'

# Chapter Forty-Four

*My life is a lie.*

The blurred landscape whizzed past Jayda's window. Somewhere in the recesses of her mind she acknowledged that Seth handled a stick-shift a helluva sight better than she had. If she'd known, she would have let him behind the wheel of Bec's car sooner. Or perhaps not. Her father always said she was a control freak.

*Her father.*

Over-long nails cut into her palms. Her knuckle would probably start bleeding again, not that it mattered. The blood would wash out.

Her jaw jammed tight. Her parents were in on it. Had Bec been in on it, too? The lies, the deceit. The entire cover-up that was her life. She didn't think so, but how could she be sure?

Tom and Mary Clarke may have died in a house fire twenty-five years ago, but they weren't her parents. Roan Madden was, along with some unknown entity even her real birth certificate couldn't name.

The genuine article lay in the folder on her lap, along with other documents and a smattering of newspaper articles that filled part of the 'black hole' that was Madden's missing years.

She had a serial killer as a parent, and once her squad found out, what little involvement she had in this case would be gone. If they'd believed she was too close before, now they'd consider her swamped. There was even the possibility she'd become a suspect in the recent murders. Her time of freedom to work the case was limited. Once Will checked Madden's DNA against the police database her secret would be out. That left her with a matter of days, a week at best.

'Turn the car around!'

Seth glanced her way, her skin burning beneath his gaze. It was nothing to the burn razing her entrails.

His eyes returned to the road. 'We're on the motorway. I can't just chuck a U-ey.'

She faced him then. 'Turn around, Seth. I don't care if you can't do a U-turn. Take the next exit, ram through the crash barrier if you have to, whatever it takes. I need to get to that prison.'

'You need to go home and process this first.'

'I know what I need, and right now it's answers.'

He glanced at her again and she averted her gaze. The grassland outside offered no judgement.

The car accelerated, and her elbow hit the door as they swerved into the left lane. A large green service station loomed ahead, and her tensed muscles almost sighed when Seth took the exit and re-entered the Princes Highway to go back the way they had come.

Out of the corner of her eye, she saw him glance her way again. 'Do you want to talk about it?'

'No.'

'What do you plan to do?'

'See Madden.'

'And . . .?'

'Find out how that sick sonofabitch could possibly be my flesh and blood.' They exited the motorway, Seth's hand braced on the gearshift as they slowed. 'They might not let you in.'

'I won't give them a choice.'

She clamped her lips and glared out her side window. Seth seemed to take the hint, or maybe it was simply that he had nothing else to say.

Whatever the case, his reporter instincts must be churning overtime. It'd almost kill him not to print this one, not that the media wouldn't find out soon enough anyway.

That had to be *his* plan—drag her down into his squalor.

They turned onto Koo Wee Rup Road, the landscape as stark as their destination. Ironic how the morning's sun seemed to have fled, looming black clouds now rolling across the sky. Cliché had finally won out.

The road was smooth until they turned into the prison entrance and hit the gravel of the car park. Damp slathered her palms. She never sweated.

'Sure you want to do this?' He slid into a parking spot and her hand was already reaching for the door before he'd engaged the handbrake.

'No. But let's do it anyway.' She didn't wait until he'd locked the car, because if she stopped she wasn't sure she'd be able to keep going.

She was about to meet a man who had brutally killed and maimed more women than she could bear to count. And as if that wasn't enough to make her chuck her guts, another, even larger gem screamed for attention—this man had once been her mother.

*This is a bad idea.*

Seth scrubbed his fingers through his hair for the third time in as many minutes as he followed Jayda towards the cluster of grubby white buildings. Barging into a meeting with Madden without taking time to process what she'd discovered seemed like the worst thing Jayda could do.

She needed to talk about it. Purge.

Something he did ad nauseum, or so his parents said. After Callum had died, he'd wanted to talk—*needed* to talk—but they hadn't. They'd just moved on, worked harder than before and buried their emotions beneath a thick mass of steel.

Jayda braced before pushing against the heavy outer door. He followed her into the tiny antechamber and waited as she buzzed to be let into the gatehouse. He got why she didn't follow normal visitor protocol and enter through the ion scanner. From what he'd read, the machine was super sensitive, and any trace of gunpowder could trigger the alarm.

Not something she would risk today.

The iron door shuddered as it was yanked inwards. A young prison officer dressed in Pakenham Prison's signature blue uniform stepped aside to allow them to enter. She pushed back a wisp of blonde that had escaped from a blue hair tie and her formidable features softened. 'Jayda.'

'Trace.' Tension seemed to sigh from Jayda's shoulders and he watched her force her lips to return the other woman's smile.

He'd heard talk of the cold war between prison staff and police. An 'us and them' saga that made no sense when you considered both parties barracked for the same side.

Whatever the case, it seemed they'd struck gold in getting one of the few prison officers who didn't view visiting detectives with disdain. The relief in Jayda's expression said she thought the same.

Trace moved back and waved them both through.

Jayda stepped onto the blue mottled carpet. 'How's Howie?'

The other woman rolled her eyes and grinned. 'Better. He slept through for the first time three days ago. We're walking on egg shells hoping it's not a teaser before he slips back into those ungodly 3 am feeds.' She let the door go and it slammed heavily behind them.

'So, who're you here to see?'

'Roan Madden.'

'Your squad's already been and gone. Left less than ten minutes ago.'

'I know. Something's come up and we need to speak to Madden again. Any chance there's still time on the 464B?'

'Let me check the paperwork.' Trace slipped behind the counter to a large computer screen and gave a couple of clicks with a mouse. 'Ah, here it is.' Another click and she nodded. 'You're in luck. It doesn't expire until three.' She glanced at the clock on the far wall. 'That leaves you half an hour.'

'I'll take it.'

'I need to run it by the supervisor, although I can't see there'll be a problem.' She disappeared into a room behind the desk, and he watched as Jayda's neck stiffened again, her back so ramrod straight it was a wonder she didn't snap.

Trace returned seconds later behind a woman with stark white features he guessed seldom smiled. She glanced at the computer screen before resting brown, almost black eyes on Jayda. 'ID?'

A fine sheen glazed her brow as steady but taut fingers slid the leather wallet across the countertop. The supervisor flipped it open and stared first at the ID then the screen.

'You're not listed on the application.'

'If you check, you'll see it covers anyone from Pacu task force.'

The woman tutted, and hummed—a power play if he'd ever seen one. 'I don't see what you need to ask that you couldn't have asked him before.'

'New information came to light just a few minutes ago.'

She lifted a brow. 'That was quick.'

'It's like that sometimes.' He watched Jayda attempt a smile, but the twist of her lips was too forced for humour.

The woman studied Jayda through narrowed eyes, as if by doing so she could burrow holes in her story, find reason to refuse her entrance. Something she had every right to do, regardless of applications and time remaining.

And there was a part of him that wondered if that would be for the best. For Jayda to get the time she needed to think things through more clearly first.

The supervisor's lips thinned, her eyes never leaving Jayda. 'We'll get the prisoner again, but only if he's willing. You'll have twenty minutes once he's ready.' She turned to Trace. 'Officer James, make the call to ready Mr Madden.'

A brief smile in their direction and then Trace disappeared again through the far door.

'I'll need you to sign in your firearm and then we'll get you through the ion scanner and X-ray.' She looked past Jayda towards Seth. 'ID?'

Jayda didn't give him time to reply. 'He's not coming in.'

The words were unequivocal, her eyes latched on the supervisor as she reached under her jacket to unholster her gun. Regardless of his instincts, he didn't argue. He got that she needed to do this alone. And she seemed calm. Icily so.

It wasn't until she slid her gun across the white laminate that he noted the quiver in her hand. The supervisor secured it in a locker, recording the number before passing the book across for Jayda to sign. By the time she picked up the pen, her hand was steady again. How long until her shock passed and reaction set in?

A sharp trill blasted from a speaker above the desk.

His body jolted. Shock passed through the room and he wasn't the only one to flinch as the siren continued to peal. Inner and outer doors shuddered before the long grate of metal scraping against metal indicated bolts sliding into place with a resounding thud.

'Stay here!' The supervisor's bark was almost lost in the din, but her glare spoke volumes. *Move at your peril.*

Not that there was anywhere for them to go. Every door in sight was bolted. Thick, no nonsense, lead-lined barriers, impermeable to pretty much anything. No way in, no way out.

The supervisor was the last to disappear through that back

doorway, leaving the gatehouse suddenly empty but for them and the infernal ringing.

His eardrums vibrated painfully and he grabbed Jayda's elbow, yelling to be heard. 'What's happening?'

Her eyes scoured the area, and he knew if she'd had a choice she'd have vaulted over the reception desk and joined in with whatever was going on over the other side.

'Jayda?'

She finally looked his way, lips pinched, the rapid, jerky rise and fall of her chest blaring out her frustration. He could feel it like a tangible thing—real, overwhelming. All-encompassing.

'The prison's in lockdown.'

That much he'd guessed. His chest tightened, the high wail of the alarm like a thousand needle-points stabbing at his inner ear. 'Why?'

He watched as she took up pacing the distance between the locked entrance and reception desk, a wild leopard caged, her empty hands clenching and unclenching tautly at her side. He knew her well enough to know she resented being stripped of her firearm, and even more, of being excluded from whatever was going on beyond reception.

'How do I know? We're out here and they're . . .' she waved her hand at the X-ray machine and the large iron door behind it before spinning on her heels and striding back towards him.

'Any guesses?'

'An escape attempt?'

Their eyes locked and he read the question in hers.

He cleared the clog layering his throat and shifted his shoulders. 'It won't be Madden.'

It was a pitiful attempt at reassurance when he hadn't a clue whether it was or wasn't. But the brief upward slant of her lips made the effort worthwhile, even if it didn't stop her wearing the mottle from the carpet tiles beneath her feet.

'Of course it won't be him.' It was unclear whether the words were for his benefit or hers. 'That'd be too . . .' she waved her hand again.

He pitched in. 'Coincidental?'

She shook her head, staring sightlessly at the wall ahead, the loaded shriek of the siren crowding the empty space around them. Her shoulders hunched, her voice so small he had to lean in to hear it.

*'Ridiculous.'*

# Chapter Forty-Five

'**H**e was low risk.'

Jayda glared at the red-faced Prison Field Commander. 'That's reassuring now he's dead.' Only the gentle pressure of Georgie's hand on her shoulder prevented her from losing it.

*Dead.*

The ramifications of that four-letter word swirled round her brain. Roan Madden was dead, and whatever answers she'd hoped for today had died along with him.

Chase's fingers dug into her wrist as he tugged her away from her questioning, from Georgie. 'What are you doing here?'

'Tracking a killer.'

The lines on his face deepened. 'Your request for a meeting was for tomorrow.'

Of course he knew. It was his job.

She dragged steel into her shoulders and tilted her chin. 'We were in the area so I thought I'd drop by.'

'The exact moment he hung himself?'

'A coincidence.'

Something in Chase's expression didn't sit well. Something she'd never thought to see when he looked her way.

*Doubt.*

Shoving at the wrench in her gut, she glanced across at the stunned Prison Field Commander still being questioned by Georgie. Her friend's gaze darted her way and softened, shooting warmth and comfort across the distance.

She swallowed, returning attention to her less-than-amused partner. 'Were there any witnesses?'

'Undoubtedly a whole prison-load, but no-one's talking.'

'What about changes in behaviour? It's not every day a man enters prison on a single murder charge only to be exposed as a serial killer.'

Chase shrugged. 'He passed his psych assessment only two days ago. It's not a given, but it does raise questions.'

'Like whether his death was rigged to look like a suicide?'

His eyes shuttered. 'That is a consideration.'

'Hell, Chase. It's me here, not some two-bit reporter.'

Her face warmed as she bit her lip and glanced over her shoulder. Seth was leaning against the reception desk talking to a prison officer, but his eyes flicked to hers as if he sensed her scrutiny. She looked away.

She'd never imagined the day would come when she'd feel guilty for denigrating his profession.

'What do you want me to say, Jayda? We're looking into it. I can't tell you any more than that.'

'At least tell me how a prisoner can hang himself in a room with no hanging points.'

'He smuggled a mop into his cell and wedged the handle between the bookshelf and top bunk. Don't ask me how he got hold of it, because we don't know.'

'What did Madden say this morning when you questioned him?'

'Jack shit.' He scrubbed his immaculately shaven jaw. 'We looked at the visitor log and the only recurring name was Anna Jones. A long-time girlfriend, so we're told.'

'He met someone in prison?'

'Knew her before he was convicted.'

'He was having an affair when he killed his wife?'

'Possibly. We'll find out more after we bring her in for questioning.'

'Any kids?' Her heart stalled as she held her breath and waited.

'We're looking into it.'

'How about, while you're looking into things, you check out the other inmates to see if any are connected to past Night Terror victims.'

His expression hardened, and she could tell she'd pushed Chase to his limits.

'I know how to run my investigation.'

*My* investigation. As if he'd been heading it from day dot. It grated, but she bit back the retort that would send her nowhere but up shit-creek without a link to the information she needed.

'Damn, I'm sorry, Chase.' Air whooshed from her lungs. 'I'm

pissed and frustrated, but that's no excuse. It's just that every time a door opens in this case, a second later it slams in our faces.'

'Which doors are we talking about, exactly?'

'Eric, Madden.' She wouldn't mention the key. That would only hasten a disaster which would come soon enough.

'Eric was a stalker, Jayda. Nothing's shown up so far to link his death to Madden's.'

Chase was still thinking inside the box. But perhaps his inability to think wider would buy her the time she needed.

'You're right. There's too much craziness in my life at the moment.' She scraped her hair back from her face. 'Any chance you can keep me posted on Anna Jones?'

'I'll see what I can do.' His gaze sharpened further, so much she'd swear it'd draw blood if he moved any closer. 'Is there anything you need to tell me?'

'Anything about what?'

'The case. Your investigation. The reason you're here.'

'I told you why I'm here. As for the rest, I'm off the case, remember?'

'And we both know that's bullshit.'

Her chest tightened. 'What do you want me to say? My sister was murdered. What would you do in my position?'

'Find the bastard and make him pay.'

'So you understand—I need to do this.'

'I understand that he killed a friend's sister, and for that reason I won't stop until he's caught.' He sighed. 'I'll keep you in the loop under one condition. You do the same.'

She didn't hesitate, or cross her fingers and pray for lightning not to strike. 'Fine.'

'So, what can you tell me?'

'Nothing yet that you don't already know.'

He searched her face and she made sure there was nothing for him to find.

Her gaze lifted, and collided with Seth's. Warmth touched every inch of her body.

'I should go.' Forcing her lips upwards into what she hoped resembled a smile, she returned her gaze to Chase. 'It's been a long day.'

He nodded, gave her arm a squeeze. 'I'm sorry it has to be this way, Jayda.' He hesitated. She sensed he wanted to say more, for a moment even thought he might. Then he turned and walked stiffly away.

Impossible to know what his apology referred to. Was it her off-the-case-and-out-of-the-loop status or his stepping straight into her shoes the minute she was gone? Or was he talking about Bec? Not that it mattered. There was a dung-heap of stuff going on in her life—he could choose from a list more than a mile long.

'Ready to leave?' Seth sidled up to her and cupped her elbow in his palm. She lifted her chin and stayed put. She was past worrying what her squad thought.

'Oh, about five minutes ago.'

'Me too.'

She followed him out towards the parking area, nodding to colleagues as she left.

Georgie's lips fluttered into a tentative smile as she passed. Jayda couldn't stem the doubts that had pricked at her subconscious since Georgie's behaviour the day of Eric's death. And now with this tempered warmth . . . Still, she managed to return Georgie's look with a smile of her own. 'We never had that drink.'

'No, we didn't.'

'Coffee tomorrow?'

'Sure.'

Georgie didn't look sure, but no way would Jayda give her a way out. 'I can swing by at ten.'

'Let's meet at the usual on Warward Street.'

She nodded, wondering again at her friend's reluctance, not only to meeting but to Jayda dropping by her place. Georgie wasn't acting like Georgie. Another slice of her heart fell away. Just one more person in her life who seemed to be hiding something. The question was, was it related to the case or not?

Wind laced with the sun's balminess hit her face and she stopped just short of the carpark.

'I'll drive.' Seth's hand warmed her shoulder with heat that failed to permeate deeper.

She dropped the keys into his palm and moved to the passenger side of the car. His raised eyebrows were the only indication she'd surprised him with her acquiescence.

'I've got ten bucks in my wallet.'

'Really? Won the lottery, have you?'

He shook his head and fastened his seatbelt. 'I'd offer a penny, but since they're no longer in circulation, and taking into account inflation and all, I reckon ten dollars is a fair price.'

It clicked. 'For my thoughts?'

'Aha.'

Her heart twisted. Her gut told her only two of the many possibilities governing Madden's death seemed likely. One horrible, and one worse still. It took a moment for her shaking fingers to pull the belt across her body and snap it into place. She focused on the first possibility and pushed away the alternative.

'The key makes perfect sense now.'

'How so?'

'He's playing. He wanted me to be here when Madden died.'

'There's no way he knew how you'd react.'

All she could do was shake her head. The engine murmured in the background.

Seth raised a brow. 'Don't you think that's a bit of a stretch?'

'From someone who doesn't know me, yes.' An avalanche of icicles tumbled down her back, chilling her to the core.

Too many arrows pointed in only one direction. The Night Terror knew her too well to be anything less than a friend.

# Chapter Forty-Six

Seth's hands dropped from the steering wheel. 'We've already established he's someone you know.'

'Known to my father, my family, yes. Not someone I'd consider a friend.'

'You believe he's that close?'

'How else would he understand me so well? Every step of the investigation he's anticipated my actions, my reactions. I'm not that easy to read from a distance.'

*'Not from close up, either.'*

Her gaze flinted, like the spears he imagined she'd launch his way given half the chance. He hadn't meant to say those words aloud.

Rather than deepen a hole that could bury him once more in animosity, he checked the rear vision mirror and reversed. 'We need background checks on your friends and acquaintances. No exceptions.'

'Done.'

'Really?' This time he didn't care if she took exception to his tone. He shoved the gears into first and the tyres shrieked as they headed for the exit. What part of working as a team did she not get?

'Before you rag on me for not sharing, consider how shitty I felt checking up on people I once thought I could trust.'

Her words sucker-punched his conscience. 'It can't have been easy.' The negative shake of her head seemed as much agreement as it was determination to hold her emotions at bay. Her trembling lips gave her away.

He eased into the traffic, then reached across to wrap her ice-cold fingers into his palm. 'I'm sorry you have to do this.'

'I know.'

The hand beneath his tensed, turned, clasped his in return.

His heartbeat quickened. His other hand gripped the steering wheel and he closed his mind. 'What did you uncover?'

'Nothing. Not a single red flag.'

'So, what next?'

'We delve deeper. Phone records, financials, anything and everything until something shows.'

'What can I do to help?'

Her breath hitched. 'Be the voice of reason while we figure out which one of my friends wants to destroy me.'

He held his silence as she battled her tears. Most women would be ranting by now—or a screaming, blubbering mess if they'd suffered even a portion of Jayda's past two weeks. Her composure had him in awe, flushed with pride and a jumble of other emotions which warred against his better judgement.

The square of her shoulders told him when she'd won.

'We need to go via Dad's.' Although she used the word 'dad', he could tell it no longer held the same meaning.

She seemed to be waiting for a response, so he nodded. What else could he do? The confrontation wouldn't be easy, but she needed it. If for no other reason than to fill in the missing blanks in the folder at her feet.

She turned up the stereo, then turned it back down. 'Thanks.'

'For what?'

'For not judging me. For keeping our agreement and not publicising my family's private messes. For sticking with me through every one of my red hair moments.'

'No problem.' Something low in his belly fluttered. 'For the record, it wasn't a hardship. I happen to be quite partial to redheads.'

Her lips twitched. 'And I thought you were into blondes.'

'That night was the exception.'

Colour flooded her cheeks. 'Why?'

'I guess I had a feeling you were red at heart.'

She opened her mouth, closed it, instead leant forwards to turn the stereo back up.

Her other hand remained clasped in his, and Seth couldn't deny he liked the feel of their coupled palms. With that thought he should have broken contact. Instead he squeezed, and the twitch of her lips let him know she got the message. That he was there for her no matter what.

Unbridled warmth flooded his chest.

Forty minutes passed in a silence that he'd have called companionable if it weren't for the circumstances. It was altogether too soon when he pulled into the curb. 'I'll wait in the car.'

Her shoulders relaxed and she gave him an almost-smile. 'Thanks.'

'If you need me, I'm here.'

'I know.' She glanced down at their linked hands and the blush on her cheeks ripened. Her fingers seemed reluctant to let go, and when they did, they wavered before reaching for the door.

His heart stumbled.

File in hand, she stepped out of the car, still gripping the door after it was firmly closed. The look in her eyes told him more than she ever could with words.

His hands clenched against his thighs to prevent them from opening his door and going to her. Oh, but he wanted to, more than anything. To hold her, comfort her, tell her everything was going to be fine. Only he didn't know that it was. Neither of them did.

His gaze drowned in the deep green of hers and he swallowed. She may be holding it together, have guts peppered with a dash of bravado, but for the first time since they'd embarked on this ride together, Jayda was scared.

With every step through her father's post-retirement garden, Jayda willed herself not to throw up.

Anger didn't begin to cover what she felt. It was a part of it—a huge part—although the word was measly when measured against the force of her fury. And it wasn't alone. It lay muddled together with myriad emotions—in the main, betrayal and fear.

It was one thing to see the disclosure in print, but it would be altogether different to hear it uttered by the man she'd considered a father and mentor. And friend.

Her hand wavered over the freshly stained front door. It wasn't as if she expected more than an empty house. Wouldn't they already be off on their sabbatical, or whatever the hell you could call it?

Her gut said otherwise.

There was a part of her that almost hoped her instincts were wrong, because no answer would mean she could neither confirm nor disprove the facts that were even now forcing bile up into her throat.

She swallowed, held her breath, and knocked. Nothing moved, inside or out. No noise but her shallow breathing and the caw of a distant magpie.

Her heart thudded so hard every smack rammed against the back of her throat. She knocked again, once, before the wood disappeared from beneath her knuckles.

The door opened, spiralling time backwards, to her uniform days of marshalling bums from city street corners. Her father could have been any one of those unfortunate men as he braced himself against the door frame, crumpled and haggard in second-day clothes, deep, dark circles rimming his eyes.

So different from the man she'd seen at Bec's funeral. Was that really only hours earlier?

It took a moment to find her voice. 'You're still here.' She sidestepped and peered behind him into the dim hallway. 'Where's Mum?'

He scratched at the two-day stubble on his chin. 'She had to go out.'

'I thought you were going away.'

'I had . . . some loose ends to tie up first.'

'Like orchestrating Roan Madden's death?'

'Madden's dead?' His eyes bugged out of his unusually pale face. 'And you think I had something to do with it?'

Her mind glazed over the pain in his expression and instead focused on her own hurt. 'So you don't deny it?'

His gaze darted past her and out onto the street. Then he stepped back. 'This isn't a conversation for the doorstep.'

She brushed past and didn't wait for him to close the door, marching down the hall and into the living room. All signs of the OPI search were gone and the room once more resembled her father's normal brand of tidy—an organised clutter that she'd always associated with him and home.

Leather and sandalwood filled her nostrils, scents that had always made her feel safe, secure. Now they just made her heart ache.

'Is that Seth outside in the Beetle?'

She jerked around to find her father hovering in the doorway. He looked so unlike the brash, gutsy detective, not to mention the only father she remembered, that she stumbled into an answer without thinking. 'Yes.'

'He seems like a good man. You could do a lot worse.'

Her gut clenched. The last thing she needed was approval from a man who'd made a botch and a half of his own relationships.

She waved her hand, to stall not only his words, but also his movement towards her. 'This visit has nothing to do with Seth and any associations we do or don't have. It's about me questioning why you were so interested in the time of my meeting with Madden. Perhaps so you could prevent it?'

'What reason could I possibly have for doing that?'

'Oh, I don't know. Perhaps to hide the fact that he's my mother.'

She hadn't thought it possible that her father could turn paler. 'That doesn't make sense.'

'What doesn't? You hiding his existence or the fact that he gave birth to me?'

'Roan Madden is a man.'

'Who was once a woman.'

His eyes widened, then narrowed. 'That explains a lot.'

So, he hadn't known the full truth. Not that that absolved him from guilt.

'Tom and Mary Clarke weren't my birth parents. Madden and some unknown man were.'

'How did you find out?'

'It's true, then?' The nausea she'd been holding at bay rose up her oesophagus and into her throat. As she forced it back down, she realised that until now she'd been wishing it all away as a lie. An elaborate hoax trumped up by a psycho-killer so he could wheedle his way beneath her skin.

Her father's weary nod trashed that theory.

'Why didn't you tell me?'

'I wanted to protect you.' His hand fumbled for the wall, even as he took two small steps towards her.

She raised her palm, stopping him mid-step. She could tell he wanted to hug her, hug away her worries as he'd done so many times in the past. No manner of hug could do that now.

'Who told you?'

'You don't have the right to ask me that. Not after twenty-something years of lies. I want to know everything.'

'Honey—'

'Don't "honey" me.' She had the sudden urge to scream, to ram her fist through the white plaster of his living room wall. Instead, she stalked towards the far end of the room and turned, her breath coming in short, fiery gasps. 'Dammit, Dad!' Her hands dropped to her sides. 'I don't even know if I should call you that anymore.'

'Of course you should!' His face twisted. 'No matter what, I'll always be your father. Nothing can change that.'

Tears pushed against her eyelids and she blinked fiercely to keep them at bay. 'You don't get it, do you? My entire world is a lie. Until this afternoon I knew who I was—Jayda Thomasz, Homicide Detective, daughter of Dean and Lydia Thomasz, sister to Rebecca Thomasz. Now I'm . . .' She opened the file and scanned the front sheet. 'Samantha Madden, daughter of a serial killer.'

'You're still Jayda Thomasz, the same person you've always been. And you're still my daughter. Madden was a DNA donor and incubator, nothing more. Withholding the truth meant you grew up without the stigma of his actions. I don't regret that.'

'The secrecy when I was a kid, I get. But later?'

He shuffled his feet, not an action she'd ever associated with the gutsy detective who'd earned the Victoria Police Service Medal on more than one occasion. 'It wasn't something you could benefit from knowing.'

His justifications were empty and echoing.

'You should have told me, Dad.' With deliberate movements, she sat on the couch, hands resting over the folder in her lap, as though the two of them were having nothing more than a simple father-daughter chat. 'Tell me now. Everything. I have a right to know.'

His steps were slow and heavy. He pulled his mobile out of his back pocket and glanced at it before he sank onto the couch beside her. She edged further into the corner.

'You're still the same girl who sat on my knee and begged me to tell her a real, live police story. Knowing about Madden won't change that.'

A tear squeezed out from the corner of her eye and she brushed it away. 'But it might help catch Bec's killer.'

His skin stretched taut over his cheekbones, and now that he was close she sensed something else.

'You've been drinking.'

He swiped the back of his hand across his mouth. 'One whisky. But if I'd predicted this conversation was coming, I'd have had a few more.'

'You promised Mum.'

'Your mother's not here.'

'I thought—'

'Well, you thought wrong.'

'What's going on, Dad?'

He scratched his jaw. 'Too much.'

'What does that mean?'

He shook his head, evading her gaze. In typical avoidance fashion, he withdrew his mobile again and began tapping.

'What are you doing?'

'I was supposed to call someone. I'm letting them know I'll call later.'

'Dammit, Dad! Stop shutting me out. Is something wrong with Mum? Has something happened?'

He dropped the phone onto the coffee table and lifted his gaze to meet hers. 'Your mother's fine. I promised I wouldn't tell you any more than that, so please don't ask.'

She jumped up. 'This family has too many fucking secrets!' Her heart squeezed as she recalled the last time she'd uttered those words. This time there was no Bec and no pinkie promises to douse her anger.

'I met your mother through Madden. Did you know that?'

She shook her head and bit back a retort. Of course she didn't. She knew nothing but the lies she'd been fed.

'We were friends, the best. And of course, there was you.' His eyes warmed for the first time since she'd arrived. 'He had no other family, or none that I knew of. So, when he asked on your first birthday if I'd be your godfather, I didn't hesitate.'

She dropped back onto the couch. His hand reached out, as if it might touch her knee, then he pulled it back and let it fall shakily into his lap.

'He told me his wife had died of cancer, and I always knew he wanted to find the right woman to be a mother to you.'

He sat stiffly against the cushions, his shoulders bunched so tight it seemed they'd shatter with the smallest movement. 'Then one day he said he wanted me to meet the woman he'd fallen in love with.' He stared at the wall opposite. 'The moment he introduced us, everything changed. Lydia was . . .' He blinked and turned to her. 'Your mother and I knew we were meant to be. Madden took it hard at first. Of course he did. It was the ultimate betrayal between friends. But then he met Juliana and it seemed everything was going to be okay.'

'Until he killed her.'

He nodded. 'Then all I could think about was how it could have been your mother.'

'So, my nightmares . . .'

'You were hiding under the kitchen table when he did it. I have no idea if he would have killed you too, and thank God you ran so we'll never know. Somehow your leg was cut. None of your blood was found on his knife and you were never clear on what happened that night. What I do know is that emergency received an anonymous call, and we found you hours later, hiding in the reeds next to the old lake at the end of your street.'

His gaze returned to the wall. 'Madden pleaded out at trial. I always thought it was to save you the pain. Now, it seems he had another agenda.'

'All those women . . .'

'I should have known.' His head fell in his hands for the briefest of moments before he raised it and turned to her. 'Doris Thombes, his first victim. Do you remember the date she was killed?'

'June eighteenth.'

'The day I told Madden I was marrying your mother.'

The air became heavy. Onerous. Like death waiting to happen.

Thoughts stuck like barbs in the back of her throat and her breath caught, each swallow like sandpaper rasping against raw flesh. 'His victims all had blonde hair and blue eyes.'

Her father nodded. 'Like your mother.'

# Chapter Forty-Seven

$S$eth turned his head for the umpteenth time.

There was no movement, either in or around the house. No lights turning on or off. Nothing to indicate what was going on beyond that closed front door.

Twilight had slowly given way to dusk, transforming the pale-blue sky into an expanse of blue-black.

More than once he reached for the car door only to drop his hand and vow to give her five more minutes. Sixty had already passed. He couldn't fathom why he cared so much. For a woman he'd known less than a month, who prodded at every raw nerve he owned.

She'd hooked him good, drove him insane as much as she drove him to want her.

He jabbed his fingers through his hair. Sure, he wanted love, marriage, kids. The whole white picket fence hoo-ha. *When his career was set.*

The timing was all wrong. She was all wrong.

Jayda was rude and opinionated and as pig-headed as they come. A tough woman to crack, who refused to open up and trust him. Despite all their faults as parents, Brianna and Grant Friedin were solid in their relationship with each other, in their openness and trust. Qualities he valued.

Jayda was a locked, steel-enforced vault. And yet she'd melted like warm honey in his arms.

He shifted uncomfortably as the denim around his crotch shrunk two jeans sizes.

She might be all wrong but his body had a mind of its own. It wanted her. Yesterday. Now. Every darned second it could.

And why not? In a metaphorical tomorrow the case would be over and so would their partnership. Jayda would leave, more experienced and ready for the relationship she'd been seeking before her parents' divorce and the past weeks' craziness took over. And he'd leave having extinguished her well and truly from his system.

A win-win.

The rumble in his gut indicated dinner was overdue. Nothing more.

His right leg was numb, his left foot a pin cushion. He shuffled in his seat, rubbing at his thighs to bring the circulation back. Perhaps a walk would do it.

As he grabbed the door handle, movement two houses down caught in his peripheral vision.

He turned, but the footpath was deserted. Not unusual. This wasn't a busy street. Still . . . The weirdness of the past week had him scooch lower in his seat. He squinted through the condensation on the windscreen. The surrounding houses were in darkness. Whoever he'd spotted wouldn't have ducked through their front door without switching on at least one light. Unless they had something to hide.

His instincts oscillated between jumping out and searching the area, and staying put and hoping whoever it was would flush themselves out when they figured no one was watching. He stuck with the latter and edged his face closer to the window. Much as the condensation made vision damn near impossible, he was loath to rub it away. Too many late-night cop shows had taught him that much.

The longer he waited, the mistier the glass grew. Perhaps he should have searched instead of waiting. Too late now to change his mind.

He blinked. No, the movement wasn't his imagination. He edged down further, pressing himself into the back of his seat as he held still.

*A woman.* Her walk and the shape of her body in her dark, fitted pantsuit gave her away. Something in her demeanour induced him to remain hidden—the furtive side-to-side turn of her head, her stilted, wary movements as she headed straight for Bec's car.

There was no way to avoid detection if she looked inside.

Just metres separated them and she didn't waver, her eyes centred more on the car now than her surroundings. There was only one thing for it.

He pushed against the door handle and scrambled out of the seat. Without stopping to close the door, he strode the remaining distance between them.

Her head jerked up. She froze. And Seth stared into the wide eyes of Lydia Thomasz.

Jayda had never felt more like chucking her guts than now.

'All this time he's been killing *Mum.*'

Her father looked like he'd joined her in the nausea stakes. He'd have a wrestle on his hands for the toilet bowl. 'We suspect so.'

'How long have you known?'

'Not long. At least, I didn't.'

'And Mum?'

He hesitated. 'You'll have to ask her.'

'Difficult when she's not here.'

'I know, love. Try to understand—'

Something clattered on the front porch. They froze, staring at each other through the metallic grind of a key in a lock.

*Shit!* Was the bastard playing with them even now?

Jayda shouldered past her father, weapon drawn, and braced herself as the door swung slowly open.

Her shoulders slumped. 'Mum!' She lowered her arm.

A whirlpool of emotions eddied through her as she holstered her gun and searched her mother's expression. It seemed an age since she'd seen her, and if she thought her father had aged during the past week, her mother had doubly so. Her face, once barely lined, was now deep-set and tormented, and the blue of her eyes had never appeared so dull.

*'Jayda!'*

The agonised whisper had Jayda hurtling into her arms. She hadn't realised how much she needed her mother until familiar warmth folded itself around her. The hurt and fear of the past weeks tumbled away as her mother's tears fell and joined with hers.

'I'm sorry. I am so, so sorry.' Her mother's voice shook, her emaciated arms clinging to Jayda as if she'd never let go. As if Jayda were a child again, in days when a hug had the power to heal all and a mother's love was dependable.

Jayda braced and pulled back, the near constant flow of tears of the past week spent. She looked up to meet a familiar pair of grey eyes over her mother's shoulder.

Seth's expression was indecipherable, and for someone who read people for a living, she was finding it damn near impossible to read him. What she'd trade right now for his thoughts. She hoped they weren't centred on the story this moment would make.

Her father rested his palm at the base of her mother's spine, and the look that passed between them made Jayda's heart skip an entire chorus. She recognised relief, but it was peppered with so much more. Love, for one.

'Your father texted that you were here. Much as I should have stayed away, I couldn't. I've missed you so much.' Her voice cracked and she wiped the moisture from her eyes with the back of her hand.

Her father cleared his throat. 'Why don't we move into the living room?'

Too stunned to do anything but follow, she swallowed, the wash of emotion at the feel of Seth's palm on her waist as confusing as seeing her father's on her mother's. Her parents looked nothing like a couple planning to divorce. And her mother had missed her, yet she should have stayed away.

Impossible to wrap her mind around that.

'Coffee anyone?' Her father's gaze met hers. She dropped her exhausted body into one of her parents' two couches, reading the familiar—and hopeful—challenge in his eyes.

She was still angry with him. That wouldn't fade overnight. But he was right—through all this havoc, nothing had changed. He was still her father. Life was unimaginable without him in it.

She raised her chin. 'What say we open one of your unbeatable ports?'

Seth watched Jayda raise the glass to her lips, then lower it without drinking.

'You missed Bec's funeral.' She leaned forwards, eyes spearing her mother from across the room. 'Explain to me how your daughter dying screams "time for a vacation".'

Lydia's slumped shoulders sank further into the couch, the anguish in her expression a tangible thing, more so because it mirrored Jayda's.

'A mother should never have to bury her child.'

'So instead, you boycott the entire event?'

He had to hand it to the other woman, much as it would have been easier to duck her daughter's accusations, she didn't sway.

'Funerals are for the living and I didn't deserve to be part of Bec's. It was my fault she died, my fault that bastard killed her. Staying away was meant to keep you and your dad safe.'

'Because Madden loved you and you married Dad?'

Shock bolted through Seth as the white of Lydia's skin turned almost transparent. Pieces were starting to click into place. 'That's part of it.'

'And what's the other part?'

Lydia pushed forwards from cushions that threatened to swallow her. 'The day he went to prison, I knew what he'd done.'

# Chapter Forty-Eight

Jayda gripped his hand so tight, Seth wondered if his bones would crack.

'You *knew* he was the Night Terror?'

Lydia's nod was heavy, not unlike the guilt that must go hand-in-hand with such an admission. Seth couldn't help it. The reporter in him stood up and took notice, even while the man in him ached for the two women.

'He asked to see me that day, and fool that I was, I thought he was going to say he was sorry. I sat in that horrible prison meeting room, sick to my stomach with what he'd done to Juliana, to you. He stared at me, his green eyes cold and not remotely sad, and he smirked. I knew then that it was a mistake. That everything had been a mistake from the moment we'd met—our friendship, letting him meet and marry my friend. The guilt that led me to introduce them.'

Her voice trembled and Seth had to lean in to hear. 'The sense I'd always had that something wasn't quite right. As I reached the door on my way out, I heard that awful clicking thing he did with his fingers, and I turned for one more look, hoping that I was wrong. I'll never forget the words he said at that moment. "You should have loved me, Lydia. It was your cruelty that killed those women, not mine."'

She faltered, then the same spark he'd seen lend Jayda courage entered her eyes. 'I knew then what kind of monster he was. What he'd done.' Lydia swallowed. 'He already had a life sentence, and the thought of sitting through another trial, seeing his wretched face day after day . . . What would it achieve, other than to drag you and this family through the dirt?'

'It would have brought justice to his victims' families. He would have been moved to high security, watched more closely.'

'I see that now. But back then I was young and naïve and selfish. I wanted to move on and forget. The Night Terror was off the streets. I never imagined he'd train someone to start it all over again.'

Jayda squinted at Lydia. 'What I don't understand is why he killed a long line of surrogates when he could just as easily have killed you and had his revenge?'

Her father leapt to his feet. 'Jayda!'

'Take it easy, Dean. She's only asking what you would if you were thinking straight.' She touched his arm, coaxing him back onto the couch. 'I've thought about little else the past twenty-five years. All I can do is guess. Perhaps in his own strange way, he still loved me. He was angry at the world, wanted to hit out and hurt someone. And that someone came in the form of forty-two women. They died because for some warped reason he wanted to let me live. Or perhaps he wanted me to suffer, to bear the guilt of every one of those forty-two deaths.'

'This isn't on you, Lyd. It was never on you.' Dean rubbed the back of her hand, but she yanked it away and curled it into her lap. It didn't prevent the trembling.

'Our baby girl's dead and I could have done something to stop the man responsible. How is this not on me?'

'You had no way of knowing that would happen.'

'I was stupid and scared, but that's no excuse. I should have tried. There are women who'd still be alive if I hadn't been such a coward. *Bec.*' Her voice broke and she swallowed. 'I'll have to live with that knowledge for the rest of my life.'

Dean opened his mouth, but Lydia stalled him with a look. They may not have shared a blood-link, but Seth could see Jayda had inherited her mother's capacity to shoot him down.

'I thought you blamed me.' Jayda's voice shook as she stared at her mother. Lydia rushed to her daughter's side. '*Never.* You are *not* to blame for this.'

'Neither are you, Mum.' They linked fingers and Seth felt that familiar wedge in his throat.

'I need your help.' Jayda's grasp on her mother's hands tightened. 'Think. Tell me everything he ever said and did back then. Madden knew today's Night Terror, primed him to kill before he died, and now that he can't tell us who it is, something in the past will have to lead us to him.'

'You're exhausted.'

Jayda made a beeline for her computer before the front door had time to snap shut. 'Perhaps, but I'm not ready to sleep.'

'The same info will be there tomorrow and you collapsing over it won't help.' Seth slid the security chain into place, clearly letting her know he didn't intend on leaving any time soon.

The knowledge gave wings to the flutters in her stomach as she peered at him over her screen. 'I'm fine, but you look bushed. You don't need to wait up.'

He looked anything but bushed. He looked . . . *tempting.* She typed in her password and waited for the system to connect. She couldn't think about *that* now. Her list of to-dos was a mile long and Seth shouldn't have ranked anywhere near the top ten.

'If you're fine, then so am I.' He performed their ritual sweep of the apartment with the spectrum analyser while his laptop booted up. Her heart warmed as she watched him finish up in the living room before dropping into the chair in front of his computer. 'So, what are we looking for?'

Somehow she'd known he'd help and the knowledge was like a steaming macchiato, extra strength.

'Anna Jones, Madden's mistress. She'd be aged somewhere between forty-five and fifty-five. I need anything and everything on her, and whether she had a child. Presumably he or she would be between twenty-five and thirty-five. See if either of them blogs, has a social media page or has been on any of the prison forums or chat-lines. If you can locate a picture, even better. If either of them have burped, I want to know what they were eating five minutes earlier. And if we can find the father, even better. Maybe his identity will lead us to the child.' By the time she finished, his fingers were trailing their way across the keys. It was reassuring, knowing that she had someone other than herself to depend on.

Her gaze dropped to the screen. Why was he still here? Seth had what he needed to research and write the story without her, and no real reason to stick around. Her fingers wavered over the keyboard.

Was it about more than the story for him?

She didn't dare hope, but she could consider it. And when this was all over, perhaps she'd allow herself to more than consider it.

One final glance at the dark hair flopped over his forehead and she pulled up the first of nine mobile phone records she'd asked Georgie to email her earlier. A ten-tonne boulder wedged its way deep into her chest. Every one of her neighbours—some of her closest friends—were about to be scrutinised, no exceptions. And once she finished with those in her building, she'd move onto the lives of those elsewhere.

She bit her lip, scrolled through the first page and then clicked through to the second.

Silence eddied between them, a light and easy wave of camaraderie that came from working with someone you trusted.

Page after page flicked across her screen—bank and phone records, credit history, anything she could find. She discovered Garry had three outstanding parking tickets and a speeding fine, Juz had never owned a driver's license and Brett from apartment twenty-six was three months behind on his mortgage. Then she clicked over to the next screen.

'That's strange.'

'What?' Seth's fingers scrubbed through his hair, leaving a trail of spikes as he looked up. It took a moment to tamp the need to smooth her palms over the disarray. Instead she shook her head. 'It's probably nothing.'

He quirked a brow. 'Tell me anyway.'

'The lease for Darren's apartment isn't in his name.'

The other brow joined the first. 'Whose name is it?'

'Deanna Ramos.'

'Sister?'

'He doesn't have a sister. And his mother's name is Anita.'

'A Spanish form of Anna.'

'It could be coincidence.'

'Or not.' He shook his head as if she were past hope.

Not so. She just wasn't ready to jump to accusations without proof.

He sighed. 'Is it his wife, then?'

'No, he doesn't have one. At least, he's never mentioned one.'

'And would he?'

She dropped her head and massaged the pressure point just shy of her right eye. 'Before today, I'd have thought so. But after discovering my biological mother is now a man and a serial killer, anything seems possible.'

The statement sounded so ludicrous when spoken aloud, that it should have been followed by a laugh. Only nothing about Madden was funny.

'Let's see what I can find.' Seth's fingers tapped over the keys.

She wanted to tell him to stop, that it wasn't necessary. That the anomaly was small and there was a good reason for it. Only, she couldn't.

What did she know about Darren, aside from what he'd told her? Although the same could be said of all her friends and acquaintances.

*Even Seth.* A mental shake put paid to the thought. Everything he'd told her checked out and she had no reason to believe he was anything other than what he professed to be.

Damn, she hated this! Invading a person's privacy had to be about the shittiest thing one friend could do to another. Then again, it was up there with stalking and murder.

This was work, pure and simple. A means to finding Bec's killer. Nothing, no matter how shitty she felt, could be ignored.

She glanced at the notepad beside her computer. 'There's something else. Last week he made a payment for eight grand to Holloway Treatment Centre in Queensland.'

As the words left her lips the implications hit. 'Oh, God! I didn't think about it at the time, but he looked pale at the funeral and he flinched when we hugged. What if he's sick?' *Or dying?* 'What if he's just had an operation or treatment for some life-threatening condition and I'm delving into his private life like he's some kind of criminal?'

'He never has to know, Jayda. But you need to do this, if for no other reason than to be able to look him in the eye and know he's a true friend.'

Seth was right. Of course he was. But it didn't stop her from hating that she'd been forced into suspecting the people closest to her.

'I know we have to do this, but Darren helped Bec buy and build the Beetle. For months they spent every weekend with their heads bent over that grimy engine, working on it together. She loved that stupid car! And, Juz. She called him her closest girlfriend. They partied, went clubbing, filled her entire wardrobe together! The thought that either one of them could have killed her is . . . doing my head in.'

'Oh.' His fingers hovered over the keyboard. He stared at his laptop with a look that said whatever was up with Darren, it wasn't 'nothing'.

'"Oh", what?'

'You might want to take a look.'

She pushed out of her seat and took a deep breath before peering over his shoulder. 'That can't be right.'

'There's only one Holloway Treatment Centre in Queensland and this is it.'

'Cosmetic surgery? Why would Darren want cosmetic surgery?'

'You said when you hugged he seemed to be in pain?'

'He flinched.'

'What about this?'

The screen flipped over. 'No way.'

'It would make sense. A female name on the lease. His being away on the pretence of "work". The cosmetic surgery.'

'Don't you think I'd know if Darren was a woman?'

'Have you slept with him?'

'No.'

'Seen him naked?'

'Of course not!'

'There's no "of course not" about it.' Seth looked so damn smug she wanted to slam his laptop closed over his knuckles. Only she couldn't drag her gaze from the screen.

*Transgender plastic surgery. Breast removal.*

Much as the woman who considered Darren a good friend baulked at the idea, her gut told her otherwise.

She dragged the back of her hand across her eyes, brushing away one or more escaped tears in the process. 'Damn! Is nobody who they say they are anymore?'

'Some of us are.'

Seth was right on both accounts. But she couldn't think about that now. Madden had changed from female to male. Darren was doing the same. Did it mean something or was it some perverse coincidence?

She shook her head. Her friend wasn't who she'd thought he was, but that didn't mean he was a killer. 'He would have been in surgery, or at least recovering, when the last murder was committed.'

'Dates can be fudged. Some practitioners can be bribed. These are things that need to be considered. It wouldn't hurt to get a warrant for his medical records.'

'Under what grounds?'

'That he might be the killer.'

'I'll need more than conjecture to convince Chase.'

Not only would it mean outing a friend whose only crime might be wanting to be male, but it meant revealing more about the case than she was willing to just yet. And without knowing how her old partner would react. Whether he'd back her or betray her.

Either way, before she acted, she had to be sure.

'We need to look at this from our other angle. What did your search for Anna or a child turn up?'

'Anna Jones. Only child of Max and Verna Jones, both deceased. Aged forty-nine, born August sixth, star sign Leo. Attended Garfield Junior High. She left in eleventh grade and bummed around for a while before completing a TAFE course in beauty therapy. Her last known place of employment was Beautification in Bunyip, although she's no longer listed as a current employee. No sign of a significant other, so far.'

'Did you find a photo?'

'Yep.' The screen changed.

'Blonde hair.'

'Aha.'

She didn't know what to make of Anna Jones. The woman was nothing like her mother, yet everything like her. Platinum blonde hair, blue eyes, but where her mother's held warmth, Anna's were hard and world-weary, her face lined as though every one of life's trials had trekked with steel-capped boots across it.

'She looks nothing like Darren.'

'Perhaps he takes after his father.' Seth didn't wait for her to comment and flipped screens again. 'I found only bare bones on social media, no blogging. There was some activity on the Pakenham Prison forum until three months ago, but none of it I've found so far mentions a child, boy or girl.'

'Any evidence of a marriage certificate or child's birth certificate?'

'Never been married. Guess she was waiting around for Mr Right. Or was that Madden?'

'Don't even joke about it.'

'I wasn't. Most of her forum posts rant about the injustice of the justice system. I don't know what cockamamie story Madden gave her about killing Juliana, but she seems to think it was some kind of mistake. Self-defence and all that.'

'A woman obsessed.' She turned and stared out at the almost full moon through her window. 'We need to find her child. Or the father. Any men other than Madden show up in her past?'

'Nothing yet, but I'll keep digging.'

'There has to be a birth certificate. Has Anna used any other aliases?'

'Not that I can see. None of the info that could lead us to her kid seems to exist. It's as if that black hole is back again.'

'He's offering scraps, but doesn't want us to see the full picture yet.'

'Something like that.'

'Then we keep at it. If he's missed something, we'll find it, and then we'll find the sonovabitch.'

'But not right now.' Seth glanced at his watch. 'It's past midnight. I've been staring at my screen so long everything's in triplicate. Let's attack this first thing tomorrow with fresh eyes and a night's sleep behind us.' He yawned. 'Don't know about you, but the thought of a bed right now is my idea of heaven.'

The word 'bed' saw thoughts she'd managed to keep at bay flounce their way back to the forefront of her mind.

His blue-grey eyes sparkled, despite his claims of tiredness. The only indication that the day had been long was the crushed, over-worn look of his shirt. Problem was, the wrinkles didn't affect the way it hugged his torso. Worse still, she knew what lay beneath the fabric and couldn't oust the images from her head.

Heady warmth shuddered through her body.

'Point me in the direction of your spare blankets.'

She busied herself, switching off her computer, shuffling papers that didn't need shuffling, knowing that Seth was waiting for her cue. It seemed he wasn't going to push, and previously she'd have been thankful. Now she was just frustrated.

How did you say 'you don't need to sleep on the couch' without sounding eager?

After the day he'd had, all he should want was a place to lie down and a pillow to sink his head into.

Not so.

Jayda's bottom lip plumped between her teeth as she stared anywhere but his direction. It wasn't difficult to guess her dilemma, but this time the decision had to be all hers.

'I assume they're in the cupboard down the hall?' He headed for the doorway.

'You don't need a blanket.'

'I'll be cold without it.'

The computer cord twisted round her finger. 'You won't be cold.'

'I'll get one just in case.'

He moved again, biting back a grin as she jumped out of her chair. 'Seth?'

'Yes?'

*'You don't need a blanket.'*

He turned, moved in, close enough to reach out and touch her. Yet he didn't.

'Why, Jayda?'

Her gaze narrowed, then a smile skimmed her lips. 'I have a perfectly good futon you can use in the study.'

It took a moment to realise he'd been duped. Somehow she had him figured, had turned his turkey into a chicken.

He returned her smile. 'Perfect.'

The curve of her lips lost its verve. Instead of calling him on his bluff, she brushed past him for the door. 'I'll help set it up.'

'Before you do . . .' He snagged her hand and tugged her round to face him. 'I need something else.'

'Mmm.' Her eyelids fluttered closed as her lips parted.

He leaned in and heard her sharp intake of breath. 'A towel.'

Her eyes widened. She stepped back, slapping his arm.

'Ouch! What was that for?'

'Being a smartass.'

She had him. In every which way, she had him. And he couldn't stop grinning. 'I thought you were warming to that part of me.'

'Other parts warm me more.'

'Care to elaborate?'

She shook her head, then arched a beautiful brow. 'You wanted a towel, I believe.'

'I've changed my mind.' He stepped in. 'I'll need two.'

'Two towels?'

The heat of her body called. His palms found the supple band of skin between her waistband and top, sliding upwards, dragging the light fabric with them.

'One for you, one for me.'

'I'm having a shower?'

Her top slipped easily over her head. It helped that she raised her arms up for him.

His heart stampeded like a bull at a rodeo. '*We're* having a shower.'

# Chapter Forty-Nine

**H**er breath hitched, but he wasn't sure whether it was the idea of showering together or his mouth drawing on her bra-clad nipple that caused it.

She sighed, fingers pressing into his skull, pulling him in as her chest arched out and her head fell back. He took the invitation at face value and made a beeline for the other breast. He unsnapped her trousers, dragged the zipper down as he tugged at her nipple and drew a moan from her lips.

His hand curved down her tummy and beneath the denim. *Hot.* The practical cotton of her panties was soaked through. He groaned, sliding his hand in further, dipping his finger in as far as the fabric barrier allowed. Her hips bucked and he pushed the fabric aside. This time his finger dove in deep, her flesh gripping tight, pulling him inside.

'*Seth.*'

It drove him crazy to hear her breathe his name that way. As if he were everything she'd ever wanted.

But now he'd started, how the hell to stop? He'd promised her a shower. And for this, their second time, it had to be perfect.

He pulled back. 'You have way too many clothes on.'

Colour rose on her cheeks. 'You too.' Her breath escaped in gasps, and as he reached for her jeans, she reached for his too.

Somehow they managed it, through fumbling fingers, impatience and all. Then, naked, he led her to the bathroom. Once the water ran warm, they stepped under together and Seth reached for the shower gel, rubbing a generous portion quickly between his palms. 'Can't have a shower without a good lather.'

'I'm partial to lather.' Her pupils were so dilated, the black had almost completely swallowed the green.

'Me, too.' He started at her shoulders, small, circular strokes that slid out over her arms, down to her fingertips, then back up again, over and over until she trembled. Her breasts were next, supersensitive flesh thrusting greedily into his palms, begging for attention. With her hands braced against his hips, he squeezed and plumped, eliciting moans that said she wanted more, that she was ready whenever he was.

He'd been ready the moment she began her teasing in the living room. And when they'd stepped beneath the spray, the stream spilling over her breasts and between her legs, he'd wondered how the hell he could last the shower long. He was rock hard, painfully so. But as her silken skin quivered beneath his touch, he found he wasn't anywhere near ready to stop.

Adding more soap, he followed the trail of water and suds over her breasts, branching out over her ribs to her hips, then trekking inward towards the juncture of her thighs. Her legs parted, inviting him in. He complied, revelling in her shuddering acceptance, pushing her until she quaked and throbbed, and with every stroke whimpered his name. Begged for him to continue, and more.

Then he stopped.

Jayda's eyes shot open. 'W–what?'

Gentle hands framed her face, warm lips brushing hers with the sweetest of caresses. 'I want to take you to bed, Jayda Thomasz.'

Her body still trembled from being so close, yet so far. Now her heart trembled too. It was that look again. It encompassed her and made her believe in the impossible.

He swept the water from her brow and she reached up to rest her hands over his. 'I want that too.'

Renewed heat flared in his eyes as he took her hand and led her from the shower stall.

She floated through the next moments as if her feet had wings. Seth's gaze never once left hers as they dried each other before moving to the bedroom. Crisp, cool sheets crinkled beneath her back as he lowered his body over hers. This time when he entered her, she was ready. The pain was less, the passion overwhelming.

Her body bounded towards weightlessness, every nerve a firing, riotous wave of sensation before she shuddered into climax around his throbbing flesh.

He held himself suspended above her, dipping once to swallow her gasping breaths into a kiss. Then he rolled onto his side, disappearing for mere seconds before returning, wrapping his arms around her, his warm, hard body spooning hers from behind.

His fingers brushed her neck as he tucked her hair to the side and feathered hot kisses over her bare skin. Impossible as it seemed, her sex pulsed in hunger. She wriggled her bottom and felt the hard thrust of aroused muscle right where she wanted it. Again.

She was beginning to need Seth Friedin too much. Half of her wanted it to be okay, wanted to trust him and lean on him, and yes, give in and follow the hint that was insistently nudging against her buttocks. The other half was scared shitless.

If there was one thing she refused to do, it was scared.

'I was in grade two when I discovered I was adopted.' She pushed the words out in a rush so she couldn't pull them back.

The lips on her neck froze, and her heart froze with them.

Oh, God! Was this the wrong time? Then again, was there a right time to open up and bare weakness? Letting people in had never come naturally. Yet, for some reason, two seconds ago it had felt right, until—

'*So young?*' The words may have been whispered, but they yelled acceptance.

Her and her overreactions. Another tendency that went hand-in-hand with the emotion-rich red of her hair.

Those heat-seeking lips continued and she let out a sigh as his arms tightened about her waist.

'Smart-ass Lucy Turner thought it her duty to inform me that two blue-eyed parents couldn't make a green-eyed child. I now know it isn't true, but she was the smartest kid in the class, so I never considered back then that she could be wrong.'

The images appeared as if it was only yesterday—her eight-year-old self storming into the kitchen, schoolbag on back, red hair in chaos, the hem of her uniform torn from climbing a tree to rescue McHenry's old tabby.

Her mother stood at the stove, her father at the bench, and they shared one of their looks before turning calmly to face her. She'd waited for them to shoot down Lucy 'Troublemaker' Turner's accusations. It had never occurred to her that the dissimilarities between her and her family were anything more than a random spin of the genetic wheel.

'My parents barely blinked when I confronted them. I guess they'd been waiting for a time to tell me, and that day was as good as any.'

His hand fanned over her tummy as he whispered into her hair. 'A tough way to find out.'

'Crappy. But I never felt hurt or had a wild urge to discover more about my birth parents. Maybe it was because I always thought they were dead. I'm more inclined to believe that I felt so loved and wanted and happy that I couldn't imagine any other life.'

She drew in a deep breath. 'I accepted it. Told Lucy to shove her theories into very awkward, uncomfortable places, and moved on. It seems funny to say, but being adopted just made sense. Unlike what's happening now, which makes no damn sense at all.'

Her heart pounded against her eardrums even as a sense of calm washed over her. Amazing how good it felt to talk about something she hadn't talked about in forever.

His lips fluttered over her ear, seeping warmth through her body. 'At least you had a family who loved you.'

'There is that.' She found his hand and wrapped her fingers around tight. 'Have you considered that rather than not wanting to talk to you, it could be that your parents didn't know what to say?'

The hand in hers tensed. 'That'd be a great happy ending, wouldn't it?'

'You don't think it's a possibility?'

'After twenty-nine years of staring at their turned backs, I doubt it.'

'Their lack of interest doesn't define you, Seth.'

'I know.'

'What matters is how you view yourself.'

He exhaled, and the weight of his pain tore at her insides. 'All I've ever wanted was to make a difference.'

'You do make a difference. To a lot of people.' She swallowed. '*To me.*'

The arms around her squeezed and he nuzzled into her hair, breathing in deep as if he wanted to drag the very essence of her inside.

'Thank you.'

She nodded, unable to find the words to thank him back. Just for being with her. For it no longer being about the story.

So many thoughts rambled through her mind, each one clamouring for attention. It wasn't the time or the place for contemplations over her future and where this would all lead. Complacence was a categorical no-no when there were so many other priorities vying for the top spot on her list.

Closing her eyes, she pushed aside everything but the cocoon of hard muscle at her back and a manner of peace she hadn't felt in long time.

Then she slipped over the edge into deep, restful sleep.

*Hey, sleepyhead.*

She scrunched her eyelids and fought against the pull from dreams that were peaceful and rather enjoyable.

Where was she before—

*You called and here I am.*

The whisper shivered across her skin before a warm mouth caught the lobe of her ear and sucked. Damn if he hadn't found another of those killer erogenous zones. Her entire body was a bevy of them.

His palm took a delicious ride across her waist and over her hips, heading on a collision course to the aching throb between her thighs. She opened her legs, moaning as his fingers feathered across flesh still tender from the night before.

Regardless of the tenderness, she wanted more. Blood thrummed through her veins.

'*Seth.*'

*I'm here.*

The warm tickle of breath on her neck hit a direct path to her tummy. Then he kissed, his lips caressing the shell of her ear, the tickles moving lower, her hips slowly bucking, searching for fulfilment. *Him.*

His expert fingers found the spot almost immediately, their play gentle, unlike her reaction. Or her need. She wanted it hard, and she told him so, his sharp intake of breath indication enough that he wanted the same. That and the nudge of hard, male muscle as he thrust into her.

Her nails dug into his back and she urged him on, unsure where the words were coming from, only happy that this was a dream because she'd never have the courage to say and do all of this if it was real.

She'd heard talk of women seeing stars when they made love, always considered it a load of baloney. Now she knew the truth. He thrust again and she screamed his name, her body splintering to the heavens as the entire Milky Way galaxy exploded across her vision.

Blissful heaviness engulfed her as she drifted to the sound of his breathing in her ear and the luxurious warmth of his body wrapped around hers.

She sighed, the smell of pine and man filling her senses. Then sleep and dreams filled her mind again.

'Hey, sleepyhead.'

Jayda's body jumped.

Her hand jerked back, preventing coffee from flooding the laptop on her knees, the front of her top taking the brunt of the spill instead.

Dumping her mug and computer onto the coffee table, she peeled her top away from her skin and looked at the deliverer of words direct from her dream. A dream she had a scary suspicion was more reality than she'd have liked.

'Damn, Jayda! What is it about you and hot liquid burns?'

The coffee was her second and she'd been nursing it the past fifteen minutes while hunting for any mention of Anna Jones's kid. But Seth didn't know that.

'I'm fine. You just startled me.'

He pulled her up and tugged at her tee. 'This needs to come off.'

She swatted his hands away. 'Are you kidding?'

'Do you know how many people suffer severe burns from hot beverages in Australia each year? It's in the thousands.'

'Most of whom would be kids pulling a cup down from the kitchen bench or table.'

'That's not the point. Do you really want to be another statistic?'

'If this is your way of getting me naked again, it's pretty weak.'

'Hey, if I wanted you naked, all I'd need to do was this.'

Before she could step away, his mouth was on her neck, making a direct course for her ear before delivering the same treatment to her lobe that he had last night.

*It wasn't a dream.* And neither was her reaction.

Sliding her hands between them, she ignored the contraction of muscles beneath her palms, the desire to discard his black shirt and toy with the taut skin and smattering of fine hairs beneath.

'I need to change.' She pushed past him and almost sprinted for the bedroom.

*Get a grip, Thomasz! Don't lose it now.*

Only it was too late for that. She'd already lost it. Had screamed for Seth to take her, to suck and lick and—*oh God!* Had she really begged him to do all that stuff?

Her face burned as she discarded her top, not bothering to soak the stain. She had more pressing problems, like how to look Seth in the eyes again without combusting from embarrassment or melting like ice cream in the hot summer sun.

She'd bared her soul, then her body, with little thought of the future.

Just proved that her first instincts were right. Sex changed everything. And it contravened common sense. She hadn't shown a bit of the stuff since Seth and lust for him had filled her brain.

And the kicker? She liked it.

The drawer's brass handle dug into her palm. Damn, why shouldn't she? For a woman who'd waited pretty much all of her life to feel what he made her feel, she had a helluva lot of catching up to do. And she wanted to do it with Seth.

Her heart stuttered. It didn't mean anything. She felt good when she was with him. Alive. Sexy. He was a constant in the past weeks' craziness, the only one who was exactly who and what he professed to be.

She sifted through her drawer and grabbed the third top that came to hand. One that hugged her in all the right places and deepened the green in her eyes.

After last night's reveal-all with her parents, the case had gained a direction which she intended to follow until it was done. Then the killer would be off the street and she'd be back in the job she loved.

That would be the time to rein in towards perspective and sense.

In the meantime, if Seth provided support peppered with the odd moment in which she forgot the hell of her life and found a slice of heaven, then so be it.

When she returned to the living room, it was to find the man of her thoughts bent over her computer. He looked up. 'You've been looking into Darren.'

'He's a suspect until proven innocent, like everyone else.'

'Even Juz?'

'If I uncover something suss about him, then yes.'

That seemed to appease him. She wished she could feel the same calm detachment. But someone she considered a friend was killing identikits of her mother, had killed her sister and Eric, and had orchestrated Madden's death. There was no doubt in her mind that at some stage in his game he intended to kill her.

The only question was when.

A deep breath tamped down the turmoil in her gut. Another pushed the thought further to the back of her mind.

She moved in closer, ready to forget, if only for a moment. Her gaze trained on Seth's as she tugged at the hem of her top. She'd chosen it because she knew she looked good in it. But while his expression agreed, the hitch of his breath as she dragged it over her head and dropped it to the floor said he preferred to see it there. And right now, so did she.

Her hand reached for his waistband and she barely had to tug before his body was hard against the length of hers. There was no soft or gentle now, his lips were fierce and demanding, his hands moving to her back, pulling her in closer still. He stole her breath, along with every sane and rational thought, and it was wondrous.

She dragged her lips away, her hands already working at the buttons of his shirt.

'Tell me again what you planned on doing once you got me naked.'

# Chapter Fifty

Everything pointed to Darren.

Even Juz—who liked most people—had disliked him at first sight. Plus, there were still things that didn't add up, would never add up until she confronted him and demanded answers. Something she would do once she had more than circumspection to go on.

Jayda turned the hot tap a fraction further and closed her eyes as the warm spray coursed over her.

The killer had to be computer savvy. Something Darren was. But that wasn't enough.

Then there was Garry. His father worked in the rare book room at Melbourne Museum. Again, the discovery wasn't enough. It didn't mean he had access to methyl cellulose glue or knew how to make his own paper. Still, it did warrant a closer look, something that so far had garnered little success.

Every avenue she followed found her staring at a brick wall. The vault at Black Keys Security was rented under a bogus identity and paid for in cash. As secure as the storage facility was, there was no video footage. In fact, there never seemed to be video footage when the Night Terror struck.

She rubbed shampoo into her hair, the scent of green apples filling the shower stall as she lathered.

What she needed was concrete not conjecture, some cold, hard evidence to back up the layers of speculation. She refused to accuse a friend with less.

Problem was, every passing hour propelled her closer towards disaster. Any day now, Will would discover her DNA was a partial match to Madden's, indicating a familial link. When that happened, her investigation would be quashed and—even worse—she could become a person of interest in his death.

The hot stream washed away the suds, not so the strain.

Three days had passed since she'd discovered her true identity and laid herself bare and vulnerable before Seth. During that time he'd barely left her side, and they'd worked together tirelessly to find something that would lead them to an arrest. Her jaw clenched. *Her squad* to an arrest.

Not that *they* were any closer either. Something she'd discovered when Chase and Georgie swung by to check up on her. Was it only yesterday? She'd lost all sense of time.

They'd stayed for coffee, openly updating her on the case, or so she would have believed if she hadn't known better. Not once did they mention the disparity between Madden's sex and his DNA. And she hadn't let on that she knew. Whatever scraps they were willing to share were better than no scraps at all.

None of the inmates had obvious links to Night Terror victims, past or present, or any connection to Madden past a shared address. Yet questions still remained around how he would have obtained a mop. He must have had help.

How much help and how far that help had contributed to his death were as yet unanswered.

Then there was Anna Jones. It was as if she'd dropped off the face of the earth. Three months ago she checked out of her rental address in Garfield and no one, friends, acquaintances, neighbours, had seen or heard from her since.

Was her disappearance by choice or something more sinister? There was no evidence of either.

Regardless, yet another avenue of investigation found them traipsing up a dead-end alley, and any initial hopes they had that the killer could have slipped up and left a clue were beginning to fade.

Time was ticking towards the Night Terror's next move and resources in the Department were stretched. Her duo of babysitters had long since passed their twenty-four hour vigil and returned to engage in real policing, as well they should.

Through all the frustration, the wall-pounding and head-banging, Seth had been there. Sure, he'd capitalised on their discoveries, submitted a string of news-breaking reports to his editor. But not once had he broken his promise to her about Bec and her family. The knowledge made her hope. And, dare she say, dream.

The nightmares had gone. Whether from having Seth by her side each night or her new-found understanding of what had happened in her past, she couldn't tell.

All she knew was that their time together was intense. So intense, she welcomed the breathing space his drink with a friend was giving her this evening.

She snatched up the conditioner and squeezed too much into her palm. Dumping the bottle back onto the shelf, she jabbed the cream into her hair, working it through from the scalp to the ends. Then, closing her eyes, she allowed her head to fall back, the full force of the hot stream hitting her upturned face.

Good to have time alone to regroup. Rejuvenate. Recover from living in each other's space for the past three days.

A door outside slammed.

Her lids jerked open, a mix of water and conditioner burning her eyes. Scrunching them closed, she fumbled for the towel before rubbing her face, all the while her heart skipping a happy dance in her chest.

He was back early. Thoughts of their last shower together saw the skipping move lower.

'Seth?'

No answer.

'Seth, is that you?'

Something crashed in her bedroom followed by a shattering of glass. Her gut lurched. Now all her heart could do was thump.

Frozen, ears supersensitive, she waited, straining for another sound. *Nothing.* Leaving the water running, she eased the shower door open and slipped into her robe. Knotting the belt, she scanned for a weapon, anything, cursing the gun still lying in her bedside table drawer.

Hairdryer clutched in one hand, nail scissors in the other, she turned the handle and edged open the door.

Her room was empty, the window behind her bedside table wide open. It had been closed before she entered the shower. She was sure of it.

The blinds clattered, a haphazard stirring as they caught the breeze, and beneath them lay her lamp, the spiral energy-saving globe smashed into her carpet.

A thud sounded from the living room.

She traded the hairdryer and scissors for her gun. The door was ajar and she crept towards it and listened. No sound.

Leading with her weapon, she sidled down the hall with small, soundless steps. Her heart pounded. Everything else was silent. Still. A scan of the living room found it empty. Almost.

A bundle of mottled black-and-grey fur mewed before jumping awkwardly down from the couch to wrap round her ankles. There was a waver in her chuckle as her shoulders dropped. Her body relaxed. The Night Terror, this case, it had her so jumpy she didn't know herself anymore.

'Tumbles, you naughty boy. What will Juz say when he hears you've stooped to breaking and entering?' She dropped to her haunches and the cat leaned into her palm, rubbing his ear against her fingers as he purred loudly.

He bucked his head into her hand and she sighed.

Her hand jerked.

In freeze-frame motion, like the pause and rewind of a tape in her mind, something clicked. Breath caught in her throat. The fingers around her gun tensed as an image tugged at her subconscious. Slowly she stood and turned towards the far corner of the room.

Vacant eye sockets gaped from a face singed with the burn of strong alkali. The body slumped the way bodies do with the loss of muscle tone, the torso jutting awkwardly to the left.

Ignoring the attention-seeking mew of the cat, Jayda's head jerked right, then left as she backed up until she could feel the wall against her shoulders. She called Chase and he said he'd be there in five. Then, with methodical precision, she moved from room to room, clearing each one as she went.

Not until every cupboard was opened, the underside of every bed and couch and table checked, did she allow herself to stop and feel.

She didn't know what to do, so she sat on the couch, Tumbles purring contentedly on her knee, no less relieved to discover the body was a mannequin.

Her gaze dropped from the lifeless stare to the paper pinned to its chest. Blood-red letters bled into the fibre.

*Your turn next.*

Seth jumped out of the car and bounded up the two flights of stairs to the apartment.

*He got the job!*

The grin wouldn't wipe from his face, even if he tried. He'd done what he set out to do. Made it.

He couldn't wait to tell Jayda.

His heart leapt. Who'd have thought? After spending almost every minute of the past three days together, he wanted more.

Not once had claustrophobia hit. And he'd waited for it. Lain silent in bed, her body curled into his as he listened to the even keel of her breathing and waited for his flight mechanism to overtake the warmth and rightness of the moment.

He was still waiting, but he doubted it was going to show. Which was why he was so damn eager to get back to her now. She had no idea of his real reason for leaving this afternoon, and he'd hated the omission. But he was ready to share and celebrate now the job was a certainty. He knew just how to celebrate.

His groin tightened with familiar need. One that roamed hand-in-hand with a sassy, headstrong detective who had lush green eyes and hair like a halo of bright, red flames.

Scaling the stairs, his strides long and quick, he pushed through the fire door. The hard wood slammed against his back as he barely stopped himself from stumbling over his feet.

Crime scene tape surrounded her apartment.

A uniformed officer glared at him from outside her door, catapulting his heart into his throat. He tried to swallow past the pain.

Her security detail had finished their token twenty-four hour stint. Stretched resources, they'd said. Idiocy, more like it. She was the target of a madman and needed protection. He'd vowed to provide it, and apart from today's meeting with Carson, he had.

Realisation slammed into his brain. He'd failed her.

*No!* She couldn't be . . . he wouldn't say the word. Not now, not when everything about them was beginning to make sense.

His legs worked independent of his brain, every step bringing him closer to his worst nightmare. He made to duck under the tape only to be blocked by the cop on the other side.

'You can't come through. This is a crime scene.'

The pound of his heart bellowed in his ears. He scuffed his fingers through his hair, craning his neck to see beyond the man. There was nothing to see but a closed door and an inordinate amount of blue-and-white tape that screamed disaster. 'It also happens to be my girlfriend's apartment.'

He waited for the weirdness to hit. Nothing but rightness followed. That and a sense of loss.

'Wait while I let the detectives know you're here. Name?'

'Seth Friedin. Is she . . .?' The words gagged at the back of his throat.

The man squinted then grinned. 'As a doornail.'

Red exploded across Seth's vision and he wanted to beat every nuance of the man's smirk from his face. His fists clenched and he stepped forwards.

'Seth.'

'Jayda?' His head jerked back. The woman he wanted to see more than anything stepped through the doorway. He'd never felt so happy to be wrong in his life. 'You're alive!' He side-stepped the officer, skirting the tape to wrap her in close.

'Did you think I wasn't?' Her body shook as she sank into his arms. Hell, he never wanted to let her go.

He buried his face into her hair, breathing in fresh, green apples and Jayda. 'When I saw the tape . . . I . . .'

The man beside them didn't even try to hide his interest.

He moved Jayda aside. 'I have something to tell you. But later.' He tilted her head and stared into eyes he wanted to wake up to every day for the rest of his life. The realisation was like one of her strong, steamy espressos on a cold winter's day—flavoursome and comforting. Not an ounce of claustrophobia in sight.

'What happened?'

'He was here.'

'The Night Terror?'

She nodded, her knees wobbling, her steps unsteady. Seth swore. Arm wrapped tight about her shoulders, he pushed the apartment door open and lead her inside. A couple of uniforms stood beside the window, heads together, hushed voices, while a forensics officer dusted for prints in the far corner. As they reached the couch, the officer turned and only then could he see what she'd been dusting.

'Shit!'

Cavernous eye sockets gaped out from a face dulled through death, the mouth and nose burned white with chemicals. His gaze dropped to the left hand, and sure enough, the ring finger was severed cleanly at the joint.

*It could have been her.*

His arm tightened about Jayda's shoulder.

She touched his elbow. 'It's not real, Seth. It's just a dummy.'

The body skewed stiffly to one side and another glance revealed the waxy sheen of its skin. The officer's smirk suddenly made sense. Not that it excused his insensitivity.

His gaze staggered over the plastic form, taking in the short black skirt and top. 'Is that—'

She nodded. 'My clothes.' The outfit she'd worn to dinner at Antonio's.

'The bastard! What the hell is he playing at? What does he want?'

'Me.' She shuddered again. It was just one crack in the veneer of her control. Then he felt her body tense as her chin kicked upwards and her eyes fired.

God, he loved that about her. The fight. The sass. She had a shell as hard as titanium, but her centre was soft. He knew, because she'd let him in, let him see how soft.

Then he saw the note.

The threat of loss taunted him. He'd felt it just before, staring at the crime scene tape webbed across her front door. He felt it now with the killer's intention outlined so clearly in blood red.

His mind screamed. He wouldn't—couldn't—allow Jayda to be ripped from his life. Not now. *Never.*

The truth was so clear to him, but he needed time to convince her. That she was his future.

# Chapter Fifty-One

**W**ide hazel eyes stared out from the corner of the room. The creature huddled between the sofa legs, shaking, *knowing*.

His throat clogged and he switched his gaze to the powder-blue walls.

The drug had taken effect, the cat's three working legs now as useless as the fourth. Soon it would lose consciousness and know nothing past perpetual sleep.

His breath quickened.

Car tyres screeched from the road below and his fingers faltered around the knife handle. He'd never been one for hurting animals. His art was of a different variety, his canvas set through actions other than his or the pitiful creature sprawled out before him.

His gaze shifted and his legacy came into focus. Testimony to all he'd achieved.

*Power up, pussy boy!*

He turned the blade. It sliced easily through his skin, red beading along the wound as it spread. Old scars making way for new.

He focused on the pain, as he had so many times before.

*Stop your whining, boy. Take it like a man.*

*Pain is power.*

He closed his eyes, lost himself in the sensation. His nostrils flared. The metallic tang rolled across the back of his tongue, an old friend, as he and pain became one.

He inhaled. Exhaled. Slow. Steady.

His eyes opened.

He moved to the bathroom and cleaned up—his skin, the knife. A bandage put paid to the blood.

Then, knife in hand, he re-entered the living room, ready for what had to be done.

# Chapter Fifty-Two

Seth shot Jayda that killer grin of his—the one that dimpled his chin and made her body quiver.

'Make yourself comfortable while I get coffee.'

He left the room. Jayda's feet remained glued to the polished floorboards as she looked around. Any other circumstances and she'd jump at the opportunity to gain insight into his life.

But she wasn't in Seth's living room by choice. Her apartment was a crime scene, her building no longer safe. Hackett's words. This time he'd informed her in person while pushing her out her front door.

She hadn't fought particularly hard. Sleep wouldn't have come easily with the memory of that mutilated hunk of plastic in her living room, despite forensics having hauled it away. She'd known that eventually the Night Terror would grow tired of taunting her and move in for the kill. She'd just imagined she had more time.

The slap of her overnight bag on the floor echoed through the open area. She took a few tentative steps forwards, if only to leave the direction of her thoughts behind.

All she wanted was to shuck her shoes, curl her legs up and sink back into the warm, comfortable cushions of a couch. Only Seth's couch didn't look like the kind one curled up into. Pristine black leather aside, it looked as if it wasn't a day over . . . a day old. Weird since she knew he'd lived here for the past five years.

She perched on the edge, her only concession to 'relaxation' toeing off her shoes. She tugged the edges of her jacket together and looked around.

Very little she'd seen so far of the Victorian cottage fit with the man she'd come to know.

The living room radiated an unused air, barren but for the essentials. The absence of family photos was no surprise, given his ailing relationship with his parents, but there was a blatant lack of anything else personal. No tatty magazines or newspapers, no half-open books or knick-knacks or *stuff* littering the coffee table or sideboard. Nothing to show outside interests or life beyond his work. The furniture appeared new but belonged to another era—Grandpa Joe's. Even the Turkish rug looked as if it had rarely seen a pair of feet.

*Sterile.* The word was perfect for this home without a heart. Was the rest the same?

Her gaze darted in the direction Seth had disappeared. Damn! She'd forgotten to remind him no instant on the coffee.

It occurred to her that she could follow, but she was too exhausted to care. Instead, she gave in to need and shuffled backwards until she leaned against the resistant, upright leather. Her eyes closed, her mind adrift. From some distant place she felt her head slump to the side. Her breathing slowed.

Dull ringing filled the world. The dark flickered, then burst with colour—a vision all too familiar, yet different. The images vivid this time, the lines sharper, more focused than ever before.

*The child craned her neck. Her slight body trembled, eyes wide as she peered through the red-splattered chair legs. The splotches looked like paint, like the day she'd dropped her tub in art and thick red had oozed down her easel and onto the floor. Only this time was different. This time the red was blood.*

*She tucked her knees closer into her body, hugged them, as if by curling up tighter she might be able to disappear.*

*A woman was crying. Red curls cascaded over her shoulders and down her back, the same colour as the girl's, but for the blood. There was a lot of blood. She scuffled backwards, hiding deeper under the dining table until she bumped the chair on the other side.*

*Her breath stuck like syrup in her throat. Slowly, he turned. She couldn't see his face. Had never seen it. All she knew was it was evil.*

*The woman screamed. 'Run, Sammy. Run!'*

*The girl scuttled out through the jumble of chair legs and belted for the open front door. The woman screamed again, a gurgling, horrifying wail, then there was silence.*

*She didn't look back, didn't stop. She ignored his call, kept running, legs pounding out over the concrete, lungs burning until she thought she would die.*

*She ran, knowing she ran for her life.*

*Strong arms enveloped her and she struggled. Caught! She twisted and punched and kneed, wanting to hurt him, wanting to make him pay—*

'Jayda, I've got you.' The smell of pine surrounded her. 'Shh, it's okay, I'm here now.' She collapsed into the familiar warmth. She was safe. He made her safe.

'Jayda?'

Soft lips brushed her hair, one hand curving over her cheek, combing a strand back from her face. Her eyes flew open and Seth's face filled her vision.

She tried to think past the thunder in her ears. 'What happened?'

'Another nightmare.'

Her heart still pounded, her skin was cold and clammy beneath her clothes. The same as every other time. Only something was different.

She pulled at the dream, struggling to remember. Something dragged at her subconscious. Something important.

'What is it?'

'I saw something. Something that made everything else make sense.' She clenched her eyelids closed, willing the dream back. 'Dammit! Why can't I remember?'

'You've had a scare.'

'I don't scare.'

Bravado talking. Her erratic heartbeat didn't lie. But an admission would mean giving in to so much more than the fear. It meant giving in to the Night Terror—both old and new. And *that* she refused to do.

'I know you're tough. You're one of the strongest women I know. But it's okay to be scared. Someone out there wants to kill you. Anyone in your situation would feel the same.'

Fathomless blue dragged her in, her words of denial powerless to move past her tongue.

'We have to get him.'

'We will. I won't let anything happen to you.'

'You might not have a choice.'

His hand reached for hers. 'You're right. I haven't had a choice since you ran away from what could have been a swinging success the first time we met.'

Despite herself, she had to smile. 'Swinging success?'

'Too cheesy?'

'Just as well you write better than you pick up.'

'I'm not interested in picking up. Not anymore.'

Happiness crept through her as she allowed his words to sink in. Dare she believe in something she'd given up all belief in? Now was the worst time to lose focus and become entrenched.

Or perhaps it was the best.

Seth had seen her at her lowest and hadn't run, much as she'd given him every reason to. The knowledge warmed her like nothing else could. What was she supposed to do with it?

She pushed away from the back of the couch. 'What happened to coffee?'

He handed her a black mug from the coffee table. 'It'll be cold by now. I didn't want to wake you.'

She sniffed. 'It's perked.'

'You don't drink anything else.'

'Before you met me, you didn't know percolators existed.'

'Before I met you, I had no reason to.'

It wasn't the cold now that made her shiver. He'd bought and kept a percolator. For her. The action more than hinted at permanence. It screamed it from the rooftops.

One more sniff and she discarded the mug on the clear glass tabletop. He shifted it to a coaster then dropped his hand to her knee. Wild flames sizzled up her leg.

She shivered.

'You're cold. I'll make you another.' He made to stand.

She pulled him back. 'No.'

He dropped down. 'No?'

'That's not what I want.'

One tug separated his shirt from his waistband. Her fingers fumbled over the buttons.

The lethal slide of a grin across his lips melted her—inside, outside, every place that remembered the feel of him, the taste—and she wondered that a look could hold so much heat. Was it possible to orgasm on promise alone?

'It's not?' His palm edged upwards, then stopped.

'I think you know what I'd prefer.'

'I'd still like to hear it.'

She lost herself in the blue of his gaze. 'I want you, Seth Friedin.'

His fingers slid higher as his lips lowered, brushing hers with the softest of sweeps. She tasted coffee, and something far more intoxicating—*him.*

She quivered, inside and out. All that filled her thoughts, her awareness, was Seth, and how much she needed him, now, more than now.

Something in his eyes held her, consumed her, made her breath catch in her throat.

'That's good, Jayda Thomasz. Because I want you too.'

It was unclear who led who to bed, and it shouldn't have mattered. But when Jayda took his hand and drew him near, his heart stuttered in a way that was entirely new to him.

Her eyes were wide, her red lips moist and waiting for him to take them. He'd never wanted anything so much.

'You're beautiful.'

She was. With a beauty that stretched beyond looks.

Much as the creamy curve of her shoulder made him want her in the most basic of ways, his response went deeper. To the world she was Detective Thomasz—hard-headed, tough, distant—but he'd glimpsed her vulnerability. She'd let him in, and that meant more than any story ever could.

The job, the success, that front-page headline he'd chased for so long—none of it made him whole. She did that.

It wasn't so much a realisation as a journey's end.

Her fingers slipped beneath his waistband, banishing every thought other than how much he wanted her. This. And how he didn't want it to end. The thought should have brought panic, instead it gave him peace.

They shed their clothes and came together, Jayda showing none of her previous hesitation.

He pulled her on top, growling as she spread her legs across his body and slowly took him inside. The fit was snug, right, and she closed her eyes, letting her head fall back as she lifted and then sank back down, taking every last inch of him in once again.

He gripped her hips and held her still until she opened her eyes and stared at him through a haze of passion. His hands scaled her ribs, cupping her breasts, palming, squeezing, until her breath hitched and her nipples tugged into tight, elongated pebbles. When her eyes closed he stopped again.

He needed to watch her unravel. And she, too, would watch. Watch him loving her.

'Look at me, Jayda.'

Her lashes fluttered open and he could die drowning in those hazy green depths. Then she smiled, lifted her hips, and slowly edged her way down. Her head dipped, her tongue darting out over his nipple before she grazed it with her teeth. The sensation shot straight to his groin and he groaned. 'What you do to me!'

Her eyes glinted as she nipped again. He grabbed her buttocks and thrust up and into her, deep.

She moaned. 'Tell me, Seth.'

At some stage in the past five minutes his brain had sunk below his waist. That had to be why her words made no sense.

'Tell you what?'

Her lips rubbed across his nipple before she took it into her mouth and sucked. Sliding him into a gaping abyss with no way out.

She lifted her head and licked the moisture from her lips. 'Tell me what I do to you.' Colour rose from her neck to her face.

He'd never been so turned on in his life; Jayda splayed across his body, blushing, asking him to talk dirty.

Her bottom lip clamped between her teeth. It was ripe red and he knew how good it tasted, how much he wanted to taste it again.

She clenched the flesh around his, dragging a growl from his throat.

'What do I do, Seth?'

He barely registered as she bent her head and let him taste her lips. She was everything he ever needed, and more than he'd ever hoped for. When she pulled back, her gaze questioned his and he gave her the only answer he could.

'You make me love you.'

# Chapter Fifty-Three

Jayda's heart gunned AK-47-style.

It didn't mean what she thought it meant. What she wanted it to mean. It was a heat-of-the-moment thing, *right?*

Seth's expression said it wasn't.

*I'm glad.*

The thought surprised her, although it shouldn't have. She'd always dreamed of what her parents had—a partnership, love and understanding, the unconditional kind. The knowledge that you need never be alone again. That one person to fill your world, your heart, make you whole in a way nothing else could.

Albeit the dream had dwindled when she'd believed they were separated, but now they were together again and she understood why they'd split, the dream was back. And she wanted it with Seth.

She wanted Seth to love her.

The realisation should have brought peace. Instead it tied her chest into knots. The timing sucked.

How had she let this happen? Complicated was the last thing she needed. And any involvement with Seth would be just that. Falling in love. Needing someone so badly she didn't know what she'd do if he was gone.

*When* he was gone. Because that would surely happen once he realised *his* dream and became a full-time reporter at the paper. He'd have his story and no reason to stay.

Even with her lack of experience, she knew words said in the heat of passion belonged to the heat of passion. Great sex wasn't a precursor to happy ever after.

The knowledge saw the knots in her chest tighten.

*But he's here now. Make the most of it.*

*And maybe, somehow, you'll make him want to stick around.*

'Jayda?' His grey-blue gaze pierced her uncertainty as he ran his knuckles along her cheekbone and under her chin.

She shivered. 'Make love to me, Seth.'

The blue brightened. 'With pleasure.'

He rolled her onto her back, feathering kisses across her face, down her neck, easing in and out, slowly at first then, as her breath hitched, faster. She tilted her hips, wrapped her legs around him, and discovered it heightened her sensitivity. His too, if his drawn out groan was any indication.

Her nails dug into his back and she knew she'd leave marks. As he would when he clamped his lips to her neck and suckled, drawing the very essence from her soul.

She didn't care, not about anything but the moment and Seth loving her. She couldn't think past that. Wouldn't. There were too many uncertainties, his true feelings for her only one. She needed to find the bastard who killed Bec, who wanted to kill her. But as she did, she needed to enjoy every moment as though it were her last.

Because there was every possibility it may be.

The stroke of Jayda's finger over his eyebrow made him tremble. Almost more than making love to her just now had done.

Her. Her touch. They did something that no other woman had been able to. They made him believe in more than his career. They made him believe he could be enough without it.

He shared her pillow, the front of her body a perfect fit against the front of his. As if their bodies were one and the same.

When he'd seen the crime scene tape surrounding her apartment he'd known—he would have swapped his newly gained job just to see her walk through the door. Then she had and his next thought had been *thank God*. He'd been handed his chance and damned if he was going to let it go that easy.

'What happened here?' Her caress over the raised skin above his left eye warmed him in a way the memories chilled.

'An old war wound.' He drew her hand away and kissed the palm, feathering kisses up her arm.

'Really?' She looked half dubious, half believing, and wholly gorgeous. He moved to her mouth and tasted her again, never wanted to stop tasting her.

She pulled back. 'It was one of the first things I noticed. That and your eyes. You looked like such a bad boy, I couldn't stop thinking about you.'

'And now?'

'I still can't stop thinking about you.' Blush powdered her cheeks and his heart moved from his sleeve to his lips. What was it about her that fuelled this almost permanent soppy grin on his face?

'I like that. Let's discuss it some more.' His lips moved back to the curve inside her elbow and he felt her shiver.

Her eyelids fluttered, almost closed, then they opened and she drew in a deep breath. 'Or not. How'd you get it?'

Like a douse of cold water, the memories rushed in.

He blanked his mind. The silk of her skin beneath his palm helped.

'A fight. But that's not nearly as interesting as your thoughts.' He moved his hand over her hip and inwards, and whispered into her ear. 'Like now. What are you thinking about now, Jayda?'

Her sharp intake of breath as he found the heat between her thighs gave a clue. The green of her irises became inundated with black as she captured her bottom lip between her teeth. He stroked and she moaned.

'Penny for them, Jayda.'

Her eyes flew open and she pushed his hand away. 'You're stalling. Why?'

He sighed and jammed his hands under his chin. Even aroused, the detective inside her wouldn't let go. And wasn't that why he admired her? Why she'd managed to burrow her way beneath his skin like no one else?

'It was just a stupid fight.'

'You've never struck me as stupid or a fighter.'

'I'm not.'

'Then what happened?'

He trailed a forefinger down her chin and over her throat. 'Your imagination is more exciting than my story.'

Her hand stalled his before he could reach her body beneath the covers. 'I'm not looking for excitement, Seth. I'm looking to know more about you. Isn't that what you do when you're a couple?'

'*Are* we a couple?' He held his breath.

She licked her lips. 'I'd like to think so.'

Again, that adorable red found her cheeks, but her eyes didn't waver from his. When she looked at him like that, gave him her heart in the only way she knew how, he was powerless to deny her anything.

'Henry Jenkins was a prat and Callum's best friend.'

'What did he do?'

'That's just it. He didn't *do* anything.'

'I don't get it.'

He'd have pitched for a diversion if he'd the slightest suspicion that it would work. She'd shown she was too sharp for that.

Instead, he dragged in a breath and sunk his teeth deep into the proverbial bullet. 'He wasn't particularly special, not even a science nerd, which makes you count in the eyes of my parents. But his father was some lordly scientist in the CSIRO. Perhaps two degrees of separation from a person of importance in a highly respected scientific organisation made him worthy of notice. Unlike their son.'

Bitterness spiked the back of his tongue. He hated its familiarity. Hated that he still lacked the balls to not care what his parents thought. Even more, he hated that Jayda was now privy to one of the chinks in armour it had taken years to build. A weakness that made him less desirable, even less the tough bad-boy she'd been drawn to at that first sighting.

'He had the gall to call me a loser before school one day, so every opportunity after I showed him just how much of a loser I was.'

His finger idled along the curvature of her upper arm, her waist, her tummy. Not once did she flinch. It gave him the courage to continue. No sense in baring half his soul. He'd gone thus far, what was a little more? For any chance at a future together, she'd need to see every flaw. He amended—every flaw but one. If she knew the rest, knew just how unlovable he was . . .

He shoved at the thought. 'They may have hated me for the fights, but they sure as hell couldn't continue to ignore me.'

At first he thought he'd botched it.

Then her hand covered his on its journey up over her ribs. 'I notice you.'

His hand stalled, his heart expanding so he thought it might burst.

Then she squeezed. 'I would always notice you.'

Jayda waited for the walls to close in again.

Love filled Seth's eyes. She knew because she'd seen it before. Her parents shared the same look. It had heat. Seth's look was packed with heat. It consumed her.

And God, it felt good.

'I—' She drew in a deep breath. 'I know the timing sucks, and us working together is about the story and the case. *Was* about that. It's still about that. But it's become more for me. I *want* it to be about more for me. And I want it to be about more for you.'

Damn! She was rambling. When had she ever rambled?

Seth looked as if he just discovered aliens ran Gloria Jeans. Not that the news would be all that surprising—what would aliens know about good coffee?

She rolled her eyes, a burn rolling up her neck and out over her cheeks. 'I suck at this.'

The heat in his eyes spiked. 'No, you don't. You're amazing. It's perfect. *You're* perfect.' His palm cupped her cheek. 'And in case you haven't guessed, I want more too.'

His head edged across the pillow and his lips met with hers. It felt good. Right. As if this was where she was always meant to be.

She returned the pressure, opened her lips when his tongue requested it. Let him in, rolled out the red carpet and welcomed Seth into her heart. He urged her back, threading his fingers through hers, pressing her hands into the pillow either side of her head.

Making her breathless and happy and wanting all at once.

When the need for air overtook their need for each other, he dragged his lips from hers. His gaze told her all she needed to know, but still she had to be sure.

'Does this mean we're a couple?'

His grin made her knees weak. Lucky he already had her flat on her back.

'We're a couple.'

Her heart melted, the scent of pine filling her with each breath, melding fantasy with reality. She hadn't been looking, but somehow she'd found the future she'd always dreamed of. With a man she wanted to know inside and out.

'So, I get to ask you couple-y questions?'

'Aha. And do couple-y things.' One hand carved a path down her arm to cup her breast, his tongue tasting and taunting until she thought she might die. 'Like this.'

She closed her eyes and sighed. 'I like couple-y things.'

'Me, too.'

He moved to kiss her again.

'I have a question.'

He pulled back, quirked a brow. 'Only one?'

'For now.' She grinned. 'What's with this place? All your furniture outside this room looks like it just left the warehouse.'

His expression closed. 'I'm house-sitting.'

'I knew it! Whose house?'

'No one important.' He tilted his hips and hard muscle nudged at her thighs, a reminder of more pressing things that required attention.

'Think we should make our couple status official?' That quirky grin did things to her body that shouldn't be legal. Things that shouldn't be possible with just a look.

She felt her lips curve as he dipped and found the racing pulse at her neck, chasing every thought from her brain other than how much she wanted him. It took a while for her limited brain function to allow words to form. 'What do you have in mind?'

'I think I'll run with instinct.' His palm drifted down her tummy and she shivered. 'You can follow my lead.'

She wrapped her leg around his buttocks and pressed her palm into his shoulder, flipping him onto his back. 'Or as a twist, you could follow mine.'

His chuckle shuddered against her breasts and her nipples tightened.

'Where'd you learn to do that?'

'Did I forget to tell you I'm a taekwondo black belt? You're pretty much at my mercy, right now.'

'Gotta love a detective who knows what she wants.' His body relaxed and his eyes shone deep blue as they stared into hers. 'I'm all yours.'

Now she had free reign, where was she supposed to start?

So many possibilities . . . Her fingers smoothed over the planes of his chest, but that wasn't enough. She dropped her body to the side so her lips could follow the trail of her hands, tasting salt and something else that was intrinsically Seth. She moved her mouth lower still, until her eyes were level with his very obvious, very aroused flesh.

Dare she?

He'd given her so much pleasure, on more than one occasion. More than anything, she wanted to give, to show Seth that he mattered, that he was special. Maybe with her actions she could say more than with the words she struggled to find.

Her fingertip skated upwards to the tip and she felt his sharp intake of breath. This time she did the same but with her tongue, and a growl escaped from deep in his chest. Salt and musk rolled across her taste buds, the seep of her own arousal soaking her thighs. He buried his hands in her hair, emboldening her to open her mouth and take him inside. He tensed and his breath hitched as she completely enveloped him.

She drew back, running her lips along his length, and then took him in once more. He lifted his hips, needing her to accept more of him, and she did. She throbbed from wanting him, but more, from the pleasure of giving to a man who had already given her so much.

She had no idea what she was doing, but with every groan and grunt, she had to be doing something right.

When his breathing was fast and he fumbled at her shoulders, she let him pull her up, locking lips with his in a kiss that tugged at her heart, filling it like a balloon ready to soar through the heavens.

She reached for the condom on his bedside table, and sat astride him, her hands shaking as she attacked the foil.

Dark eyebrows hovered above eyes filled with passion as he watched her. Then he grinned, giving more cause for her heart to flip-flop and her fingers to fumble.

'Need any help?'

# Chapter Fifty-Four

*D*amned impossible packaging!

Jayda's fingers were all thumbs as she tried to ignore Seth's scrutiny. The manufacturer preached safe sex. It was their main frigging selling point. Yet how many people tossed the idea of protection in the heat of passion when the foil wouldn't rip? It didn't help that her hands were shaking like crazy.

She hadn't trembled like this since their first time. Only the feeling now was more nerve-racking, more intense. It was no longer just about the case.

She lodged her tongue between her teeth and willed the telltale nerves in her hands to still. 'I'll let you know.'

With a sudden *rip!* the packet split open and a condom slid out. She stared at the little round disc in her hand.

There ended the easy part of the process.

She'd never done this before, but surely it was a matter of logistics. Much as a penis wasn't a cucumber, the principles couldn't be that different to old Miss Hamstead's demonstration in high school sex-ed.

She pinched the end of the latex, trying to still her hand as she rolled it up his length. His breath hitched, his eyes following her movements with a fire that made her burn with wanting. It wasn't as easy as she remembered in twelfth grade, but then again, the sight of a cucumber hadn't made her hot and horny like the image of Seth naked and wedged between her thighs did.

As she reached his base, she squeezed.

He groaned. 'Done?'

'Not even close.' She grinned. 'But at least you're ready.'

*'Not even close.'*

No time for a comeback. Before one could form, he had her flat on her back and breathless. He scooched down her body and soon the clutch of the sheets was the only thing that prevented her from sliding onto the floor in a writhing heap.

Where the strum of his fingers stirred her body to life, the lilt of his tongue shot liquid fire through her veins, every limb, every organ, her belly, her breasts and the folds deep between her thighs singing as he worked his magic.

And when she thought she couldn't take a moment more, he eased upwards, his eyes locked with hers as he entered her, each thrust driving her to need and want him more than she ever imagined she'd need or want a man.

Sensation splintered outwards, infusing each and every cell in her body. She clung to him, wrapped her legs around tight, let herself drown in the feel of Seth filling her completely until all she knew was his flesh joined with hers, and the pulses that dragged him so deep into her that she could almost believe they were one.

He kissed her soundly then left the bed. He disappeared for only a moment before returning to her side, holding her tightly as if he would never let her go, and for the first time in too long, Jayda felt a way beyond the hell of the past weeks.

She would get through the nightmare, survive, with this man by her side.

Seth tightened his arms around Jayda.

Her expression was peaceful. He'd put it there.

The slow roll of her breathing soothed, lulling him towards rest. He closed his eyes, the weight of the past day lifting as he allowed conscious thought to slip away. Random thoughts tumbled through his mind.

His eyes shot open. He still hadn't told her about the job. Should he wake her, share the news? They could celebrate, make it real, give it a meaning that only sharing it with Jayda could.

Because gaining the position without her wouldn't mean half as much.

The realisation brought with it a strange sense of calm. There was no panic, no desire to escape. He edged closer, touched his lips to her hair, losing himself in the scent of fresh apples and their loving.

He had time. She'd be there in the morning. And the morning after that. And if he had anything to do with it, every morning thereafter until he could no longer count.

She'd never been soppy or the slightest bit maudlin.

Yet as Jayda rolled away from Seth's warmth and slipped into jeans and a shirt, she almost lost herself in that one, fatal backwards glance. Almost chucked her clothes on the floor and crawled back under the black-and-gold covers, unable to stall the regret that she was leaving when all she wanted to do was stay and curl into him.

She didn't have a scarf, instead she turned up her collar, her fingers running across the tender patch of skin on her neck. Memories of how it got there saw her body temperature hike as she paused for one more look.

The sheet draped over the rise of his buttocks, providing an eyeful of bare, male skin. He lay sprawled on his stomach, one arm flung over the spot she'd just vacated, the other wedged under the pillow. *Temptation incarnate.*

A lock of black draped over one eye and the black ink of his lashes brushed the olive of his skin. How had she not noticed those lashes before? Her best guess? Other attributes had stolen the limelight. Not least of all the broad musculature of his biceps, his shoulders, pecs she couldn't see right now, but sure as hell her mind could. It seemed where Seth was concerned, her memory turned photographic.

Time to go before she didn't.

She tiptoed across the cream carpet, taking in the cluttered surface of the dresser, marvelling again at how little the room resembled the remainder of what she'd seen of the rest of this place. The house belonging to someone other than Seth made sense. It also made sense that the areas he frequented most would appear more lived in, more like him. What she didn't get was why he'd chosen this smaller, darker room over the master bedroom, which would surely have been more comfortable. Unless it was a condition of his house-sitting agreement.

She touched the door to the frame but didn't close it for fear of waking him. Treading softly through the living room, she collected her purse and keys and made for the front door.

One check through the security peephole showed a deserted doorstep. Still, it didn't hurt to be careful. Turning the knob, her other hand moved to the gun at her hip. She wrapped her fingers around the familiar coldness, and braced the weapon in front of her body as she pulled the door towards her and peered outside. Still clear.

The click of the door closing was louder than she'd have liked and all she could hope was that Seth remained asleep in his bedroom. Time was sparse.

The soft soles of her shoes barely dented the idyll of the morning. A twig snapped in next door's front yard, and her gun was already raised as a magpie stepped out onto the path. The black-and-white bird glared at her, then cawed and flapped its wings, taking flight to a large oak across the street.

Luckily, the Beetle started first try and she eased it onto the road. It wasn't long until the shop she'd noticed the day before loomed up on her right. It was early still, and there was barely a queue. Within minutes she was back behind the wheel, the engine humming.

The smell of coffee and fresh pastries filled the car, but that wasn't the reason for her smile. Anticipation had dragged it to her lips. Seth was always doing things for her—buying pastries, the right kind of coffee, drying her tears, being her rock. It was time she gave something back. She wanted to give something back.

The car shuddered into the curb and she jiggled the key until it slid easily from the ignition.

She reached for the door only to fall back into the seat. Her heart was racing. She flipped down the sun visor and stared into the mirror. The woman who stared back was barely recognisable. She looked . . . happy. Something she had no right to be. Bec was dead. A close friend wanted to kill her. She should be focused. Driven. And she was, but she was so much more.

The man who put the flush in her cheeks, the hope in her eyes, was nothing like the man she'd wanted growing up, yet everything she needed right now. He was strong and gentle, funny and dependable, and honest.

She was thinking about him too much. Wanting him too much. Every moment apart was spent in anticipation of seeing him again.

She needed to take a step back. Several, in fact. She deserved good in her life. And right now, good meant Seth. The future was another story, one she was refusing permission to unfold. She couldn't get too comfortable, too attached. Too complacent whilst there was a killer out there gunning for her.

She frowned. She could be happy now. Just cautiously happy.

She glanced at the dashboard. Nearly 8 am. Time she was back inside and on the case. There were calls to make, an appointment to keep with Anna Jones's old landlord. And a man waiting who deserved coffee and pastries in bed.

She grinned as she opened the door and grabbed the large paper bag and tray. There was a lightness in her step she'd never imagined could be put there by a man. The sky was the palest of blues, not a cloud in the sky. It was going to be a beautiful day.

Her inner child almost skipped to the front door.

*No!*

Her toe caught on the top step. She stumbled, fell to her knees. Coffee and pastries spilled onto the path.

*No.*

A corner of her heart splintered.

She pushed herself up and reached for her gun. Squinting through tears, she scanned her surroundings. Not that she expected to find him. He hurt and then left her to shatter—that was his MO. And this hurt was meant to cut in a way none of the others had.

It came laced with the promise of more.

Her eyes flew back to the bloodied mass on the welcome mat. She knew instantly what it was, and what it was meant to convey. What she didn't know was how much further the bastard was willing to go to send his message and what she would find once she crossed the threshold.

She skirted what remained of the battered body without stopping to check for life. Tumbles was dead.

She dragged her gaze away. No cat could suffer what he had and survive. Pain sliced her chest as she thought of the man she'd left very much alive less than half an hour ago.

Agnostic or not, she murmured a plea as she fumbled in her pocket for the spare key Seth had handed her yesterday. A courtesy she'd never extended to him. Not the time to think about that now.

She unlocked the front door and braced herself for what waited on the other side.

'Jayda! What the—'

Seth lowered the phone from his ear and stared at the gun in her hand. All Jayda wanted to do was drop her weapon and hurl herself into his arms. Not the done thing when there could be a killer nearby.

'He was here. The Night Terror.'

His head jerked right then left. 'How do you know?'

'He killed Tumbles.' Her eyes darted around the room as she reached back and locked the door. 'I need you to stay behind me and call Chase while I clear each room.' She passed him her mobile. 'Speed-dial four.'

'Shouldn't we wait for backup?'

She shook her head and raised her gun, moving towards the kitchen. Seth fell in behind her and she heard the beep, beep of the keypad as he made the call. Ten minutes later they were back in the living room, waiting for Chase. The house was clean. She doubted the Night Terror had moved past Seth's front doorstep.

Seth handed back her mobile. 'Where is he? Tumbles.'

'On the welcome mat.'

He moved towards the door and she grabbed his arm. 'Wait until Chase comes.'

At first she thought he'd ignore her, then he nodded. 'Why the cat?'

She swallowed and met his gaze, still wanting to go to him but unsure how. It was as if the killer were standing beside her, mocking her, letting her know that every time she felt safe, every time she felt ready to move forwards, he would be there to cut and slash and drag her back down.

'Because I love him. Because he wants to destroy everything that matters to me.'

'If he wanted to do that with the cat, why wait until now?'

She strode towards the front door, then spun on her heels and stalked back the way she'd come.

'Killing Tumbles and dumping him at your door was a message. That he knows exactly how to hurt me. And that no matter where I go, he'll find me.'

She turned just as a car door slammed outside. Chase. She peered out the security peep hole as realisation curled around her heart. There was a third message, one she would keep to herself until she figured out what to do with it.

That if she dared to love Seth, he'd be next.

# Chapter Fifty-Five

Something was up.

Seth busied himself at the buffet—repositioning the butt-ugly Egyptian vase, swiping at a speck or two of dust with his finger—when in reality all he wanted to do was crash the private party taking place only metres away.

He looked over again as Chase shook his head. Jayda blinked, her jaw locked in a telltale sign that she was feeling the pressure. Even from across the room, he could tell that Chase had discounted the link between the cat and the killer. The man had to be blind. Either that, or something else was up.

Did he believe by screening the truth he was protecting Jayda, or was his agenda more sinister? Either way, it wouldn't hurt to take a closer look at her old partner. He locked the idea away in his mind for later. Jayda need never know.

Forensics had already removed the cat and doormat. The surrounding bloodstain and its significance still remained—the killer wouldn't let up until he destroyed the woman Seth loved.

That meant Seth was locked in the killer's radar, just as Tumbles had been. Not that it made a difference. He wasn't going anywhere. And more than ever he was determined not to let Jayda out of his sight.

She nodded. The other man took her into his arms and she appeared comfortable there. Seth's gut churned. Again, he questioned their relationship. Was he a fool to believe she'd continue to want him over her partner? Chase and Jayda might not see eye-to-eye on this case, but that wasn't a clincher when it came to love. They had a history together. Didn't opposites attract?

Was Seth merely a filler until Jayda returned to her old life?

The thought made his chest tighten until he wondered that he could still breathe.

Over Chase's shoulder, Jayda's eyes opened and caught his. What he saw relaxed him, albeit marginally. It didn't stop the feeling that something between them wasn't as right as it had been when she'd fallen asleep in his arms mere hours earlier.

The two parted. Chase nodded Seth's way, then he and Jayda both headed for the door. He whispered in Jayda's ear, causing her to shake her head and cast a glance towards Seth.

Then he was gone.

'What was that all about?'

'Nothing.' Her eyes seemed focused anywhere but on him. He worked at giving her the same glare she sent his way when she wanted him to come clean. She must have sensed it, because she sure as hell didn't see it. With a sigh, she spoke as if to the front door. 'Chase wanted me to stay with him.'

The tightness returned.

'And what did you say?'

She turned to him then. 'That I can look after myself. That I was as safe here as I would be anywhere. That he needs to catch the killer so I don't have to look over my shoulder every damn waking moment!'

'He doesn't believe this is linked to the Night Terror.'

Her eyes widened. 'He didn't say it quite like that . . . How did you know?'

'I know you. That's enough to get the gist of a conversation I wasn't privy to.' He hated that he sounded jealous, but dammit, he was. And he had every right to be after last night.

She shook her head. 'I was after information and had more chance of getting it without a reporter present.'

'What's the story with you and Chase?'

'There is no story. We work together, we're friends. That's it.'

'I sense more.'

'On his side, perhaps. Not mine.' Her eyes bored into his and he knew she was telling the truth. 'Shouldn't you be more interested in what we discussed than in our non-existent love affair?'

'Now you've cleared that up for me, yes.' He raised his brows and waited.

'They found Anna Jones' great-aunt just north of Sydney in a place called Wyong.' She rubbed her eyes and pushed her hair back from her face. 'She suffers from dementia, drifts in and out of clarity and the local detectives haven't been able to get any sense out of her so far. The staff says that Anna called her great-aunt every Friday at 5 pm for the past ten years—until three months ago. After she missed two Fridays in a row, the administrator tried to contact her, only to find both her mobile and home number disconnected. He spoke to the local police who told her that on the sole evidence of a couple of missed calls, they were unable to open a missing persons case.'

'Do you think he killed his own mother?'

'Do you?'

'It's not unusual for serial killers to have mummy issues. Why should the Night Terror be any different?'

'My thoughts exactly.'

Their eyes locked, but as he leaned in to press his lips to hers, she twisted her head. He would have kissed her ear instead—an action that had melted her in the past—but she sidestepped out of reach.

Mobile in hand, she latched her focus to the screen. 'I thought I might call all the secondary schools in and around Bunyip to see if Anna registered a child there around sixteen years ago. Then I have a couple of interviews, one with her landlord and the other with an old colleague who's just returned from Bali.'

'I have a few calls of my own to make. What time do you need to leave so I can be ready?'

'Eleven.' For every step he took towards her, she took two steps back.

He grabbed her hand. 'Are we okay?'

'Sure. There's just a lot to be done.' She wrangled free of his grasp and moved towards the door. 'Do you mind if I make my calls from the study?'

He shook his head at her retreating back. The renewed distance between them was about more than just a dead cat. Whatever it was, Jayda wasn't sharing. She'd closed off again, was backing away.

*Not gonna happen.*

There'd be no more secrets between them. About the case, that is. He'd wait until they were in the car, with nowhere for her to run, then he wouldn't let up until he found out what the hell was going on.

*'Where the heck have you been?'*

Seth yanked the phone from his ear and glared at it in lieu of Richie.

'Seth?' Even at arm's length, his friend's booming voice rang loud and clear.

He brought the mobile cautiously back. 'I've been busy.'

Richie snorted, then proceeded to mutter something about women and bulls. Reassuring to know some things never changed.

'I hear congrats are in order. Thanks for letting me know you got the job.'

'Sorry, Rich. It's been so damned crazy, I haven't told anyone yet.'

'Even Jade?'

'*Jayda.* And yeah, even her.'

This time he grunted. 'So, what's this big exclusive you've promised Carson?'

'Where'd you hear that?'

'You know the newsroom has ears.'

'That muffin boy is a nuisance.'

'But his double choc-chip and raspberry muffins are worth the angst.'

He couldn't help but grin. 'Much as I agree, I didn't call to talk muffins. I need a favour.'

'Of course you do. You never call, you never write, and you never send me a six-pack of beer—unless you want something.'

'Three words. Corporate. Seats. MCG.'

'Whadoyou want?' Richie's words tumbled head over heels down the line. His footy mania made him suitably predictable. But, hey, no foul if they both came out the other end of the deal winners.

Seth grinned. 'There's a detective who works with Jayda—Chase Durant. I need you to use your sources to dig and see what shit you uncover.'

'He's a detective? I could get my ass kicked for this.'

'Then do it carefully.'

'Why didn't I think of that?'

'Because I'm the brains of this outfit.' He glanced towards the door. Not that he expected to see Jayda appear, now that she seemed so determined to avoid him. 'And while you're at it, look into a Georgie Tanneras.'

'Don't tell me. Another detective?'

'Get me info on these two detectives plus a couple of others and there's an annual club membership upgrade in it for you.'

'Give me their names and I'll see what I can do.'

He read out the list of Jayda's friends and colleagues, Juz, Garry and Darren at the top, and gave Rich all he knew about Anna Jones. Rich had a wealth of contacts—Seth didn't know who, where or how, and he knew better than to ask. The man was a bank vault when he needed to be, which had suited Seth on more than one occasion, so he saw no reason to complain about the secrecy, as long as he was able to reap the benefits.

There was a rustle of paper and a click of a pen. 'And what about the story?'

Seth's grip on the phone tightened. 'I haven't got it figured out yet.'

'Don't tell me you're that close to a detective whose sister was murdered and there's no dirt. Did you hear her father was being investigated by the OPI?'

'How do you know that?'

'It's my job to know. It's called reporting.'

'Touché.'

'Save the smarts for some other sucker. It's not just your ass if you don't deliver—I'm the one who convinced Carson to hire you over Ben Priestly.'

'Priestly applied for the job? Knight Investigative Journalism Award winner two years running Ben Priestly?'

'Is there another? His wife's pregnant and he's quit travelling to be an in-the-picture dad. I convinced Carson that you'd scoop the shit out of him with less than a quarter of the prima donna attitude. Now Priestley's working for the *Sydney Herald*, he's off the table. If you prove me wrong, I'll be up shit creek without a canoe, let alone a frigging paddle.'

'Damn. I'm sorry, man.'

'Don't be sorry. Be productive and write the story.'

Seth closed his eyes and Jayda's deep green ones stared back. Trusting him, as she trusted no one else right now. She needed someone to lean on, to be there for her, and as much as he wanted that promotion, he wanted her to need him so much more.

Richie's bark broke the silence. 'You're not going to do it, are you?'

'I can't, Rich. Everyone close to her has let her down. I won't do that too.'

'You've gone and fallen for her.'

The words still sounded good to his ears, even peppered with derision. His heart stuttered. 'Hard.'

His friend sighed. 'You've turned into a sap and a half. We need to cut this conversation before it leaches through the phone line and turns me too.'

'So, we're good?'

Richie harrumphed. 'After I voodoo your sorry ass from here to Jamaica, sure.'

'What'll you do about Carson?'

'I'll figure something out.'

'Tell him I *will* discover the identity of the Night Terror and I *will* get him the story. He won't regret giving me the position. And neither will you.'

'I've been thinking.'

Seth jerked the car into fourth gear and clenched his jaw. Jayda over-thinking wasn't a good sign. In fact, it was about as good as the uneasiness wedged between them since Tumbles had wound up on his front doorstep.

Mind you, she *had* let him drive. A concession, in her words, to males being more familiar with the operation of a stick shift. He wasn't quite sure how to take *that*.

The heady scent of fresh apples filled the car and he tried not to lose himself in it. It wasn't easy. He'd grown used to how good it made him feel. How he'd no longer needed to second-guess every move, could grab Jayda and pull her into a kiss, knowing she'd kiss him right back.

Now he was back to second-guessing, and he hated it.

Jayda sat in the passenger seat, meticulously folding and unfolding the hem of her top. She couldn't even look at him, when previously her eyes couldn't get enough.

'You need to take this back.' She fumbled in her purse. Next thing he knew, she was holding his key out for him to take. 'I should find somewhere else to stay.'

His head began to pound. He glanced at her, ignoring the shiny new metal he'd only just had cut. 'Why?'

She dropped her hand into her lap. 'You're house-sitting and I'm being hunted by a psycho who won't think twice about collateral damage.'

The headache faded. He breathed easier. It was so clear now—her distance, her change in mood. He didn't need her protection, but the fact that she was determined to provide it spoke volumes.

'Like Tumbles?'

She nodded, her eyes still fixed anywhere but his direction. 'Everyone I care about is fair game.'

'So what you're saying is that you care about me?'

Liquid green stared at him across the car interior. 'You know I do.'

He cocked his head. 'It doesn't hurt to hear it once in a while.' He grinned. 'Not that it matters. You're not going anywhere. And neither am I.'

Her head jerked back. '*You know?*'

'The moment the Night Terror left Tumbles on the doorstep I guessed it was his sick way of saying that I'm a target. And it doesn't change my decision.'

She stared, wide-eyed and so gorgeous he wanted to pull over and kiss away every line on her heart-stopping face.

*What the hell.*

The car jerked as he twisted the wheel. Jayda's hand shot up and braced against the dashboard as they skidded into a bus zone. The old lady sitting in the shelter shot him a dirty look. He shrugged, then as an afterthought flicked on the hazard lights.

Jayda let go of the dash and turned, looking at him like he'd lost his mind. Little did she know he had, from the very first moment he'd laid eyes on her.

'What are you doing?'

'This.' He released his seatbelt and covered her mouth with his before she could say another word.

He couldn't imagine what the woman outside thought now. Not that it mattered. As the flashing lights indicated, this was an emergency.

His palms bracketed Jayda's face, his tongue breaching the seam of her lips to taste the wonders inside. She moaned, straining against her seatbelt to kiss him back. Her palms fluttered across his chest and up over his shoulders. She would have crawled into his lap if there was room and he cursed Volkswagen for not building the Beetle more like a sedan.

The gears pressed uncomfortably into his thigh and he shifted, trying not to break contact. Her hands slid back down to his chest, and where before they'd pulled him towards her, they now pushed him away.

'You're trying to distract me. It won't work.'

'Seemed to be working just fine.' He flashed her a grin. 'But we could always try again.'

She shook her head and edged back in her seat, placing as much distance as possible between them. 'This isn't a joke, Seth. I won't be responsible for you getting hurt.'

'You aren't responsible for anything that madman does. That's all on him.'

'I couldn't bear it if he hurt you.'

'Then we're at an impasse, because I couldn't bear it if you left.'

'So, what do we do?'

He grinned and cherry red bloomed across her already flushed cheeks. But, just in case she hadn't read his thoughts . . .

'I'd say carry on where we left off, but that'd finish the old dear outside.' He indicated at the woman under the shelter, who looked one breath short of apoplexy.

A horn behind them solved their dilemma. The large bumper of a city bus loomed in his rear vision mirror, and he waved an apology before hitting the accelerator, leaving it and their audience behind.

'I'm serious, Seth.'

'So am I. Being with you is serious. It's what I want and nothing that psychopath does will change that.' He scrubbed his fingers through his hair. 'I don't believe splitting up is the answer. We're so much better together.'

He reached for her hand.

She took it and squeezed. 'We *are* pretty good.' Her smile was like sunshine.

She slipped the key back into her purse. 'So I guess I'm staying.'

His heart gave a mental fist pump in the air. 'I guess you are.'

# Chapter Fifty-Six

Jayda glanced over her shoulder at Seth sitting two booths away.

A couple of weeks ago she'd have resented his protectiveness, his unwillingness to let her out of his sight—considered it a slur on her ability to take care of herself. Now it made her feel loved, a feeling she'd nearly given up on.

The coffee mug between her palms was more like a small soup bowl than a cup, and the rich aroma of freshly ground beans stole some of the knots from her shoulders.

Of all her interviews today, this was the most difficult.

'So it's serious, then?'

She looked up from her drink to meet the question in Darren's gaze. 'I think so.'

'You don't know? You've got the poor sap wrapped so tight around your finger, he's about to snap with jealousy.'

He slid his hand across the white Formica to wrap it around hers. Then, in typical Darren fashion, he shot a large grin Seth's way and wiggled his fingers in a wave.

Jayda tugged her hand free. 'That's not funny, Darren.'

'Wow, you have got it bad.' He raised his hand, effectively stopping her from agreeing or denying it. 'And the fact that he does too makes it perfect. You deserve some of the good stuff, Jayda. And lover-boy looks like he'd be particularly *good* at the good stuff, even if he is glaring at me as though he'd like nothing better than to rip me limb from limb.'

'He's looking out for me.'

'And I'm glad he is. I can't believe someone killed that mangy old cat.'

'Tumbles wasn't mangy.'

'Unlike his owner.'

'What *is* it with you and Juz?'

'Something about him doesn't sit right. Like he's not quite who he makes out to be.'

'We all have secrets.' She looked directly at him then. 'You must have things you've never shared with me.'

He barely wavered. 'I don't mean little stuff like failing math at school or wetting the bed. I'm talking big.'

'So am I.' She bit her lip then launched into the question she'd come to ask before she could talk herself out of it. 'Was your entire week in Queensland about work?'

His gaze sharpened, the line of his cheekbones staining with red. 'You obviously know the answer already, if you're asking that question. You tell me.'

'I'd rather hear it from you.'

He sagged backwards into the cracked red vinyl. 'I wanted to tell you, Jayda. A million times, I wanted to tell you. I just didn't know how.'

'Straight up usually works fine.'

'Not when your family no longer wants to know you. When you've lost all the friends you've ever known. When you couldn't bear to lose another.'

It was like watching a fresh green leaf waste away under the harsh rays of a desert sun. The confident man she knew seemed to shrink and wither before her very eyes.

This time her hand reached across for his. 'Tell me now.'

His pain was a metal vice clutching her heart. Their hands remained linked, his tightly gripping hers as he revealed a past she'd never once envisaged.

Confusion. Denial. Rejection. Banishment.

A child wanting GI Joe when other girls wanted Barbie. Wanting to wear black pants to his sister's communion and crying when his parents forced him to wear a dress. Hating the changes in his body that made him less like the person he saw himself to be.

Wishing for death rather than having to live a lie.

'Self-acceptance has been a long road. Long and lonely.' The hand in hers shook. She squeezed.

His lips wobbled into the semblance of a smile. 'I've gone through years of psychotherapy, hormone replacement therapy, building a life as the only true me I know. Now that I finally have a job I love, friends around me I care about, I wasn't ready to jeopardise the first bout of happiness I've experienced in years.'

It hurt that he hadn't shared his secret with her. That he hadn't believed their friendship was strong enough to withstand it. But as he spoke of watching people he loved turn their backs, she understood. 'I just wish I could have been there for you.'

'You are now.' The wobble left his smile, his eyes filled with so much—pain, relief, love.

He wasn't the killer. She just *knew*.

And if her gut wasn't enough to rule him out, his alibi was. He'd been in surgery at the time of the last murder and nothing about the timing had been fudged or faked. He hadn't 'wangled' it as Seth had surmised. They'd discovered as much this morning when she'd spoken to his physician. He'd revealed very little, under the constraints of doctor-patient confidentiality, but he'd said enough.

'How did you find out?' The dreaded question.

Something of her feelings must have shown in her expression. Seth jumped up, spilling water from his glass in his rush to get to her. She shook her head, stalling him midstride so that he hesitated, reluctantly returning to his table. She could tell he wanted to ignore her signal to stay put, and loved him all the more for the fact that he didn't.

*She loved him?*

She shook her head. But the thought wouldn't budge. It fluttered slowly through her mind, followed only by a sense of rightness.

*I love Seth.*

The realisation came like the first sweet-smelling breath of spring. She wanted to go to him, tell him, throw every apple she had into that one, incredible basket and feast on it. Of all times to discover what deep down her subconscious must have known for an age . . .

'Jayda?' Darren's hand waved across her vision, pulling her back. 'How did you know?'

First she had to explain to a friend that she'd suspected he was a murderer. How she'd breached the borders of friendship and rifled through his life.

She inhaled, closed her eyes. When she opened them again, it was to find Darren staring at her, no accusation, just curiosity.

The feeling wasn't as bad as when she'd believed her mother blamed her for Bec's death, but it came close. She deserved accusation, not trust and understanding.

It was more than difficult to find the words to explain. But she had to try.

'Sure you won't join me?'

Everything in Jayda trembled as Seth brushed her hair aside and pressed his lips to the back of her neck. Her fingers slumped onto the keyboard and a line of incoherent letters raced across the computer screen. She really should remove her hands, but the amble of his lips across her skin robbed both her strength and inclination.

'I promise to wash all your difficult to reach bits.'

She dragged her hands into her lap. 'I told you, I need to finish this.'

He swivelled her chair and kneeled between her legs, pressing the lever beneath her seat. It squealed, and with a whoosh of air, slowly lowered her to eye level. Murmuring approval, his palms rested on her hips and his mouth gained better access, this time to the racing carotid on her throat. 'You've been working at it for hours. Haven't stopped since we arrived home yesterday. Don't you think it's time for a break?'

His fingers inched inwards, igniting the need to touch him back. As her palms spanned the breadth of his chest, she wondered if she'd ever get tired of knowing she could. That his body had become as much hers as hers had become his.

'What about if I pay particular attention to the less difficult to reach and more fun parts?' He stopped long enough to waggle his eyebrows and then leer sexily at her, before continuing the journey with his lips, which were almost lost in the cleavage of her new, burgundy lace push-up bra.

Yes, she'd finally gone and done it, splurged on a collection of new underwear while they were out yesterday afternoon. Seth had insisted on tagging along. For her safety, he said. And in between acting all tough and bodyguard-like—which made her laugh since *she* was the one with the gun—he'd spent the time offering suggestions, even offering to help fit each item and provide feedback when necessary.

She'd breathlessly declined, preferring to wait until they'd returned home before she modelled the garments for him. Not that they'd stayed on much longer than the time it took for him to stand back, admire, and then unclasp and slide them off.

Even now, she didn't know what turned her on more—the gossamer feel of satin and lace against her skin, or the heat in Seth's expression every time he looked at her.

At the moment his look, not to mention his touch, were hands-down winners. She turned to the screen and tried to refocus on her list. Now the Night Terror had changed tack and come after her, the case was worth another look from that angle. When things turned personal, killers tended to become sloppy. She could only hope their killer fell prey to this same logic.

'I need to finish this.'

'Really?' He glanced at the screen, then back at her askew neckline, and as his fingertips worked her nipple through her top and bra, she gasped. Her head fell back, pressing her breast even deeper against the hand that cupped and squeezed her towards heaven.

'Sure I can't convince you?' His mouth returned to her neck, doing delicious things that made her want to melt right onto the floor.

She dragged in a breath and wriggled back into the chair, pushing against him with both palms. 'You're not playing fair, and I really do have to finish this.'

'Really?'

'Yes, *really*.' One look at his woeful expression and she bit back a laugh. 'But if you're good I promise to make it up to you later.'

'Promise?'

This time she did laugh. The man was impossible.

'I promise.'

He tugged at her neckline and peeked down her top. 'The only thing I love more than this colour on you, is this colour off you.'

She swatted his hand. 'I said be good.'

'You didn't say what at.' Again his eyebrows waggled.

She pointed at the door. 'Go. Shower. Now!'

'Boy, you're bossy.'

'You only just worked that out?' As he sauntered towards the bedroom, she didn't even try to hide how much she appreciated the way his butt filled his jeans. He turned to face her and she amended her thought. How *everything* filled his jeans.

He quirked a brow. 'There are times I quite enjoy it. Last night, for instance.' Heat hit her face while the memory struck places lower and much, much deeper. What he'd been doing when she'd begged him—*ordered* him—to go faster, deeper, harder. Damn! How the hell was she supposed to concentrate now?

He grinned. 'Shame you don't need a shower as much as I do. Guess I'll have to suffer through all that soaping and scrubbing alone.'

Then he left her, squirming, steaming; brain anywhere but on the case. Imagining all that naked, bronze skin, wet and lathered. She knew how it felt, smelt, tasted.

Now she did need a shower—one that was ice-cold.

Instead she poured herself a glass of water from the fridge, drinking half and tipping the remainder into her hand. She sluiced it over her face and down her neck. If basic physics were to be believed, the cooling effects couldn't help but travel south.

It took a while to highlight and delete the gibberish which had jumped all over the screen. Once that was done, she leaned back in her chair and stared at what remained—a sequence of events that had a large red flag stuck square in the middle.

She doubted it was paranoia making her believe that the Night Terror had anticipated her every move since early in the case. As if he'd read her, seen exactly what she was planning and when, as though—and she knew how crazy it sounded—as though he had a direct link into her mind.

*How?* Was there a leak in her squad? Immediately Georgie's face appeared. Their catch-up had been a partial success, resolving some issues while raising others in turn. None of which, it seemed, related to the Night Terror.

Georgie's presence in the building that day had been explained away. She'd been visiting a new love interest and wasn't ready to share their identity.

She understood her friend's need for privacy. How she didn't need her own Liam incident rushing in and wrecking her career. News spread through the squad as easily as butter melting over hot toast, and the ribbing would have been just as liberal. Georgie had already survived one very public relationship and breakup. It made sense she'd want to keep this one under wraps until she was sure about it, which was probably why she was still holding something back.

There was more to her story than met the eye.

A mental sift through every male on her floor had none leaping out as an obvious candidate. Unless she should consider the women? That might explain Georgie's reluctance to share. She shook her head. It didn't matter. As long as they—male *or* female—made her happy.

It was unthinkable that her friend would contravene her sworn oath as an officer. She'd lost her father twenty-plus years ago to a stray bullet in a robbery gone bad. It was the reason she'd joined the force, the reason she believed far too deeply in justice to be anything but on the right side of the law.

So, if Georgie wasn't the leak, who was? Chase? Despite being a dick at times, he was no criminal, to the point where before joining homicide, he'd been instrumental in blowing the whistle on police corruption in Victoria.

One by one she discounted the members of her team. She had to be missing something. *What?*

She rifled through the papers beside her computer to locate her notebook. Writing her thoughts rather than typing them always helped her see things more clearly.

Her continued search yielded no joy and, more importantly, no pen. There were times when it felt as if odd socks and pens lived a doomed existence, all of them sucked through the same universe time warp, never to be found again.

Yesterday she'd had three pens, today she had none. Surely Seth must have one. Somewhere.

Running water still hummed from the shower. She glanced at the buffet with its array of drawers, then back to the door. It wasn't as if the house were Seth's, so she shouldn't feel guilty about searching it when he wasn't around. And searching in the living room felt less invasive than entering the more private domains he'd adopted as his study and bedroom.

It wasn't as if she were searching for more than a pen.

She pulled out one drawer, sifted through a bunch of old crocheted doilies and embroidered napkins, then opened the next.

Her jaw dropped. Her gaze darted to the closed bedroom doorway, then back. Seth hadn't lied. Not exactly. Half-truths were just that, a mix of what you were willing and unwilling to share.

Although why he hadn't shared this . . . The house wasn't just anybody's.

She shook her head.

The frame on top was gilded black and the photo inside could have been any family if it weren't for the younger but recognisable version of Seth on the right.

She'd wondered at the lack of photos, but hadn't for one moment imagined it was because he'd hidden them from sight, had hidden the fact that he wasn't house-sitting for just anyone.

She stared at the photo, as if sharper scrutiny would reveal something of its past. A family of four stared back.

Seth's father was greying even back then, with round glasses and deep frown lines bordering his mouth. His dour face was a perfect match for his wife's, but she had Seth's raven hair, and grey-blue eyes that lacked the humour and sparkle of her son's. The child between them, unsmiling and non-descript, had to be Callum.

Then there was Seth. He stood at his mother's side, arms straight, shoulders squared, like an army cadet. His chin jutted outwards, an almost desperate determination in his expression which made her heart ache for the child he once was.

There were other photos, all taken before or around the time Callum must have died. None existed after. And in none of them did Seth appear happy or connected to his family.

She dropped all but the first back into the drawer, unable to drag her eyes away from the Seth of back then.

'Jayda?'

She turned, the photo still grasped in her hand. 'Why didn't you tell me this was your parents' house?'

# Chapter Fifty-Seven

*G*enius. *Pure fucking incredible genius.*

The splay of his lips widened across his teeth. His hand hovered, then tapped *send*.

*It was done.*

Fingers flexed, then bent, as if wrapping round pulsing skin and bone. A bloody cough hacked into laughter.

His grip tightened. He pictured her, pleading, anguished, the light in her witch's eyes fading as he extinguished what remained of her life. Her last thoughts that she'd lost everything she loved.

The end was close. Squeeze.

Squeeze.

*Squeeze.*

# Chapter Fifty-Eight

Seth stood in the doorway, gorgeous and wet, hand gripping a white towel wrapped low on his hips.

'You rummaged through my drawers?'

'I don't know about *rummaging*. I was looking for a pen, not family secrets.'

'I don't have any family secrets.'

'Really?' She tapped the photo in her hand. 'You hid this.'

He blinked before returning his gaze from the frame to her face. 'Why does it matter?'

'It didn't until you chose not to tell me.'

'The house belongs to my parents and I'm minding it. End of story.'

'If it's such an issue, why not get your own place?'

'It's not an issue. I have my own place and it's rented out. I stay here because it's convenient.'

'For who?'

'Both parties. Does it matter?'

'I don't know. It mattered enough for you to keep it secret.'

'That's where you're wrong. It just didn't matter enough for me to make a big deal of it.'

'What about these, then?' She waved the photo at the others stacked in the drawer. 'Why hide them?'

'Why do you always add two plus two and come up with fourteen? No photos out means less dust. I hate dusting.'

'Really?'

'Yes. Really. If that hideous vase had fit into a drawer, it would have suffered the same fate.'

She didn't believe him. Not for a second. But nothing would be gained from pressing him further. He'd revealed and shared so much of himself in the short time she'd known him. Was she unreasonable to want more?

She carefully placed the photo back on top of the others and closed the drawer.

He moved closer, dragging her thoughts away from the buffet to the towel that hid and revealed so much. Scents of fresh pine and man beguiled her senses.

'You promised you'd make up for missing the shower.' The whisper of his words shivered across her skin.

She stepped back. 'I haven't finished yet.'

'What say I help you finish, then you do the same for me?' The dimple was back.

She fought a grin, instead giving him 'the look'. 'Are you kidding?'

He glanced down and her eyes followed his. The tent in his towel told her he was indeed serious.

She dragged her gaze upwards. 'You'll have to put some clothes on.'

'A waste of time when I don't intend to stay dressed for long.'

'If you insist on helping in that get-up, my brain won't be able to focus long enough for me to finish.'

'Then turn your focus here and once we're done I promise, like the good Boy Scout we both know I'm not, that I'll help you to finish. I'll even wear clothes to do it.'

She sighed. Her father always said the sign of a good sportsman was to know when you're beat. To be able to pick yourself up and see if your end game couldn't be won via another avenue.

She ran her hands down his torso then tugged at the towel until it fell to the floor. Stormy grey invaded his eyes as her hands found what his towel had failed to hide. She dropped to her knees and his breath hitched, his body frozen in anticipation. The heat already thrummed through her body, the flesh between her thighs pulsing with want. Her lips were so close, she tasted him on every inhaled breath.

She glanced up to find him watching her beneath hooded eyes.

'I have one more proviso.'

He nodded and closed his eyes, losing himself in the sensation of her hand running up and down his cock. She could have asked for the moon and he would have handed it to her without a word.

Luckily for Seth, she didn't want much.

'I need you to find me a pen.'

'The building's not the same without you.' Juz's words brought a smile to Jayda's lips as her still sticky-taped phone pricked against her ear.

She leaned back in her chair, languid and sated from Seth's loving. 'Tell the building I feel the same.'

'At least you've still got your sense of humour.'

'And my head.' Silence. 'Juz?'

'Not funny, Jayda.'

'I guess. But if I don't laugh about it, I'll cry.' She swallowed. 'I'm sorry about Tumbles.'

'He was a good cat.' His voice wavered. 'He'd been through so much.'

Words clogged in her throat. Some memories never fade. A kitten's poor, broken body dumped in the gutter outside their building. Juz's gentle hands cradling him, his soft voice soothing until the vet could put all but his rear right leg back together.

'You saved him.'

'Not this time.'

'You'd have to be a monster to kill an innocent animal like that . . .' Her vision blurred and she blinked. 'Sometimes I feel as if I'll never get this bastard.'

'You'll find him. I know it. What do we always say in class? If your opponent's good . . .'

'*You need to be better!*' They finished it together and something a lot like yearning filled her throat. 'I miss you, Juz. You always know what to say.'

'That's what friends are for, hon. You sound in dire need of a hug.' He gave a throat-clearing cough and then his voice regained the old Juz quality she knew and loved. 'Is that an indication that we're not getting enough?'

'*We* are getting more than enough, and that is all I'm saying on the subject.' No need to see his face to sense his disappointment at her restraint. Juz didn't do well when not *in the know*.

'When am I going to see you?'

'This case makes it impossible for me to plan anything.' Instead of staring at a computer screen that refused to yield answers, she stood and began to pace. She heard a sigh. 'Juz?'

'Yeah?' Another sigh, his tone uncharacteristically flat. Something was up.

'What's wrong?'

'Garry moved back to Sydney.'

She stopped so fast she nearly tripped over her feet. 'He *left* you?'

'He was offered a too-good-to-pass-up job at the Nicholson Museum.'

Jayda's hand tightened around her mobile. '*Telemarketing?*'

'No. Antiquities. Restorations, from what he told me, which wasn't much.'

Her heart began to race. 'Repairing old books and artwork?'

'Don't know. Does it matter?'

'Has Garry been acting strange lately? Being secretive, or doing things out-of-character?'

'Why? What are you thinking?' His voice cracked. 'Do you think there's someone else?'

She bit her lip. It wasn't as if she could share her suspicions with Juz. Not when she lacked proof and he was already hurting.

'I don't know what to think. Are you sure it can't be fixed?'

'I don't even know how it broke.'

'You were so good together.'

'We were, until we weren't. This past week he seemed distant. I thought it was to do with crap going on at work. Then a friend called two days ago, and the next thing I know, we're having "the talk".'

'Oh, Juz! I'm sorry.'

'Me too.' His voice trailed, and her heart ached for him. He cleared his throat again. 'If it's okay with you, I need a good old-fashioned debrief, even if it is over some of that syrup you call wine.'

'I still have half a dozen bottles from the box you bought at Christmas.'

'Then bring a bottle when you come.'

'I'll try to sneak away.'

'Don't tell me reporter boy is the possessive type?'

'More like protective.'

'And you have to ask permission to meet a friend?'

'I don't *have* to do anything.'

'But you do?'

'I don't know. It hasn't come up yet.'

'That'd be the only thing that hasn't.'

She rolled her eyes and snorted. 'If you're angling for details you'll need more bait than that.'

'Spoilsport!'

'Ah, but you love me.'

'How could I not?'

Five minutes more of banter and she ended the call feeling refreshed. And with direction.

She moved back to her computer. She needed to take a closer look at Garry. His guilt wasn't a given, but neither was she ready to rule it out.

Then there was Juz. Logic said he was still a suspect. But that same logic argued that he was a friend who never failed to make her feel better. He struggled to use his iPhone most of the time, let alone any type of computer. And he loved cats—Tumbles in particular.

'How's your boyfriend?'

She looked up from the screen to find Seth lounging against the wall. A sight that never failed to send shivers up her spine and heat into her blood.

'Single.'

'Garry left him?'

'Don't sound so happy. Juz is miserable.'

'Poor Juz. Perhaps we should go see him.'

'We?'

'Sure. Why not? He'll need the support of friends. Your friends are my friends. Unless they happen to be a killer, that is.'

Lucky for Seth, Juz was right and she hadn't lost her sense of humour. She rolled her eyes. 'Really?'

'Too soon?'

'You think?' She pushed out of her chair. 'Want to guess where Garry's working now?'

'No. Want to tell me?'

'Where's your sense of fun?'

His chin dimpled. 'Right where you left it,' he checked his watch, 'just over an hour ago.' He closed the distance between them, his gun-metal gaze igniting an inferno on her senses. 'Want to find it again?'

Fire rolled across her cheeks. She remembered exactly what they'd been doing an hour earlier, and from her body's reaction, it was more than ready for a replay.

'*Nicholson Museum.*' She stepped back. 'Garry's working in antiquities at the Nicolson Museum.'

The flirtation left his expression. 'And you think he had access to the methyl cellulose?'

'It's a possibility we can't overlook. I just don't get his relationship to Anna Jones. No adoption came up in his history, so unless he was swapped at birth . . .'

'Which is more Hollywood than Garfield.'

She shrugged. 'Yet not so outlandish that it hasn't happened before.'

'Maybe this will help. One of my contacts has found a birth certificate listing Anna Jones as the mother. He's emailing it across now.'

'The name?'

'He didn't say. We'll know soon enough.'

*I'm gonna make him an offer he can't refuse.*

Seth pulled his phone from his pocket and checked the caller ID. 'I need to take this.'

Jayda nodded then disappeared into the kitchen, her departure followed by coffee-making sounds that made his mouth water. He was getting more than used to her personal brand of coffee, and instant hadn't tasted the same since. In fact, since she'd entered his life, nothing was the same.

He put the phone to his ear.

'*Seth!*'

He pulled it away and winced. 'Richie, hey. Tell me you sent that email.'

'It's on a cyber course to you now.'

Jayda returned to the living room and shot him a smile that promised more than coffee once he put down the phone. With that thought his jeans grew uncomfortably tight. He moved towards her with nothing in mind but what was about to occur.

'Thanks, man. I need to—'

'That's not the reason I called. *Have you seen today's "On the Inside"?*' Richie's voice stampeded across the phone line and into Seth's eardrums. 'Great story! I'm glad you changed your mind. What I don't get is why you sent it to such a low-down *rag?*'

His eardrum echoed from Richie's inability to have a phone conversation on any volume other than full. Maybe that's why it took a few moments to grasp his friend's meaning. 'What are you talking about? Change my mind about what?'

'Get your head out of your pants and focus, man. The story.'

'The . . .' He skirted a stunned Jayda and flipped up his computer screen. It took only seconds to find the scandalmonger's front page news.

'Son of a bitch!'

'Seth?'

'What the . . .?' Every word that scrolled upwards with the click of his mouse made the boil in his blood bubble up and threaten to overflow.

*Fuck!*

He slewed his hand through his hair. 'Rich. I'll call you back.'

He didn't wait for an answer. He ended the call and tossed the phone onto the table.

It was all there. He corrected himself. *Almost all.* Mercifully Jayda's link to Madden was missing. Small comfort. His mind jumped to the computer file on his hard drive—every detail of their joint investigation, their conversations. Evidence that somehow he was responsible for this monstrosity.

'What is it?' Her breath at the back of his neck didn't warm him as it would have moments earlier. It just set the lump in his throat and made it impossible to breathe.

He jammed his hand onto the mouse and closed the screen.

'What was that, Seth?'

The coldness in her voice said he'd reacted seconds too late. She'd seen, and he had no idea how to explain away the irrefutable evidence that he'd betrayed her, regardless of the fact it wasn't true.

The article was written in his voice, albeit not in his paper, but under his by-line.

'I haven't worked it out yet.'

'Worked out how *The Inside Story on the Thomasz Family* got out?'

'It wasn't me, Jayda.'

She reached over and gave the mouse a couple of clicks. The headline flashed up again, his name proudly stamped beneath it.

'That *is* your name?'

'It's not my story. Someone else wrote it.'

'Who the hell would do that?'

'I don't know. He must have hacked into my computer like he hacked into yours.'

'So you've been keeping notes.'

He nodded, hating the disbelief in her expression.

'Why? Why would you keep notes on a story you weren't going to write?'

'To help me think it all through. There was never any danger of me using it like this.'

'But someone else did. You wrote stuff I told you in confidence, about Bec, about my parents. Stuff I've never shared with anyone, stuff I never would have shared if I'd thought it would go on record.'

How could he explain he used the notes the way most people used diaries? The way Jayda used her lists.

Writing helped him process information, work out how he felt, how he'd cope. He had folders of files dating back to his teens, to days when the only one who would listen was his old clunky keyboard and hard drive.

She scrolled down, then stopped and swallowed. 'Shame you didn't go further. *The inside scoop on Jayda Thomasz, and yes, I've been inside!* Wouldn't they love to know *that?* You have so much more you could have told them about the daughter of the biggest serial killer Melbourne has ever seen—innocent-come-slut, a screamer in the bedroom who loves it when her supposed boyfriend goes down on her. Now that'd sell papers and get you that wonderful promotion you're chasing.'

He knew she was hurting, that she was just trying to hurt him back. But the idea that he'd kiss and tell, do anything to injure her, made him want to ram the computer and every bit of the story against his parents' perfect, white-washed wall.

'I'd never do that. Jayda, come on. Do you really think I would?'

The cold in her eyes was only just outweighed by the scepticism. 'Let's say for argument's sake that you didn't write *this*.' Her hand waved at the screen. 'The fact that you had the material meant someone else could. Or was it that you intended to write it, you were just waiting for something more to happen before you did?'

'That you'd even consider such a thing says you can't possibly know me.'

'You're right. I don't know you.'

The defeat in her voice almost killed him. It hurt more deeply than her anger.

'Tell me you don't still want that promotion.'

What killed him almost as much was how her hard-earned trust had turned to dust. And how he was about to provide the final clip of ammo that would seal her belief of his betrayal.

'I already have the promotion.'

'You *what?*'

'I got the offer on Monday. I meant to tell you. But after meeting my editor, I came back to your apartment being a crime scene, then I brought you here and Tumbles was killed, then we've been working round the clock to solve this case. So much has happened, I never got the chance.'

'You said you were meeting a friend that day.'

'I didn't want to tell you until it was a certainty.'

'You lied about it beforehand, and then after you didn't tell me at all.'

'I've just given you my reasons.'

'*You never got the chance.* What about last night in bed? This morning? Or even five minutes ago before the phone rang?'

'I forgot.' It may have been the truth, that it had been the furthest thing from his mind these last few days, but it sounded so damn lame, even to his own ears.

'The job you want more than anything, the reason you approached me, seduced me, wanted to work with me, and you *forgot?* Would you believe you right now?'

'I'd want to try.' He reached for her hand. 'I love you, Jayda. Through all of this, you have to believe it.'

She wrenched out of his grasp and it was like someone ripped away a piece of his heart. She dropped her phone into her bag, grabbed her keys and headed for the door. 'I don't know what I believe anymore.'

'Jayda, at least stay and we can talk about it.'

'I'm not like you. I don't *talk*, and last time I tried it brought me to *this*.' Again her hand waved towards his computer.

'It's not safe for you to leave.' He tried to grab her hand again and she evaded him.

'And it's not safe for me to stay.'

Next thing he knew he had a gun barrel pressed between his eyes. 'Follow and I'll shoot.'

She backed away, her free hand disappearing behind her to twist the doorknob and open the door. She didn't say another word, but she didn't have to. The look in her eyes said it all.

He'd lost her. And if that was possible so quickly, so easily, he wondered if he'd ever really had her at all.

# Chapter Fifty-Nine

$J$ayda's mind whirled.

*Liam all over again.*

Only this time it was so much worse. This time her love was real.

She gripped her head in her hands and squeezed. The whirling didn't stop. It only intensified, and now everything had become a blur. The reason became obvious as the first tear skidded down her cheek and dropped from her chin onto her jeans. She scrubbed the next before it had a chance to fall and willed the rest to stay back.

*Do. Not. Cry.*

One shaking hand gripped the wheel, the other jabbed the key in the ignition and jiggled. The car roared to life.

Funny. Her car had been ready for pick up from evidence for the last two days, yet she'd felt no great rush to do so. She could have blamed it on the case and being too busy to take time out to collect it. Could have blamed it on Seth for distracting her to the point that she'd no longer cared whether she got her car back or not.

The truth was much simpler. Driving the Beetle made her feel close to Bec. As if her sister was in the car with her, laughing with her unique brand of humour. Providing comfort when she needed it.

She needed Bec now. Needed her comfort more than anything. Only she was so very far away and she was never coming back.

The light at Seth's front door flickered on. Before he could follow, she skidded onto the road, only just missing a passing car. The screech of brakes and beep of the horn brought her back to the moment.

Where to go?

Her apartment was a crime scene and one of her friends was trying to kill her. She could go to her parents', but there would be questions she wasn't ready to answer yet.

She slid the gear shift into fourth and came to a decision.

She would go to the person who knew her best. The friend least likely to be a killer.

Damn, damn, damn and . . . *damn!*

Jayda was gone and she'd made it pretty clear she didn't want him to follow. He could still feel the chill of cold metal against his temple, while a corresponding chill lodged itself deep in the chambers of his heart.

The room already felt empty without her. He wasn't ready to consider what her absence would mean to his life.

What was he supposed to do now?

*Solve the case.*

The voice of reason. He had no idea where it came from, but it was as good a suggestion as any.

The birth certificate should have hit his inbox by now.

He logged into his private email, found two unread messages—one from Richie, one from his parents.

If humour was something he still owned, he would have laughed out loud at the irony.

They'd obviously read his last message. His decision to move out of their place had earned what his achievements had failed—their attention. He waited for the familiar wrench—it didn't come. Their inability to love him no longer mattered. Neither did anything they had to say.

He clicked on Richie's email, then the attachment, and scrolled through the document until he found what he sought.

The mouse dropped from his hand.

*Shit.*

His breath clogged as his worst fears were cemented in the distinct black scrawl.

He now knew, with absolute certainty, the identity of the Night Terror. Grabbing his keys, he rushed to the door only to remember his car was still waiting in evidence for him to collect it. He'd been in no hurry to pick it up, hadn't planned on going anywhere without Jayda, and they'd been using Bec's car.

He dialled Jayda's number hoping she'd answer, not expecting much. She lived up to the expectation. The woman was as stubborn as a damned mule, and didn't he love her for it? The message he left was brief and much as he hoped to God she'd check it, there was no guarantee.

Cursing again, he dialled the number for St Kilda police station and prayed he'd get hold of Chase before it was too late.

'One glass of Moscato coming up!' The welcome *clink* of wine glasses echoed from the kitchen. 'And I know you said no food, but chocolate doesn't count!'

Jayda's lips twitched into an almost-smile.

She wandered aimlessly through the familiar living room, the layout so very like her own.

What was she meant to do now? The man she loved had been collecting data on her. Extensive data. He was a reporter at heart, and now he'd become one in title. His most recent by-line proved the story would always come first, whether he'd written this particular report or not.

Didn't the data's existence suggest intent?

It was the same damned circle she'd been round a hundred times since she left him. And it led her nowhere but migraine-central. Not that she suffered from migraines, but if there was ever a time for one to hit, now would be it.

She stood at the sideboard, fingering miniature Turkish bowls dusted within an inch of their lives.

Did Seth write the article? She doubted it. He'd never stoop to writing for a rag like *On the Inside* and his shock was too honest to be anything but genuine. Plus, he'd promised he wouldn't, and somewhere inside she knew that he'd meant it.

Then why was she so angry?

*The notes.* Not about the case. She had more than enough of those herself. It was the other stuff. Personal stuff. Thoughts, feelings, anecdotes, about Bec and herself, her parents. Things that no one had been privy to until he'd typed them up and left them on his computer, ready for someone to hack into.

And then, of course, there was the doubt.

Seth *thought* he loved her—had even said it a few times—but could he really? He loved his job, wanted a promotion more than anything. She got that. She'd been the same when it came to earning her detective badge. But he'd just achieved the biggest leap in his career, the dream he'd worked for, seduced her for, *and he hadn't said a word.*

What was she supposed to think?

Her gaze scanned the bookcase without seeing a single title. He'd told his reporter friend. Had he told his parents?

Why hadn't he told her?

That same circle. Only this time she had an answer.

This wasn't about anger. It was about the knife that plunged so deep into her heart she doubted it would ever come out. Seth hadn't shared his biggest triumph. Hadn't wanted to. Hadn't *needed* to. And that knowledge was slowly killing her, because she'd believed he wanted to share his life with her.

He thought he loved her, but from where she stood, it seemed he'd just got it wrong.

She picked up the Lladro kitten. It really was beautiful. All the more so because it had been lovingly carried from halfway across the globe. Maybe that's what she'd done wrong. She should have travelled. Seen the world and experienced it enough to tell when a man truly loved her.

She turned the fine porcelain in her hands, until something caught her eye. *Weird.* She squinted. A *Made in China* stamp? On a genuine Lladro bought in Spain? The ink was faint, as if it had been scrubbed clean. Only it hadn't been, not quite. Funny that she'd never noticed it before. Then again, she'd never picked it up and looked at the underside before.

She checked the hummingbird beside it. Nothing. Including the stamp that would make it genuine.

Her gaze roamed then latched onto the canvas covering the greater portion of the wall above the sideboard. She took a couple of steps and stopped. She'd never looked at it so closely, always glanced at it across the length of the room from the couch. The oils were vibrant, the strokes precise. A woman, her head and shoulders, blonde hair flowing, her tears a swirl of droplets that sprung from moist blue eyes.

Jayda's heart pounded so hard she could feel the throb of it behind her temple. The picture had always made her uneasy but there was something more than that now. She moved closer. Funny how she'd never noticed that the tears were works of art in themselves. Tiny ceramic-looking dewdrops, each skilfully painted and unique.

And if she wasn't mistaken, something about them had changed. Were there more? Her eyes latched onto one with a blue background and burnt orange sunflowers. *Van Gogh.*

Her vision blurred. The porcelain hummingbird slid from her fingers and shattered at her feet.

At the explosion of ceramic, her dream—her memory—came to her.

*'Run Sammy. Run!'*

*The girl scuttled out through the jumble of chair legs. As she ran through the living room, she couldn't help but catch a glimpse of the painting on the far wall—a woman crying as if her world were about to end.*

*Then a scream erupted from the kitchen and the girl belted for the open front door.*

Jayda reached for her gun. How ironic she'd finally found him now.

She turned to the sound of fingers cracking. Then pain exploded against the back of her skull and everything went black.

# Chapter Sixty

**D**amn, but her head hurt like hellfire.

Jayda stifled a groan and tried to focus through the pain. Her eyelids were crusted shut and the thought of prying them open made the pounding in her head go wild. At first she didn't try. It was important to get her bearings, to ensure she was alone before letting on that she was awake.

She worked to steady her breathing and remain still. No mean task when she was slumped awkwardly against the metal pole to which she seemed to be tethered. Her shoulders ached from the pull of her hands behind her back, coarse rope cutting deep into her wrists and ankles. The floor was damp and its chill seeped through her jeans and deep into her bones.

The stench of sweat and musty carpet overwhelmed her nostrils and with every swallow, the copper tang of blood struck at the back of her tongue.

Aside from the occasional creak of old pipes and the low hum of an air-conditioning unit, there was no sound.

Continuing to feign lifelessness, she detected no movement, no changes in air pressure or sound. Nothing to indicate she was anything other than alone.

Slowly, painfully, she opened her eyes.

Her vision blurred. She blinked. Squinted. A distorted mish-mash of colours and lines slowly merged into focus.

The room's only lighting came from a blue security lamp. That and three strategically placed skylights ensured it wasn't so dark that she couldn't recognise a weights room when she saw one. Equipment haphazardly cluttered the gym floor that she knew extended over most of the building's second level. Some sections were covered with large white sheets, in others equipment had been pushed and stacked together.

The room didn't smell of paint, but it did project an air of impending renovations. Any hopes that a die-hard exercise fiend might turn up and save her dive-bombed then died.

She blinked, wishing she could scrub at whatever caked her eyelids. Grime and God knows what. Blood, perhaps. She could smell it, taste it. A red trail stained her t-shirt and no doubt more matted her hair where she'd been struck.

She raised her head and a scalding poker arced through her skull. But nothing came close to the pain in her heart. Her best friend had deceived her. Said he loved her when he'd secretly loathed her *for years*. She shuddered. He'd murdered Eric. Tumbles. So many women. *Bec.*

This time when she blinked it was to drive back the tears.

The mountain of hurt threatened to push her towards helplessness. She dragged oxygen into her lungs and shuffled until her back lay flush against the pole and the pull on her wrists relaxed. Her knuckles scraped against something abrasive and she winced. Twisting her neck, she gulped back the nausea that swilled in her throat. She might have been grimy and bruised already, but she refused to chuck and add rancid to her list of offences.

Her fingers stretched out. The roughness they reached felt like textured plaster. Her heart leapt. This was her light, when until now her day had been an endless tunnel. If she could yank the pipe from its brackets, there was a chance she could break free.

She dragged in a deep breath, ignoring the tenderness of her ribs. Using the pole and wall as leverage, she bent her knees and dragged her bound ankles closer to her butt, then pushed her body backwards and up. Muscles burned. Scrapes and bruises she hadn't felt until now screamed in protest. Her head swam and she almost lost those stomach contents again.

But she was standing, and that brought her one step closer to freedom. Her body felt heavy and stiff. She had no idea how long she'd been lying there tethered like an animal, no idea even of the time.

No idea why she was still alive.

She shuddered. Rather than questioning her bounty she needed to make the most of it.

No sense in waiting for a rescue that wouldn't come. She'd walked out on the only person who would have realised she was missing. And in case that hadn't sufficiently cemented her fate, she'd held a gun to his head and threatened to shoot him if he followed.

*Stupid, stupid, stupid!*

She smacked her head back and the room swam. She'd botched up royally. Instead of taking off half-cocked she should have stayed, should have talked.

*Seth isn't Liam.*

And Liam was nothing more than a blip in her past. She'd let him rule her life for too long. She wouldn't let him rob a second more.

She loved Seth, and God help him, he loved her. He wasn't responsible for the article. She was sure of it now.

Although, hadn't recent events showed her gut was less than trustworthy these days? Hadn't she discounted the wrong suspect when it came to the Night Terror? Dammit that she couldn't trust her instincts. Her gut was so twisted that it had led her every which way but the right one.

But whatever the reason Seth had for collating that information, her heart told her it wasn't suspect. She should have known he'd never give a bottom-dwelling rag like *On the Inside* the time of day, far less every detail of her private life. And she should have given him the chance to explain, instead of allowing blind anger to take over.

*Stupid.*

First thing she'd do when she escaped this godforsaken hell is tell him so. *If* she got out. She just had to get out.

She was spiralling again. Running in circles when she needed to think straight.

*Get it together, Thomasz. First things first. Free yourself and catch the sonofabitch who hogtied you to this post. Then fix your life.*

Wishing things were different wouldn't change them. Only action could do that.

And while she hoped to heaven that the birth certificate in Seth's inbox would lead him to search for her, she couldn't count on it. The only thing she could count on now was herself.

She tugged at her bindings. The pole shuddered, giving her hope. She yanked harder. The knot at her wrists tightened and she gasped, blinking back tears.

*Suck it up. No time for histrionics.*

She worked her fingers over the knot, hoping to loosen it, and sharp pain sliced across her knuckles. She bit her lip as a stickiness soaked the back of her hand. The knot refused to budge, but she had another idea. With slow, meticulous movements she dragged the rope up and down against the sharpness jutting from the wall—perhaps a nail?—feeling the friction against the fibres. The noise thundered in her ears. Lucky no one was around to hear it.

Where was he?

Her head swung right and a blur of white and chrome filled her vision. She bit her lip and held her breath. It didn't stop the room spinning, but it did slow the motion. Gradually this time, she turned the other way and peered into the expanse of mirror that covered the wall to her left. She was sure she was alone. There were places he could stay hidden, but why would he?

Then again, why would he leave her alone with all ten fingers and breath still in her lungs for escape? It didn't make sense.

Nothing made sense.

Her hand slipped. 'Ouch!'

The distant crack of knuckles splintered through her body like a snapped whip. *Where was he?* She twisted her head, searching, but there was no sign of the man she'd called friend.

'Jayda, Jayda, *Jayda*. Always fighting, always resisting. Don't you think it's time you relaxed and accepted your fate? I know *I* have.'

There was a movement behind the bench press to her left and she turned to watch as he stepped out from the shadows. His olive skin was unusually pale, and the brown eyes she'd once considered warm now glowered with so much hate she wondered how she'd never guessed.

Even now, with the irrefutable truth before her, she still found it hard to believe.

'Why, Juz?'

'Ahh, such a wide-ranging question.' His grin stretched broadly across his bared teeth. He took a step closer and dipped his head, trapping her gaze in the wild, glassy brown of his. 'Because it was so much fun.'

His obvious glee made her feel physically ill, but her mind raced through every training manual she'd read. How did you handle someone who'd charged completely off the rails? Who'd perhaps never been on them in the first place. Could anything he'd ever told her be trusted? Doubtful. That meant she had to start from scratch.

*Keep him talking until you work out a platform for negotiation.* Words from her Crisis Hostage Negotiation trainer. Great in the classroom, but how did you negotiate your way out of madness?

*Find a weak spot and exploit it.*

Juz's cold assessment didn't waver as he stepped closer and his fingers trailed her temple before slowly winding a lock of hair behind her ear. She bit her lip to stop from shrinking away, but couldn't prevent her body from stiffening.

His nostrils flared, like the beast he was, scenting her fear.

He dropped his hand, skimming it along her arm and down towards her bound wrists. 'I'm pretty much an expert at knots. Just so you know, this one's a constrictor. The more you pull, the more it tightens. You're not going anywhere, *my friend.*'

His fingers trailed to the tips of hers. An army of cockroaches couldn't have made her more nauseated.

Her mind latched onto the one thing that hadn't changed with Juz's Night Terror transformation—his ego was still colossal. Perhaps she could work this to her advantage.

'Well done, Juz. You had me fooled every step of the way.' She nodded in what she hoped looked like admiration and pushed a smile into her stiff lips. 'But you're my best friend and feelings that strong aren't easily turned off. Why don't we try to figure a way out of this together?'

'Cut the negotiation bullshit, Jayda. It won't work with me.' He slashed his fist through the air and her gaze flew to the blink of metal in his hand. Her body chilled. How had she missed that he carried a knife?

A knife, her gun. How many ways did the bastard have to kill her? She clenched her fists and gasped at the burn of rope against her skin.

She had everything to live for, but that meant she had so much more to lose. And the look in Juz's eyes said he knew it.

*Dammit! No more.*

He'd played his game one step ahead of her. That reign ended here.

Her parents deserved happiness. They wouldn't lose another daughter. Plus, there was a man out there who loved her and she planned on spending the rest of her days loving him back. Provided he still wanted her.

But there were so many things to do before she could think about winning Seth back.

She stared at the monster in front of her. The bastard who'd broken her heart and left her floundering in self-doubt.

The game started now.

With slow, minimal movements, she continued scraping her bindings against the metal behind her back. 'You're right, Juz. I won't pander to your ego. And you've shown me I can't outsmart you.'

Her voice shook, but if he picked up on it he'd only sense her fear, and that was real enough. It would no doubt make him feel powerful and she could only hope that the headiness of that power would make him sloppy. A long shot, but wars had been won on less.

'Ahh, Hostage Negotiation 101. Establish rapport.'

'I assumed rapport was something we already shared. Considering you sang karaoke at my last birthday.'

His lips twisted. 'And how I hated every minute of it.'

'Your acting skills really are remarkable. I never once guessed.'

'Of course you didn't. You were so desperate for approval, it was pathetic.' His words were meant to cut and they did, with a surgeon's precision. But there was no place here for sentiment. Juz wasn't the only actor in this production.

She blinked back tears she wished were wholly counterfeit and lifted her chin. 'Why even bother with the ruse of friendship? If you wanted to kill me, why not do it then?'

'Ahh, well done. I see what you're playing at now. Encourage me to talk until rescue arrives. It'll be quite a wait, though, so why don't we make ourselves comfortable?'

He patted the cushioned seat of a shoulder press machine, then sat down. Dead eyes observed her with calm detachment. His ankle balanced carelessly on his knee and his hands rested in his lap as he fondled the knife with casual ease.

He couldn't have been less than three metres away, yet she felt the chill of his soul as though he sat right beside her.

A soul that had once warmed and comforted.

'Relax, Jayda.' His grin slithered towards a sneer. How had she ever thought his smile warm?

'I will if you loosen these ropes.'

'Nice try. It's good you still have fight left. It'll make it all the sweeter when I take it from you.'

She suppressed a shiver.

He twirled his blade through the air. 'There won't be any rescue, you know.'

She hadn't expected him to comply, but she'd managed to get him talking, and while he talked he wasn't using the knife. She bit her lip. Her arms and shoulders ached with the constant cutting movement and her vision was beginning to double. She blinked and forced her eyes to merge the two monsters into one.

'It's just you and me, Jayda. No one knows you're here and the gym is closed until the asbestos crew comes next week to clean it up.' He gestured towards a jagged opening in the far wall. 'And I doubt your faithful puppy will follow you after enjoying the feel of your gun at his temple.'

Her head jerked back. She gasped as it hit the pole and pain ricocheted through her skull. 'How do you know about that?'

'The same way I know everything. I'm not nearly as computer-illiterate as I've led you to believe.'

Her fingers fumbled and pain sliced through her palm.

She drew in a deep breath, fighting the tremble in her nerves that threatened to overwhelm her. 'It would have taken a tech genius to hack into Seth's computer and make it look as though he sent that article to *On the Inside*.'

'I'm that genius.'

What she'd give to slap the smugness from his face.

Long slender fingers caressed the blade in his lap. 'The web is such a glorious mine of information. Did you know there are sites that let you send emails from one address while making it look like they've been sent from another? And redirecting incoming emails is even easier.'

He glanced at his watch then returned his cold gaze to her. 'Everything I wanted was laid out with step-by-step instructions. And for those few things beyond my own capabilities, I enlisted help.'

'Eric.'

'Alas, poor Eric, I knew him well.' He chortled as if his Shakespearean misquote made joke of the year.

She stamped down her anger. *Be positive, be calm, be unthreatening. Engage your captor. Plan your escape.*

'What I don't get is how you persuaded him to help.'

'I can be quite charming when I want to be.'

'Much as I agree, it would take more than charm to convince Eric to break the law.'

'How right you are. Because, of course, you *know* him. You *bewitched* him. You made my job so easy.' He cleared his throat. She thought she detected a flinch, but it was so fleeting she couldn't be sure. 'I played to his weakness. *You.* The poor sap believed he was in love and when he thought you might be in danger from that dreadful Night Terror character, he jumped at the idea of setting up some surveillance.'

'And then he cottoned on, so he had to die.'

'Oh, no. No, no, *no*. I wasn't the one to let him down. Eric's death was all on you, *my dear friend*.' His lip curled. 'You signed his death warrant the moment you asked him to recover your generous gift to charity. After all, I couldn't allow him to blab all his dirty secrets to you in a fit of lovesick guilt.'

Her knees buckled, slamming her back against the pole. This wasn't on her. *It wasn't.* She gasped, then tensed her shoulders to prevent herself from sliding to the ground.

'Who's the murderer now, Jayda?'

She shook her head. 'I didn't murder anyone.'

'You don't have to wield a knife to have blood on your hands. Take the old man, for instance.'

'Madden?'

'Oh, go on, Jayda. Why not call him Daddy?'

Jayda held her breath and counted to ten. *This is your game, not his. Stay detached. Stay on track. Don't let him draw you in.*

'Madden died in prison. There's no way you could have been responsible for that, and neither was I.'

'You underestimate me, Jayda. But, that's always been your problem. You fail to believe anyone could be as clever as you. Guess I proved you wrong.'

'I know you left the key behind the photo so I'd be close to the prison when you revealed my past. I know you wanted me to rush over there, wanted me to get that close to the answers I needed before you took away my only chance of gaining them.' She didn't wait for his nod. She already knew she was right. 'What I find difficult to believe is that you could have a man killed when he's behind bars.'

'Oh, Jayda. Money buys a multitude of other men's sins. There are any number of individuals out there who would be thrilled to kill you. For the right price, of course. That, however, is a pleasure I've been saving for myself.'

'So, you paid someone to smuggle a mop into Madden's cell, then they used it as a hanging point and made his death look like a suicide. Why? What harm could he do you from behind bars?'

His hands fisted, white knuckled and shaking in his lap. It was the first chink she'd witnessed in his veneer.

'What would *you* know about harm? A Portuguese man-of-war's tentacles can reach for miles beyond its body. It has means.'

'By means I guess you're talking about your mother.'

'I don't believe we were talking anything but metaphors. Your dear daddy is dead because you wouldn't leave well-enough alone.'

'He's no more my father than he was yours!' The words shot out before she could drag them back. Her body shook and she almost lost herself in those cold, dark eyes. A momentary flicker crossed his expression, then vanished, replaced with an air of careless nonchalance.

'You *are* the talented detective, aren't you? When that fiery hair of yours doesn't get in the way. I see the plan—draw me out, make me brag, uncover all my dirty secrets so you can use them to lock me away once you've been rescued.'

He stood and the room crowded inwards.

'That's how this would work in your perfect world. What you have yet to realise is you're in my world now. There'll be no rescue. You're alive at my whim. Your very existence is something I could end at a moment's notice.'

He turned the knife slowly in his hands and she dragged her mind back from how that blade would feel at her neck.

His lips stretched tightly across his over-white teeth, leering, predatory. Then he sauntered slowly towards her.

# Chapter Sixty-One

Juz approached the way a hunter would stalk live prey caught in a death trap.

With every step, the precious seconds she needed to cut through the rope slipped away. She wrenched at her hands and the pole shuddered. She heaved again. This time a nail flew out and skidded across the concrete floor.

He stepped over it and stopped, barely half a metre before her.

She was so close. Another strand of the rope snapped and she felt a loosening at her wrists. Her heart thudded. The metal blade glinted in his hands, but she refused to remove her eyes from his face.

'It hurts, doesn't it? To realise someone you loved didn't love you back. That they were only using you to play out some sick, demented plan.'

Pure evil slid across his lips and she wanted to kick him. Wanted to slap the filthy smirk from his face and put a bullet straight through his skull.

In seconds that could be her last, she swore she'd die fighting and tried again.

'I get it. You're looking for love. Well, you'd already found it. You've always been like a brother to me. I loved you.'

Masking her disgust at the lie that was their relationship wasn't easy. She doubted the residual bitterness on her tongue would ever fade.

His gaze narrowed. 'Yes, *loved*, past tense. Nothing lasts forever, Jayda. Every fire burns itself out with time. I prefer to be the master of my own destiny.'

'By killing everyone who loves you before their love has a chance to die?'

'Simple, but effective.' The blade turned in his palm. 'Detective school taught you well.'

She wrenched at her hands, wincing as the rope chafed against raw skin. He stepped closer and his minty breath fanned her cheek. Her bravado dwindled. Her throat clogged and her vision blurred.

*I don't want to die.*

Juz shook his head. 'Always the fighter, always refusing to admit defeat. Take this case. If I hadn't fed you information every step of the way, you'd still be poring over old files with that patsy partner of yours, wondering why you just didn't get it.'

His hand inched towards her waist. She flinched. He lifted the hem of her t-shirt and the knife's blade flashed.

'If there's one thing that good-for-nothing prick in prison taught me, it was that pain is relative. You think that what you're feeling right now is pain, but it's nothing compared to what it could be.'

Fire slashed across her stomach. Her body jerked and she watched the slow bead of blood cut across her skin. Tears welled against her lids and she blinked them back. 'You bastard!'

'How right you are. You are too though, in case you forgot.'

He let go of her top and the slow seep of red stained the grimy, already blood-smattered white. He slipped a cloth handkerchief from his pocket and carefully wiped the blade.

'A mere scratch. I don't mean to kill you for a while yet. We have so much to talk about and I've waited too long for this moment to have it end so soon.'

She tugged and felt the resistance on the ropes. Then it eased. As the final thread snapped, her right fist shot out in an upper cut straight to Juz's throat. His eyeballs bugged from their sockets as cartilage crushed beneath her knuckles. With a wild gurgle, he fell to his knees, a mobile skidding out from his pocket as he hit the floor.

Ignoring the burn from her wound, she grabbed the knife and cut the binds at her ankles. The phone was cracked, but it still had power and signal. His fingers wrapped around it and she stomped on his knuckles, cringing at the sound of splintering glass that followed. He gave it up with a wild howl and she slipped it into her pocket, although the phone was near useless now, as indicated by the blank, cracked screen.

She kicked his stomach. Hard. 'That's for Bec, you bastard!' She sniffed, dragging the back of her hand across her eyes and nose, and kicked again. 'And that's for Tumbles and Eric and all those women.'

He writhed on the floor. She knew he was in pain, knew his windpipe was damaged, possibly snapped, and that in time the area would swell, restricting speech, restricting breathing.

She paced. Temptation dangled like a ripe, juicy carrot. If she left him, he'd be dead within a few hours. Possibly fewer if his trachea was snapped. He'd killed so many, did such evil really deserve to live?

The pacing gave her no peace, and in truth, she hadn't expected it to. Much as she believed he deserved to die, it wasn't her decision to make. She'd taken an oath when she'd taken on her badge, and that oath bound her as tightly as the ropes had only minutes before.

She didn't care that Juz was suffering, but she did have to get help. Difficult to know what to do with no cuffs. The broken rope wasn't sufficient to restrain him, and much as she was tempted to leave him to his fate, she couldn't risk a sudden recovery or escape. She needed to tie him up and go for backup, all before he fell unconscious and died.

Every class she'd ever taken on CPR leapt to the forefront of her mind. She hoped to hell it wouldn't come to that. The irony of breathing life into the monster who'd sucked the life out of so many didn't escape her.

As he lay gasping on the floor, she patted him down for her gun or other weapons and came up empty. Biting her lip, she braced herself against the pain at her stomach and looked around. She could rip the sheets into strips.

She backed towards the closest shroud of white. One eye on Juz, she hacked at the cloth with the knife. His gasps quietened, the guttural breathing slowing almost as if he were slipping toward unconsciousness.

The cutting was slow and every jerk of her arm pulled at her stomach. She lifted her tee and inspected the wound. It had dried at the edges, and blood seeped rather than dripped from the cut. Most of all, it still hurt like hell.

She let go of her top and tugged the last strip of cloth free. She turned.

*Shit!*

The floor was empty.

She tightened her grip on the knife and scanned the area.

What the hell was wrong with her? She wasn't a damned recruit, knew better than to remove her eyes from a suspect, regardless of whether they'd seemed incapacitated on the floor or not. Did the man have superhuman strength? She'd seen a blow to the throat disable bigger adversaries for longer than Juz's measly few minutes.

Slowly she backed away, eyes darting side-to-side. At least she knew he didn't have her gun. Not that he was likely to use it. Yet. His ego wouldn't allow him to kill her until he'd finished with her.

The thought gave her little comfort.

*I'm not ready to die!* She was spiralling again. *Stop!*

She had the knife and the upper hand. If she could keep him talking, keep him busy, he'd eventually collapse and this time she'd restrain him immediately. She wrapped the strips around her torso and tied them like a belt low on her hips.

'Turn yourself in, Juz. That pain in your throat is your trachea. It's either broken or fractured. You need to see a doctor before it swells and blocks your airway. If you do nothing, you'll be dead within an hour.'

A deep bark—laughter?—sounded from her right.

Heart thumping against her ribcage, she veered left until she had the wall at her back and a large piece of cloth-covered equipment shielding her. The exit beckoned to her right, but she ignored its draw. Not while a killer was still walking, breathing and—by some stretch of the imagination—in her custody.

'Perhaps you should worry more about your own mortality, Jayda.'

Like a game of tug 'o war, she had to gain back control. At least when he talked, she knew where he was.

'You were telling me about Madden.'

'Yes. Let's continue our dialogue while the little cogs in your brain work out what to do.' She heard the hiss as he drew in a breath. 'Want to know why he broke his own protocol and killed the *lovely* Juliana?'

'She discovered who he was?'

'And how might she have done that?'

Her mind reeled with possibilities too horrible to contemplate. 'I don't know.'

'How disappointing.' His laughter broke into a hacking cough. 'The bitch received an anonymous tip-off that her adoring husband was cheating. Such a pity she picked the wrong time to investigate. Instead of finding Madden with my mother, she watched him strangle his forty-second victim. He had no choice but to follow her home and kill her before she could reveal his secret. And, of course, the police received an anonymous tip-off about the murder. The blood was still fresh on his hands when he passed his legacy to me and promised that one day, I too would become famous.'

The pride in his voice shivered its way up her spine.

'You were there?' Suddenly, one more jigsaw piece clicked into place. 'You cut my leg!'

'I'd have finished the job if the bastard hadn't stopped me. You always were his Achilles heel and my misfortune.'

What could make a person so sick, so twisted?

Impossible to wrap her head around it all. He must have been about ten at the time—*a child*—wielding so much destruction.

Time to contemplate that later. She had to remain detached. Couldn't allow him to drag her in to his madness.

*Keep him talking.* 'You mentioned his legacy.'

'The canvas.'

'A record of his killings.' The thought dragged a shudder deep into her bones. 'All those teardrops. Each one hand-painted to represent the victims.'

'You're not just a pretty face, after all. Did you like your sister's? I thought it fitting that her favourite piece of art become a little part of mine.'

Her heart twisted and she pushed back the pain.

'The tears. What are they made from?'

'Why, fingernails, of course.'

His voice seemed closer and she edged away.

'A masterpiece years in the making. You can thank Lydia for her part in its creation.'

Every word out of his self-satisfied mouth made her sick.

His laboured breathing filled the silences between his sentences. Eventually his throat would swell so that speech and breathing would become impossible. All she had to do was bide her time until then. Keep him talking, even if she didn't like what he had to say. Even if she wanted to ram his tongue so far down his throat that he'd never utter another supercilious word again.

'What about my mother?'

'Surely you know of their love affair?'

She didn't answer. Instead, she skirted a row of steppers and hunched behind a leg extension machine, all the while ensuring she had the wall at her back.

'It'd make a great story. Perhaps I'll write it someday.' He coughed. 'Ironic to think that Madden changed sex to marry my mother, to make us his legitimate family. I already called him "Dad" and he said it was just a matter of paper before it became real. Then he fell in love with your whore of a mother and that paper burned along with any hopes I had for a normal life. Your family ruined everything for me. So I guess it's only fair I return the favour.'

Something clicked in her mind. 'You reported my father to the OPI.'

His voice radiated delight. 'I wondered when you'd connect the dots.'

'Is any of it true? The allegations? The infidelity?'

'What do you think?'

'The affair took place years before we met.'

'Yes, it did.'

Her head whirled and the catch in her throat made it near impossible to speak. 'You had this planned back then?'

'I've been planning this forever. My life's work. It wasn't difficult to find a woman willing to be photographed with your father performing . . . questionable acts.'

There was a crash to her right, and then a hand weight rolled between two steppers to stop at her feet. Her heart pounded in her ears.

'I grew up knowing you had everything and I had nothing. Let's just say I've enjoyed evening the score.'

# Chapter Sixty-Two

**S**_he's not here._

Seth tugged at the paper mask that made it near impossible to breathe. _Of course she isn't._ He scrubbed his gloved fingers through his hair and only just stopped from ramming his fist through the wall.

It'd be too easy for Juz to take Jayda to his apartment. And nothing about the confounded man—or the case—had been easy so far. Why start now?

_Because the woman I love is in danger._

It had taken him twenty-nine years to find happiness, the least the universe could do was line up and make this chaos go away.

Again he wanted to hit something. Preferably the face of the bastard who'd captured her.

The moment he'd seen the birth certificate he'd guessed the killer's identity. The father's Spanish descent, the name of the child, Justino. The coincidences were too great for it to go any other way.

This was all his fault. Stupid pride had made him hesitate before going after Jayda. But it was that same stupid pride that wouldn't allow him to quit now. He'd find her and love her and never let her go.

But first, he had to find Juz.

His gaze combed the living room and the forensics team scouring every inch of it. He gave a tight smile to Georgie and the other officer beside her as his fingers flexed at his side and he clenched them into fists. Damn but he itched to join in the search. But at the threat of being bodily removed from the scene, he maintained his distance.

His gaze flitted every which way, willing his eyes to find something to lead them to Juz. In the meantime, what the hell was he supposed to do?

He took to pacing the Turkish rug, his disposable shoe coverings swishing against the carpet fibres. He was walking in Jayda's footsteps, the way he'd seen her pace on so many occasions. The action made him feel closer to her. Connected.

As he turned, he telepathically willed her to be safe, anywhere else but with Juz. A hope he knew to be futile. Little doubt the bastard already had her. The first thing he'd noticed as he followed Chase into the apartment was Jayda's purse and mobile left brazenly on the coffee table for them to find. The phone's display showed a trail of his missed calls. It gave him little comfort to know she hadn't been deliberately ignoring him.

Worse still was the smear of blood on the carpet near the sideboard . . . Chances that it was Juz's, not Jayda's, were slim. And it'd be days before forensics could confirm either way.

They didn't have days. He doubted they had hours. To find Jayda alive, they had to find her now.

For want of anything better to do, he moved into the hallway and towards the study.

A techie sat at Juz's desk. He looked like a kid just out of school, with black rimmed glasses and a ponytail of blonde hair trailing down his back. The boy—he couldn't think of him as more than that—was analysing the laptop, scanning files that proved Seth's innocence in relation to the article, and showed that Juz had also hacked into Jayda's computer, as well as her bank account.

The screen flickered. Seth froze in the doorway. A live video feed of his house's front entrance appeared. Two girl guides stood on his doorstep with a box of what he presumed was their signature biscuits. With another click of the mouse they disappeared and the screen flipped to the hallway outside Jayda's apartment.

The knowledge that they'd been monitored despite their precautions made him physically sick. His daily scans with the spectrum analyser had been worthless.

'I've found something!' The techie's fingers flew over the keyboard and Seth rushed to the computer, almost colliding with Chase as he did the same. The mouse clicked like thunder in one of those dry, ominous storms. His stomach surged to his throat, his hands gripping the head of the boy's chair.

The screen had split.

Juz filled the left, seated on some bench seat like he was hosting a Sunday afternoon tea party. He waved his arm through the air. A giant vice grabbed Seth's chest and squeezed. The bastard had a knife.

He switched focus to the right and his nightmare bolted to life.

Jayda stood, hands bound behind her back, blood smeared across her face and down her top. She seemed unaware of the camera, her wide eyes fixed on her captor. Her shoulders slumped, but her head remained high. He knew her well enough to know she was scared, but that spunk he loved and admired forbade her from giving Juz the same satisfaction.

His gaze slid back to the left. Juz raised his chin and stared into the camera, his smile a ghoulish split of lips across over-white teeth. Seth's greatest fears came to life with that one look.

The picture stuttered, then jumped. He watched the same feed run again.

A looped video, which meant old footage. How old? And what did that mean for Jayda?

*They would not be too late to save her.* He wouldn't allow any other outcome. There had to be something. *Anything.* And if the kid at the keyboard didn't act fast, he'd find himself on the floor and Seth in his place.

He scanned the screen. It didn't reveal much. Large white sheets covering, what? Furniture? Were they in a warehouse? A storeroom? Or an attic, perhaps?

'Can you get a location on the feed?'

Chase shot him a "you're pissing on my turf" look. He didn't care. He'd piss all over this case if it meant getting Jayda back alive.

The boy looked to Chase who nodded, then turned back to the computer, his gloved fingers dancing like a seasoned performer across the keyboard. He seemed to know what he was doing. If only he'd do it a damn sight faster.

Seth squinted, caught something in the corner of the screen. 'Can you freeze that?'

This time the kid didn't wait for permission.

'Rewind it back a little . . . That's it. *Stop.*'

He stared. He hadn't imagined it. What looked like a stack of weights poked out from beneath a sheet left of the screen.

A gym, perhaps. But gyms were like milk bars—everywhere. So, where to begin?

He turned to Chase. 'What gym does Juz work in?'

'Prahran Health and Fitness. But they're closed at the moment.

Asbestos.'

That was it. 'We need to get down there. *Now.*'

*Boom!*

His hands flew to his ears. Too late. A rapier sliced his eardrums, then a splintering *crack!* echoed through the apartment.

Chase pushed him back, racing from the study, drawing his gun. Seth regained his balance and with one last look at the screen ran after him.

'The bedroom!'

Chase stopped outside the door. 'Shit!'

Seth skirted the other man and slammed straight into Garry's blue-green gaze. Wide. Lifeless.

Agonised.

Chase pulled him back from the snow of white powder. Plaster flakes coated his hair and the cream carpet at his feet. Seth shrugged the other man's hand from his shoulder and stared at the ceiling. It gaped in a perfect, premeditated circle. Through the shattered plaster hung a rope and from the rope hung Garry.

The detective holstered his weapon. 'Forensics!'

A woman brushed past wearing the signature white overalls and yellow vest. Chase took a couple of steps towards her then stopped. 'Tell me what we've got.'

She surveyed the body. 'Three stabs to the abdomen, one cut to the throat.' She took a closer look. 'He was dead long before he was trussed in the rope.' She looked up. 'Looks like the ceiling was weakened and some kind of explosive finished the job.'

Seth followed her gaze to the floor. Two seconds before he saw it she extracted a small device from the rubble with gloved hands.

'A timer.'

Chase's gaze met his. Seth recognised the instant he reached the same conclusion.

He turned to the pitiful remains slumped forwards into its noose. Juz had planned the exact moment he wanted them to find it. Had planned it to the second.

They had all the evidence they needed for a conviction. Nothing was hidden. Nothing encrypted. Juz had set the party, laid out the welcome mat and invited them in.

His eyes strayed to the knife jutting from Garry's chest, and the bloodied paper it pinned there.

His heart pounded.

*Beat the clock.*

A pocket stopwatch hung from the blade and he watched it click over from fifty-nine minutes to fifty-eight. Blood thundered through his veins, building to a heavy throb against his temple.

Juz had sent a message and that message was clear. His game was nearly up and he had no intention of coming back.

'Wait. There's something else.'

The woman extracted a pair of tweezers from a pouch at her waist and with a gloved hand she pried open Garry's mouth. It was then he noticed something wedged between the dead man's teeth.

Carefully she extracted a folded piece of paper.

'What does it say?'

Chase shot him another look and he returned it. If the man didn't ask the questions, he would.

She opened the note and her fingers shook. *'Boom!'*

This time the look they shared was consensus.

*'Run!'*

# Chapter Sixty-Three

Jayda swung her head left then right.

*Where the hell had that dumbbell come from?*

Juz hadn't moved. She could still hear the wheeze of his laboured breathing from across the room. She dodged behind a large multi-gym, moving towards the sound. She needed to see him.

Her shoulders ached. Her arms, her neck, her trembling legs only just managing to hold her upright. Every part of her ached. Not least of all, her heart.

Difficult to believe that every single shitty thing in her life could be linked back to the actions of one man.

'You attacked my father because he was my hero.'

'There would be no reason to drag him down if he wasn't. Everything I've done so far has been because of you. Bec, Eric, your father, my mother, Tumbles. Even Garry, once he began spouting your virtues. They each have you to thank for their demise.'

'You killed Garry too?'

'He never was the smartest tool in the shed. But even idiots must die if they start asking awkward questions. I moved all the evidence out of the apartment and into the *conveniently* out-of-order lift. But when he still wouldn't quit, it was time for him to go.'

She sagged against the wall. It was ridiculous, really. With everything Juz had done, she'd imagined she'd known the extent of his hate. But Garry? His only crime—loving the wrong man. And then the discovery that Juz had been making plans while they were children . . .

She'd been raised inside her parents' protective bubble, oblivious to her past, unaware that she was anything other than a normal child with a normal past and a normal future ahead.

Juz had grown up under Madden's umbrella. It had twisted his mind and blackened any loving, healthy portion of his heart. He'd orchestrated her stepmother's death, ensured Madden was caught and imprisoned, set her father up so he could later use the information to bring him down. All to hurt her.

The realisation was a dagger in her chest that Juz was slowly, methodically twisting.

By hiding the truth, her parents had saved her from a similar fate. Yet, when she'd discovered what they'd done, she'd laid blame at their feet. Not once had she shown gratitude or thanked them.

Her fingers tightened around the knife handle and she tilted her head up to the water-marked ceiling. *Please give me the chance to thank them!*

With a shaky hand she pushed away from the wall. 'Garry loved you, so he had to die.'

'All this talk of *love*. Such a pointless emotion. Madden wasted all he had on Lydia, and in return she dragged his heart through the dirt and married his best friend.'

She moved closer still and caught a glimpse of him through a line of treadmills. He held a mobile in his hand, and every few seconds his gaze dropped to the screen. Where the hell had it come from? There'd been no mobile when she searched him earlier. She'd swear to it.

*Damn!*

This whole situation brimmed with madness, and where Juz had hidden a phone was the very least of her worries.

With a flare of his nostrils, he bared his teeth. 'What? No comments on mummy Lydia's betrayal?'

'She never loved him, you know. And she didn't lead him on to believe she did.' Jayda bit her lip to prevent herself from saying more. *A calm negotiator encourages a calm hostage environment.* 'Madden may have imagined they had a love affair, but they never did.'

'Is that what she told you?' His eyes glinted almost black. 'Lydia Thomasz is a liar as well as a whore.'

Jayda's teeth ground down on her lip. *Don't engage. Stay calm and stay alive.* She waited, blood thundering through her veins.

'He was going to leave mother for Lydia. When Lydia rejected him, he married her bitch friend and committed my life to a purgatory with my whining excuse for a mother. I was promised a father, stability, Friday night football and Sunday afternoon roasts. Instead I got leftovers. *Yours.*' His fingers twisted and her body chilled with every knuckle click. 'He gave you everything and left me scraps. I never forgave him for that.'

'Yet you continued his legacy.'

'It was the only promise he made that he kept. Even then, passing me the Night Terror reins was more for his profit than mine. He always was a self-centred sonovabitch.'

He gripped onto a weights stand, fighting for breath, his voice a laboured rasp. She strained to hear it.

'Not that it mattered. Becoming the Night Terror helped pass the time while I worked at fulfilling my own destiny.'

'Why Bec?'

'Why not?'

'She had nothing to do with you.'

'You loved her and therefore she had everything to do with me. She was a snotty, spoiled little brat. Killing her was worth the old man's wrath.'

She recoiled from the snap of his words. 'You broke victimology.'

'Another point, Sherlock. Have you worked out my unsanctioned father's predilection for virgins?'

'He wanted to possess them unspoiled?'

'Correct again. Any idea why?'

'To be their first, the way he couldn't be my mother's.'

'Top of the class.' The wide spread of his lips made her skin crawl. It was so far from the smile of the friend she remembered. 'And the significance of the severed finger?'

She shook her head.

'Jayda? I can't hear when you shake your head.'

It was as if the security camera above winked. She edged further behind the hulking metal. Whilst it offered limited cover, what it did offer was concealment.

'I don't know.'

'Come, come. Don't stop while you're on such a roll. Or perhaps you need a little incentive.'

Metal flashed in his hand and a 9mm projectile whizzed past her left ear. Plaster sprayed out from the wall behind her.

She threw herself to the ground. Pain ripped across her cut stomach and she gasped, dragging white powder into her mouth and nostrils. Dust hit the back of her throat. She gagged, spluttered, spat it out. Ironic that if a bullet didn't get her today, the asbestos would. She would have laughed if she wasn't damn well bawling. She scrubbed her eyes while her heart tried to beat its way out of her chest.

*Where the hell did the gun come from?* Her *gun. Had he left it hidden? Had he planned on her breaking free?*

Juz was still anticipating her actions, manipulating her even.

She blinked back the tears. She was tired. Of the game. Of wondering whether she'd see the people she loved again. Her parents. Seth.

Struggling for breath, she crawled closer to an expanse of white sheet and sat up. Juz's feet still remained firmly planted where she'd seen him last. Why couldn't he just collapse and die? Or had her blow to his throat missed its mark?

'Jayda? I missed deliberately, so I know you're still there. I'm waiting for an answer.' Through a tear in the sheet she watched him raise his hand again. 'Or should I keep going?'

What was it about the finger? 'It's . . . it's the victim's ring finger!'

He nodded and dropped the hand with the gun. Tension leached from her shoulders and she released the breath she hadn't noticed was wedged in the back of her throat.

Her semi remained in his hand, a reminder that while he still breathed, he still held the balance of control. 'Significance?'

She gripped the cold metal of the equipment and pulled herself up. With the hem of her tee, she mopped her face. As the fabric fell, she sucked in a lungful of air and searched for the strength to continue.

'Wakey, wakey!'

This time the bullet hurtled to her right. She shrunk into the sheet, body quaking beneath the rain of plaster. Anywhere else and she could hope that someone would hear the shots and call the police. Not so in this sound-proofed space.

With thoughts that his third shot might just reach its mark, she searched for an answer. 'By removing the ring finger, he ensured his victims could never wear another man's ring. They'd belong to him alone.'

'Bravo.' Hoarse coughs racked his body. He pressed his wrist to his mouth and when he removed it, the sleeve was soaked with red.

That wasn't from her blow to his throat.

Realisation swirled through her mind as the implications of that blood clicked into place. 'You're sick.'

He didn't appear surprised she could see. But then again, the placement of the two bullets indicated he had a pretty accurate idea of her location. That he may have access to the security camera feed didn't help. She moved further behind the sheet, knowing it provided little more than a semblance of protection.

'Oh, I'm much more than that.'

Realisation transformed any residual hopes into indulgence. *'You're dying?'*

He glanced again at the screen of his phone, his expression like the big bad wolf seconds before he ate Little Red Riding Hood's grandmother. Why'd he look so damned pleased?

That thought was closely followed by another—Juz had nothing to lose.

# Chapter Sixty-Four

'**Y**es, I'm dying. Another legacy from the bastard you get to call Dad.'

She bit her lip and swallowed the denial on her tongue.

'Ever heard of chronic poisoning?'

She shook her head, then remembered the whirr of the bullet past her ear. 'No.'

'Long-term exposure to a toxic substance. You'll laugh when I tell you what. Want to guess?'

Dying didn't seem to faze him. He clutched the metal stand for support, his lips spread thinly across his teeth in a sickening grin. This was all just a game. A fun-filled afternoon.

His life's work coming to fruition.

Her mind raced. How did he mean to catch and kill her now she'd escaped? The semi held fifteen rounds so thirteen remained, including the one in the chamber. Randomly shooting until he hit the jackpot wasn't his style. The worst of it was that he didn't appear concerned. If anything, he looked confident. The knowledge made her uneasy.

She fumbled for something. Anything. 'Cyanide.'

He shook his head and tut-tutted. 'If it were cyanide I'd be dead already. Don't throw just anything out there. *Think.*'

'I can't give a diagnosis if I don't know the symptoms.'

'Watching?' Without waiting for her answer, he extracted a clean handkerchief and rubbed at the underside of his jaw and down his neck. The olive she'd always associated with Juz was slowly overrun by sallow.

He wore makeup?

'Pale and peeling skin. You've seen me cough up blood. Then there's sensitivity to light, loss of appetite, nausea and vomiting, bone pain, and most important, the kidney damage that's killing me even as we speak. Any ideas now?'

Toxicology wasn't her strong suit. It was something she left to forensic anthropologists like Teddy. 'None.'

'How disappointing. Not that I'm surprised. Who'd have thought you could be poisoned by something that's supposed to be good for you? A vitamin, no less. Any guesses which one?'

'A?'

'Top of the class. Although I suspect it was more luck than educated guessing.' He pushed away from the stand, and now that she knew his condition she picked up the stiffness in his movements. Funny how she'd never noticed before.

'They say eavesdroppers never hear anything nice. I learned the hard way how true that is. Never imagined I'd catch mother and Madden in a phone discussion on how much I needed controlling, how illness would tie me to them in a way nothing else could. Turns out they'd been systematically "controlling" me for years.' With a bark he cleared his throat. 'Ever questioned why you've been feeling so sick lately?'

Before she could dwell on whether the words held substance or were uttered purely to scare her, he glanced at his phone and murmured. *'It's time.'*

His words clutched at her chest, squeezing the air from her lungs. *Time for what?*

He tilted his head. 'Where was I? Ah, yes. My mother, your father. They both got what they deserved. Perhaps I have too.' Glittering black returned to her. 'And now, so will you.'

Every pound of her heart drove the copper taste of blood to the back of her throat.

*What had he planned?*

She slipped the mobile from her pocket and stared at the cracked screen. No signal. She'd had crappy luck lately with phones. It'd be funny if it wasn't so damned inconvenient. And downright distressing.

She had one more chance. It was a long shot, but a long shot was better than no shot at all. She hard-reset the phone and winced as the corresponding click seemed to bounce off every one of the room's four walls.

She stalled. 'I had as little control over the course of my life as you had over yours. Things could just as easily have been reversed and neither of us is to blame for this situation. It's not too late, Juz. It's never too late. I can help you.'

'Again with the psychobabble. I expected more from you, Jayda.' Even as his body hunched over, one hand braced against the weight's stand, he reached into his pocket and she strained to see what he pulled out. 'Before you become my last victim, it's important you realise the true extent of your loss.'

His hand shook as he aimed what appeared to be a remote control at the largest of three LCD TVs. The screen jumped to life. It took a moment to recognise what he meant her to see—Seth, Chase, her team, other members of the force, all scouring Juz's living room.

Her heart leapt. They'd figured it out, were looking for her.

Her eyes were drawn to one man—Seth. Pacing, angry, impatient. Like a cobra bracing to attack. She drank in every last agitated inch of him.

Something changed.

Everyone froze. Chase ran from the room, Seth close at his heels. The screen flickered and Jayda stared in horror as Garry bobbed midair, hanging from a noose suspended from the ceiling. Seth raked his hair in that agitated way of his, and her fingers itched to smooth the black strands back into order. While she was still living, breathing, she would strive for the moment when she could do just that. She closed her mind to the rest.

'It's a funny thing. *Love.* It makes people weak. Careless. Like your ridiculous excuse of a partner. His emotions make him blind. I wonder, have you asked him lately what's up with his wrist?'

She couldn't drag her gaze from the screen, much as she knew watching Juz was more important.

*Why was he showing her this?*

'Shame you won't get the opportunity.'

She turned her eyes to him then. He wheezed, hand clutching his throat. Not long now until he wouldn't be able to speak at all. She lived for that moment.

'Then there's lover-boy. Do you really believe he sees you as anything more than a stand-in for his parents? Too late now to find out.' He dipped his head to the side. 'He's got a helluva story. His dream job. Lucky he hooked up with the girl who could get him both.'

They were just words. A sick bastard's way of manipulating her into doubting everything she had that he envied.

*Don't let him get to you. It's what he wants.*

'For the short time you have left, I want you to know everything that happens next is because of you.'

The film continued, everyone searching for her, placing themselves in the firing line of whatever Juz had planned. And she couldn't do a damn thing. She wanted to scream, but her throat was constricted and dry, and she couldn't drag her eyes from the scene she had no power to stop.

Blind desperation trilled through her voice. 'You don't have to do this, Juz. You have me. Do anything to me, just leave Seth and the others out of it.'

'Sweet sentiments, but it's too late. It's already done. These are just the highlights I saved for you.' Each rasp of his chuckle sliced away another portion of her heart. 'Wait! Here's my favourite part!'

A forensics officer turned from Garry, something small clasped in her tweezers. Was it paper? With slow, meticulous care she unfolded the tight ball and read. Her words swept through the room like Jack Frost in a grassy meadow.

They scrambled for the door, their panic tangible, a fist-punch to Jayda's heart. Behind them, black smoke billowed out from the closet, swallowing the room, them, everything in sight. Debris scattered through the haze, then fire captured the cloud with a burst of bright, burning gold.

A roaring inferno, the consequences of which she couldn't tell.

A whimper slipped unheeded from her lips, every bit of staunch stolen from her spine.

'Brings new meaning to "going out with a bang", don't you think?'

The words ricocheted through her brain. She wanted to ram that supercilious voice back down his throat until he choked on it.

She crept forwards, still shielded by the equipment, as if by closing in she'd see more. Get some indication that they'd survived. All she got was grey smoke and flames.

Her legs buckled, pain shafting through her chest. She gripped the metal beast beside her to prevent herself from crumpling to the floor. He couldn't be dead. Wouldn't she feel it? The wrench. The burn as her heart ripped in two and the best part of it disintegrated to nothing.

She lifted her chin and willed Seth to be alive. Vivid orange and yellow licked at the screen, mocking her prayers.

Then the image flickered and she found herself staring into her own wide-eyed gaze. A light below the security camera just ahead of her flashed red, proving her right, that Juz had somehow hacked into their feed and was recording her even now. To what end?

Who knew what else the sick bastard had planned.

The knife weighed heavy in her hand and she wanted nothing more than to sink it into his heart the way he'd cut and thrust his hatred into hers.

She took two steps towards him, but something in his expression stopped her from taking a third. The one shred of sanity she had left held her back. He'd lived for this moment, to see her lose everything she valued. Her dignity. Her life.

Much as it took all her willpower, she wouldn't give Juz that last slice of victory he so obviously craved.

'You bastard! You've taken everything.'

'Oh, but that's where you're wrong, Jayda. You have one thing more that I want.' Again she heard the sickening crack of his knuckles. 'Your last breath.'

Adrenalin steeped her veins, hurtling her blood through her body so fast it made her head spin.

'So what are you waiting for? Come get me, you sick sonovabitch!'

He made no attempt to move, his lips slithering into a thick, wide arc.

Something was wrong.

With jerky movements she scanned the area, eyes so wide they hurt. Nothing had changed. But it felt as if the room had shrunk, the walls caving slowly in around her.

Two metres to the left, the door loomed. Something instinctual drove her to leave now, and without a thought, she moved towards it. She clicked the phone back on and sent a prayer up to whichever god cared to listen.

*Two bars.*

Iffy, but better than no bars. It was a chance.

Eyes fixed on the barely moving Juz, she skirted a line of hulking white ghosts, pressing her back to the wall. His body may have been hunched, but the glassy brown of his eyes followed her with unwavering precision.

She steeled against the drag of that gaze. The chill that could so easily freeze every remaining hope she still clung to if she let it.

With shaky fingers, she dialled the number and held her breath. She needed Seth to answer, needed it more than she needed her next drag of oxygen.

The obligatory five rings blasted her ear before the call clicked over to voicemail. She heard his voice, a robotic recording telling her to leave a message after the tone. As she watched Juz gasp for breath, she left a message for the man she loved, unsure whether he would ever get it.

She clutched her stomach and her heart ached.

For all his strong words, Juz leaned heavily against the metal stand. Only his firm grasp on her weapon stopped her from rushing him now. As she watched him clutch his throat, she rang Hackett.

'Homicide.' The clip of her boss's greeting had never sounded so wonderful. Emotion welled in her throat so she had to clear it to speak.

With her back hard against the wall and Juz clearly in her line of sight, the door remained less than a metre to her right.

She heard a click, then the hungry squeal of oil-starved hinges. Cold air charged across the side of her neck.

'End the call, Jayda.'

Like a freeze frame in one of those old-time reel-to-reel movies, she turned to face the barrel of another gun.

# Chapter Sixty-Five



For the first time since the nightmare had begun she allowed herself to relax.

'Thank God you're here. Juz is the Night Terror. He's injured but still armed. Over there by the treadmills.' She waved in his direction.

*I'm safe.*

She peered over her friend's shoulder. 'Where's back-up? I saw the bomb. Is everyone okay?'

'I said end the call, Jayda. Or would you rather I end it for you?' The Smith & Wesson lifted until it levelled right between her eyes.

Realisation dawned. Like a young leaf spiralling down from the heavens into the murk, her sudden hope vanished and the nightmare returned. With her every inroad towards escape, the universe dealt a blow to drag her right back in.

Jayda bent slowly, dropping the phone at her feet. With any luck Hackett was still on the other end.

She stared at her colleague, her friend, wearing the badge that dictated she *uphold the right*, and every bit of stability she'd reclaimed by knocking Juz to the ground and escaping vanished. The hollow in her heart widened.

Georgie nodded. 'Now the knife.'

The blade followed the path of the phone.

'Hands up where I can see them.'

She raised her hands, flinching at the pull of skin on her stomach.

Georgie surged forwards, urging her back with a wave of her weapon. Two stamps of her heel ground the phone and any hope of rescue into the hard floor. Then she retrieved the knife and waved it towards the treadmills.

'Get moving. Any tricks and your last thought will be a bullet as it slams through your brain.'

With leaden legs, Jayda made the death march across the gym room floor. Georgie rushed to Juz's side. His body slumped against the rack of weights, his breath barely a whistle. Gun still trained on Jayda, her free hand fluttered over his face, his chest. 'I'm sorry I took so long.' The warmth in her brown eyes hardened when they lifted to Jayda. 'What have you done?'

'Less than he deserved.' She stared at the woman, with whom she'd shared her deepest fears, her darkest secrets, bending over a man she'd loved like a brother. Reality pitched and she felt herself sliding the incline. Was anything real anymore?

'You and *Juz*? I don't understand, Georgie.'

'That doesn't surprise me. After all, why should you change now?'

She still didn't get it. But with an M&P 40 calibre to her head, it wasn't the time to let on. Her mind was a muddle of jigsaw pieces, so she started with the bits she could process first. 'But Juz is *gay*.'

'That changed when he met me.'

'Seriously? Don't tell me you swallowed that line.'

'It wasn't a line.' Georgie stepped closer and she flinched as the shiny black barrel loomed in her vision.

Juz pushed up with his free hand, the other still holding Jayda's weapon. Georgie fumbled to help him. He gasped, tried to speak even, but the blow to his vocal chords seemed to be working its magic.

If only it'd work a damn sight faster and finish the job.

Georgie leaned towards Juz and he whispered in her ear. She glared at Jayda. 'Untie the material from around your waist and toss it to me.'

'Think about what you're doing, Georgie.'

The gun waved again. 'Do it!'

Jayda fumbled with the knots, her mind racing. 'He doesn't love you. He's just using you.'

'Shut up!' The weapon in her hand trembled until Juz placed his palm on her wrist and she relaxed.

'If you do this, your entire career is shot.'

'It's already shot, but at least this way I have a chance at happiness.'

Jayda dropped the material to the floor.

Juz raised his gun and Georgie grabbed the strips. 'Hands behind your back and turn around.'

'Your happiness will be short-lived if you think it involves a life with Juz. I broke his windpipe. Hear that wheeze? Once the swelling increases, the little oxygen slipping through right now will become zilch. If you really want happiness, call an ambulance.'

Georgie's trapped deer eyes flitted to the door then back. Again Juz touched his hand to hers. Some silent communication occurred between them and once more Georgie seemed to relax and focus, her fingers flexing over the gun's trigger, the barrel directed unswervingly at Jayda's heart.

She flinched. Swallowed against the lump in her throat and tried again. 'He'll die without medical attention, Georgie. Is that what you want?'

'Shut up and turn around.'

She turned, unable to stop her body trembling. Death was suddenly all too real, all too close.

'I'm going to tie your hands behind your back. Try anything and you're dead.'

She wasn't stupid enough to believe she'd live if she complied. The odds weren't even close to fair. Her body braced. Cold fingers contacted with her wrists.

Jayda sidestepped. Her palm struck Juz's gun from his hand, then she elbowed Georgie in the chest. As she turned to finish the job, sharp pain smacked against the back of her head and the world retreated into night.

'You bitch!' Georgie's shriek was barely recognisable as her fist smattered into Jayda's jaw and the black exploded into stars.

Her hands were yanked behind her back and roughly tied together. Then she was hauled to her feet, stumbling. Georgie dragged her, pushing her into a chair, tying her bindings to whatever equipment was behind her.

*This is it, then.*

There'd be no escape, no more cutting ropes or hopes of a miraculous rescue. Nothing she said or did now would make a difference.

She rolled her jaw and winced. Fresh blood coated her tongue.

Her chest squeezed. She wouldn't give up. Not now, not ever. Not while she still breathed and there was a chance. 'The Juz you think you know is an illusion, Georgie. He traps people with his lies and turns them into his pawns. He kills. Brutally. He murdered Bec, for godsake! Once you're no longer useful, he'll do the same to you.'

She felt a sharp tug at her wrists. Everything below the bindings was already numbing. A perfect match to the void in her heart.

'We love each other.'

'Everyone who loves him dies.'

'That's because he never loved them back.'

Jayda shook her head. 'Juz is a psychopath. You've done the training. He's incapable of love.'

'So incapable that he cooks for me? Knows what to say when I'm down? Braves the rain just to buy my favourite ice cream?'

*Orange choc chip. In her freezer.* How could she not have guessed?

'When Ben dragged my heart through the gravel, who picked me up and stopped me from finishing it all at the end of a rope? You? Slim chance you'd drag your nose out from your ass long enough to notice anyone else's life but your own.' Georgie blinked, her gaze softening briefly as it brushed over Juz. Then razorblades returned as she glared at Jayda. 'Only one friend saw how close I was to losing it, and he made sure he was there for me every single day. Surprise, surprise, that friend wasn't you.'

'It's all part of his act.' Jayda bit her lip. The urge to scream bubbled up in her throat. What the hell could she say to break through this brainwashing? 'He's a cold-blooded killer, Georgie.'

'You have no idea what he's been through. He didn't want to do it. Madden manipulated him. Taught him, only made him feel special when he followed orders. He had no choice then, but now that Madden's gone, Juz is free.'

Jayda gasped as an entire jar of pennies dropped. 'My God! You were in the prison that morning. *You* killed him!'

'Madden was the devil. He didn't deserve to live.'

'That wasn't your decision to make.'

Georgie moved to stand before her. 'Who the hell are you to preach when you stole any chance Juz had of a normal life?'

'That wasn't my fault.'

'Nothing ever is, and yet your very existence creates havoc for the people around you. You've tried to take everything away from me. Stole my best friend, even though you didn't want him for yourself.'

Her mind was still reeling from Georgie's first accusation when the second one hit. 'Who are you talking about?'

'Think about it, Jayda.'

Her mind raced. 'Chase?'

Georgie's narrowed gaze said she'd guessed right.

'I know you guys spend a lot of time together but I never tried to change that.'

'And yet as soon as he fell for you it changed anyway.'

'You should have told me, Georgie.'

'So you could pity me? Pass me your scraps? It got to the point where all he talked about was "Jayda this" and "Jayda that". I'm so sick of your goddamn name! Sick of the hordes of men who think you're so goddamn wonderful they ignore the people who really matter in their life. Now I've met someone who puts me first, and once you're gone, things will only get better.'

The words sliced through Jayda's heart, jab by painful jab. Any hope that some care, some love for her remained in Georgie was gone.

Georgie turned to Juz. 'She's ready.'

Jayda's mouth turned to sand.

She watched Georgie return to his side, watched him pull her to him for a kiss. Georgie glowed and her words echoed through Jayda's mind.

If only . . . her mind scrambled. *If only what?* What good to wallow in *what ifs* when she should be working towards escape instead? Her fingers fumbled over the thick knots. They weren't moving and there was nothing sharp this time for cutting.

She turned away from the happy couple rather than watch. Her last memory wouldn't be a kiss shared between the two people who'd betrayed her.

It was too late to question whether telepathy was real. She tried it anyway. Thought of Seth, thought of her parents, sent messages out that might just be her last. She prayed that Seth and Chase and the rest of her team had survived. That her parents could withstand the loss of another daughter. That they would at least have each other. She tried to focus on the good rather than the regrets. The memories rather than times she'd hoped for in a future that was never to be.

A loud *squelch* shattered her thoughts. Then came a muffled grunt that sounded all too familiar.

Her head snapped around in time to witness Georgie's surprised gurgle before she slid to the floor. Her eyes were wide, pleading, the sky blue of her shirt swallowed by a growing circle of red. Juz withdrew the knife from her chest as if she were a slab of butter, and stabbed her twice more in the abdomen. By the time he slit her throat the light in her brown eyes was gone.

He wiped both sides of the blade on Georgie's trousers then straightened. 'How does it feel to be right, Jayda?'

Her throat constricted and she gasped for air. For all her sins, Georgie didn't deserve this end. But then again, neither did she.

It seemed Juz had found his voice again. It may have been laboured and weak, but the bastard was still living and breathing and able to do what he'd promised. Rob her last breath.

She began to shake.

'Oh, come now, no need to panic. Your end won't hurt half as much.' He stepped forwards. Jayda jerked her shoulders and twisted her wrists.

Georgie's perfect rope-tying prevented her from further movement.

The bloody blade brushed against her cheek and she twisted away. Cold metal slid over her ear, towards the warmth of her beating jugular. She flinched.

'No need to worry, that's not the fate I have in store for you.' The laughter rasped out from his throat as he dropped the knife. 'Nothing but the full Night Terror treatment for you, my dear *friend*.' He touched his fingertips to her lips. 'This moment could be quite beautiful if you stop fighting and relax.'

She snapped her teeth, barely missing his fingers as they skipped without hesitation towards her collarbone.

'I hear that when the body is deprived of oxygen it feels like you're drifting, as if you're falling into a peaceful, deep sleep. Give up the fight, Jayda. It's over.'

'I'll never stop fighting, you sick fucker.'

'Never say never.'

'Go to hell, Juz.'

'Yes, I will. And I have every intention of taking you with me.'

Her heartbeat belted against her eardrums. A light flickered above and the world receded until there was nothing but Juz. He filled her vision, her entire universe. His minty breath became her air, his touch on her cheek, her neck, her sole link to reality.

His fingers wrapped around her throat, surprisingly warm, surprisingly gentle. She twisted her head side to side, but the fingers remained, and slowly, gradually, they began to tighten.

The roar of a thousand oceans filled her ears. Her head floated, then her body followed. Fields of clover spanned out before her, mesmerising, inviting. Light transformed to dark and warm turned to ice. His mouth moved to cover hers. Her brain screamed. Her limbs heavy, lethargic, too weak to resist.

Thunder clapped. Then again. The grip around her neck relaxed. Then came silence as a dark, cold world consumed her and awareness became a thing of the past.

# Chapter Sixty-Six

'Juz Callum! Raise your hands and step away from the victim!' Chase's bellow could have been a whine for all its effect.

There was no talking a psychopath down, and Seth wasn't about to stand around and watch while this one killed the woman he loved.

He dodged the front line of detectives, their weapons all levelled at the lowlife. Ignoring Chase's shout, he ran, wanting nothing more than the crack of bone beneath his fist as he pummelled the bastard into the ground.

Juz's lips latched to Jayda's like a leech to its life-giving host.

Blood roared through Seth's veins. He couldn't have survived the blast only to be too late to save Jayda now.

The parasite pulled back, eyes glazed, teeth bared, fingers wrapped firmly around Jayda's neck. He turned and his demented glee slipped.

Seth was almost upon him and only then did the villain's hands drop to reach for his waist. Seth saw a gun and leapt. The blast thundered in his ears and ceiling plaster rained over them as they toppled to the ground. Air whooshed from his lungs and all he could hear was laboured breathing, Juz's and his own, accompanied by shouts from the surrounding detectives. He pushed himself up.

Now he knew what it was to stare into the eyes of a madman.

Juz glanced deliberately towards Jayda's limp body, then back to Seth. Blue lips stretched taut across teeth that released a hiss. *'I win.'*

Seth growled and punched him straight between his beady killer eyes. The nasal bone didn't crack beneath his knuckles. Instead, sharp pain shot through his fingers and up into his arm. Juz's head juddered and his eyes closed. A hollow victory. There wasn't time for more. Seth scrambled up and rushed towards Jayda.

Firm hands wrapped around his wrist and yanked him back before he could get further. Chase's pretty-boy face hijacked his vision and Seth tried to wrestle free, tried to see around the big oaf.

An officer rushed past, cuffs in hand, and kicked the gun out of Juz's reach.

Chase jabbed his chest with his free hand, effectively pushing him backwards and further from Jayda, his nostrils flaring like a dragon ready to spit fire. 'What the fuck do you think you're doing?'

'Your frigging job!'

Seth tried to wrench free, but Chase's grip tightened, his eyes narrowed. 'Don't make me cuff you, Seth!'

'Dammit, Chase. I need to know she's okay.'

'And you will, when the paramedics do *their* job.' Seth winced as Chase jabbed his finger hard into his chest again. 'Which part of "stay back" didn't get through your thick skull?'

*'Officer down!'*

Seth spun around. The officer who'd rushed past only seconds earlier writhed on the ground, hands clutching at a knife and blood seeping from his abdomen.

Juz sat up, the officer's cuffs dangling from the wrist of one hand, his gun gripped in the other. He raised his arm and levelled the black barrel at Seth. Pain smacked through his chest as Chase's palm connected with his ribs. He stumbled backwards, heard the *crack!* before he saw the gun in the detective's hand.

Juz's right shoulder jerked backwards. He pushed himself up. Would the sonovabitch never die?

Again he raised the weapon.

Chase's second shot found its mark. Juz slumped to the ground, the hole in his chest blooming slowly into a circle of red.

Two officers converged on the body before it could spring to life a third time. Others escorted a team of paramedics towards Jayda and the officer at her feet.

Before he could join them, Chase hauled him over to the exit. He craned his neck. Both Jayda and the officer had disappeared beneath a sea of blue uniforms. Much as he was tempted, punching the lights out of Jayda's partner would do nothing but get him even further removed from her.

Chase thrust him towards two officers. 'Watch this idiot! If he moves, cuff him!'

The men sized him up and nodded. Both held their palms against their batons. Not that he'd consider defying them.

'Don't think I won't shoot your ass if you so much as sniff at my crime scene.' With a final wilting glare, Chase stalked away, barking commands at every officer in his path.

Seth raked his hand through his hair. He couldn't see shit. His gut had twisted into so many knots even a sailor wouldn't have a clue where to start. And all he could do was comply with Chase's dictates. He'd never felt so damned helpless in his life. Not even when the speeding car had slammed into his parents' sedan and he'd gaped into the bloodied, lifeless eyes of his older brother.

Chase's back receded beyond the blue. Seth squared his feet and waited—alone in the furore and at the mercy of his imagination.

*No pain.*

Jayda floated downwards on a sea of warmth and softness. Waves rolling over sandy beaches lulled her ears while a white glow teased at her eyelids, beckoning for them to open.

And there was peace. Eternal peace. This had to be heaven.

Nothing in her past warranted a trip to that other place. Sure, she'd been no angel growing up. But she'd been no devil either. One of the good guys, fighting for truth, justice and the good ole Aussie way.

Cops and robbers had been her favourite game back as far as she could remember. At the age of seven, armed with a set of two dollar handcuffs and plastic .38, she'd apprehended Bec the Burglar, considering the subsequent shattering of her grandmother's crystal vase necessary collateral damage. Unfortunately, her father hadn't seen it that way. She and Bec had lost TV privileges for an entire week.

At ten, Benjamin Carmichael had told her that the perfect way to prevent a car from starting was to stick a potato in the exhaust pipe. What he didn't add was that it could also blow the exhaust valve. The experiment cost her TV privileges for a month and over a year's pocket money, plus change.

Thirteen had seen her take pot shots at her mother's prize pumpkins with a pellet gun, but by this age she'd gained street smarts. Tilly, next door's crazy terrier, had shouldered the blame for the yellow splattered mess all over the backyard. The poor pup had also received a stern reprimand for the tunnelled prison escape beneath the back garden fence.

The warmth of those memories rolled over her.

Mischievous, yes. Bad, no. Not enough to discount her from floating among fairy floss clouds in glorious, perpetual sunshine.

*Jayda?*

The name wafted through the mist and into her consciousness. Something pressed against one fingernail, then another. Pain shafted through the third and she gasped.

She tried to open her eyes, but it proved more difficult than she'd expected. Her eyelids felt heavy, her hand too when she tried to lift it. Her lashes dragged, then fluttered open, and her surroundings melded into a kaleidoscopic blur. Low voices filtered through the cottonwool. One in particular sent familiar tingles down her spine. It sounded distant, but it stood to reason that if she were in heaven he'd be there to meet her.

If he'd failed to survive that blast.

Her heart twisted, the sharp pierce in her chest unexpected. Was it possible to still feel pain after death?

'Seth?'

Someone rubbed her hand. A face emerged—olive skin, beach blond hair. There were others around her, two close enough to recognise. None of them the face she wanted to see.

The clearest of the faces spoke. 'I'm Michael, a paramedic. I'm here to check that you're okay. How do you feel?'

The haze in her head sharpened. 'I'm not dead?'

'You're very much alive.' His fingers rested against the flying pulse on her neck. 'Can you tell me your full name?'

Her mind whirled. She was alive! A tiny corner of her heart twisted when she realised she wouldn't see Bec—not now, not for a while longer—but there was another part that leapt for joy at her second chance at life.

She sensed the bustle around her, felt the charged energy of an active crime scene. Uniforms and detectives hugged the periphery of the room whilst forensics did what forensics did best.

She craned her neck for any sign of Chase, anyone from the Pacu task force. Or Seth. Had she heard his voice earlier or was that all part of her pre-awareness daze?

Michael rubbed the back of her hand, pulling her thoughts and gaze back to his overly blue eyes. 'Your name?'

'Jayda Marie Thomasz.'

'Do you know where you are, Jayda?'

She blinked. The ghostly outlines of covered gym equipment swam into focus. That included the multi-gym to her right, still sporting her material bindings.

She shivered. 'Prahran Health and Fitness.'

Michael nodded to another paramedic who passed him a thermometer. 'That's good, Jayda.' He ran the nozzle back and forth across her forehead until it *beeped*. 'Are you cold?'

She shook her head and bit her lip as the room swam again. Someone covered her body with a blanket. The wiry fibres scratched in her clenched palm. 'The man who did this to me, his name is Juz Callum. Is he still here?'

Michael's cool hand covered hers. 'You're safe. He can no longer hurt you.' The standard, non-committal response didn't tell her nearly enough. She pushed herself up and immediately regretted it as the room swirled. She allowed Michael to ease her back down. 'Is he in custody?'

'I'm sure the detectives will be able to fill you in as soon as we're done. Look at me, please.' He flicked a penlight across one eye and then the other. When he finished, he checked her pulse again. 'Can you tell me where you hurt?'

'You don't understand. *I'm* a detective and this man is dangerous.' She grasped his wrist. 'I need to know what happened.'

'At the moment you're my patient. Once I've determined you're okay, we'll see what we can find out. So, tell me, do you feel any pain?'

Arguing the matter meant drawing on energy she didn't have. Instead, her mind merged with her body and the subliminal gave way to reality.

Her fingers ran over the puffy skin stretched across her cheek. She winced. No wonder she could barely open her eyes. She licked her lips. *Blood.* Then she remembered Juz, his lips covering hers . . .

Her stomach heaved. She rolled over just in time to spill her guts onto a pair of overworn white runners.

Someone cursed.

'Jayda?' Michael's voice again. Soft. Reassuring.

Strong arms supported her back as cool, professional fingers pushed her hair from her face.

'Everywhere. I hurt everywhere.' *Most of all in my heart.*

*No fixing that.*

She had to know. Good news or not, she couldn't bear not knowing. 'A bomb detonated in St Kilda. Was anyone hurt?'

'I heard something about an explosion but I didn't attend the scene. I'll see what I can find out for you.' Again he nodded to one of his counterparts. 'In the meantime, we're going to get you onto a stretcher and take you to St Vincent's. You've had a couple of nasty blows to the head which need monitoring, and I'd like someone to take a closer look at your stomach. You may need stitches.'

She opened her mouth to tell Michael she wasn't going anywhere without answers, but the room began to spin and it took all her energy not to chuck her guts again. Next thing she knew, Michael had a syringe and he was checking the inside of her elbow for veins. 'Do you have any allergies, Jayda?'

'No.'

'Good. Here's something for the pain.' She felt the cool rub of alcohol and then pressure on her arm. 'Deep breath now. It'll only sting a little.' Her skin burned, then cold flooded her vein.

Cool hands checked her pulse, her forehead, then lifted her up. Someone called her name. It sounded so much like Seth. But then the spinning intensified and she had to close her eyes.

*Another dream. Flickering. Floating.*

*Wind-swept clouds, wafting gently over her.*

She let them.

It was easier. Welcome. Because dreams were heaven-sent, and that meant Seth would be alive.

# Chapter Sixty-Seven

'Jayda!'

Seth strained for a glimpse beyond the huddle of royal blue. Seeing through a hurricane would have been easier.

Was she hurt? Alive?

Damn Chase for being such an ass! Leaving him to stew over a multitude of possibilities, each horrible likelihood scrambling for equal footing.

All he could do was wait for news while taking comfort in the fact that she was surrounded by paramedics rather than forensics.

He pressed forwards. Once again, a restraining palm stopped him from moving beyond the tape. He shot the officer his best man-to-man look. 'Come on, man. It's my girlfriend in there.'

'It's also a crime scene and orders are orders.' Déjà vu. Only this time the reality of his possible loss hit him square in his pounding, aching heart.

Juz was sprawled inert on the floor, the bloodied Georgie not far beyond him. There was no satisfaction in knowing that the man who'd betrayed Jayda so brutally was dead. Not until he knew whether she was alive.

Someone grabbed his shoulder and he swung around.

Chase's hand dropped. His expression had lost its edge, although warm and fuzzy it was not. 'She's going to be okay.'

If he didn't know better, he'd have said there were tears in the other man's eyes. Not that it was easy to see through the moisture in his own.

'Thanks.'

'Much as I should arrest your ass for the stunt you pulled back there, I'm going to do my damnedest to get you off the hook. If you hadn't uncovered that birth certificate, we might never have found Jayda in time.'

He could see how much the concession cost Chase. As though every word was a razor blade swallowed. But regardless of delivery, it was a truce.

Seth nodded. 'At the end of the day, we're both after the same thing. Jayda's safety.'

He left it at that. They both wanted more, but there could be only one victor in that department, and it wasn't Chase.

A pathway cleared as Jayda's stretcher was wheeled to the door.

'I want to go with her.'

Chase shook his head, his expression hardening.

Seth's resolve hardened with it. He drew Chase to the side and whispered in his ear. 'What if I promise to shut my mouth and keep what's under that bandage from your superiors?'

Chase pulled back, his eyes darting from side-to-side as he gripped his wrist. 'You bastard! What do you think you know?'

'The truth. Amazing the dirt that rises when you begin to dig.'

'You looked into me?'

'I looked into everyone with a connection to Jayda. What? You can't tell me you didn't do the same.' He glared at the other man through narrowed eyes. 'Do we have a deal?'

Chase looked ready to explode. But he had to know he'd been beat. He hesitated, then nodded.

They trailed the medical team down the two flights of stairs and out onto the front lawn. He had no idea what Chase said to the paramedic—he didn't much care, as long as the discussion reaped him a seat in the ambulance.

He couldn't drag his eyes from Jayda. Her ashen face, her swollen skin a mottled purple and yellow. A large lump erupted from her temple, a large bruise spanned her cheek and split, bleeding lip. And then there was her hair—the rich red was matted and dulled with red of a different shade.

In fact, there was an awful lot of that. *Blood.* Smeared everywhere. Over her arms, her legs. The front of her t-shirt was caked, with barely any white remaining.

Thunder roared through his skull. Given another shot at Juz, he wouldn't stop at a single punch.

He clambered into the back of the vehicle, taking the seat the paramedic indicated. The man opposite rechecked Jayda's vitals before readjusting the flow of clear liquid into her arm. 'I've given her a mild sedative for the pain so she'll be in and out of consciousness for a while now.'

'Is she going to be okay?'

'Her doctor will be able to tell you more after a full examination.'

Seth gritted his teeth. That was the medical profession, infinitely reliable in their tight-lipped bureaucracy. God forbid they gave loved-ones a straight answer.

'Can I hold her hand?'

'Sure. Just watch the needle.'

*As though I wouldn't without the heads-up.*

He cupped her icy hand between his palms and willed his own heat and energy to transfer. Then he began to talk.

He ignored the other man and talked as if nothing had happened since Richie's call and the discovery of that damned scum article. He talked about the weather, his work, the times they'd share together when life was back to normal. He talked about how she was never allowed out of his sight again.

Then the words stuck in his throat.

Her eyes fluttered open and his heart stumbled.

Jayda blinked.

Even through a hazy cloud, Seth looked damned good.

His hair had that frazzled, windswept look and the shadow on his chin spanned way past five o'clock. His clothes were sooty and wrinkled, which made perfect sense considering what he'd been through.

'*You're alive.*'

'Very much so.' The hand around hers tightened as if to prove it.

'Georgie was working with Juz. She loved him and he killed her. I thought he killed you too.'

His eyes widened. Then he shook his head, seemed to sense she wasn't ready to delve further into yet another betrayal. 'Juz won't kill again.'

She swallowed, her throat like two sheets of sandpaper chafing.

'He's dead?'

'He stabbed an officer and threatened Chase with a gun. It was self-defence.'

She couldn't fathom the sadness that followed Seth's words. Regardless of the monster Juz had revealed over the last few hours, he'd been a good friend for years before that. Difficult to believe it had all been lies.

Her mind felt woolly, the fight to stay awake like hacking through thick forest undergrowth. The world began to sway.

Confetti rained across her weighted eyelids, the world around her slipping. She clung to Seth's hand and dragged deep breaths into her lungs.

No time for sleep now. *So much more to know. To say.*

She opened her eyes.

'The officer. Who was it? Are they okay?'

'The wound missed all vital organs. That's all I know.'

She swallowed. 'I saw the explosion. You escaped. How?' Words so clear in her mind slurred thick and heavy as they left her mouth, but Seth seemed to understand.

He leaned in and she caught a whiff of pine and burnt carbon. 'The blast you saw was more theatrical than functional. A whole lot of smoke and not much else, which makes sense, since Georgie was in the apartment at the time. I doubt she had any intentions of dying.'

'Yet she died anyway.'

'You can't make a deal with the devil and expect to come out unscathed.'

He was right. But it didn't make her any less sad. Emotions were beyond logic and a part of her knew she would always mourn Georgie's loss. She'd wanted what Jayda had been lucky enough to find. If only Georgie had searched for it anywhere else but in Juz.

Her vision blurred and she blinked. 'I thought I'd never see you again.'

'You can't get rid of me that easily.'

Her head spun and she closed her eyes. The brush of his hand on her cheek was wondrous. Then his lips stroked her forehead. 'Are you okay?'

She felt the rush of moisture against her eyelashes. Before she could second guess them, she pushed the words weighing on her mind to her lips. 'It hurt that you didn't tell me about the promotion.'

The soot-stained lines on his face deepened. 'I didn't keep the news from you deliberately.'

'You didn't rush to share it with me, either.'

His eyebrows knitted. 'No.'

'Why?' She held her breath. Did she really want the answer?

'I thought it would change us.'

'Not telling me did that anyway. When everyone was hiding something, you were the one person I thought I could trust. It hurt, Seth.' She swallowed. 'You convinced me to open up, to let you in. Then you shut me out.'

The ambulance stuttered to a stop. With the lack of motion, Jayda's world began to spin.

*'Jayda?'*

Dark spots eddied across her closed eyelids and it was harder to hold on. Everything stable slipped. Voices surged, then receded. Michael. Seth. Others.

*Jayda?*

She fought to focus, fought to open her eyes. Chase swam across her vision. He still wore the bandage. She clenched her lids. Juz's taunts goaded her, then ebbed slowly away. Someone checked her pulse, ran their knuckles across her breastbone. She flinched, but her eyelids seemed glued together. That same person pulled her eyelid back and flicked a bright light across her vision.

*She's fine. Just the sedative.*

Odd words and sounds. Echoes.

An abyss, dark and looming, rose before her. Her body suspended over the edge. Her fingers scrabbled, grasping, frantic. Nothing stuck.

Her heart pounded.

She stumbled, slipped. Then slowly she began to slide.

Cold air hit her face and her body dropped. Dream and reality merged.

Words wafted through the murk.

*Sorry . . . never shut you out again . . . love you . . . marry me . . .*

Then there was nothing.

Jayda allowed her gaze to roam.

She took in the whitewashed walls. The scrubbed-within-an-inch-of-their-life grey floors. The spotless over-starched bed sheets. And a needle stuck into her left arm that attached to a drip.

From somewhere nearby came distant clatters, muted footsteps and the occasional *bleep* of a machine—all signatures of a hospital environment.

How long had she been here? A day, perhaps? Difficult to gauge when she'd drifted in and out of a drug-induced haze for what seemed like forever.

She turned her head towards the cracked vinyl chair beside her bed. Her father sprawled awkwardly in the seat, his head tipped to the side, open mouth releasing deep breaths that bordered on snores. His hair, which had greyed more in retirement than it had through years on the force, was in dire need of a cut. It stuck out at all angles, a thick tuft flopped over one eye.

Deep lines cut shadows into a face that was haggard and pale. Even in sleep, his exhaustion was evident.

Her heart twisted. What hell he must have gone through in the past few weeks—losing one daughter, almost losing another.

*Your very existence creates havoc for the people around you.*

She flinched. *No. Not true. This is Juz's doing, not mine.*

It didn't change the fact that her father's pain was due to her. The two chairs beside his sat empty.

He snorted, opened his eyes. Their gazes clashed and the pinch around his mouth eased into a tight grin. He pushed himself up and moved stiffly towards her, negotiating the rolling stand and tubes trailing into her left arm. His fingers shook as he captured her hand and gently rubbed it. 'How's my girl?'

'Tired. Sore.' Her free hand moved to her face. The swelling had gone down, but her muscles felt stiff. Even talking hurt. 'What day is it?'

'Wednesday. You've slept for over eighteen hours. The doctor cleaned and taped your stomach,' he winced, 'and a CT shows your head is clear of serious injury. You're going to be fine.'

He scrubbed at the stubble on his chin, every one of his worries etched deep into his expression.

She squeezed his hand. 'How are you, Dad?'

'Better now that you're safe. You need to stop being so much like your old man and listen for a change.' He snorted. 'So much for promising myself I wouldn't lecture.' He shot her a sheepish grin.

She laughed, and everything that hadn't hurt while she'd floated in the clouds, hurt again.

He tensed. 'Do you need something for the pain?'

'I'm fine. A little worse for wear, but I'll cope.' Her eyes scoured the room, and then what she could see beyond the doorway. 'Where's Mum?'

'I convinced her to step out for a few minutes. She's barely left your side.'

*Or yours.* The thought gave her comfort. *Bec should be here to see her plan working.* The comfort waned.

'It was good to see you each time I woke.' Her gaze slipped beyond his to the black smear on the far wall. 'And Seth.'

He nodded. 'For a reporter, he's not half bad.'

'High praise.'

'And it doesn't come lightly.' Her father's stamp of approval. What more did she want?

*Seth's honesty. His trust.*

She bit back the pain that accompanied that thought and his very marked absence now. 'I guess he's back at work?'

'Don't know much about that. What I do know is that Chase threatened to throw his butt behind bars if he didn't get that same butt down to the station to make a statement. Doubt he would have left otherwise.'

Her heart pitched. 'Why does Seth need to make a statement?'

'He threw himself at Juz during the raid. I imagine Chase has a lot of explaining to do, starting with why he allowed a civilian to attend in the first place.'

Warmth fluttered its way through her stiff body. Seth had come through, like he always did.

Was it unreasonable for her to want more?

It shouldn't have mattered that he kept his promotion from her.

She'd prayed for this moment—to be free, to have the opportunity to be with him. None of that had changed. But reality always came at a price, and hers was doubt. He'd said so many things, before, while she'd been drugged to the eyeballs. Was any of it real?

'Did . . . did he say much?'

'He said a lot.'

'And . . .'

Her father looked at her as if she were a soft drink short of a six-pack. 'And what?'

*And I think he asked me to marry him, Dad. Kind of, in a dream. Do you think he meant it?*

Only she couldn't say the words. And the question wasn't one her father could or should answer.

'And, when do I get out of here?'

His internal sigh was unmistakable. Dean Thomasz didn't do D&Ms well. 'Another twenty-four hours of observation just to make sure you're okay, then you're good to go home.'

*Home.* There was a time when she knew where that was. But now . . .

She nodded at the man who—melodramatic as it sounded—had saved her life. He'd given her a home, a family, a clean slate when he changed her identity, and for that she'd always be thankful.

Sagging back into the pillows, she closed her eyes. Deception had been intrinsic to the process, she could see that now. It didn't mean she had to like it. Or that she was willing to continue living in the midst of half-truths and lies now that the secret was out.

*Home.*

Her heart said home was with Seth. Her head said slow down. Something had held him back from sharing his promotion with her. Until she knew what that something was, until she could make certain it wouldn't wedge itself between them and fester, her heart would stand aside and allow her head to rule.

She loved Seth, wanted to share her life with him. That hadn't changed. But after living in the shadow of a lie for the first twenty-seven years of her life, she needed truth and honesty before she could ever hope to leave the past behind and move on.

# Chapter Sixty-Eight

Jayda walked through the door past Seth and headed straight for the couch. It still looked like it just arrived from the warehouse, was stiff and cold and hard, but it was a wonder to her weary body.

Weary, *relieved* body.

Her stomach was healing well, the rope burns on her wrists and ankles fading fast. Even the worry of death by asbestos was moot. The gym was clear of the stuff. It seemed the scare was one of Juz's many ploys to protect the scene for his final act. Proof again of his cunning in his plans to destroy her.

Those plans, it seemed, included abnormally high levels of potassium in her blood, explanation as to why she'd been spilling her guts so readily over the past weeks. Tests on the wine in her fridge revealed the source—Juz's Christmas present, five bottles of which she'd already consumed. Luckily, blood tests showed her body had sustained no lasting effects.

She was going to be fine.

Fists clenched, she pushed thoughts of Juz aside. He no longer factored in her life, so it followed he should have no place in her thoughts.

A yawn escaped her. She let her head fall back against the hard-as-rock headrest. After being pricked and prodded by a trail of doctors and nurses alike, she was ready for bed.

Seth shucked his jacket onto the back of an armchair and moved towards her. The lean fit of his tee and jeans suffused heat into every portion of her that until now had been suffering fatigue. Yep. Bed looked mighty fine about now.

He bent and lightly pecked her forehead. 'I'll make coffee.'

Her heart freefell. She bit her lip and nodded, closing her eyes.

Questions still hovered unchallenged between them. She'd been waiting for the right time, only the right time hadn't come. And if she were honest, she'd admit she simply didn't have a clue how to start.

It was four days since her discharge from St Vincent's. Four days of pecks and pats and abject indifference.

Four days of limbo.

The consensus from her doctor and family was that she should take it easy for a while, avoid going home to her apartment, and even more, that she avoid going home alone. Seth had adopted his habitual role of protector. She hadn't argued. Hadn't felt the need. It was what she wanted, to be with Seth. And he wanted it too.

After all, he had asked her to marry him. Sort of. Then he'd never mentioned it again, making her doubt whether she ever really heard the words at all.

Since he'd taken her into his care, he'd been more the solicitous friend than the irrepressible lover. And it was driving her crazy.

Just less than a week ago she'd escaped death. If nothing else, the experience had taught her it was time to start living. Time to embark on her future. Not tomorrow or next week or even next month. *Now.*

That future included Seth. Didn't he want it too? Why else would he insist she come home with him? It wasn't so they could sit silently opposite each other at the breakfast table, each lost in thoughts the other couldn't begin to guess. And it definitely wasn't so she could sleep in the spare bed while he slept all alone in his room at the end of the hall.

That was the part that killed most. Agonising over whether he still wanted her. Whether his life-changing realisation did or didn't mirror hers.

Whether he ever considered chucking gentle and caring to the wind in favour of tossing her onto the bed and taking her with nothing less than abandon.

The coffee-making noises from the kitchen lacked the comfort of the past. Her gaze roamed the living room as if somewhere there she might find the answers she needed.

If only she could be more sure of his feelings. Then perhaps she'd find the words to start the discussion that even now slumped like avalanched rocks in her stomach.

Had he really proposed, or was it all part of a drug-induced dream? Did he want to share his life with her or was the part of him that cleaned her vomit and tucked her safely into bed just intent on completing its altruistic duty until she was well and they could both go their own separate ways?

Should she wait until he broached the subject, or bowl on in and force him to break the news to her now?

Was she ready to hear whatever he had to say?

Kneading the pressure points either side of her temple, she closed her eyes and willed the craziness to stop. If only the act of willing meant it would be done.

'Drink it while it's hot!' The cushion beside her dipped and she opened her eyes.

He arranged two drinks on coasters on the coffee table before gently taking her hand. Her heart leapt. He was finally going to answer all those questions driving her on a one-way trip to Loonyville.

'Here.' He dropped two headache tablets into her palm and then passed her mug. 'Okay?'

She dropped the pills onto the table. Turning towards him, she stared into grey-blue oceans devoid of even a hint of desire and gulped. 'Do you still want me?'

His head jerked back as if she'd socked one to his chin.

*Damn!* Days of uncertainty had blocked the filter which allowed her to think the question without actually blurting it out minus an appropriate lead-up.

'Why would you ask me that?'

'In the four days I've been here, not once have you tried to kiss me properly, let alone . . .' A slow burn rolled out over her cheeks as she spun her hand through the air.

The corner of his mouth twitched. 'Are you saying you want me to kiss you properly, as well as . . .' His hand gesture mimicked hers.

'Have you thought about it?'

His voice cracked. 'Every waking moment.'

'Then why haven't you . . .' Again she waved her hand.

He reached for it, his touch anything but solicitous. Heat filled his gaze. 'I've been waiting.'

'For?'

'Your check-up. A sign that you're ready.'

'Hell, Seth! I've been ready since I checked out of hospital!'

This time his lips slid into a smile that made everything below her waist melt. 'Ready for what, exactly?'

Her heart stuttered. 'This.'

She leaned in, losing herself in pine and pure Seth. Her tongue fluttered across his lips and his breath hitched, the blue of his irises darkening to gun-metal grey. His mouth opened and she took up the invitation, her lips roving hungrily over his. His hands skimmed her shoulders, her arms, resting on her hips, pulling her closer. As if he had no idea where to start. As if he couldn't get enough.

Liquid fire pooled in her abdomen and she wriggled on the rough leather as the rampant heat spread lower.

It had been days, a lifetime if she counted what they'd both been through. The hard planes of his chest felt wondrous against her palms as she pushed him back. She straddled his hips, and didn't doubt his need matched hers when she slid lower. She rubbed against him and sensation zapped straight to her core.

His hands crept up to cup her breasts through her top. He kneaded and she moaned. He palmed and squeezed and tugged at her nipples and she nearly lost her mind.

His palms skimmed down past her waist and she barely winced as his fingers ran over her stomach.

He yanked them back. 'Oh, God, Jayda! I'm sorry. Are you okay?'

'I will be once your hand is back where it belongs.' In case he didn't get it, she tugged it towards the throbbing flesh between her thighs.

He rubbed and she thrust against him. He groaned, his fingers scrabbling at her waist. 'Dammit, woman! You're wearing way too much clothing.' He tugged at the hem of her top. 'How could you doubt that I want you? Now. Forever.'

Something inside her froze.

Impossible to fathom what her brain considered 'the right time', but that's exactly the message it sent out and for the life of her, she couldn't drive it back.

She gripped his hands, heart racing, body crying out for her to stop this nonsense and keep going. She couldn't. All she could do was hope that what she was about to say would mark an intermission rather than their final curtain call.

'Seth, we have to talk.'

Jayda didn't talk.

The words shafted through Seth's chest as her palms trembled over his skin. What was with her sudden turnaround? Second thoughts?

She'd seemed happy to see him in the ambulance. Overwhelmed, even. And her response had led him to believe he was forgiven.

But since the hospital and coming home, he'd wondered if it was a case of the anaesthetic talking. A vacuum had settled between them and all conversation, all contact, had become stilted.

Which meant she wasn't ready to hear his renewed, unfumbled marriage proposal. One delivered while she was *compos mentis* and fully capable of tossing back a rejection.

And wasn't that what had held him back?

*Until now.*

Correction. Until two minutes before now and the icy shower that was her 'we have to talk'.

She clambered off his hips and leaned back against the arm of the couch, legs folded beneath her, arms crossed. Closed. Unreachable.

He sat up and shivered, the room suddenly cold, as if someone had turned the aircon on full and opened all the vents.

He forced a grin to his lips. 'Since when do you talk?'

'Since not talking nearly destroyed us.'

The overstuffed leather barely gave as he fell back and chewed over those six words. He nodded, then spoke with slow deliberation. 'O-kay. Let's talk.'

The green of her irises nearly swallowed him whole. Her bottom lip plumped between her teeth and he resisted the temptation to coax it out from its confines. Serious as Jayda was about having a conversation, now she had his full attention, she seemed lost for something to say.

There could only be one reason—she was bracing herself. And that couldn't be good.

He bit back the ball of pain clutching his throat. She wanted him, no question. Her skin still glowed from her display of how much. But wanting him now didn't mean she wanted him forever. Or, more immediately, past the time it would take for her to recover and move out of his life.

A chill seeped through his clothes and into his bones. 'Let me guess. You're looking for a way to let me down gently?'

Her arms wrapped tight around her legs, hugging her knees into her chest. 'Is that what you want?'

'Isn't that what you want?'

Their conversation would be ridiculous if it wasn't so painful. And in another life, he would have nodded and walked away. Only, this wasn't just any life. It was the one he wanted to span into his future.

*So, what now?*

*Fight, you fool! Run through fire if it means you come out the other end with Jayda.*

She looked uncertain. Lost. Light flickered in the tunnel that was their conversation. Had he got it wrong?

'What do you want, Jayda?'

'The truth. About everything.'

Funny. What she said made absolutely no sense, yet it was the clearest thing she'd said over the past days.

The moment was one of promise and foreboding. That instant before a tightrope walker steps out from the platform and onto the wire.

He had two certainties. The first—that words were his life. He knew their value, made them work for him every single day. And now he needed their power for what came next. *Jayda*. He loved her. More than anything or anyone, ever.

There he arrived at certainty number two—that he wanted Jayda in his life, to have and to hold, in sickness and in health, till the world stopped spinning and time was no more.

And even then he doubted he could let go.

Which meant it wasn't an overstatement to say he was about to fight for his life.

# Chapter Sixty-Nine

Jayda watched the emotional reel flit across Seth's face. She had no idea what he was thinking or if she'd made enough sense for him to understand what she was asking of him. Hell, she wasn't even sure herself.

What if he didn't get it? Or didn't want to?

She hadn't thought past this moment. Considering a future without Seth was like considering life without breath.

*So, Thomasz, what if he doesn't give you what you want?*

The twist in her heart was her answer. She'd take anything she could get, for as long as he was willing to give it. And although it would hurt, living without Seth would hurt a helluva lot more.

He opened his mouth and she felt the unconscious halt of her body as she held her breath.

'My name is Seth Bartholomew Friedin. I'm twenty-nine years old, a reporter for the *Melbourne Telegraph* and madly in love with a sexy red-headed detective.'

His grin arrowed straight to her heart. Heat billowed into her blood and she wondered that the entire neighbourhood couldn't hear its stampede through her veins.

'Although I've told you what my life was like before Callum died, I haven't described what happened after.' He exhaled in a rush. 'It started when I was nine. Some kid in a beat-up blue hatchback ran a red light and slammed straight through our back passenger door. I remember sitting next to my brother's crumpled body, his blood splattered over my arm, sad, yet so surreal and detached. And I couldn't help thinking *maybe Mum and Dad will love me now.*'

His voice shook but he barely took a breath before continuing. 'It's horrible, I know. When I let myself think about it now, I'm sick to my stomach. My brother was dead and apart from being freaked out over all the blood, I felt nothing. Then I did feel something—guilt—but I still couldn't stop myself. I'd wanted Callum's place for so long, it was like the universe stopped the world and said, "Hey, Seth, here's your chance."' He took another deep breath and his shoulders squared against the hard back of the couch. 'So I gave up writing to study science.'

It took a moment to realise her mouth was gaping. She snapped it shut and shook her head. 'But . . . Oh, Seth. You *hate* science.'

He nodded. 'But my parents loved it. This was my chance to make them love me, too. So I took up something I hated to make them happy, the way they were when Callum was alive.'

Her heart ached. For the boy he once was. For the man sitting beside her now, hurting in a way no son should ever have to.

What stung most was the outcome of this scenario, which she could picture so clearly. He'd struggled to do what they loved, hating every minute of it, yet none of his efforts had been good enough. His parents had still turned their backs. And *that* was the biggest disappointment of all.

'Science wasn't your passion. So what if you couldn't do it? At least you tried.'

'Oh, but that's where you're wrong.' He pushed up from the couch and began to pace. Since when did Seth pace?

He stalked halfway towards the front door, then turned. 'I did more than try, I succeeded. I won at the school science fair three years running, topped all three science classes, earned a choice of scholarships for two of the top private secondary schools in Melbourne.'

He spun on his heel and shot her a half grin, although she doubted the sparkle in his eyes stemmed from happiness. 'For years I did what I thought they wanted me to do and I kicked science butt.'

'That must have made them proud.'

He froze. As if her words had formed a blockade in his mind and all he could do was stand and stare. But not at her or anything in this life.

It was only when she moved to shuffle the stiffness from her legs that Seth's head jerked back. His gaze sharpened and he sank back into the couch.

'Wrong again.' His fingers scuffed through his hair and she tamped the urge to reach across and smooth the raven tufts back down. His hand dropped to clench against his thigh. 'After the first presentation they never came to another. I kept hoping, searching the crowd, kidding myself that if I pushed myself more, achieved more, it would make a difference.'

He grunted what she guessed was a laugh. 'I was seventeen when I won a scholarship to join CSIRO's engineering program. That was eight years after throwing myself into someone else's shoes for all the wrong reasons. And I would have kept going . . .'

The pain in his expression was so raw it twisted her heart.

'But?' She bit her lip. Damn if that filter hadn't failed her again!

Seth's only reaction to her insensitivity was a stiff shrug. 'My father told me to decline the offer and go back to writing.'

She felt her jaw drop and stalled it midway. *'Why?'*

'You can't guess?'

She was sure she could, but she'd give anything to be wrong.

He didn't wait for her to answer. 'That was the moment I finally got it. They'd never loved Callum for his love of science. And because of that, science would never make them love me.'

His voice dropped so she had to lean forwards to hear. 'It was too painful for them to see my success in a field their dead son should have been in.'

She opened her mouth, then snapped it shut. He didn't need false assurances. Much as she longed to say he'd got it wrong—that surely his parents had loved him but didn't know how to show it—she doubted that was the case. And honesty had to work both ways.

She reached across and took his hand. It felt good in her palm, even better when his hand turned and held hers back.

There was a quaver in his throat as he cleared it. 'I don't kid myself that it was anything less than guilt that made them pay for my first year of uni. The second year I worked two jobs, cleaned a department store before classes and washed dishes at a local cafe after. I paid my own way, worked my butt off and refused to accept anything more from them. I was eighteen when I left home, determined to pay every cent back and be great no matter what they believed. Not that they wanted to hear about my successes. And they wouldn't take my money. Guilt again, I guess.'

Too stunned to say anything, she gritted her teeth. Seth was worthy of more than the morsels his so-called parents had tossed his way. Deserved more than their rejection or indifference.

She squeezed his hand and earned a heart-stopping smile. It warmed her, even through the chill of his story. Seth seemed not to notice her outrage. His speech wavered, but not for one second did it stop.

'I heard through a friend that they'd landed an assignment in Libya, otherwise I'd never have known my parents were leaving the country. It was my idea to housesit. If they wouldn't take my money, then I'd work for them and wipe the slate clean in my own way. I don't deny that in some warped part of my mind I hoped that while I was living in their house they might realise they wanted me in their life. Fat chance, right? I'm a lot wiser now.'

He scrubbed at the shadow of stubble on his chin. 'Funny how I received my first email from them six days ago.'

She found her voice. 'But that's great! What did they say about your promotion?'

'I didn't tell them and they didn't ask. They wanted to know who would housesit once I moved out.'

'You're moving out?'

He nodded. 'I emailed them the day after we became a "couple".' His fingers bobbed in the air, his smile so goofy it warmed her heart.

'Spending the past two weeks with you made sense like nothing else could. It made me feel whole, showed me I don't need my parents to give me what I already have the capacity to give myself. Acceptance.'

His hand slashed through the air. 'No more guilt and no more living in the past. I'm done trying to be anything other than true to myself.'

There wasn't an ounce of hesitation in his words, and her heart told her he meant every one.

'I still don't know why they loved Callum and not me. I guess I'll never know. Sometimes a couple have two kids and they love one more. It happens. Maybe for no other reason than they're incapable of loving two children. Or perhaps I was a mistake—they planned for one kid and instead they got two. Whatever the case, they could have done a lot worse than not love me, and for that I'm thankful. It means that I'm here right now and able to do this.'

His eyes bored into hers. Her breath lodged in her throat and she tottered between wanting to speak and waiting in hope for what was about to happen.

'I'm letting go. Of the past, the guilt, chasing love where it doesn't exist. Since you came into my life, I see happiness in my future, if I can just let myself look for it. And one thing I know for sure is that I don't need to look any further than right here.'

He slid from the couch and onto one knee.

Her heart thudded.

'I can't think of anything I want more than to spend every day by your side, for the rest of my life.'

A tiny black box found its way into his hand. He opened it and she gasped. Inside lay a delicate gold band encrusted with a string of tiny diamonds, two larger stones flanking the deepest, richest emerald she'd ever seen. Her vision dimmed, but for the first time in too long her tears were happy.

'*How did you know?*'

'That you're partial to emeralds? Your father may have mentioned it once or a hundred times.' He grinned. 'With this ring on your finger and you by my side, I know I can do anything, be anything. Most of all, for the first time, my life will be complete and everything will mean so much more because I can share it with you.'

His hands shook. 'I want to share the best perked coffee and make a gazillion lists about how much you mean to me. I want to love you and hold you and cherish you, and keep you safe. And most of all, I never want to keep a single thing from you ever again. I'm an open book and yours to read every day from now on, as long as you want me.'

He tugged the ring from its nest and it glinted between his fingers.

'Jayda Thomasz, will you marry me?'

She stared at her birthstone and the man offering it, handing her more than merely a ring and a promise. It was the life she'd envisaged before the hell of the past weeks. Possible now. More than possible—*real*.

She'd waited so long to give herself to a man again, and the man she'd given herself to had turned out to be the right one. The only man she could imagine spending the rest of her life with.

She'd found her happiness.

Blame it on the moment, the lingering anaesthetic, the words she'd never thought to hear . . . With a hefty sniff, she began to cry.

*Hell!*

Not the reaction he'd been going for. Surprise, maybe. Excitement, even. Not . . . *tears.*

He saw it all clearly now. Jayda was overwhelmed. Not with love, but with pity.

Cement clagged in his gut. The future, so distinct seconds earlier, was now a billow of dust.

*Pfft!*

He stuffed the ring back into its box, and shoved it in his pocket before rejoining Jayda on the couch.

'If you don't want to get married though, that's fine.' He ignored the pain in his chest and ploughed on before he lost his nerve. 'We could try living together instead.'

Her shoulders slumped. She snuffled and wiped the back of her hand across her eyes. 'Is that what you want?'

It was the beginnings of that ridiculous conversation again. This wasn't the time for circles, or pretending he could read her when, for the life of him, he hadn't an inkling of her thoughts right now.

He shoved the hair back from his forehead, shoving back the doubts that threatened to overwhelm him. 'Talk to me, Jayda. Tell me what you want. I can't keep guessing.'

He held his breath.

She reached across the table and snagged a handful of tissues from the box. Mopped her eyes, sniffed, blew, all the while leaving him hanging like a man on death row.

Unsteady fingers scrunched the soggy mess into her pocket and she sniffed again. Then her gaze trapped his and she dragged in a deep breath. 'I want you.'

The shackles around his chest lifted. Her words filled his heart like sunshine after the blackest of storms.

She scooched towards him and next thing he knew her hand was rummaging around in his front jeans pocket. The tears were gone and from the light in her eyes he guessed his body's immediate reaction hadn't gone unnoticed.

'Now, where did you put my ring?' She fished around some more.

He groaned. 'You're doing that on purpose.'

'Doing what?' Her fingers climbed the length of his erection, her eyes glinting innocently as he nearly lost it. He tried to pull her hand away and failed.

'Minx!'

She laughed and it was the most wondrous sound in the world. Thank heavens, she eventually found the box and offered it to him. 'Ask me again.'

His heart drummed. 'Are you going to make me beg?'

Her lips quirked. 'Would you?'

'I don't know. Do I have to?'

'Try me.' She grinned, and he grinned right back.

Once again he dropped to one knee. Only this time was different. This time he didn't doubt her answer.

'Jayda Thomasz, will you marry me?'

'Yes!'

He'd never got that thing with women and happy tears, but he was sure as hell glad he knew they existed. Because they were in Jayda's eyes once more and he wouldn't make the same mistake second time round.

He slid the ring onto her finger and she threw herself into his arms, toppling him backwards. His head barely missed the edge of his glass-topped table as his back slammed against the hardwood floor. He gasped, dragging air into his stunned, oxygen-deprived lungs.

She straddled his hips and he was more than happy to let her do just that, and anything else that took her fancy. That included appeasing the building throb between his legs.

Breathing suddenly lost its importance.

He swore. 'You've got to stop putting me through hell like that.'

'And you've got to stop assuming the worst. I love you, you idiot!' She slapped his chest. 'I've loved you since you brought me coffee and pastries and walked me into the shower then put me to bed. You're exasperating, thoughtful, gentle, kind and sexy. And I love every infuriating inch of you.'

He ran his hands over her ribcage and revelled in her shudders as he cupped her breasts. 'You forgot funny.'

Her lips twitched. 'No, I didn't.'

'I'll have you know there are people out there who think I'm hilarious.'

'And I'll have you know that not everyone has the impeccable taste I have when it comes to humour.'

'Ouch! That smarts.'

'I have a feeling you're about to get over it very,' she pulled her tee over her head, 'very,' she reached back and unhooked the scrap of white lace hugging her breasts, 'soon.'

His mouth dried.

She tossed the bra over her shoulder. 'I've never made love to a fiancé before. It's about time that changed.'

She wriggled back and unzipped his fly, easing his erection from his jocks. Slowly her palm ran over his flesh and she dipped her head, lips poised. His cock twitched, so damn hungry it hurt. Then her breath caressed him and the gates to heaven opened wide.

She tilted her head and eyes of rainforest green swallowed him whole. 'Love me, Seth.'

Coherent speech was hopeless, but he managed one word as he encouraged her upwards.

'Always.'

# ABOUT THE AUTHOR

Michelle Somers is a bookworm from way back. An ex-Kiwi who now calls Australia home, she's a professional killer and matchmaker, a storyteller and a romantic. Words are her power and her passion. Her heroes and heroines always get their happy ever after, but she'll put them through one hell of a journey to get there.

Michelle lives in Melbourne, Australia with her real life hero and three little heroes in the making. And her writing companion, a black cat named Emerald who thinks she's a dog. Her debut novel, *Lethal in Love*, won the 2016 Romantic Book of the Year (Ruby) Award and 2013 Valerie Parv Award. It was first published in 2013 by Penguin Random House as a 6-part serial, then re-released a year later as a complete story. The sequel, *Murder Most Unusual*, was released in 2017.

Michelle loves hearing from her readers, so please visit her website www.michelle-somers.com or chat with her on Twitter, Facebook or Instagram.

# ACKNOWLEDGEMENTS

This moment, the unleashing of *Lethal in Love* into the world, is a dream come true. And behind dreams there are always angels.

I'm blessed to have many angels in my life, and I'd like to acknowledge some of those who've helped me on my journey into published authordom.

My editor, Lex Hirst. Thank you. For your excitement from the very first moment I pitched *Lethal in Love* to you and Penguin Random House. For loving Seth and Jayda's story almost as much as I do. It's been a privilege and pleasure working with you, and you've made my first experiences in the world of publishing a joy.

To my cheering squad, Mich, Nena and Shazz. You girls are my sanity. You bolstered me up during every one of my doubting moments and celebrated my achievements almost as heartily as I did. Your friendship and love keeps me on the right side of sane, along with the odd shared glass or two of wine.

Robyn Grady, my mentor and my friend. Your guidance and friendship has meant more than you can imagine. Thank you for being the first to show me that an onion has more than one layer and so, too, do our characters.

Valerie Parv. What can I say? You are amazing. In all that you do and all that you give. You're my inspiration and my year's mentorship with you was one of the highlights of this journey. I'm proud to be deemed one of your minions.

My critique partners. Those wonderful people who have read *Lethal in Love* in part or in full and whose feedback smoothed out the wrinkles and made it work. Joanne Levy, Lauren Bradford, Amber Bardan and

Sarma Burdeu, and my beta reader, Ariel Moy.

The inspirational women of the Melbourne Romance Writer's Guild (MRWG). My journey to publication began from that very first meeting four years ago. I treasure your friendship, laughter and support. You guys rock!

Romance Writers of Australia (RWA). That body of writers that gives tirelessly to its members. Thank you for nurturing and growing all who enter your ranks. And a mega thank you for the conference pitching program which put me and my story in front of Lex.

Thanks to those experts whose advice brought authenticity to my story.

Gordon, for an in-depth, and at times humorous, insight into Victoria Police, and for keeping my 'artistic license' on a loose leash.

Belinda at the Department of Justice and Regulation, for answering my questions on Victoria's prison system.

Ray Povh for delivering the blow that brought a killer to his knees. Josephine Caporetto for schooling me in the Italian language of love.

Much as *Lethal in Love* isn't time travel, I'd like to leap into the future and thank one special group—you, my readers. You are the barometer for my success. If I've made you forget this world for another, if you've laughed, cried or trembled while reading my book, then I've done what I set out to do. Thank you. Your ongoing support allows me to continue to do what I love. I hope *Lethal in Love* gives you as much pleasure as it's given me.

I believe that family provides the roots that enable us to grow. Mine is no exception.

Mum. I don't remember a time growing up when books weren't part of our lives. Thanks to you and Dad, I travelled the world, embarked on adventure after adventure and married princes every single day, and all before bedtime.

Love and kisses to my three beautiful boys: Josh, Nathan and Gabriel. Each one of you is a blessing and a joy. Thank you for encouraging Mummy to follow her dream and celebrating when it came true. You make me believe that anything is possible.

And last, but by no means least, Danny. My husband, my rock. You show me true love every day. This book is for you.

**LOVED LETHAL IN LOVE?**
**THEN TRY MY SECOND BOOK IN THE MELBOURNE**
**MURDER SERIES, MURDER MOST UNUSUAL**
**Copyright Thrasher Publishing 2017**

SHE WRITES.
HE WATCHES... HE WAITS... HE KILLS...

Romance novelist Stacey Holland doesn't believe in love; marriage to a manipulator taught her as much. So she hides away in her fictional world, penning the perfect romance, intertwining the perfect crime. Excitement is for her books – worlds where the mortality of her characters is governed by a tap on her keyboard and the heroine always gets her happy ever after.

Homicide detective Chase Durant's cases are real and gritty and one wrong move could be his last. The Force is his life – he doesn't have room for more. Love and relationships hold no place for a man whose fate is predetermined by the genetic roll of a dice. With uncertainty on the horizon, he won't promise a future he can't guarantee.

Then a sadistic killer breathes Stacey's gruesome murders to life and the pair are thrown together in a sick game of murder and lies.

When tempers flare, and the murders get personal, can author and detective fight their growing attraction all-the-while fighting the killer determined to destroy them both?

*Read on for an excerpt . . .*

# Prologue

*They make it look so easy in books. Murder the victim, move the body.*

Stacey Holland adjusted her grip on the mannequin and puffed the hair from her eyes. Squinting through darkness, she shrugged off the wish to be somewhere else. Warm wouldn't hurt. The Bahamas. Or curled up on her couch, a good book in one hand and a spiced cider in the other. And a tub of the best choc-chip cookies in the universe.

Instead, she was Arctic-blast cold, plotting the perfect murder for her perfect manuscript. Because nothing less than perfection would do.

Damn the drill of her mother's voice. *Fame's not won from the back-row seats, my girl. Get out there, get dirty and get it right.*

She scrunched her nose against the crack of mud on her skin. Yep, if nothing else, she ticked that second-to-last box, tenfold.

A cow mooed in one of the far paddocks and another answered its call. The chill night air sliced through her wet clothes, labour's sweat covering her skin, a trickle running down her collarbone and falling between her breasts.

She tightened her grasp on the fibreglass hand, breathed deep and heaved. Planting her gumboots into the rain-soaked grass, she braced, leaned back, used every last kilo that usually made her despair but now gave her leverage.

*Plop.*

The ground slammed hard against her butt. If she'd shed those extra inches the fall would've hurt a helluva lot more. As it was, the jar slammed her tailbone and juddered up her spine.

Mud soaked through her jeans.

*Great.*

Goose pimples pricked her skin. Needled her blood. Chilled her bones. She shuddered. Slumped toward her bent knees. Stuck.

Her choc-chip-cookie obsession prevented her from slumping

further than a few inches forward. Her head dropped to her palm, the squish against her forehead barely registering on her *icko-meter*. What was a little more mud?

She'd never been a "why me?" kinda girl, but now was as good a time as any to start. On paper the corpse would have moved.

*Reality's a killer.* Her lips twitched.

*So, why am I butt-deep in what better be mud?*

*Because death and despair are my fictional friends. And simply, superbly delicious.*

The snort left her lips before she realised it had formed. It didn't matter that the alliteration was as ridiculous as her ass dancing the hippo-shuffle through mud puddles and paddies.

Cold shivered through her body, a sensation chased closely by a sharp, "so what?" shrug. If it took mud-dancing to reach bestseller status, then she'd schlep a whole vat of mud back to her car.

Her heart skipped a heady cha-cha through her chest. She grinned, shook herself off, slithered and squelched her way to her feet. Her butt still protested, but it could have been worse. Could have been *her* arm broken, not the mannequin's.

She brushed the muck from her hands, then crouched and clicked the ball joint back into its socket. Too thunderous for stealth. But thankfully, no one was around for miles.

Not that it mattered. She wasn't doing anything wrong. *Much.*

*Not long now.*

Light winds fluttered the leaves above, eddying musty scents through the air. A promise of more rain.

He squinted through his night-vision lenses, his steel-tipped boots planted firmly in the muck.

A head-lamp bobbed through the black—distant, indistinct, like a lone firefly in search of its mate.

He dropped the binoculars, letting them hang from his neck, drawing on his cigarette, watching the smoke curl upward and mingle with the frostbitten sky.

Expectation slinked like a wild dingo up his spine. Stealthy.

Ravenous. *Insatiable.*

A crack echoed through the paddock. He tensed, cigarette dangling between his lips. The faraway yellow flickered, bobbing its leisurely way toward the barbed boundary fence. Then a car door slammed. Another.

Dark swallowed the light. An engine growled then dulled as a double-wide beam tore through the ankle-length grass.

He pressed back, tree bark pricking his neck like a goad of conscience, had he been prone. The headlights bounded through the entry paddock until swallowed by the shadows.

His nostrils flared, drawing in smoke and icy anticipation.

Ten minutes of darkness ensured she wouldn't return.

*Stacey Holland. Author extraordinaire.*

The beat of his heart quickened, the heady scent of imminent death pricking his senses. She thought she knew loss. Pain, even. She didn't know shit from shitake. But she'd learn soon enough. He was one hell of a teacher.

And soon she'd lap up every one of his lessons. Would drop to her hands and knees at his feet, greedily begging for more.

His lips spread wide, the smile of a lover seconds before satisfaction. He stubbed his cigarette into the ground. Dropped it into a zip-lock bag and into his pocket. It paid to be careful. Others had been caught with less evidence.

His Ute wasn't far. A hundred metres or so away, behind the hay barn. He opened the boot and wide eyes stared out from the cramped plastic-lined interior.

'Showtime.'

He withdrew a tiny bottle from his pocket, grinning as the man shrunk further back, like a steer roped and ready for a butcher's knife. He found the racing pulse at his neck. Felt the blood course its tribute through the body for the last time.

'It's useless wasting your energy, trying to change destiny. You can't. Fighting will only prolong the pain.' He snatched the blue collar and dragged him closer. 'Be a good boy and I might let you go. What do you say?' He didn't wait for an answer. Truth? He didn't care. Either way the man would die, the method already prescribed.

He patted his inside jacket pocket. The knife hadn't moved.

Palm braced against the man's temple, his thumb and forefinger folded back the eyelid. Clear liquid spilled from the nozzle onto the red-rimmed iris, pooling at the edges as if clamouring for escape. There was none.

He increased pressure against the sweat-soaked temple, stalling movement that might see the liquid spill free. He didn't have to wait long. Life's force raced its death march through the trembling flesh until it could run no more. The body spasmed, stilled. The pulse at his neck sprinted erratically, then stopped.

Extracting the body from the boot was easy. It hung limply over his shoulder, still limber, still warm. Muscles flexed, he steadied, then began the trek. Only a kilometre to the spot she'd chosen for him.

Only a kilometre to her scene of the crime.

### 2 days later . . .

*It's just research, you nut.*

Rain streamed down Stacey's hood, plops the size of elephant's tears dripping onto her already sopping face. She rolled her eyes and huddled further under the building's narrow eaves.

*Try telling that to my heart.*

Driving tight fists deep into her pockets, she blew, but no amount of puffing dislodged the hair plastered across her cheek. She relented, dragged a hand out and pushed the strands back, before returning her frozen fingers to the warmth.

Somehow imagination helped romance flow easily onto her pages. Suspense was a different, prickly-thorn-in-your-butt story. Hence the reason she stood outside Detective Chase Durant's precinct, sodden and shivering, in the wettest May on record for twenty years, trying to still her senses before she bowled inside and had to unglue her tongue from the roof of her mouth. Again.

He did that to her. *Why?*

She'd never been a sucker for broad shoulders and fathomless blue eyes. Or a smile that made her knees fold like the billows of an accordion. She wrote sexy detectives, and he happened to be a *particularly* sexy detective, in the flesh. Maybe that was it. Or her overactive imagination getting the better of her. Or maybe she needed to take Shazz's advice and get out more.

Either way, wavering outside his place of work wouldn't catch her anything but a cold, something she needed less than his amused tolerance and a desire to prove she deserved otherwise. It didn't matter how he viewed her, as long as she left today with enough info to finish her book.

Another bracing lungful of frost and her hands left their warmth for the two-way double doors. Her palm connected with the glass and it sprung outward, driving her back. She stumbled, overcorrected, propelled forward into a solid mass—strong arms, warm, spicy scents, and muscles both delectably superhuman and male all at once.

Murphy's Law chuckling at her expense.

Chase's fingertips dug into her upper arms, pushing her back. 'Lurking outside police stations now, are we Stacey? Hoping to catch a killer? Or maybe a detective?' Humour tumbled across his lips, calling her resident kittens to romp and roll across her stomach lining. 'I guess it's your lucky day. You found one.'

She stepped back, giving the kittens a stern back-in-your-basket warning. Chase yanked her from the path of a passer-by and she toppled back into his body.

*Firm, muscular, warm . . .*

Before she became too comfortable or kidded herself that she'd enjoy the wrap of his arms and the press of his lips too much, he dragged her through the station doors.

Her skin tingled, not from cold.

She shrugged free of his grasp, tossing the rain from her hair, avoiding his gaze. There it was again, that amused forbearance she hated so much. It hauled her back two-and-a-half years. Made her feel worthless and small, and left her questioning how far she'd come.

And whether she'd ever really moved on from being nothing at all.

Stacey's lips tightened like a bow seconds before the arrow's fired.

Chase's first impulse was to lean across and drown in the scent of honeysuckle and woman. His second was to get the hell away before he did something stupid. Like kiss her.

'What are you doing here, other than wreaking havoc on everyone within bomb-blast range?'

One-and-a-half metres of curvaceous irritation uncoiled, like a taipan ready to strike. 'You bowled into me, buddy, not the other way round!'

He bit back a retort. Rolled his shoulders and winced. His troubles were no fault of hers, and projecting them only added guilt to his ever-growing dung-pile of emotions.

Still, that didn't change the fact that Stacey Holland was trouble, with her dripping blonde ringlets, bright pink cheeks and wet ruby lips. He had no time for distractions. The Night Terror had struck again, killing a friend. That was his focus—that and stopping the bastard before he murdered again. That and showing he deserved his lead role on the case.

He had so much to prove.

The second hand on his watch hacked at the last threads of his patience. 'I have to go.'

'But we have a meeting.'

'Tomorrow.'

'Today.' To prove her point, she shoved her mobile in his face.

He read: *Appointment. Detective Durant. 1.30 p.m.*

The words were a mental slap about his head. As if things weren't bad enough, his memory had become another dud bullet in an already dwindling chamber.

He pushed the phone away.

She snatched her hand back as if his fingers were the last thing she wanted against her skin. Or maybe they were the first?

He couldn't help it. Her reaction tugged a dry smile to his lips. 'Appointment? Don't you mean *date*?'

'This is work, not pleasure!'

Red flooded her face and he bit back a laugh. 'Ouch! Yet another slap to my ego. If you're not careful, I might think you don't like me.'

She had that startled deer look—wide eyes, ready to bolt—and his laughter slipped into a chuckle. 'Work and pleasure aren't mutually exclusive, you know.'

'They are for me.'

'Live a little, Stacey. Life's too short.' Which reminded him. His real appointment awaited. He side-stepped and pushed open the door. 'Call and we'll make another time.'

She scampered up beside him, didn't notice the puddle until she ploughed through it, splashing water halfway up his leg. *Great!*

Water plastered her trousers to her calf, but she didn't seem to notice, or care. 'Can't we at least walk and talk at the same time?'

His right arm spasmed. Reason enough to end things here. His squad believed he was following up on a lead and he didn't need some ditsy romance writer catching him on the lie. He stopped, and pulled her in before she pitched into a lamppost. How the woman survived her day without him was a mystery. Wide green orbs stared up through the rain, her lips parted and ready . . .

He released her and stepped back. *Not now.*

'I'm busy in the real world, solving real problems, catching real killers. I don't have time for pretend.' He glanced at his watch. *Dammit, if he didn't move, late would be an understatement.* No brisk walk to clear the cobwebs now.

He raised his hand to a passing taxi and sighed inwardly when it pulled into the curb. He brushed past her and this time she didn't follow. 'Call me and we'll have that date. Just not today.'

Her frown deepened. No sense of humour—that was her problem. And he had neither the time nor the inclination right now to help her find one. Stacey lived in a fairytale world where princes rode in on white horses and the damsels they saved were young and perfect and innocent; where life always ended with a happy ever after.

*Fiction.* He wasn't fool enough to think life even remotely resembled that. His fist clenched in his lap as he tried to hold it steady.

That didn't mean he was willing to give up hope.

# Chapter One



***11 months later . . .***

. . . ***A****nd the RuBY winner is . . . From Mishap to Murder, Stacey Holland!*

The Cloverleaf Ballroom erupted in a frenzy of applause, friends and associates standing, cheering. Celebrating. For her.

Champagne bubbles clogged in Stacey's throat. She knocked back another mouthful to wash them down, and spluttered.

*Great move, Einstein.*

Shazz slapped her none-too-softly on the back and she almost leapt from her seat.

'Ouch!'

'Complain now, thank me later,' her friend whispered. 'At least you're no longer choking your way toward cardiac arrest.'

Stacey straightened. Damn, she was right! Who knew bubbles scared the same as hiccups?

*Romantic Book of the Year.*

She won.

Difficult to move past the whirling spinning wheel that was her thoughts.

Shazz pulled her out of her seat and into a hug. 'Go get 'em, Stace. Romance Writers of Australia's biggest award, and it's yours. This is your moment.'

It was. One she'd envisioned since her leap into romantic suspense three years ago.

Agent, Beth Samuels—"Morticia" to her friends—unfolded her lithe frame from her chair and sandwiched Stacey's hand between her bony ones. 'Well deserved. You aced it this time.'

Rita Hayden, her editor, flicked back her fiery bob before wrapping Stacey into her curvaceous frame. 'I knew you had it in you.'

Ethan Miklem tugged her into a not-so brotherly embrace, his low whisper delivering a gopher-trail of goose bumps across her neck.

'Another rung on your ladder to success. I'm glad I get to share it with you.'

People wanted to hug her, shake her hand, tell her she'd done good.

She'd been trying to tell herself that for years. Now perhaps she'd believe it.

Her head whirled and she gripped the back of a chair.

She'd avoided going heavy on the alcohol all evening for just this moment. A RuBY nomination was the Australian romance authors' equivalent of the Oscars. No mean feat. Exciting. Elating. Thrill-the-pants-off-overwhelming.

RWA President Jermaine Hart had pitched into the lead-up and Stacey had thrown caution all the way to Antarctica. This was *the* moment—a stepping-stone toward New York Times best-seller status.

Recognition. *Validation.*

Reason her mother had to be happy now.

She blinked, champagne effervescing through her blood and into her brain.

Jermaine's speech had her biting nails she'd never bitten before, and steadying her nerves had become more pressing than the need for temperance. She'd grabbed Shazz's second glass of bubbly and downed the lot in one hit.

She hadn't considered the subsequent steam-train rush of alcohol to her brain.

A path cleared before her.

Paper scrunched in her palm. Her speech.

Daubing moisture from her eyes, hoping her mascara was as waterproof as professed on the label, she made her careful way to the stage through the cheering crowd. Over-polished marble and stiletto heel collided. She tottered, caught her breath, adopted a nothing-to-see-here-but-drunk-woman-in-heels smile, then continued toward the stairs. The hellish heels transformed the remaining metres into a marathon.

*Don't trip. Don't trip. Don't trip.*

She made it past stair number one. Only four more to go.

*Don't trip.*

The toe of her borrowed Armani sandal caught on the second step and she pictured Shazz's cringe, her protect-those-shoes-with-your-life speech forever engraved in her mind.

'Got you!' Jermaine grabbed her arm and guided her up the remaining stairs.

Air whooshed from her lungs as she made it to the podium, all vital body parts miraculously intact. Jermaine pressed the award into her hands and she didn't hear a thing past that moment. The angular-cut glass felt cold and unnatural, heavier than it looked. She tried not to think of how the shards would scatter if it were dropped.

*Great murder weapon.*

Not an ideal time for plotting.

She stared out at the crowd of upturned faces, an entire litter of kittens prancing through her chest. *Everyone out there is on your side. They want you to win.* Her editor's words. Comforting in theory, not so easy to remember under a bright spotlight and five-or-so hundred pairs of eyes.

She rested the award on the slanted wood, smoothed her crumpled speech with her free hand, cleared her throat and launched in before the tentative grasp on her nerves slipped.

'As many of my oldest friends will attest, I've been dreaming up bad guys and bad boys since I was old enough to appreciate the difference.'

Chuckles rippled through the audience, providing her with courage enough to stem the waver in her voice. 'I've always felt that authenticity is the key. Every piece of action, every murder that makes it into my books is performed until I'm satisfied it's plausible. If I can't do it, I don't write it.'

She looked up from her notes. *Big mistake.*

Cut glass dug into her palm as she lost herself in familiar eyes of tropical blue. Butterflies joined her resident kittens, tangoing in tandem across her stomach.

*Breathe.*

Oxygen dragged into her lungs, diffusing the jitters.

*How dare he!* Trespassing on *her* day, *her* moment. Making her all fuzzy and warm and melty in front of her friends.

*No!*

She clenched her jaw, ignoring a heartbeat that would challenge the most rigorous Riverdancer. The racing heartbeat wasn't him. It was the champagne.

Awareness was not allowed in places that shouldn't be aware. Not over Detective Chase Durant.

Her grip on the award tightened. She stared at her crumpled speech and forced the scrawled black into focus.

'My characters are everyday people who get caught in not-so-everyday circumstances. They're true and honest, they hurt, but they always mend. Such is the way of romance, a genre which gives so much pleasure to so many of our readers. It's why we as authors push through the uncertainty, through the pain, the tears. But this moment, accepting this award, makes every tear, every heartache worth it, because it says that in some small way I've touched the hearts of the people out there. And as writers, that's all we ever strive to do.'

This time when she looked up, she avoided the front row's far left table.

'My list of thank-yous is long, but I'll try to make it quick. First, I'd like to thank . . .'

Before she knew it, her speech was done, the crowd was standing and concertina legs were carrying her back to her seat. His table stood in the opposite direction to hers, so avoiding him should have been easy.

Her gaze met his. Deep, probing, accusatory.

'What happened up there?'

Stacey snapped her attention to Shazz. *Safer.*

She dropped into her seat. 'Chase Durant happened.'

The presentations wrapped up and wait-staff descended on the room with trays of chocolate berry mousse and crème brûlée.

'He's here?' Shazz swivelled in her seat, an excited oh-my-god-I-just-saw-Hugh-Jackman shrill in her voice.

Stacey grabbed her arm. 'Don't be so obvious.'

'Oh, like you?'

'Very funny.'

'Not so if the look on your face is anything to go by. Why do you let him rile you?'

'Oh, let's see, because he thinks I'm a flake and a disaster. Plus, last time I asked him for help he fobbed me off.'

'Wasn't he working some serial killer case at the time? I'd say that's reason enough for not being as *available* as you'd have liked.' Shazz winked on the word "available", as if that bugged Stacey more than the info she'd needed for her now award-winning novel. It *so* wasn't. 'Far as I can see, with the way his eyes superfix-follow you, the only disaster in this equation is his emotions.'

Damn, she couldn't help it. Shazz's words had that fuzzy feeling back again. She bit her lip rather than ask her for more.

'Forget about him. He doesn't matter.'

She said the words with a toss of her hand. Even turned to the table and smiled at Ethan across the swanky chocolate centrepiece. But as others joined them and drew her into another round of hugs and congratulations, she knew the words were a lie.

Her speech was so close to a confession, its sweetness glazed his tongue.

She was brazen, he'd give her that. And too goddam sexy in the green, filmy get-up that clung and revealed and . . . well, *revealed.*

The Muscle Man deep in conversation with her seemed to think so. His palm brushed her upper arm as he leaned in. She gazed into his eyes, didn't pull away.

Chase pushed out of his seat. Time to clear his head, of her, in the dress. *Out of it.* He tossed back his lemon, lime and bitters. Better if it was whiskey. Only this was work, albeit off the clock. He had a hunch and he had to follow wherever it led. Which meant keeping his head.

*Focus.* Not easy with a certain strawberry blonde needling at his concentration. But he'd prevailed under worse pressure. And there were worse things than surveilling Stacey Holland.

Even if she was willing to kill for a good story.

His glass clattered onto the table. Difficult to believe the woman could plan, let alone execute a murder. But too many indicators pointed her way and until he could rule her out, she was stuck fast under his radar.

And Muscle Man's, it seemed. The bastard could barely tear his eyes off her.

With a growl, Chase headed for the double glass doors leading out to the rose garden.

'What the hell are you doing here?'

His hand paused on the cold of the glass, then pushed, and he slipped through, toward the scent of roses, leaving the plush scent of honeysuckle behind.

The door opened behind him, as he knew it would.

'Chase?'

Even angry, her voice contained a lilt that tugged at his gut. Low.

He turned to meet her flinted-green glare, her face a soft contrast of shadows under the muted lighting. So not the face of a murderer.

He crushed the thought before it wheedled its way through his reserve. He'd worked homicide long enough to know murder had many faces, some of them just as exquisite as the one looking up at him now.

'Funny how fate keeps crossing our paths.' He grinned.

'Does "pull the other" ring any bells for you?'

The daggers in her expression said she missed the humour.

One day he'd see her laugh.

Another thought to bury. And he'd heap on weedkiller, just to make sure. He had no business making the stern Stacey Holland laugh. Enjoying the view, on the other hand, was free fodder, and who in their right mind would pass up such a bargain? He indulged in a slow perusal of that dress close-up, enjoying the way her skin flushed, the red disappearing beneath her strapless neckline.

His spike in temperature had everything to do with spring moving toward summer, and nothing to do with the view. Or his reaction to it.

He switched focus from his reaction to hers. 'Why am I here? To celebrate the success of women in writing, of course.'

'Something I'm sure your date is most grateful for.' She frowned the moment the words left her lips, the grate of her voice matching the porcupine-prickles in her stance.

His grin couldn't help but widen. His "date" was busy networking inside, and Gracie's bestie. And while dating his sister's friends was something he'd partaken on occasion in the past, this, right now, was work.

That didn't mean he couldn't enjoy it. 'Jealous?'

She even snorted cute. 'I write fiction, I don't live it, detective.'

'You called me Chase before.'

'And many other things, but I think for all intents and purposes "detective" is fine.'

He stepped in. 'Why? Because it helps you keep your distance?'

She tottered backward on those ridiculous heels. Heels that made her legs go on forever, tempting a man to explore and dream and want. He reached out and the only way to steady her was to pull her in. He was a practical guy, after all.

Her chin tilted up, the set of those plump raspberry lips unimpressed, even whilst the green of her eyes became overtaken by black. By a need almost equal to his.

'Why are you really here, *detective?*'

She pressed every single one of his buttons, and he was tempted to press back—hard. Against the wall, on the carved wooden bench . . .

*A life without living is worthless.* Why his father's words came to him now, he had no idea. He was all too familiar with the weight of regrets.

*Damn!*

Killer she may be, but cold she was definitely not.

Why was he there? 'For this.'

Her lips parted, an invitation in any language. He accepted like the gentleman he was. She tasted of chilled champagne and strawberries dipped in dark chocolate mousse. His hands moved from her waist to her hips and he pulled her in closer still. Just as he'd imagined back when she bowled into his precinct almost a year ago on the pretext of research.

His heart gunned like a V8 eating up ground on the Grand Prix's home straight. Her mouth moved tentatively under his and he groaned. *If only she wasn't . . .*

He jerked back. *What? A cold-blooded killer?*

What the hell was he doing? Angling to be her next vic?

Kissing a murder suspect wasn't the stupidest thing he'd ever done, but it ranked pretty damn close. Even if he found her to be innocent, fraternising within an investigation was taboo, and could spark the end of a career.

He took another step back, ignored the draw of her body, the memory of how damn fine she tasted. Distance meant sanity, something she sucked from him like a succubus drew life from its victim.

Some moves were inexcusable, regardless the excuses. 'That should never have happened.'

'Damn straight, it shouldn't!' Her bottom lip trembled, as if she were vulnerable. Hurt. Despite the fact she'd kissed him back.

He had a crazy desire to do it again, to kiss her pain away. His right wrist began to tremble. He stilled it with his other hand and turned away. He was not weak. Life would not do that to him. He dropped his hand. *She* would not do that to him.

He turned back. Now she looked pissed. Well, she could take a frigging number.

'Nice speech up there. I hear there are writers who'll do pretty much anything for their craft. Is that true?'

She caressed the green stone nestled between her breasts and he imagined those same fingers slowly caressing him. His groin tightened.

*Was she doing it on purpose?*

She licked her lips and he almost groaned out loud.

'How far would you go to close a case?'

He shook his head. 'That's not the same thing.'

'You think not?' He dragged his gaze from her hand to her face and hated the knowing look she shot him. 'Do you love your job, detective?'

His fist clenched. Not as strong as he'd have liked. 'I can't imagine doing anything else.'

'Then we're a lot alike because neither can I. And if I need to go the extra mile to turn a good story into a great one, I'll do it. Even if it means talking to a cranky detective.'

When she smiled, the right side of her mouth quirked and her eyes filled with mischief, *knowing*, as if she held a secret. It made him want to know it, want to get it from her in any way he could.

He gritted his teeth. 'I'm not cranky.'

She arched her brow. 'Did I say you were?'

'You said—'

'I know what I said. It's what you assumed that I find interesting. You think you're the only detective I know?'

Time to pull the rug back under his feet from where she'd dragged it. 'You were telling me how far you'd go for a good story?'

'More to the point, does it bug you that I might know more than one detective?'

Barely two seconds passed between his question and hers. She was deflecting. Well, it took two to ping-pong and he was an ace at the backspin and block.

'From memory, last time you wanted help around interrogation techniques. Well, here's a quickie, no charge. Stacey Holland, where were you on the evening of Thursday, fourteenth of May?'

Her glare suggested he hunt for lost marbles. The hand on her hip suggested he watch out for thin ice. 'I'm not sure where you're going with this, but how would I know what I was doing eleven months ago?'

'A knee-jerk response about seventy per cent of suspects give first-up. Now think, what was happening in your life around that time?'

Her brow furrowed, then cleared. She bit her lip and he pulled his gaze north of temptation.

'I was finishing *From Mishap to Murder*. So, I guess I'd have been writing.'

He nodded. 'Now what if I told you the fourteenth was the first dry night after a week of solid rainfall? In fact, it was the wettest May on record for the past twenty years.'

He spotted the moment she remembered and tried to act like she didn't. Her frown frosted over, her expression clouded, and her gaze dipped beyond his left knee. 'I was researching a scene for my book.'

'What scene was that?'

Her head jerked back. 'What's this really about?'

'Helping you.'

'Can we at least be honest?'

'You first.' He rolled his hand.

She watched like it was bug-infested, or riddled with leprotic boils. 'You think I'm lying about something?'

'You tell me.'

Air puffed through her lips disturbing the blonde wisps slung low over her brow. Then she rolled her eyes in that typical stop-yanking-my-chain look. 'Why are you really here?'

He searched her expression. 'I'm on a case.'

Her reaction was immediate—a war between curiosity and feigned disinterest. If he'd been a gambler, he'd bet all his chips the writer in her would triumph.

She wavered before moving closer, winning him his bet amidst a flurry of honeysuckle and heat. 'Anything interesting?'

Funny, but this time he'd swear she wasn't holding anything back. Or maybe the awkward-and-absurd act concealed a damned good liar.

'Only if you view murder that way.' Still no reaction. She was good. Better than. Her talents were wasted in books when she could easily have graced the widescreen. 'But it's an ongoing investigation and off limits.'

'That's a shame.'

'Undoubtedly.' His hand spasmed and he clenched it before it started to shake. 'I should get back to my date.'

Her poker face didn't span past masking murder. It seemed that jealousy was harder to hide.

Her palms smoothed over her thighs and only a dead man would miss how the material hugged every curve she'd pressed against him when they'd kissed.

'See you around, Stacey Holland.'

She tilted her head. 'You know one thing I believe in less than fate?'

He raised his brows.

She raised hers in return. 'Coincidence.'

# Chapter Two

'I'll take one, no, make that two metres of the three-strand rope. And this.' Stacey dropped the fishing line onto the counter and dug into her bag.

'Going fishing?'

Heat flooded her face. She ploughed around for her purse, looking anywhere but into eyes that stripped every scrap of sense from her brain.

*Was the confounded man stalking her? Today of all days, with her shoddy pre-weight-loss tracky dacks and hoodie.*

Not that her wardrobe or the frizzy wildness of her hair should matter.

*It didn't matter.*

'Maybe.'

'No maybe about it.' His voice was as dry as her not-so-honey-blonde split ends. 'Fishing tackle, boat anchor rope. That smells of fishing to me. Can I come?'

She slanted her gaze upward of denim and muscle-hugging cotton until it met with eyes fifty shades of irritating and irresistible. Her heart rate spiked. Why'd the devil have to look so damn hot in blue?

Her fingers contacted the smooth leather of her purse. She dragged it out, shooting Chase what she hoped was a cactus-wilting glare. 'You may think you're funny, but it's just delusion.'

'Ouch! That's a kick right where it hurts.'

'I'm sure you've enough ego to spare.' She pushed the items across the counter to Burt, or so his nametag said. It also said he was there to help in any way he could. Shame that didn't extend to tossing an overzealous detective out of her life. 'No doubt I have fate to thank once again for bringing you to Hook, Line and Sinker the exact moment I happen to be here. Are you stalking me, detective?'

Burt leaned in, no pretext of anything but lapping up their

exchange. Her glare did nothing but elicit a wide grin from both men.

Burt's behaviour, she could understand. Their "conversation" had to be reels more riveting than fishing-talk. Chase, on the other hand, had no excuse. His hip rested against the counter, his arms folded across a chest she'd experienced up close and personal only a week ago.

The gleam in his eyes said he knew exactly the effect his presence had on her equilibrium. 'And why would I do that?'

Flames swept across her face. All she needed was for him to add one plus one and come up with a window. This was anger, not attraction.

'Boredom?'

'You underestimate yourself, Stacey. You are anything but boring.'

She slapped her card against the payWave reader, then stuffed her receipt and purchases into her bag. Time to leave Burt and his over-eager interest behind. If she was lucky, Chase would take her none-too-subtle hint, stay put and keep the other man company.

She strode to the exit and pushed through the heavy wooden door. Her luck had to come in at some stage. Just clearly not today. The wind whipped about her hair as Chase joined her on the footpath.

She gathered the frizz-ridden strands in one hand, holding them back so she could see. 'Okay, let's get this awkward stuff over with. If you're angling for a date, forget it. I don't date.'

The blue in his eyes deepened. Then his lips curved upward and she locked her knees for fear of crumpling like a house of matchsticks to the ground.

'*Interesting.*'

At least the cold on her cheeks provided a reason for the red. 'Not really. Just reality.'

'Yet nothing exists for no reason. Why don't you date, Stacey?'

Heart conga-drumming in her ears, she lifted her chin. 'Why do you need to know?'

'Curiosity.'

'Just as well you're not a cat.'

His gaze narrowed. 'Otherwise you'd write me into one of your books?'

'I don't kill cats.'

'But you do kill people?'

'With a pen.'

He cocked his head. 'Painful death.'

'Like this conversation.' She backed up. 'I have somewhere else to be, so goodbye *detective*. And next time you have an inclination to follow me, don't. Just for the record, you're not my type.'

The wind urged her on as she turned and strode away. If wishes were guaranteed, that'd be the last she'd see of Detective Chase Durant.

Congo heartbeats amped up to techno.

'I wasn't angling for a date.' His laughter pranced about the wind, meandering playfully through her mind. 'And just for the record, you're not my type either.'

Gloved fingertips *bump-bumped* across rows of spooled fishing line, the dry thuds matching the dry empty thud of his heart. Dust eddied and unsettled, drifting downward and showering the muddy brown of his steel-tipped boots.

Red bloomed across her cheeks. Through cracks in the shelving he could see she was riled. Flustered. A wildcat on heat. Over an idiot detective who wouldn't recognise a clue if he rammed it up his tight ass and lit a match to it.

He flicked the grime from his gloves, then turned his head, found sudden interest in the array of rods as the bitch stormed past and slammed through the store's front exit.

Dick on a lead, the pig-cop followed. Her voice grated through the glass, anger and denial in one overwrought outburst. Her trembling body told another story. She wanted him. Wanted him to fuck her until she couldn't remember her name, or his.

It would be her downfall. Always picking the wrong man.

The fishing line slipped easily into his pocket. Strolling the aisle, he added sinkers to his basket. A packet of hooks joined his pocketed nylon. He smiled at the young assistant straightening a display. She flushed, smiled back, invited. *Tempted.*

He headed for the ropes, ignoring the weighty need that filled and tightened his balls. His path was set. Straying, no matter how sweet, was not an option. Not yet.

He fingered the nylon strands. His gut told him the climbing rope would be better, but he picked up the three-strand anyway. It was her choice. The drama, the deliverance, the death. Her choice.

All but the finale, the last bow. They would be his.

Stacey threw her bag onto the table and her body onto the couch.

*After* she'd tossed the flowers from her front doorstep into the trash, curbing her breath and her temper all the way. She wasn't stupid enough to believe that Brad's fortnightly delivery signified more than control. Three years divorced and he was still manipulating her and her emotions. Still making her feel small and insignificant, and a damned laughing stock.

Something the entire male population seemed intent on these days. Or at least the male population she came into contact with. *Very close contact.*

The thought flicked a switch and heat flooded her body.

*Damn!*

Had she just made a blithering fool of herself?

Of course she had. Hence the reason—well, okay *one* reason—she didn't date. She could write a relationship in a matter of hours, minutes even. But give her a real, live man and she couldn't connect enough words to start a shopping list.

*Idiot!*

She banged her head against the back of the couch. Relief factor— zero. And now her head was a bass drum in a marching band.

What had seemed the most logical explanation for his turning up every which way the past week, was wrong. Very wrong. He didn't want to date her.

*You're not my type either.* Her heart did that little dive-bomb thing that came latched to the feeling labelled *idiot*. Of course, a man like Chase Durant wouldn't fall for someone like her. Not with a choice of clichéic willowy blondes or stunning redheads like his partner. And that was a good thing.

He was too close to the kind of man she'd sworn to stay clear of.

Memory clutched her chest, squeezing until she thought her ribs might shatter. Her father. The yelling. The hurt. The last time he walked out their front door. The reasons he left her behind and never turned back. Brad's control. His need to change her a rejection itself. Thoughts she'd mulled and turned over time again, cutting deep into old wounds.

Neither man deserved her energy, her time. They'd robbed too much of both already.

She plucked a loose thread till it unravelled, the hole growing in sync with her unease.

*Why have you been following me, detective?*

Since the awards dinner, something niggled. Something in their exchange made little or no sense. Something past the kiss she would not think about.

She crossed her legs, clenched her thighs. *Mind out of the rose garden and into reality.*

What date did he mention? May fourteenth? In seconds she was at her desk, tapping her keyboard. A lead weight slammed her chest. She clicked on the link. Dropped her jaw all the way to the overworn cream carpet.

It was a joke. It had to be a joke.

The front page headline slashed that theory to shreds.

*Nine Knife Slasher Strikes Again.*

The more she read, the deeper she fell into a fictional world that was *From Mishap to Murder.* A fictional world she'd created which had suddenly become real.

*No!*

*No-no-no-no-no-no-no-no-no.*

This wasn't happening. In Hollywood, yes. Melbourne, Australia? No way. Not with her story. Her murder.

Her head spun, a spinning-top off its trajectory and heading straight for trouble.

Oh, god! Was that it? Chase believed she was a murderer. That she killed to make her murders authentic?

She stumbled up from her chair and dashed for the bathroom. *Do not vomit. Do not vomit.*

She made it to the toilet bowl just in time. A sinful waste of toast, eggs and perfectly seasoned avocado.

She dropped to the floor, jarring her knees, her nerves.

Bile lurched in her stomach and surged up her throat.

Whoever said positive affirmations worked didn't know shit from sugar-free strudel. They sure as hell never worked for her. She was better off without them. And him.

He'd kissed her, for what? Not because he was attracted. *Oh, no.* He'd kissed her for a confession, for her to trust him and tell him she killed people.

She gagged. Waved farewell to another lot of good cuisine. Probably last night's Thai tofu and noodle salad. She rinsed, then wiped her mouth with a wad of toilet paper, tossed it into the bowl and flushed.

She'd acted out her book, then someone had gone and acted it out for real. As if her book were a prescription. *A recipe for murder.*

Great name for a TV crime show, not her life.

Comprehension shuddered through arms and legs that struggled to push up from the floor. Slowly, shakily, she stood. *He* knew. That whole conversation, the flirtatious chit-chat, the supposed advice for her novel . . . He knew and not once had he let on. He'd followed her, led her to believe he was interested . . .

A sluice of cold water over her face and a vigorous rub of the towel replaced anger with disgust.

Since when was seduction a prescribed interrogation technique of Melbourne police? All the time she'd worried over trespassing on private farmland, he'd been looking to convict her for murder. Naive fool that she was, she'd read his continued presence as interest. How he must have laughed after their exchange outside the store. How he must be laughing still.

Only this was nowhere near funny.

Clutching the white marble sink, she blinked at the mirror. *Coincidence.* A pale reflection of herself nodded back.

Once the cops looked closer, the murder would appear nothing like her scene. There'd be differences. *Big differences.* Then the police would have no choice but to continue hunting for the killer elsewhere.

It didn't matter that she didn't believe in coincidences. She didn't believe in love either yet, like yesterday's trash, it was littered all around her.

The pound against her skull mushroomed until she thought her head would explode.

She'd make Chase see sense. Self-preservation aside, she had an obligation. If the police were looking at her, it left the killer free to kill again. *If* that was his plan. Something she didn't doubt. She'd researched enough psychopaths to know gratification killers rarely stopped at one. It was her responsibility to change that. Fast. Whatever the consequences.

Which meant a visit to Chase's precinct and a long conversation. The thought of seeing him made her skin burn. The burn lower and deeper she chose to ignore.

Luck dangled the entire weekend before her. Time enough to prepare for their confrontation, and time enough to stew. Still, come Monday, only one more exchange and she'd sever him from her life forever. Like the sharp, clean rip of a scab from a healing wound.

It wasn't as if she'd done anything wrong, so what on earth could he do?

Arrest her for mannequin murder?

## AND THERE'S MORE!

Like a free romantic suspense novelette?

Get a copy of COLD CASE, WARM HEART when you sign up to
my newsletter on my website

www.michelle-somers.com

# ABOUT COLD CASE, WARM HEART

### *Three deaths, one clue and twenty-four hours*
### *before it's too late. . .*

Homicide detective Calamity Dresden has twenty-four hours to catch
a killer before he kills again and disappears underground. Estranged
lover Sebastian Rourke wants justice for his murdered father and every
other victim of Melbourne's sadistic Trifecta Terror.

But when the two are forced to team up and danger closes in, can they
keep their minds on the case and their hands off each other?